# STATE *of* GRACE
## Sandra Moran

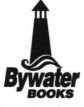

**Bywater**
**BOOKS**

Ann Arbor
2016

Bywater Books

Copyright © 2016 Sandra Moran

Bywater Books First Edition: August 2016

Printed in the United States of America
on acid-free paper.

Cover design by TreeHouse Studio

Bywater Books
PO Box 3671
Ann Arbor, MI 48106-3671

*www.bywaterbooks.com*

ISBN: 978-1-61294-091-5  Print
ISBN: 978-1-61294-092-2  Ebook

For Cherie and Cheryl

# Foreword

*State of Grace* is the first book Sandra wrote. It is the book that started her writing career. When asked why she chose to tell THIS story, she simply would say, "No reason other than to prove to myself that I could write." Well ... she could write.

After she completed the book, she began reaching out to literary agents. She knew, to give herself the best chance to be successful as a writer, she needed an agent. An intern with Marcil-O'Farrell Literary, LLC was given the story to read. She liked it enough to suggest that the owning partners read it. They, too, liked the story and signed Sandra as a client. They worked with Sandra a great deal on the story. They also suggested she hire a professional editor, which she did. After those changes were incorporated, the agency did its best to market it to several big publishing houses. Sadly, it was never picked up by any of them.

While all of this was occurring, Sandra kept on writing. She wrote *Nudge* next, followed by *Letters Never Sent.* The work involved with publishing and promoting those books simply left *State of Grace* waiting in the wings. Sandra never gave up on this story, though. About the time she was wrapping up *All We Lack* she decided she wanted to revisit *State of Grace* and focus on its publication.

She felt her original story had gotten lost with the multiple rounds of edits. She got out her original version, made some changes she now felt important, included some from the professional edit, and then sent it to her beta readers. She incorporated many of their suggestions and had it the way she wanted it on September 14, 2015.

The story had been lost and now she had it back. It was HER story again.

Because of this, it was paramount to me, and to her family, that *State of Grace* be published precisely as she left it. I did not want to see it edited again. Perhaps the story could have been improved upon by editing. To me, that is irrelevant. This is the last book any of us will ever read that is from the amazing mind of Sandra Moran. I believe you will enjoy it, just as it is. And, as you read, you will know, she completely approves of every word you are reading.

—Cheryl Pletcher (Sandra's spouse)
*Lenexa, Kansas*

# STATE *of* GRACE

# Prologue

Were you to ask my friends and family, they would tell you I am not the most reliable of storytellers. They would warn you to question everything I'm about to say.

But, were you to ask me, I would tell you that they're wrong because the story I'm about to tell you is the truth. Granted, it's from my point of view—but it's still the truth. That's not to say I don't take creative liberties. I do. I admit that. But they're important details if you're truly going to understand what happened the summer that Grace Bellamy was murdered—and how the brutality of that event affected the rest of my life.

It's a complicated tale and if I mislead you as a result, I apologize. I just know of no other way to tell my story.

Part I:
1981–1988

# Chapter 1

I grew up in Mayberry.

Actually, that's a lie—although, for anyone familiar with the television show, and who has also been to Edenbridge, Kansas, they would know it's not too far from the truth.

It's a place most people never see unless they're heading to or from Oklahoma on Highway 69, running on fumes and knowing they won't make it someplace bigger to fill up. But those outsiders who have no choice but to venture off the interstate and onto the county road, they find Edenbridge—a small, outwardly quaint village where life moves at a slower, simpler pace. Today, most of the businesses have closed down or been replaced by ambitious start-ups that have no chance of success. But in the '80s, when I was young and ran wild through the town with my friends, Edenbridge was a place of endless adventure.

We had the required cast of characters: the town drunk, the town lawman, and more than a few town eccentrics. Each had their own story—though, over time and multiple retellings, no one really knew what was real and what was embellished. In the end, it didn't really matter because the fiction became the accepted truth.

A perfect example of this is Puddin' Puddin'. Today we would say he was "developmentally disabled," but in 1981, there wasn't such a thing as cultural sensitivity. Puddin' Puddin' was simply "a retard." His real name was Edwin and he was the son of Otis and Sarah Glenderson, an elderly couple who lived south of town on a scraggly piece of property that abutted Brush Creek. The lot, which was overflowing with abandoned vehicles on concrete blocks and rusted appliances that no longer worked, looked like a junkyard. It

7

was an eyesore and the cause of more than a few muttered comments when the subject came up over coffee at the town mercantile. Still, folks would say with a shrug, what can you do?

Though it was clear when he was born that he "wasn't quite right," no one realized how much so until he flunked out of the first grade four times. Eventually he was kept at home and spent most of his days prowling the woods behind his house. As he got older, his territory extended to include Brush Creek and the town of Edenbridge. By the time I was old enough to know about him, he was a child trapped in a man's body—a man who spent most of his days riding a creaking, fat-tired bike around town muttering "puddin' puddin' puddin'" to simulate the sound of a motorcycle engine.

Even as a child, I understood that Puddin' Puddin' was the town's responsibility. Otis was known for his drinking and Sarah was known for putting up with it, and as such, it was our job to collectively make sure that Puddin' Puddin' was okay. It wasn't hard. Most of the time he just pedaled around town in the same ill-fitting khaki pants and long-sleeved Oxford shirt buttoned at the neck and sleeves. They were most likely hand-me-downs from his father who was at least five inches shorter than his son, but that wasn't regarded as a bad thing. Frugality was respected and hand-me-downs were common in most families—my own included. Still, many of the farmers laughed and nudged each other as Puddin' Puddin' rode past, his head bent forward, his large, ruddy face intent, his enormous hands tightly gripping the handlebars.

They also laughed—though with maybe more respect—at Bill Hawkins. "Hawk," as he was known, was a bow-legged, lanky man who lived in a small, one-story limestone house just outside of town on the banks of Brush Creek. If you didn't know better, you would have thought the house, which was more than 100 years old, was abandoned. The windows were covered with yellowed newspapers and the electrical and telephone wires had been clipped at the pole.

"No gov'ment bastard is going to tell me what to do," Hawk was quick to tell anyone who would listen. "It's like them goddamned radios and TVs! The gov'ment uses them to watch what you're doing in your own goddamned house! It's against my civil liberties as an American!"

Hawk hated the government, refused to pay his taxes, and chose instead to grow his own vegetables and keep chickens and a goat in his backyard. He fished and frogged in the creek, and to make money for the things he simply had to buy, he dug up earthworms to sell in town at the general store. Each day he would walk into Edenbridge with his bucket of night crawlers and barter with Mr. and Mrs. Gray, the owners of the Mercantile for the things he needed. Though some of the worms went into the shallow, wooden "worm box" in the back of the store to be sold as bait, most were discreetly returned to the same field from which they originated, only to be re-exhumed by Hawk the following night. It was charity that took his pride into consideration. Something I didn't understand at the time.

Hawk and Puddin' Puddin' were objects of fascination for me. I had a vivid imagination when I was young and tended to fabricate wild stories in my head about anyone who was the least bit different. I know I stared at them, sometimes too hard, in an attempt to drink in every nuance of their oddity.

"Why does he do that?" I asked one day as my mother and I drove past Hawk limping along the short stretch of highway into Edenbridge, head down, a dented bucket full of dirt and worms in one gnarled hand. Without looking to see who it was, Hawk had raised the forefinger of his free hand in a gesture that passed for a wave in our part of the country.

"Do what?" she asked, glancing sideways at me.

"Why does he dig up worms and sell them in town?" I asked. "And why does he always wear those same overalls and shirt?"

She frowned slightly and was thoughtful before answering. "Hawk lives by different rules than the rest of us. He believes things other people don't." She paused and then continued, "It's not bad. It's just different."

"Grandpa says he's a crazy SOB," I said. "He says—"

"I don't want you repeating what your grandfather says." Her tone was sharp. "He's a bigoted old—" She stopped herself from finishing the sentence, tipped her head back slightly, and took a deep breath, her eyes still on the road. After she had exhaled, she smiled slightly and glanced again at me. "I want you to make sure you're always nice to Mr. Hawkins," she said. "Do you understand?"

I nodded and she returned her attention to the road. As she drove, I studied her profile. My mother was an attractive woman. I knew this not just because of how I saw her, but also because I saw how *other people* saw her clean lines and even features. But there was more to it. She had a vitality . . . a fierceness . . . that drew people in just as much as it seemed to push them away. Despite having grown up in Edenbridge, she was different from the rest of the locals. A self-proclaimed atheist, she had managed to offend most of the town with her godlessness and disregard for social norms. We never went to church and she took great pleasure in sitting on the front porch on Sunday mornings drinking her coffee and reading the newspaper as people drove past in their Sunday best.

And then there was the Mustang. Midnight blue with a black hardtop, my mother's car was the talk of Edenbridge—not just because it was a two-door sports car in a world of dirty pick-up trucks and dusty sedans, but also because it had glasspacks and an eight-track player on which she blasted Elvis Presley and Linda Ronstadt as she rolled through town. She stood out and was different in her own right, so condemning or even commenting on Hawk's strange behavior wasn't, in her mind, appropriate. They were fellow misfits in our small corner of the world—misfits, but still accepted because they were both descendants of two of the first families to settle in Edenbridge.

The town of Edenbridge, Kansas, was founded in 1850 by three families—the Webbs, the Hawkins, and the Holloways—all of whose ancestors immigrated together to North Carolina from England in the 1700s. The Holloways were my father's people, and my mother's family was descended from the Webbs. This joint lineage to two of the founding families made my sister, Tara, and me Edenbridge royalty, if such a term can really be applied. It may seem trivial, but in places like Edenbridge, who you are, who your parents are, and who their parents were before them is of the utmost importance. It tells people what you're made of—your stock.

And from what I know about the Webbs and the Holloways, they were a hearty bunch. I suppose they had to be to survive—first in North Carolina and then later in Kansas.

I'm not sure why Hugh and Elizabeth Holloway, William and Grace Hawkins, and James and Agnes Webb decided to move to Kansas or why they decided to name their corner of the Kansas prairie after their ancestors' homeland. Maybe, like me, they had grown up hearing the romanticized stories and wanted to pay homage to them. Or maybe they just couldn't think of anything more original. I don't know. But every Pioneers Day, just before the potluck and games, we would all gather in the gymnasium of the grade school and listen to the story of the founding of Edenbridge. Usually it was read by Mrs. Gray, the elderly school librarian. We called her Old Lady Farts behind her back because she had a tendency to pass gas silently as she moved around the library reshelving books.

Each year's program was the same. Mrs. Gray would welcome everyone to Pioneers Day, we would all stand for the Pledge of Allegiance, and then Reverend Ackerman would lead us in a prayer. At first, I would lower my head and close my eyes like everyone else. But as I got older, I found that it was much more interesting to keep my eyes open and watch everyone else pray—everyone, that was, except for my mother. I enjoyed watching her watch them with a slightly amused expression on her face. Even more than that, though, I enjoyed meeting her eyes over everyone else's bowed heads and watching her enigmatic smile turn into a grin. That shared experience made me feel warm . . . happy . . . as if we were co-conspirators in some grand scheme.

After the prayer, Mrs. Gray would approach the microphone with her worn copy of *The Unabridged History of Edenbridge, Kansas* and read the story of the town's founding. As she neared the end, she would point to Mrs. Ackerman, the church organist, to play the opening bars of "Home on the Range." Dutifully, we would all stand and sing. I liked to imagine the Webbs, Holloways, and Hawkinses standing on the flat expanse of prairie that bordered the Salt Creek Valley, the hot wind blowing from the south, as they gazed for the first time at the place that was to become their home.

Much of the town's early success was due in large part to its location at a bend in the Brush Creek. It was one of the only places where a wagon traveling north to connect with the Oregon Trail could ford the Creek. Later, when the stagecoach routes were created along the wagon trails and travelers started coming through the area, Jacob Webb built an inn—a massive limestone structure that still stands today, though it's been turned into a residence and a bed and breakfast.

In its day, Edenbridge was a destination in our corner of the world. And then the railroad came. The problem, though, was that it didn't come to Edenbridge. Rather than following the stagecoach route, the tracks were placed through a town about 15 miles to the east. As stagecoach travel was replaced by rail, Edenbridge's prominence dwindled. It was a blow to the town, but there were still plenty of businesses and there were lots of farmers. Edenbridge didn't grow, but it didn't shrink either. That didn't start until the 1930s, when the impenetrable clouds of swirling, red, brown, and gray dust and grit made it impossible to farm anything. Still, the people of Edenbridge held on. "That which does not kill you, makes you stronger," they would tell each other. And they were right to a certain extent. They survived the Dust Bowl, the Great Depression, and World War II. And by the time my parents were born, though the town was a lot smaller than it had been in its heyday, there was still the general store—now called the Mercantile—a diner, a doctor's office, a dentist's office, the phone company, the post office, three churches, and two filling stations—one of which was owned by my father's father and also served as the farm implement dealership.

I'm telling you all of this not to bore you, but so that you can understand the dynamics of our community—who we were collectively because of our history. Ours was a community built on the bedrocks of family, God, and country. It was a strong foundation, but one that was perhaps outdated. The world began to change and Edenbridge, for all of its authenticity, was being left behind. Kids began to graduate from high school and move to Wichita or Oklahoma City. The town began to shrink as the

12

population dwindled and businesses began to fail. By the time I was born, all that was left of Edenbridge were the schools, a handful of businesses, and, of course, the Congregational Church.

In a town like Edenbridge, even the smallest of events are significant—which is why the rape and murder of my best friend, Grace Bellamy, stunned and, in many ways, crippled the townspeople. We had never dealt with murder—and certainly never that of a child. The closest we'd come, coincidentally happened earlier that same summer with the disappearance of Adam Walsh from a Sears store in Florida. It happened the last week of July and the entire country was obsessed by the story.

I remember the day I became aware of the significance of Adam Walsh's disappearance. It was the first day of August and about a month before school was scheduled to start. It was a Saturday. I know this because I had spent the day with my father working at my grandfather's gas station in Edenbridge. During the week, my father worked as a printer and copier repairman for Xerox. Every morning he would disappear from the house smelling like soap and Old Spice and return in the evenings with the slightly spicy odor of cigarettes, stale cologne, and some unidentifiable smell I decided was "the city." But on weekends, he would pull on his oldest jeans and a stained white T-shirt and go to the shop where he pumped gas, smoked cigarettes, and gossiped with the farmers.

Often I would go with him, playing in the greasy garage, prowling through the dusty storage area that smelled of oil, grime, and age. I explored the dirty recesses of the buildings, avoiding only the exposed drain in the corner where all the men peed when they thought I wasn't looking. Although I realize now that the men affectionately tolerated my presence, at the time, I honestly believed they considered me an equal. I drank Coca-Cola out of thick glass bottles scuffed and cloudy from use, dangled candy cigarettes from my mouth, and at the end of the day, used the same thick, petroleum-based hand cleaner and filthy nail brush the men used to remove the worst of the grime from my hands.

We drove home that evening with the truck windows down, the hot air blowing my already tangled hair around my face. "Hey

13

Jude" came on the radio and we both sang along. Dad sang the words and I enthusiastically joined in on the chorus. It had been the perfect day.

We were just through the front door, into the foyer, and were halfway to the living room when my mother came around the corner. The smell of frying chicken hung in the air and my stomach rumbled. "Birdie, bath," she said in way of greeting as she pointed down the hall toward the bathroom. She wrinkled her nose as my father continued past her to the kitchen. "You could use one, too." My father shrugged but didn't answer. Our house was one of those cookie-cutter ranch-style homes that were so popular in the 1970s. With all the rooms on one level, sound carried and it was easy to stand in one room and hear what was going on in other parts of the house. From where my mother and I stood, I heard the refrigerator door open and the clink of glass as Dad pulled out a beer.

"Dinner smells good," he said as he came back through the doorway and headed toward the living room, an unlit cigarette dangling from his mouth and a bottle of beer in his hand. He set the sweaty bottle on the end table and walked over to the television to turn it on. He bent down to pull at the worn plastic knob and then backed toward his chair as the picture slowly appeared. Satisfied with the channel, he lowered himself into his recliner to watch the tail end of the local news.

My mother glanced back down at me. "Bath," she repeated and then returned to the kitchen. In the living room, my father, his eyes fastened on the screen, flicked open his scratched silver-plated Zippo and touched the flame to the tip of his cigarette. He took a deep drag, pulled the cigarette from his mouth, and reached for his beer. I wandered into the room, hoping he would offer me a sip. Though I hated the taste of beer, I loved the feeling of inclusion in his end-of-the-day ritual. It made me feel important and grown up. I sidled closer and he grinned. "You'd better get in the bath or your mom will have your hide."

As if she could hear us, my mother's voice came from the kitchen. "Birdie? I don't hear any water running."

I was in the process of pretending not to have heard when she came into the living room, tongs in hand, and glared.

"Birdie," she began and then stopped, her attention drawn to the television.

"Authorities in Hollywood, Florida, tonight are continuing to search for six-year-old Adam Walsh, who was abducted outside a Sears Department store on July 27th," the newscaster was saying. A picture of a freckle-faced boy in a white and blue shirt and a red baseball cap, and holding a bat flashed on the screen.

"Hollywood police say that Walsh may have been in the company of a suspect described as a Caucasian male in his mid- to late-30s, about six feet tall, 170 pounds with dark hair. Anyone with any information about this case is asked to contact the Hollywood, Florida Police Department."

Below the picture and physical description of Adam flashed a red bar with a telephone number. My mother stared intently at the screen, her lips pinched together, her eyes slightly narrowed.

"Birdie. Bath. Now."

With exaggerated deliberation, I sauntered toward the bathroom. It was a petty show of defiance, and my mother's eyes narrowed as I passed. She waited until she thought I was out of earshot before she spoke.

"John," she said as I started to close the door. "How closely are you watching Birdie when she's down at the station? She's down there with all those men . . . do you keep an eye on her?"

"Nancy, she's a kid," I heard him say. "She plays in the back, she runs around, she has fun. That's what kids do. This is Edenbridge, not Wichita or Oklahoma City."

I listened to this exchange from the bathroom, the door cracked about an inch, my back against the sink.

"It may not be Wichita, but that doesn't mean that something couldn't happen to her."

I heard the wet sound of my father taking a swig of beer and could tell he was buying time, choosing his words. "Nance," he said finally. "I think you're making too much out of this. Nobody here would do something like that."

My mother sighed and I heard her muttering as she went back

15

into the kitchen. I quietly eased the door shut and flushed the toilet before turning on the spigots and adjusting the temperature of the water. In the kitchen, I could hear my mother banging things around and muttering to herself.

"Birdie," she hollered, "Dinner's almost ready. You have five minutes and I want those fingernails clean. Do you hear me?"

I made a noise of assent and then climbed into the bathtub and began to scrub.

I realize now how much my mother must have hated those days—hated the grime I never was fully able to scrape from under my fingernails, the mannish gestures I picked up from the farmers, and the fact that I was allowed to roam unsupervised in the presence of so many adult men. She was never wild about the idea of me spending my Saturdays at the station, even before what happened to Grace, but the year I turned eleven, her disapproval changed into something stronger—something I now recognize as fear.

I think I first noticed it one spring evening in April, three months before Adam Walsh disappeared. The evenings were staying lighter longer and I had been out playing with my friends until my mother called me inside and forced me into the bath. As I waited for her to finish brushing Tara's hair, I sat crouched in front of the screen of the open front bank of windows. I closed my eyes and smiled as the nighttime breeze cooled my bath-reddened skin and wet hair. I didn't realize how the light from the living room silhouetted my body until a carload of boys drove slowly past and began to whistle and whoop.

"Birdie," my mother said sharply as I ducked down below the windowsill. "Get away from the window."

The boys in the street laughed loudly before gunning the engine and racing away.

Embarrassed, I remained crouched against the wall as my mother hurried over and pulled the curtains closed. My heart thudded loudly in my chest and head as I looked fearfully up at her.

"Sweetie, you can't sit like that anymore."

Her tone was gentler.

"You couldn't see it, but with the light the way it was, to those boys you looked like you were naked."

I blushed and wondered who had been in the car. I looked at Tara, who watched us with a curious expression. My mother crouched down next to me and looked intently into my eyes.

"Birdie, you're going to be a very pretty girl. Your body is going to start changing and boys are going to start paying attention. That's why when I say you can't run around in the backyard without a shirt on or that you need to be more careful, you need to listen to me. Do you understand?"

I nodded. Even though I wasn't quite sure what she was telling me, the thought that I might one day be pretty made me very happy. I was in what my mother referred to as my "awkward stage." I was tall for my age and gangly. My body was changing, preparing for adolescence, and my coordination couldn't quite keep up. My bony knees and elbows were a perpetual patchwork of scratches and scrapes from unanticipated falls. Today, when I look at pictures of myself from back then, I'm struck by my angularity. In one photo, which was taken shortly before Grace's death, I'm sitting on the ground under the shade of a tree. We were at a picnic and my mother must have surprised me when she took the shot because my head is turned toward the camera, my mouth slightly open. I'm dressed in red shorts and a tank top that is startlingly white against my tanned skin. I'm sitting with my arms around my knees, which are pulled up to my chest. I look somewhat like a brown prairie grasshopper—all lines and angles. The upper part of my face is obscured, in part by my unruly mop of mousy brown curls, but also by an enormous pair of my mother's plastic sunglasses.

The maturation of my body wasn't the only change I noticed that summer. There were changes in my parents' relationship with each other. It was as if they had forgotten how to talk to each other. And, when they did talk, it was with words that were almost too polite—interactions that were well on their way to unresolved arguments that evolved into resentment that evolved into apathy. But that would come later. On that Saturday, my parents still loved each other—at least I think they did.

## Chapter 2

My mother's concerns were the furthest thing from my mind two days later as I pedaled my bike down the dirt path to the tree house that Grace, Natalie, and I had built the summer before in one of the towering oak trees in the woods near Brush Creek. Despite its haphazard construction, the tree house was sturdy, made from boards salvaged from a nearby barn that was falling in on itself. We called it the Nest.

Although I liked to be the first to get there, I was rarely able to beat Grace. Her lack of parental supervision gave her a freedom that neither Natalie nor I had. More often than not, I would arrive to find her pink banana-seat bike already propped against a nearby tree, and she would be curled up in one of the corners reading. Because her mother wasn't awake to cook a morning meal, Grace's breakfasts, if she bothered to eat, usually consisted of cold Pop-Tarts or crackers from a waxy sleeve of saltines she carried in her bag.

Although we didn't really talk about it, I think both Natalie and I recognized how Grace was neglected—the way her clothes were never quite clean or how haggard she always seemed to look. Of course, I say this now as a thirty-year-old, but looking back, it was more than just her appearance. Grace compartmentalized her life—separated the time she spent with us from the time she spent at home. She talked about her father only to say she had spent the weekend with him, and she never talked about her mother except to say that she "wasn't feeling well" or that she "had a new boyfriend."

Grace endured her life stoically, though to this day, I can't help but think if we had been older or better equipped emotionally to understand just what exactly was going on, we could have helped her. Maybe we even could have prevented what happened. Or maybe we couldn't have. I don't know. What I *do* know is, that Monday morning, three weeks into summer vacation, my thoughts were no more pressing than figuring out our plans for the summer. I grinned as I climbed the board slats nailed to the side of the tree to serve as a ladder and pulled myself up onto the platform. Grace was sitting in her corner on one of the torn lawn chair cushions we salvaged from the community dump, reading a library book and eating a strawberry Pop-Tart.

I didn't realize it at the time, but Grace was a pretty girl. Like me, she was gangly, though when she moved, there were different results. Where I was clumsy and awkward, Grace was graceful— her movements smooth and seamless. And there was something about the way she looked at people with her green, thickly lashed eyes. There was a depth about her that belied her years—a calmness that made all of us think she could handle anything.

"Hey," I said somewhat breathless from the climb.

She looked up, startled by my greeting. She had been so deeply engrossed in her book that she hadn't heard me come up.

"Hey yourself," she said as she stretched out her legs.

"Whatcha reading?" I asked.

"*The Outsiders*." Grace flipped it over so I could see the cover. "Not bad."

She broke off a piece of Pop-Tart and popped it into her mouth. She pushed several strands of blond hair from in front of her eyes and studied me as she chewed. The hollows beneath her eyes were smudged with shadows of fatigue. I was about to ask what time she had gotten to the Nest when a whoop of greeting came from the clearing. I peered down through the entrance as Natalie carelessly dropped her bike to the ground, jogged to the tree, and began to climb.

"What's up, chickens?" she said, rather than asked, as she heaved herself onto the platform. She was breathing heavily, her forehead and upper lip glistening with sweat.

Natalie Stewart was the leader and the smartest member of our group—not that Grace and I weren't smart; we were. But not like Natalie. She was not only smart, she was also fearless. If there was trouble to get into, rules to break, or feathers to ruffle, Natalie was typically the ringleader.

"Nothing," I said as I grabbed a cushion from the pile and tossed it at her. "How about you?"

"Hot." She settled herself on the cushion and pushed her sweaty bangs back from her forehead. "I'm probably already sunburned."

Her hair would eventually deepen to an enviable shade of auburn and her features would lengthen into smooth adult lines. But when we were young, Natalie was cursed with the bright orange hair, round freckled face, and pale complexion of her Irish ancestors. Whereas Grace and I would turn brown in the sun, Natalie's skin would redden, blister, and peel away, only to be the same shade of white as when she started. She hated her skin—but only slightly more than she hated the color of her coarse, unruly hair. For Natalie, her appearance was a source of constant frustration and because of that, she tried to pretend that looks weren't important. She covered it by being smart and fearless. But it still bothered her that she wasn't pretty. I enjoyed the fact that I knew that about her.

"So, did you guys hear about what happened to Mr. Holmes?"

Natalie's question shook me.

I shook my head, knowing that if anyone would know details of the latest gossip, it would be Natalie. In addition to being gifted at sneaking around and eavesdropping on other peoples' conversation, she also benefitted from the fact that her father was a detective with the Cherokee County Sheriff's Department. He generally knew everything that was going on in the county.

"Somebody painted nasty words on his pickup and then slashed one of the tires." I could tell from her tone that she was pleased to be able to deliver this information.

"Why would somebody do that?" I asked.

Grace raised her eyebrows, curious as well about the answer.

"Because he's black, duh," Natalie said as if it were obvious.

I frowned and then nodded slowly.

Edenbridge wasn't unwelcoming to strangers. That wouldn't

be Christian. Rather, they were polite—painfully polite. It was the Midwestern equivalent of the Southern expression *bless your heart*.

Enter the Holmes family. Not only were they newcomers to the town and the only black family, but in the minds of many people, they didn't belong because of how they got their land. It all started during the Vietnam War when Walter Hanson, the great-grandson of one of the town's founders, Emmet Hanson, gave his family's land to Anthony Holmes. Walter was the sole surviving member of the family line. A "confirmed bachelor"—I realize now what that meant—Walter farmed the family property until he was drafted to fight in Vietnam. He was a much better farmer than a soldier and no one was really surprised when he was killed in battle. What *did* come as a surprise was that just before he died, Walter deeded the land his family had held for generations to Anthony Holmes, the man who, despite leg and shoulder injuries of his own, had carried him to safety and medical attention.

At first, Mr. Holmes' claim was disputed. People in town talked about going in together and hiring a lawyer, but, without the Hanson family to object and because Mr. Holmes had documentation, there wasn't really anything anyone could do. The land belonged to Anthony Holmes—though had he known what was in store for his family, he might have sold the land immediately. But he was, at heart, an optimist and believed that this land was the first step for a better life. He was both right and wrong.

Like Walter Hanson, Anthony Holmes grew up working the land. He had a love of farming and also knew how to raise cattle, pigs, and chickens. So, when he was released from the army, it made perfect sense that he would take his wife and two children, go to Edenbridge, and farm the land that had been given to him. He was unprepared, however, for the sight that awaited him in his new home—flat land bursting with corn, wheat, milo, and soybeans. One planting season showed him that these weren't crops he was good at cultivating. Better, he decided, to raise pigs and chickens.

At first people in Edenbridge were amused. They took pleasure in making jokes at his expense. They stopped laughing, though, when the hot summer winds from the south funneled the heated stench of Mr. Holmes' animals into town. Their animosity increased when the farm crisis hit, crop prices hit rock bottom, and everyone began to lose money—everyone, that was, except Mr. Holmes. Because he focused on animals rather than crops, he was faring better than most. Rumor had it that he was even making a profit. Resentment ran high and the townspeople's treatment of the Holmeses ran from grudging to hostile. My grandfather was one of the worst in this regard.

A sour man with a hawkish nose and small black eyes, my grandfather stood barely above five feet in height. And, like many men of short stature, he tried to project the bravado of a much larger man by swaggering and bullying anyone around him, swearing like a sailor and gesticulating with a smoldering cigarette to emphasize his point. Regardless of the weather, he wore the same outfit: a short-sleeved white button-down with a pocket at the chest to hold his cigarettes, droopy gray or black polyester pants cinched below his large belly with a turquoise-inlaid, tooled leather belt, and cowboy boots.

My grandfather's belligerence scared me—as did his hatred of anyone different. Polacks . . . spics . . . niggers—my grandfather hated them all. That's why when Natalie mentioned the vandalism to Mr. Holmes' truck, I immediately thought of the conversation between my grandfather and his cronies the weekend before. I had been down at the station with my father.

"Goddamned stink," my grandfather had announced as he stepped inside the dirty garage. "Can't even take a breath of fresh air."

My father, who was head and shoulders deep in the engine of an old Chevrolet pickup, looked up warily.

"Somebody oughta go up there and teach that sumbitch a lesson."

This comment came from Randy Jenkins, one of the men who worked in the station. He was lying on his back, his legs sticking out from under the front of the pickup. As he spoke, he pushed himself out from under the truck. The caster wheels on the rolling creeper squeaked in protest. His face was dark from the dirt and grease of the old engine. With a huff, he sat up and looked meaningfully at my grandfather, who pulled a crumpled pack of cigarettes from his shirt pocket, shook one out, and stuck it between his lips.

"He better be careful somebody don't go put him in his place," he finally agreed. Despite the oil, grease, and gasoline cans, he flicked open the tarnished lighter and held the flame to the tip of the cigarette. He inhaled deeply, held the smoke in his lungs for several seconds, and then blew it out both nostrils. No one spoke and finally, my grandfather pulled the cigarette out of his mouth, hawked up a wad of phlegm and spit.

"—you know?"

Natalie's question brought me sharply back to the present.

"Know what?" I asked.

Natalie sighed in exaggerated exasperation. "You weren't listening."

"I was," I insisted. "Really."

"I *said* that my dad told my mom that he got to Mr. Holmes' place and Mr. Holmes had his shotgun out. He said he was fed up with the way people treated him and his family. He said it wasn't his fault that people were losing their farms or that his pigs smelled. He even threatened Dad."

We were all silent for several moments, no one knowing what to say. Finally, Grace spoke up. "I'm glad my dad isn't a cop. It sounds too dangerous."

Grace's father was a dentist and, like most of the fathers in town, traveled to Winston to work—or, at least, he had until the year before when he announced to Grace's mother one night at dinner that he'd fallen in love with one of his hygienists. He moved out the next day, and after that Grace visited him every other weekend in his sparsely furnished bachelor's apartment.

"It's not so bad," Natalie said almost matter-of-factly. "Besides, I get to hear all about stuff that's going on. And I know stuff most people don't."

"What do you mean?" I asked, both curious and slightly frightened.

Natalie thought for a moment and I imagined her trying to determine what information would elicit the biggest reaction from us. She had an excellent sense of timing when it came to storytelling. Her dream, she had confessed to me one afternoon when it was just the two of us, was to write murder mysteries.

"Well . . . I know about how to solve mysteries. I've seen all sorts of crime photos and I know about fingerprints and blood and stuff. I could probably solve murders if I wanted to."

We believed her—or at least I did. And I could guess from the expression on Grace's face, she did too. We were silent and in that silence everything suddenly seemed too small—too intense. The morning sounds of locusts and birds seemed somehow ominous rather than pleasant. I was uncomfortable.

"Hey, let's ride up to the store and get some watermelon sticks," I said to break the spell.

"Yeah," Natalie said. "And then we can ride over to the old Montgomery place and see if we can get in."

Sneaking outside of the boundaries of town and exploring the boarded-up house that used to belong to the Montgomery family was something we had been planning to do most of the summer, but had thus far been unable to accomplish. The boarded-up house, which had been abandoned for at least a decade, was a never-ending source of fascination for our group—and particularly for Natalie. Not only was it supposed to be haunted by the ghost of William Montgomery, the man who built the house in the early 1900s and hung himself during the height of the Great Depression, but it was also rumored to have been abandoned in such haste by later occupants that the plates were still on the dinner table.

"I don't know, you guys." Grace shook her head slowly back and forth. "What if we get caught? We're not supposed to be in there."

"Exactly." Natalie grinned and raised one eyebrow dramatically. "Which is why, my dear Watson, we need to do it. Just think how cool it will be. Nobody's been in there for years. And we've got everything we need to do it without getting caught."

When I had first suggested sneaking into the house, Natalie had jumped into action, making a list of everything she thought we'd need for a successful break-in. Per her instructions, we had each brought flashlights, gloves, ski masks, and rope. Now, Natalie turned her attention to the collection of things that lay piled in the corner of the Nest.

"We will definitely need the flashlights and we don't want to leave fingerprints so we'll need the gloves, too. But . . ." She pursed her lips in thought. "I don't think we need the ski masks. It's too hot."

"I don't know, Nat." Grace said again. She looked first at me and then at Natalie.

"So, don't come," Natalie gave a nonchalant shrug. "Me and Birdie will go, right?" She looked at me for affirmation.

"Yeah," I said with forced fearlessness. Grace looked back and forth between us. I leaned forward and touched her knee. "You should come, though. It won't be the same without you. And we won't go to jail."

Grace stared into my eyes for what seemed like forever before she gave a deep sigh. "Okay. I mean, why not?"

"Excellent!" Natalie said with satisfaction.

And that's how the decision was made to break into the Montgomery house. We were just curious girls who wanted adventure. We had no idea that we would set in motion a chain reaction that would change everything.

## Chapter 3

What I remember most about breaking into the abandoned Montgomery house was that it was like entering another world. Outside, the air was hot, muggy and the sunlight almost too bright. But inside the house, it was musty and dark; the air, though cooler, was thick with dust and an unnatural silence. We entered through a window in the back. Natalie's gloves came in handy for more than preventing fingerprints. In an attempt to keep people out, the windows and doors had been boarded up with splintery planks of varying lengths which we had to pry away. The gloves had protected our hands from the jagged shards of glass that survived a long-ago thrown rock.

One by one, we climbed through the lower portion of the window and then stood, clustered together, in the unnatural silence of what appeared to at have been, at one time, a dining room. Despite the stories of a house frozen in time, most of the furniture had been removed. All that remained was a rickety-looking wooden chair with a broken leg, a stained blanket, a pile of rotting boards, and various brands of crushed beer cans. The wallpaper had been peeled away from one of the walls and in its place someone had spray-painted the words, "Kill the PIGS!!" and "Satan worships here."

I turned to look at Grace. We hadn't turned on our flashlights, and in the gloom her eyes were wide and very white in her tanned face. Next to her, Natalie stood very still. Her already pale skin looked almost translucent in the half-light. She turned her head to look at us and seemed to realize we were waiting for her to tell us what to do next. She swallowed and then gestured to a doorway that led toward the front of the house. "Let's see what's out there."

She turned and started for the doorway. Grace and I followed. We walked silently into the main area of the house. The walls were gray and, in some places where the sheetrock hadn't ripped off, dark mold stained the surface. I stepped carefully over the warped and rotting floor and around a pile of old magazines, a discarded pair of boy's underpants, and a Jim Beam bottle.

The smell of cool, dank decay tickled my nose and I sneezed.

"Bless you," Grace whispered. She was walking in the direction of the hallway. Buckled and peeling wallpaper drooped from the wall to her right. The floor groaned under her slight weight. Ahead of her, Natalie turned toward what must have been a front bedroom, shone her light into the room, and froze.

"Uh oh."

Grace, too, halted and we both picked our way carefully to stand next to Natalie, who swung the beam of her light from a sleeping bag, to a milk crate, to a flashlight, to a book and notebook stacked neatly on top of the sleeping bag. Next to it was a familiar army camouflage jacket with the name "SULLIVAN" on a cloth badge.

"What is it?"

"It's Don Wan's army jacket," Natalie said.

I looked at Grace who swallowed nervously.

Everyone in Edenbridge knew Don—all the way back to the days when he had been Lenny Sullivan, the youngest of seven and the son of Red Sullivan, who had a reputation for abusing both whiskey and his family—generally in that order. It was after one particularly violent encounter with his father that Lenny, who still went by that name in those days, ran away and joined the army. Eventually, he was sent to Vietnam where, by his account, his army buddies christened him Don Juan because of his romantic prowess. It was only years after his discharge and subsequent name change that he realized he had misspelled Juan on the name change application. Because he always had heard it pronounced, he just assumed it was spelled like it sounded. He was wrong.

After two tours in Vietnam and an honorable discharge, the newly minted Don Wan moved to the West Coast, where he spent the better part of two years feeding his addiction to opiates. He let his crew cut grow into a shaggy mess and purchased a motorcycle, painting fantastical dragons on the gas tank. His days consisted of getting high, working on his motorcycle, and expanding his collection of hand-drawn tattoos.

No one in Edenbridge knew why Lenny/Don returned home. Some people said it was the death of his father. Some said he couldn't make it in California. Others said it had to do with a scrape with the law. All we knew was that one day he came roaring back into town on a motorcycle covered with flames. A clearly pregnant girl with stringy blond hair sat behind him, her arms barely able to span the distance created by her belly and his chest. And he wasn't Lenny, he told everyone; he was Don.

Within weeks, the girl, whose name we came to know was Tammy, left to return to wherever she came from, and the house, which was mortgaged to the teeth, was repossessed. Homeless, jobless, and with only his motorcycle to his name, Don slept wherever he could find a bed. When that didn't work out, he slept in the woods near the creek, under one of the county bridges, or in one of the many abandoned barns or farmhouses. Apparently, this included the Montgomery house. To make money, he worked odd jobs around town.

"Do you think he's here?" Grace whispered. We stood in silence and listened for any creaks or sounds to indicate he was upstairs or in an unexplored part of the house. The soft rustle of what were probably mice was the only sound.

Natalie shook her head. "We would have seen his motorcycle outside if he was around, right?" She raised her eyebrows and looked at each of us for confirmation.

We nodded.

"Okay, so . . ." She looked down at Don's things. A battered and grubby notebook lay on top of the army-issue sleeping bag. Natalie reached down and picked it up.

"Nat, what are you doing?" I could hear the anxiety in my own voice and tried to remain calm. "That's Don's. You can't look at it."

"This isn't his house," she said. "That means it's fair game. Besides, don't you want to know what Crazy McCrazerson writes about?"

I shook my head. "I'm going to see what's upstairs."

"Suit yourself," Natalie said and opened the notebook. She flipped through a couple of pages before gasping. "Guys, come here." Her tone was urgent. "You've got to see this."

Both Grace and I moved quickly to stand on either side of her and looked down at the notebook. Sketches of full-breasted women lounging in various poses jumped off the page. In some of the drawings, the women wore bits of clothing, in some, just hats or panties. But in most of the sketches, the women were nude. Some were touching themselves with long, graceful fingers. In others, they were reaching forward for something or someone outside the picture.

"Gross." Grace said. "Are they all like that?"

Natalie began to slowly turn the pages. Not all of the drawings were of nude women. Some were just faces—faces of women or girls or boys. One, I thought, looked remarkably like one of the boys in our class. Another, I saw to my shock, looked like me. Grace saw it, too.

"Birdie . . ." she said softly, "This looks like you. He drew you."

I felt sick. My arms and neck and legs began to tingle.

Natalie turned on her flashlight, shone it onto the page, and then looked from the page to my face and back again. She could see I was upset.

"It looks a little like her," she said finally. "But not really. Birdie's skinnier and her eyes look different. And her hair is longer. It's not her."

Grace looked again at the picture and then again at me. I could see she didn't agree, but she said nothing.

"Let's go, you guys," Grace said finally. "I don't like it here."

I shivered, praying that Natalie would decide that Grace was right. For once, she did.

"Okay," Natalie said, still looking at me. The shadows masked her eyes, but I could tell she was thinking. She closed the notebook. As she leaned down to put it back on top of the sleeping bag, several loose sheets of unlined paper fell to the floor. She bent to pick them up and as she did so, looked down at the images.

29

She gasped softly before quickly slipping them into the back of the book.

"What is it?" I asked. Grace, who had walked to the doorway, turned.

"Nothing," Natalie said, too quickly. "Just more of the same stuff." She carefully placed the notebook back on the sleeping bag where she had found it and then stood. She walked quickly to the door and shouldered past Grace. "Let's get out of here."

I met Grace's gaze, shrugged, and then followed Natalie out of the room. I could tell from the way she walked that she was upset about something. What, I wondered, had she seen that she wasn't telling us?

## Chapter 4

Climbing out of the gloom of the Montgomery house and into the heat of the late morning sunshine was a relief—or, at least, it was for me. The three of us blinked uncomfortably in the bright light and then started to walk, our heads down, to the cluster of trees near the old well where we had hidden our bikes. Natalie was quiet and I glanced at her several times, tempted to ask her what she had seen.

"So, what are we going to do now?" Grace asked as we hauled our bikes out of the bushes and pushed them out to the blacktopped road that would take us back into town.

"I should probably go home," Natalie said.

I turned to look at her, surprised at her answer. She never wanted to go home.

"We probably all should," she said and looked pointedly at me. I narrowed my eyes like I had seen my mother do when she was suspicious of something I had said, but Natalie ignored me.

"I think I'll go back to the Nest," Grace said.

As she spoke, we climbed on our bikes and began to slowly pedal back toward town. Within ten minutes we had reached the Lempkins' house. I grinned to see Andy mowing the grass, his T-shirt tucked in the waistband of his jeans, his skinny chest and stringy arms reddened from the sun. He smiled and raised his hand in greeting. My flushed face turned even redder as I tried to be casual and wave back.

Part of my nervousness was because I was in love with Andy. But equally significant was that everyone in town was slightly intimidated by the Lempkins. For lack of a better analogy, they were the Kennedys of Edenbridge. Or, if not the Kennedys, then the Osmonds. In addition to Ted and Alice, the family consisted of three boys and two girls who happened to be twins. Like their parents, they were all attractive with naturally wavy hair, perfect teeth, and a natural grace that made everything each of them did seem effortless. They possessed a celebrity quality that made the rest of us jealous. But you couldn't dislike them for it because they were also genuinely nice.

Often on Sunday afternoons in the fall, all seven of them could be seen in their front yard, tossing a football around or playing three-on-three while Alice sat on the front steps and watched the game with a steaming cup of what we all imagined to be cocoa. The other thing about the Lempkins was that they genuinely liked each other. You could tell—not only by all the family activities, but also by the way they subtly attended to each other at school or at town events.

Natalie glanced in my direction as we passed and snickered. My crush on Andy was common knowledge and she enjoyed teasing me about it. "Birdie's got a boyfriend," she sang. "Kissy kissy."

"Shut up," I said and pedaled faster. We were almost to the Mercantile and if we were all going home for the afternoon, I wanted to get some jawbreakers and bubble gum. "Last one to the store is a rotten egg."

We raced, then, as fast as possible to the store and only hit our brakes at the end so we could skid to a dramatic stop.

"I won," Natalie announced and climbed off her bike. "And I had the longest skid mark." She pointed at the ground.

"You're so full of it," I said. "I—"

My words were interrupted by yelling from across the street at my grandfather's service station. Parked in front of the pumps was Mr. Holmes' battered Ford pickup. Large, scoured circles that looked like gray rain clouds spotted the passenger side and the hood—as if someone had taken an SOS pad and tried to scrub off the paint. I remembered what Natalie had said about the words someone had painted on his truck.

"I'll be right back," I said to Grace and Natalie as I climbed back onto my bike and began to ride through the intersection toward the station. As I pedaled, I heard Mr. Holmes start the rumbling engine of his truck. I looked up just as he threw it into gear and stomped on the accelerator. The truck lurched forward.

"—asshole!" Mr. Holmes yelled as he flipped Randy Jenkins the bird and then gunned the truck, not stopping at the four-way stop. Our eyes met for a long moment—his furious and mine, I'm sure, scared. His eyes widened as he cranked the steering wheel at the last minute to avoid hitting me. I wobbled on my bike, thrown off balance by fright and surprise, and then fell onto the pavement. From the corner of my eye, I saw my grandfather run toward me. I had never seen him run and in different circumstances, his short-legged gait might have been funny. From the other side of the street, Grace and Natalie rushed forward. Though they were farther away, they reached me first.

"I'll kill that goddamned son of a bitch," my grandfather puffed as he panted to a halt. The tails of his shirt had come untucked from his pants and I caught a glimpse of his round, fish-white belly.

"Birdie, are you okay?" Grace asked.

I nodded and looked down at my left knee. It was bloody and raw. So were my elbow and hand. Even though it hadn't yet begun to hurt, I started to cry.

"That's enough of that," my grandfather said gruffly.

Natalie and Grace helped me to my feet while my grandfather righted my bike and began to push it in the direction of the station. By the time we reached the small, grungy office, my grandfather was on the phone to my mother.

"—better get down here," he said. "I'll explain later." As he spoke, his black eyes blazed with barely contained fury. I found out what happened only later that night, when my father came home for dinner. My grandfather had called him at work.

"Apparently," my father said that night at dinner as he helped himself to a second helping of fried potatoes and onions, "Anthony Holmes came into town to fill up a couple of gas cans. Slim was across the street getting a couple of sandwiches for lunch. Dad was in the back and Randy was manning the pumps. Randy made a comment about the smell. Anthony got angry and started yelling.

Randy yelled back. Anthony jumped in the truck and—well, you know the rest."

Within hours, different versions of the story (all from people who "had it on good authority") had circulated around town and that evening, our phone rang off the hook with people calling to glean additional details—all under the cover of calling to "see how Birdie was doing." I listened to my mother later that night as she talked on the phone to Natalie's mother. Like Natalie and I, they had been friends since childhood. They talked about everything and this was no exception.

"I know," my mother said into the receiver and then laughed. She was in the kitchen perched on the stool next to the rotary wall phone. Though it was unlikely my father could hear her over the noise of the baseball game on television, she spoke in a low tone. From my hiding place around the corner, I had to strain to hear her words.

She listened intently to whatever Mary Jane was saying.

"Well, honestly, I don't blame him," she said. "I would have . . . *exactly*."

Blame who, I wondered? And what would she have done?

"Okay, well . . . yeah, just tell Nate that we're not going to make a stink about this," my mother said and then laughed. "No, it wasn't a Freudian slip . . . yeah." She laughed again and then became serious.

"There was something else I wanted to talk to you about. It's not only about today, but it really made me think about how much the girls run around town on their own." She paused. "I know. I think that's a good idea, but I'm not sure what kind of reaction you'll get from Brenda. Half the time I'm not even sure if she remembers she *has* a daughter."

They were talking about Grace's mother.

"Well, have you seen that new boyfriend?" my mother asked. "He looks like he's nothing but trouble. I know Brenda's hurting, but she really needs to pay attention to Grace." My mother sighed and I peeked around the corner to see her coiling the phone cord around her finger. She seemed to be wrapping up the conversation.

34

"Okay, well call me if you . . . okay. Yeah. Bye."

She hung up the phone. I shrank back into the shadows.

"I know you're listening," she said.

I didn't move.

"Birdie," she said. "Come here."

Slowly, I stepped into the triangle of light that shone out of the kitchen into the dark hallway. She smiled.

"You okay?" she asked.

I nodded.

"How are your war wounds?" she asked and inclined her head toward my knees and arm. I raised my hand and the faint odor of Band-Aids and Bactine wafted upward.

"Okay," I said and shrugged. "What did Natalie's mom say?"

My mother stared at me for several seconds, wondering, I'm sure, how much she should say. "She was telling me about what Mr. Holmes said happened," she said finally. "Why he got so angry."

"Why?"

"Mr. Jenkins said some things that were mean."

"Did he call him a nigger?"

My mother blinked and sucked in her breath. Her expression was furious as she looked around the kitchen, though her eyes landed on nothing long enough to actually see it. She exhaled slowly.

"Did you hear that word down at the station?"

I nodded.

"I want you to listen to me, Birdie," she said. "That is not a word you should be using. It's a bad word. It's a . . . ." she paused. "You need to promise me you won't use that word—no matter how many other people you hear use it. Understand?"

I nodded solemnly and she studied me for several seconds. "Good." She kissed me on the forehead and then looked over my head at the oven clock. "Now, go tell Tara it's time for her to take a bath and get ready for bed. And do me a favor . . . keep an eye on her, okay? I need to talk to your father."

## Chapter 5

I woke up early the next morning, eager to meet up with Grace and Natalie to discuss the events of the previous day. I knew that Natalie would tell me what her mother said on the phone the night before and I was curious to know what people around town were saying. It was kind of fun to know that I was the subject of so much discussion—or at least part of the subject.

I sniffed the air. My mother was frying eggs and cooking bacon. My stomach growled at the aroma and I jumped out of bed, pulling my faded Strawberry Shortcake nightgown off in one swift movement. I reached for my clothes from the day before—cut-off jean shorts and a striped tank top—and held them to my nose. They smelled sweaty and were a little dirty from our adventure in the Montgomery house, but I didn't care.

"Morning," I announced as I wandered into the kitchen.

My mother stood in front of the stove, a spatula in one hand and a dish towel in the other. Tara sat on the stool under the wall phone. Her round face was still flushed from sleep and her blond curls were tousled. She smiled, her blue eyes picking up the navy of her Wonder Woman pajamas.

"Hi," she said brightly. "Guess what? We're having eggs."

"We always have eggs, stupid," I said.

Our mother spun around and glared at me.

"Don't call your sister, 'stupid,'" she said and jerked her head in Tara's direction. "Apologize."

"Sorry," I mumbled in Tara's direction, though I didn't look at her.

My mother eyed me critically and pressed her lips together.

"Didn't you wear those clothes yesterday?" she asked after several seconds. "And, when was the last time you brushed your hair?"

"Yesterday," I lied. Her eyes narrowed and I could tell she wasn't buying it. "Or maybe the day before," I amended.

She sighed.

"Birdie, I can tell from here that you haven't touched it since at least last week," she said.

I groaned. Ever since I had let the underside of my long hair become so matted and knotted that it had taken my mother two hours with a rat tail comb to untangle it, she had become much more critical of my hygiene.

"But, Mom—" I began, and stopped when she held up the spatula. Grease from the bacon fat flew off and splattered onto the linoleum. She scowled and quickly bent to dab at it with the dish towel.

"Dammit," she muttered.

When she stood, her gaze again fell on me.

"So, I've talked to your Dad," she said. "And we both agree there need to be some changes."

"I'll go brush my hair," I sighed and started to move toward the doorway.

"That's not what I mean," she said and then added, "Although, I expect you to brush your hair after breakfast."

"So, what do you mean, 'changes'?" I asked.

"What happened yesterday could have ended very badly," she said as she turned back to the skillet and slid a greasy egg onto each of the plates on the counter. "It made us both realize that too much of the time we don't know where you are or what you're doing." She looked sideways at me, her eyes narrowed. "Or, if you're doing things you know you're not supposed to. For example, what were you girls doing yesterday morning—before you went to the Mercantile?"

"Huh?" I asked, buying time.

"Mrs. Granger said she saw the three of you out near the Montgomery house. You know the rules. You are not supposed to go outside of town."

"We ..." I said and then looked at the floor and shrugged. "We were just riding around. We weren't doing anything wrong."

"Birdie, look at me."

I raised my head and she studied my face for several seconds before shaking her head. "You're a horrible liar. What were you doing out near the Montgomery house?"

I glanced up and then shifted my gaze to Tara, who was watching the conversation with interest. My mother turned back to the bacon, putting two slices on each of the plates before popping two pieces of bread in the toaster.

"Birdie?" she said, as she turned once again to face me. "I asked you a question."

"We just . . ." I began and then stopped. Lying about being there would only make the situation worse. I sighed and then said, "We just rode out there to see what was going on."

"Even though you *knew* you weren't supposed to be there."

"Geez, Mom," I groaned. "I'm almost a *teen*ager. Why *can't* I ride over there? Other kids' parents don't care if they do."

"I'm not 'other kids parents'," she said. "I'm *your* parent and what I say goes. And when I tell you that you can only go down to the Mercantile or your tree house, I mean it. You've got to learn to do what I say."

I sighed dramatically and glanced at Tara, who stuck out her tongue, clearly enjoying my discomfort. I waited for the toaster to eject the toast and for my mother to turn back to the counter before I pointed at Tara to let her know I would get her back.

"Either way, I've talked to your dad ..." She pointed at me with her index finger. "And he agrees, so don't try to play us off each other—and we both think you should stay around the house from now on."

"But that's not fair," I whined. "There's nothing to do here."

She shrugged, turned back to the counter, and began to scrape Parkay onto the slices of toast. "You can play Atari or we can set up the Slip'N Slide."

"Slip'N Slide is for babies," I said sullenly.

"Well, I'm sorry," she said firmly. "But this is not up for

negotiation." She shook her head as she extended her arm for more margarine. "I don't make these rules just to be mean, Birdie. There's a reason. What if something happens to you and you're not where you're supposed to be? How am I going to find you? There are men out there that would think nothing of waiting until one of you is off by yourself and then kidnapping you and murdering you."

"I know, I know," I groaned. "Don't talk to strangers. Don't get in their cars. You've told me a million times."

She sighed, set the knife on the counter with a thud, turned, and came to where I stood. I stepped back a half-step, sure I had pushed her to her limit already. She crouched and put her hand on my shoulder. Her tone was gentle. "Not everyone who wants to hurt you is a stranger, Birdie. What would you do if someone you knew came up to you and tried to grab you or tried to get you to go with them?"

The look in her eyes scared me more than the thought of abduction.

"I wouldn't go."

"That's right," she said. "You say 'no.' And if someone, even someone you know offers you a ride, you don't take it. Do you understand?"

Her grip on my arm tightened and I nodded. She turned and beckoned to Tara, who slid off the stool and padded over to where we stood. Our mother wrapped her other arm around her and the three of us stood, three points of a triangle. We nodded. Tara's eyes were wide. I am sure mine were, too. I felt my throat constrict when I tried to swallow. "Mom, you're scaring us."

She closed her eyes and pulled both of us close. I inhaled her scent—a mixture of baby oil, bacon, and something that wholly belonged to her. "Sometimes being scared isn't a bad thing," she murmured. "It makes you cautious." I felt her kiss the tops of our heads before standing and returning to the counter and the half-buttered toast. "But back to the new rules. First and foremost, you're getting too old to run around without a shirt on, Birdie. You're not a little girl anymore."

"Me, too?" Tara asked.

My mother seemed to consider this before nodding. "Yes, both of you. And, Birdie, I don't want you going out by yourself any more. You need to be with at least one, if not two, of your friends. And this business of going out into the woods near the creek . . . I would really prefer it if when you girls get together, you do it at our house or Natalie's."

"What about Grace's house?"

"Grace can come here. But I would prefer you not go over there."

"But, what about the Nest? Can we go there?"

She again paused, as if considering. "No," she said finally. "I don't think you girls need to be out there by yourselves. It's too private. Someone could easily find you and there wouldn't be anyone that could help you."

I thought again about being in the Montgomery house and of Don Wan's drawings. I thought about the drawing of my face and imagined what could have happened if he had walked in and caught us going through his things. Would he have killed us? If we had escaped, would he have come to the Nest and kidnapped us? What would have happened then? I knew from Natalie's vivid descriptions of crimes her father investigated that there was rape and torture. I forced myself to imagine Don with his greasy hair and his bad breath. I thought about his hands on me, undressing me. Would he rape me? Not at first, I thought. More likely he would make me pose so he could draw me. Or maybe he would make me spread my legs or touch myself so he could draw me like he did those other women.

I imagined being trapped in the house with him—in the back bedroom where his things were. It was dark except for a candle which he had set close to me. Even though I knew Don was there, I couldn't see him, only a hunched, dark form. All I could hear were the terrified puffs of my own breath and the soft scratch of his pencil on the paper. And I could smell him, the spicy, sour odor of his sweat. I thought, too late, about my mother's warning and tried not to let him see my fear. The room, still hot from the afternoon sun, was thick and moist. I tried not to move, despite the trickle of sweat running down my back.

How would he kill me, I wondered? Would he strangle me? I imagined him putting down his notebook and coming toward me, his hands suddenly around my throat, tightening—

"Birdie?" My mother's voice broke into my thoughts. She had been talking and I hadn't heard a word. I blinked, still caught somewhere between the present and my imagination. "This isn't a punishment. I just don't want anything to ever happen to you. I love you too much. Do you understand?"

My stomach tightened and I knew right then and there I should tell her about the drawings—about how one of them was of me. But, I thought, if I told her the truth, I would also have to tell her how and where we found them. And then I *would* be grounded —as would Natalie and probably Grace. It was better to pretend as if none of it had ever happened. We hadn't gotten caught and we were all back safe where we belonged.

"I understand," I mumbled.

"Good," she said with a sigh and thrust one of the plates toward me and the other at Tara, who still stood next to me. "Now eat before your breakfast gets cold."

We took our plates and walked to the tall wooden stools that ringed the outer edge of the bar. "Can I go over to Natalie's after I eat?"

She turned and shook her head. "Why don't you play here today?"

"You said we could go over to each other's houses." I sighed dramatically. "Besides, there's nothing to do here."

"Of course there is. Play with Tara. Read a book. Dig a hole to China. I don't care, just don't test me on this."

"Okay." I said the word with as much disdain as I could manage and, even though I was no longer hungry, took the fork, stabbed the yolk of the fried egg, and watched as it ran over the white. I was reminded of the day Natalie, Grace, and I tried unsuccessfully to fry eggs on the sidewalk. I glanced over at Tara, who was dipping the corner of the toast into her own yolk. She looked up and grinned. There was no way I was going to play with her. She was still just a baby.

41

"May I be excused?" I asked. "I'm not hungry."

"Finish your breakfast." My mother spoke the words without turning from the sink where she was washing the dishes.

I looked over at Tara and considered sliding my egg onto her plate, but decided it was too risky and then I would also owe her. A sandwich would be the fastest way to finish, so I put the strips of bacon on one triangle of toast, folded the egg on top, and then stuck the other triangle of toast on top of that. I shoved one corner into my mouth in an enormous bite. I chewed a couple of times, swallowed quickly, and took another bite. I was finished in less than a minute.

"Done," I announced and slid down from the stool. I took my plate over to my mother, who turned to look at Tara's plate to make sure I hadn't pushed my food off onto hers.

"You're going to make yourself sick eating like that." She took the plate and put it and my fork into the soapy water. "Go brush your teeth and your hair."


As soon as I finished brushing my hair, I wandered back into the kitchen. Mom was in the bathroom putting on her makeup and Tara was in her room. I climbed up onto the stool and called Natalie and Grace to let them know I was, at least for the time being, stuck at home. No one answered at Grace's house, but Natalie picked up on the second ring. Our conversation was whispered and rushed.

"I know," Natalie's tone was angry. "Me, too."

I twisted the phone cord around my finger like I had seen my mom do. "So, what are we going to do?"

I heard a sigh on the other end of the line. "I don't know. I need to think about it. But for now, keep cool."

"Okay." I hesitated, wanting to ask about Don Wan's notebook, but also scared to. I took a deep breath. "Nat, what did you think of those pictures—the ones Don Wan had in his notebook . . ." I swallowed.

"I thought they were creepy," she said. "Really creepy."

I remembered her reaction when she looked at the papers that had fallen out of the notebook. "What was on the papers—the ones that fell out?"

"Nothing."

"Nothing?"

"No, nothing. Just more drawings."

I swallowed. "Of . . . ?"

"Just of people," she said. "Why do you care?"

"Were any of them of me?"

Natalie was silent and I could tell she was deciding whether or not to tell me what she saw. "No," she said finally. "They were of Grace. They were all of Grace . . . naked."

"We need to tell her." I felt the panic rise up in my chest. "We need to tell our folks."

"She's probably at the Nest." Natalie was quiet. "Would your mom take you out there?"

"Probably not," I said. "She's in a bad mood today."

At the mention of her, my mother came into the kitchen and pointed at her watch. "Time's up," she mouthed and whirled her finger in the air. "Wrap it up."

I nodded. "Mom's making me get off the phone," I said in my normal voice and then quickly added, "Wanna come over tomorrow?"

My mother, overhearing the invitation, frowned and shook her head. "Birdie," she hissed, "You should have asked me first."

I covered the mouthpiece even as I could hear through the earpiece Natalie hollering out to her mother, "Mom, can I go over to Birdie's house tomorrow?"

"Sorry," I whispered back and then amended, "But you said they could come over here. Please? You won't even know we're here. I promise. Besides, you said . . ."

My mother opened her mouth to speak and then, seeing something in my expression, began to laugh. I could tell I had already won the battle. I heard Natalie having a muffled conversation with her mother. Suddenly, she was back on the phone. "Yeah. Tomorrow works, but I can't come over until after I clean my room." I heard her mother in the background. "Okay, *Mom*. Sorry. I'm back. Want me to call Grace and see if she can come, too?"

"Yes," I said and smiled at my mother, who shook her head. "See you then."

At the same time I was plotting how to circumvent my mother's new rules, Tommy Anderson sat in the kitchen of his grandparents' house and thought about how much he hated being stuck in Edenbridge for the summer. I, of course, didn't know Tommy then. It was only after we became friends that I learned about his experience that summer. He had been sent from Chicago by his parents with the hopes that living with his grandparents would help straighten him out. More than anything, though, it simply made him angry.

He was bored and every day was the same. Sleep in, eat breakfast, and try to ignore the sounds of the daytime soap operas his partially deaf grandmother was addicted to watching. He knew the schedule by heart: *The Young and the Restless* at 11:30 followed by *As the World Turns* at 12:30 followed by *Guiding Light* at 2. Saturdays were dedicated to cleaning and chores, so the television was off, but on Sunday mornings it was back on so anyone passing by could appreciate the efforts of the television evangelists, preaching fire and brimstone and cajoling viewers to change their evil ways and donate money.

Tommy hated Edenbridge. In Chicago, there had been a lot to do. But that, according to his parents, was part of the problem. In Chicago, he had gotten into trouble, cut class, been involved in several fights, and was twice caught shoplifting. His parents were concerned, but it wasn't until they found the drugs in his closet that they decided drastic measures had to be taken.

They thought his friends were the problem. When he told me about this later, he laughed. His friends weren't the problem. What his parents didn't realize was that they weren't leading him . . . he was leading them. It was *his* idea to skip school and hang out at the park and smoke. With his dark hair, lean body, and sly smile, *he* had been the one who had come up with the idea of luring the cruising fags into the filthy park bathrooms and then rolling them for cash. It had been lucrative in more ways than one because more often than not, the men they beat and robbed also carried drugs with them. Weed, coke, poppers . . . each man was different. But Tommy and his friends didn't care. A hit was a hit, and trying new things was fun—especially when supplemented with the beer or alcohol Emilio's cousin, Lawrence, bought for them.

That, he thought, was the worst part of being in Edenbridge—the lack of drugs and alcohol. He had only been here for two weeks and he was itching for a fix. He didn't care what it was, just as long as it was something. Finding it was the trick. Because he was from a place where public transportation made having and driving a car unnecessary, at the age of seventeen, Tommy had neither a driver's license nor the skills necessary to drive a car. His grandfather had promised to teach him, but thus far, had managed to avoid fulfilling that promise—likely at the behest of Tommy's parents.

So, day after day he sat in the house with the television blaring and dreamed of escape. Sometimes he would explore the town. Other times he would walk down to the Mercantile and exercise his five-fingered discount. His latest acquisition was a hunting knife. It hadn't been hard to steal, given that the owner of the store was deaf, dumb, and blind. It had been easy, in fact. Tommy imagined the looks on his friends' faces when he returned to Chicago and flashed his knife. He imagined the fear in those fags' faces when he pulled the knife out and held it to their throats. He felt a tingle in his belly at the thought.

He had considered asking his grandfather to take him hunting. He wanted to try killing something and the thought of shooting a gun sounded fun. Emilio's cousin, Lawrence, had an old .357 Magnum he found in a dumpster. The one time Tommy held it, it felt big, heavy, and powerful in his hands. He had gripped the handle, hefted its weight, and shifted it from hand to hand. Holding the hunting knife made him feel the same way. He liked the power that seemed to flow through his hand and up his wrist and arm.

Maybe it was time to try it out, he thought. Get a feel for the weapon. He glanced into the living room at his grandmother. She was midway through *As the World Turns*.

"Grandma," Tommy said. "I'm going to go for a walk."

"Eh?" his grandmother said, glancing around.

"I'm going to go for a walk," he said slowly and distinctly.

"Okay," she said. "Stay out of trouble."

Tommy nodded exaggeratedly before turning and tromping upstairs to his room. The knife was wrapped in a T-shirt and stuffed between the box springs and the mattress of his twin bed. He slid his hand inside, searching for and then finding the soft bundle. He unwrapped the knife and looked at it. The blade was shiny; the dark wooden handle deeply grained. He held it, feeling once again the power it contained. He moved to stand in front of the mirror, liking what he saw—a man who was fearless and could take what he wanted. He felt that tingle again in the pit of his stomach.

He considered how to carry the knife and it occurred to him that perhaps he should steal a leather case—something that would not only protect the blade, but also protect him when he wore it on the inside of his clothing, against the skin. That's how he wanted to have it—close to him. He grinned, rewrapped the blade, and stuffed the bundle in the waistband of his pants. Pulling his shirt over the front and turning sideways, He could still see a bulge. But, he thought, if he changed into a looser shirt, he could probably get it out of the house without notice.

As he changed, Tommy considered where to stash the knife while he stole the case. The garage was a possibility, but if he did that, there was the chance that his grandfather would find it. The same applied to the tool shed. The best place, he thought, would be someplace where no one went. Immediately, he thought of the woods near the creek that ran behind the store. He could stash the knife, walk back to the store, steal the case, and then go back to reclaim his knife. Maybe he could steal a sharpener, too.

He grinned, imagining how he would sharpen the knife to a razor sharp edge. And maybe, he thought suddenly, he could find some animals in the woods that he could hunt and kill. Suddenly, the summer didn't seem so bad.

Tommy walked awkwardly down the stairs, unaccustomed to the feel of the bundle against his stomach. He let the screen door bang shut behind him and squinted into the harsh light. The noonday sun was unforgiving and the hot wind carried a sour stench that even his city nose recognized. He grimaced, shook his head, and again wondered how people lived in a place like this. It seemed so different from what he remembered from his childhood visits. Then, it had seemed magical. The days had seemed to stretch out forever before slipping into the violet hues of evening and, finally, firefly-sparkled nights. But this, he thought as he scanned the faded houses of the neighbors and the yards that seemed drained of life and color, was just pathetic.

He bounded off the front porch and headed toward the cracked sidewalk. Like Edenbridge, it too, had seen better days. Roots had burrowed under the concrete and caused it to buckle. Grass grew up between the cracks, and in some places the sidewalk was nothing more than a spiderweb of oddly shaped chunks of cement.

The Mercantile was two blocks from his grandparents' house. The woods that ran alongside the town side of the creek were a ten-minute walk from the other side of the store. Tommy planned his route carefully. His short criminal career already had taught him that it's best not to call attention to yourself if you can avoid it. And, walking back and forth in front of the store on his way to and from the woods was something that even the old fart who owned the store might notice. He decided to take different routes to and from the woods—make it look like he was just taking a walk, checking out the town.

At the end of the block, he made a right turn, walked to the end of the block and then turned left, heading in his original direction, but a block beyond the store. He would, he thought, take this street past the main drag and on to the woods, where he could find someplace to hide the knife. Then he would go back to the store, get what he needed, and return for the knife. As he walked, he scanned the trees for squirrels or other animals he could hunt and kill. He saw a cat and made a mental note. It would do if he couldn't find anything else. A cat would be a disappointment, though, because he really wanted the thrill of stalking something wild. Maybe he could find a raccoon or a deer.

As Tommy neared the woods, he noticed a path that seemed to lead from the edge of the cornfield into the trees. He turned and followed it. As he walked, he realized that it wasn't an animal trail but one made for and used by humans. He looked for evidence of people but saw nothing. The path was at a slight incline and as he crested the small hill, he found himself in a clearing. Directly in front of him was an enormous tree anchored by a massive tangle of thick, knobbed roots. He pulled the bundle from his waistband, placed it in the crevice between two prominent roots, and quickly covered it with sticks and leaves. He stepped back, surveyed his work and, convinced that only someone looking closely would be able to see it, turned and walked back along the path out of the woods.

I learned this part of the story later from Grace, who, unbeknownst to Tommy, was lying on her back in the Nest, her eyes closed, her head resting on the cleanest of the cushions. She wasn't sleeping; she was thinking. Unlike Natalie and me, her mother didn't insist she stay home—not that she would have wanted to. At home, she had to deal with her mother's depression and Reggie's unwanted attention. She preferred the solitude of the Nest. It was one of the few places where she felt safe and at peace. So, while Natalie and I tried to figure out how to escape, Grace walked her bike along the dirt path to our clubhouse, stowed her bike in the bushes, and climbed to the solitude of our fortress.

And there she was when she heard the noise of something moving through the trees. At first she thought it was a deer and crept silently to the edge of the tree house to look out. What emerged from the trees wasn't a deer, but a tall, slender boy with dark hair who wandered through the clearing toward the large elm we called Goliath. She watched as he looked around the clearing, pulled something from under his shirt, and then knelt to hide it in the heavy tangle of exposed roots.

From her bird's-eye perch, Grace watched him leave and wondered what was so important that he would hide it in the woods. She considered climbing down to investigate, but ultimately decided not to. Later, when I asked her why, she said that it was out of respect for the boy we later came to know as Tommy.

"Sometimes," she said cryptically, "It's nice to have something that's all yours."

# Chapter 6

After I got off the phone with Natalie, I wandered aimlessly around the house, stopping occasionally to sigh dramatically. My mother, who was dusting, ignored me for about five minutes before she said, "It's not going to work, Birdie. I'm not going to give in just because you're moping around the house."

"But I'm *bored*," I whined.

"Go read," Mom said as she picked up the stack of coasters and wiped under them. "Or go outside. Just do *something*."

I grunted and huffed off to my room. Only the main rooms of the house were air-conditioned, and during the day the bedrooms were shut off from the rest of the house, making them easily twenty degrees hotter. A box fan wedged in the lower half of the open window listlessly circulated the humid morning air. After the cool of the living room, I immediately began to sweat.

I didn't have to stay in my room, I reminded myself. I could go back out into the living room. Or sit outside in the shade of the enormous oak trees in our backyard. But the thought of being someplace other than my oven-like bedroom seemed inappropriate. I needed to think about the events of the past twenty-four hours. My near miss with Mr. Holmes' truck. My mother's increasingly extreme behavior. Don Wan's drawings. It was unsettling. All of it. I was unsure what to think—or what to feel.

I closed the door to my room and went to the bed. My pad of drawing paper and rubber-banded collection of pencils lay at the foot. The realization that I shared this hobby with Don made me feel suddenly nauseous and I quickly slid them under my pillow, where I couldn't see them. With a sigh, I walked over to the window and stood in front of the fan. The hot air blew my hair around my face and I leaned in close. "Ohheeeeohhhh." I spoke the words into the whirling blades and listened to their fractured sounds as they came through the other side. After a minute of this, I turned, walked to my bookshelves, and surveyed the yellow spines of my Nancy Drew mysteries. One of my favorite things to do, as a child, was read—a love affair with the written word which began at the hands of my mother during too-hot summer afternoons when I was too young to ride my bike around town.

When it was very hot, my mother would close down the house, draw the thick, heavy curtains together to block out the sun, and turn on the air-conditioning unit that was set into the wall of the living room. The living room, kitchen, and dining room would become dark, mysterious, and deliciously cool in the absence of sunlight. I would sit on the couch and drink in the chilled air and enjoy the goose pimples that sprang up on my arms and legs.

In the afternoons, when the temperature outside was at its hottest, my mother would sit me on the couch, go into her bedroom, and return with a book. She started with *Little House in the Big Woods*. It was the first book *her* mother read to her as well. As a child, she had loved the adventures of Laura Ingalls Wilder and wanted to share that with me. She would pour herself a glass of iced tea and settle herself onto the couch. I would snuggle in next to her as she opened the book to the spot where we had ended the day before, and began to read.

For my mother, there were rules when it came to reading books. First, at no time should you write in a book. Books were precious and writing in them served no purpose. Although that might have been a rule designed to prevent me from using the pages as an impromptu coloring book, the rule stuck and even in college, I found myself almost unable to highlight passages or make notes in the margins. Ultimately, it worked to my advantage because when I forced myself to part with the books at the end of the semester, I often received the premium buy-back price because of their pristine condition.

The second rule was that it was unthinkable to mark your page by folding down the corner. A coupon, the brown paper from a

Reese's Peanut Butter Cup, or a bobby pin were fair game and often used by my mother to mark her place. But folding down the page was sacrilegious.

The third rule was that when reading—especially reading aloud—it was necessary to always reorient one's self by rereading the last page of the chapter or section. That would, according to my mother, "get your mind back where it needed to be." And so that's where we would start, slightly before where we left off the previous day. My mother would open the oversized paperback book and begin to read. She read clearly, with inflection, but made no attempt to distinguish between the voices of the characters. I would watch her finger as it moved beneath the words and breathe in the sweet, earthy scent of pipe tobacco that perfumed all books purchased from the joint bookstore and smoke shop. It was the safest I had ever felt in my life and probably why even today, when I am upset or scared, I turn to a book.

But somehow, after talking to Natalie about the drawings, the idea of sitting and quietly reading was unappealing. I ran my fingers over the spines of my Nancy Drew books. What, I wondered, would Nancy Drew do? She and Bess and George would expose Don Wan, who would move out of town. And then, they would fix things so my mother would stop worrying. But I knew I wasn't Nancy, and Natalie and Grace weren't George and Bess. We were girls and we had no power. We were girls who were kept at home where there was nothing to do. I didn't want to go to Grandma's. I didn't want to read. I didn't want to dig a hole to China. Or, I began to wonder . . . did I? If I had to be miserable . . . maybe she should be, too. She had said that morning she didn't care what I did. She had, in fact, suggested digging a hole to China. I grinned at the thought. It was perfect. I would get my way without breaking rules. I *would* dig a hole to China—a big hole.

I opened my bedroom door and stepped out into the cool air of the hallway. "I'm going outside," I yelled as I pushed open the storm door, hopped off the side of the front porch, and made my way to the detached garage. Inside, in the back corner with the gardening tools, was the shovel my mother used to plant trees she pulled up from along the banks of Brush Creek and replanted in our yard. I hefted it over my shoulder and headed out of the garage in the direction of the fence separating our yard from that of Mr. and Mrs. Spencer. Of the two sets of neighbors (my grandparents on one side and Buck and Edith Spencer on the other) my mother preferred the Spencers, for no other reason than she detested her in-laws.

Building on the lot next to them hadn't been my mother's idea. Having grown up in "the country," living in a town—even one as small as Edenbridge—made her feel claustrophobic. She wanted the space and freedom that came with acreage. My father was agreeable to the idea until his parents, who had a corner lot in Edenbridge and owned the land on both sides of them, offered to "sell" one of the lots to him for a dollar. Always eager for a bargain, my father jumped at the deal, signed the paperwork, and commissioned the builder—all without consulting my mother who, when she found out about the deal, was furious. It was just one skirmish in their long-standing battle of wills that always seemed to have something to do with my grandparents.

My mother resented my father's parents for a variety of reasons, most of them centered on what she saw as their "interference" in our lives. As proof, she would point emphatically at the backyard and the zoysia grass that was slowly overtaking the fescue she had used to seed the lawn just after the house was built. It was an old argument that was replayed every spring and summer.

"That goddamned grass," my mother would announce as she stomped into the house after mowing the backyard. "Have you seen it? I can't, for the life of me, figure out what you were thinking when you let them convince you to plant it."

"They said zoysia didn't have chiggers," my father would mutter. "I thought it would be good for the girls to be able to play and not get bit."

It was at this point that my mother would throw up her hands in frustration.

"*All* grass has chiggers, John," she'd say. "It's grass. It's in its nature to have bugs. Besides, it wasn't about chiggers. It was just another one of their attempts to control us. It's just like that stupid truck."

53

Mention of "the truck" always made my father wince. It was a story that had become legend in our family. It had been a Saturday afternoon less than a year into my parents' marriage. My mother and her sister, Glenda, had driven into Winston to see a movie and because my mother had just washed her black 1959 Chevrolet Impala convertible, my aunt drove.

"I loved that car," my mother would sigh each time she retold the story. "It was my first car and it was so *pretty*."

Having heard the story so many times, I almost feel as if I had been there for what happened when my mother and aunt returned home and saw the dented, white pickup truck parked in the spot previously occupied by the convertible.

In my imagination, my mother storms into the house calling my father's name.

"Where is my car?" she asks when she finds him. Her voice is anxious and panicky.

My father, I can imagine, looks up from whatever he is doing. When they were first married, he was rail-thin with a dark flattop, thick black glasses, and big ears. In my mind, he is fixing something or tinkering with a radio or something. I imagine him poised with a screwdriver in his hand and a cigarette smoldering in a nearby ashtray. Buying time, he picks up the cigarette, takes a drag and looks at my mother.

"I traded it," he says through the smoky exhale. "Dad heard about this good deal down at the station and—"

"You traded it," she interrupts tightly, a statement rather than a question. "For what? And don't tell me it's that battered truck outside."

My father shrugs, trying to appear calm, but also knowing that the arguments he crafted in his head all the way back from my grandfather's service station, would only dig him deeper into the hole he had created.

"We needed a truck," he says.

My mother stares, angry, disbelieving.

"We needed a truck?" she repeats. "Really. *We* did? John, that was my car. *My* car. You had no right to trade it without my permission. If *we* needed a truck so badly, why didn't you trade your car for it?"

"I thought you could drive my car," he says. "I'll drive the truck."

I can only imagine my aunt taking in this discussion, her eyes darting back and forth as she watches this verbal tennis match.

"John, I don't want to drive your car," my mother says acidly. "I want to drive my car—the car I brought to this marriage. I want to drive the car you traded without my permission and the car you're going to go get back. If you want that stupid truck so badly, trade your own damn car."

My father shakes his head.

"I can't," he says and jumps up to come around the table and stand in front of my mother. "It's done. But I've got good news. I got $100 on top of the trade. We can buy that new vacuum you want."

Later my mother would say, "I should have known then that this marriage was going to end in divorce." And it did. But that would come years later after many unresolved arguments.

One of the things my sister and I had to be careful of when we played outside was not to get on the nerves of Mr. and Mrs. Spencer. My mother insisted they were nice people, just old and, because they never had children, unused to the noise and chaos. My sister and I knew better, though, having more than once been on the receiving end of Mrs. Spencer click-clacking down the back steps onto their patio to tell us to quiet down because she was "having one of her spells" and we were making it worse.

"She's just nasty and mean," I complained to Natalie one morning at recess.

She shook her head. "Actually, it's because of her vapors. I heard Mom talking to someone on the phone about it. Probably your mom."

I frowned. "What are vapors?"

"I looked it up in the dictionary. It means she's not right in the head. Mom said it's because of what happened during the war."

"The war?" I shook my head. "What war?"

"World War II, dummy," Natalie said. "Someone broke into her house while Mr. Spencer was away at the war. It made her mean."

As was often the case with Natalie's eavesdropping, she only got part of the story correct. She was right in that Buck had been stationed in Italy during the war. And Edith, who was a schoolteacher, had indeed stayed by herself on the farm. But what happened the night a man broke in while she was asleep remained a bit of a mystery —mostly because Edith never shared what happened. What people pieced together after the fact was this: One night while Edith was asleep, a man snuck into the house. Even now no one locks their doors at night, so it is likely he simply slipped in through the front door. Whether he was there to steal something or to take advantage of the fact she was alone in the house, is unclear. In either case, the next day she showed up in Edenbridge in Buck's battered old Chevy with two suitcases in the bed. Her eye was blackened, her lip split, and her jaw bruised and swollen.

"I won't be staying at the farmhouse anymore," she said when asked. "I'll be living with my parents until Buck gets back and then we'll figure out what to do." That was all she said on the matter, though the fact that she refused to contact the sheriff confirmed for many that what happened was too painful and embarrassing to admit. The external wounds soon healed, but the same couldn't be said for the emotional damage. What happened that night made Mrs. Spencer ill-tempered and suspicious. Even though she continued to teach, she no longer was active in the community, preferring to go straight to her parents' home after school.

The hope was that things would be better when Buck returned from the war. But, if anything, the exact opposite was true. Instead of returning to the farmhouse, they sold it to Buck's brother and bought the lot next door to the house that would one day belong to my parents.

"It was 'that night,'" people said with a sad shake of their heads whenever Edith Spencer's name came up. "It made her scared of her own self."

It also made her paranoid. Nothing happened in the vicinity of Edith Spencer's house that went unnoticed. She spent much of her time looking out the windows. Everything that happened was noted in her spidery handwriting complete with date, time, and the manner of the event. When she died, dozens of boxes of notebooks were found, labeled by date and year. Infractions ranging from barking dogs and suspicious cars to detailed accounts of the activities of her next-door neighbor's rambunctious children were noted.

I'm sure one of the events she detailed in her notebook was the conversation we had the day I decided to make myself so much of a nuisance that my mother released me from house arrest. I was determining where to start digging random holes in the space between our garage and the fence that separated our lot from the Spencers'. I could hear Mrs. Spencer working in her backyard garden and whistled to let her know I was there.

"Nancy, is that you?" she called over the fence. "Nancy? John?"

"It's me, Mrs. Spencer," I said. My mother was adamant that my sister and I call any grown-up Mr. X or Mrs. Y until they gave us permission to use their first names. Mrs. Spencer never gave that permission.

I heard a soft grunt from behind the fence and knew she was climbing onto the stone bench so she could look over. Within seconds, her pale, wrinkled face appeared over the top of the wooden slats. She studied me for a moment and then frowned. "What are you doing with that shovel, Birdie?"

I looked up at her, unsure about how to answer. "What do you mean?" I could hear the defensiveness in my tone and cringed when she gave me one of her meanest "don't you sass me" teacher looks in response.

"You're holding a shovel and you look like you're going to dig something up," she said. "That *is* what one usually does with a shovel."

I hesitated and searched my mind for what I could say that wouldn't cause her to call my mother and tell her what I was up to. "I'm . . ." I looked down at the shovel. "I am going to dig a hole . . . for my hamster . . . Darwin. He died. Heart attack. He was eating his Hartz pellets . . . you know, the green ones, and he was stuffing them in his pouches and I guess he got one lodged in his throat because he began to cough. And then a big chunk of green food flew out and then he sort of just grabbed his chest and died. It was really sad."

She narrowed her eyes. "That makes no sense." She studied me for several seconds before shaking her head and disappearing behind the fence. I assumed she had returned to her gardening, but after a few moments, I heard her voice again. "I'm sorry for your loss."

"Thank you," I said. "He was very special." When she didn't reply, I moved away from her property and began to dig.

By the time my father pulled into the driveway, I had blisters on my hands, mud caked to my shoes, and smears of dirt and clay on my face. The hole was easily a square yard in size and a foot and a half deep.

"What are you doing, Birdie?" he asked as he got out of the car.

"I'm digging to China," I said. "Mom won't let me go outside of the yard, so I decided to see how long it would take me to dig to China."

He stood over the hole and surveyed my work, a smile tugging at the corners of his lips.

"Ummmm," he said. "Well, it looks like you're off to a good start."

"I am." I was surprised he wasn't angry and decided to up the ante. "By the end of summer I should be halfway there."

"Umm hmmmm." He looked toward the house. "Do you know what we're having for dinner?"

I looked at him, both irritated and exasperated.

"Dad, I'm busy," I said. "I'm working on something and this might not be the right spot. I'll probably have to dig in a couple of places to find the right one. There could end up being holes all over the yard."

"Well, be careful," he said and began to walk toward the house. "Don't fall in."

I stood in the hole and watched him jog up the stairs, pull open the door and step inside the house. The door banged closed behind him. *Unbelievable!* I stared at the closed door. *This has to be part of their plan*, I thought. But they don't know who they're dealing with. This was just the first of many holes. And if that didn't work, well, then, Natalie and I would figure out a new plan. Between the two of us, we would outsmart our parents at their own game.

# Chapter 7

I stood in the shadow of the house and watched as the man drove slowly down the street, headlights off, navigating by the light of the full moon. Although his face was obscured by the darkness of the car interior, I could sense his eyes raking the yards and houses, casing the neighborhood. The car itself was long, gray, and silent as it slid past our house. What, or who, was he looking for? I found myself imagining his motives, picturing the contents of his trunk. A knife? Rope?

The car rolled past with a quiet crunch of grit under tires and I took a deep breath, exhaling slowly. He was gone. We were safe. I turned and began to walk toward Natalie's house. I wasn't sure why I was going there. I just knew I had to talk to her. I wore dark clothes to blend in with the night and felt slightly giddy at my invisibility. In my fist, I clutched a butcher knife I'd taken from the kitchen. It was my protection against people like the man in the car. In some ways, I felt like the predator. I walked quickly and quietly, looking from side to side as I went. One block down, one to go. Natalie wasn't expecting me, but somehow, I knew she would be up and that she would come outside. There was something I had to talk to her about—something that only she would understand. There was urgency to my step. I wanted to be there already. The pleasure I used to have of sneaking out of the house and moving silently in the night was lost in the knowledge I now had of the dangers that were everywhere. Rather than enjoying the freedom of being outside without anyone knowing, I was jumpy, on edge. I had to get to Natalie's. I had to talk to her. I was single-minded, which is why I didn't see him until it was too late.

He was crouched behind a car parked in Mr. Tucker's driveway. He was tall and dark and moved quickly and silently. He, too, had a knife, I realized as he grabbed me and put a gloved hand over my mouth. My body tensed and the butcher knife I had brought for protection dropped uselessly from my hand.

"Don't say a word," he hissed in my ear. "I have a knife and I would think nothing of gutting you like a fish. Do you understand me?" My heart thudded in my head. My chest hurt. I couldn't breathe. I couldn't think. My body ached. My bladder released. "Do you understand me?"

I nodded.

"You didn't think I saw you, did you?" he whispered in my ear. "Oh, I saw you, all right. I've been watching you a lot more than just tonight. I've been watching you with your friends . . . at school . . . around town. You've been playing hide and seek with me, but I knew where you were all along. You broke into my house and saw my special pictures. Well, now I'm gonna' show you what them pictures mean. We're gonna have some fun, you and me."

It was Don Wan.

He picked me up, hand still over my mouth, and carried me to his car, which was parked down the street. He was breathing heavily by the time we made it to his car. He fumbled in his jeans pocket for the car keys. He held me pressed against him. His body was hard and unyielding. His breath came in short gasps and I felt him tremble slightly as he located the keys and opened the trunk. Inside I saw the rope and the gray roll of duct tape.

"Now, I'm gonna take my hand off your mouth so I can get a couple things out of the trunk and you're gonna promise me that you will not make a peep, okay? Because if you do, I'm gonna knock you out and when you wake up, you won't like what happens to you. Do you understand?"

Again, I nodded.

He slowly removed his hand, watching me carefully to see if I would disobey.

"That's a good girl," he said as he reached into the trunk and felt around for the rope and tape. His eyes never left mine and he smiled as he watched me tremble with fear. "You're scared, ain't you? You shouldn't be. This is gonna be fun. By the end, you'll be begging me for more."

I don't know how I summoned the courage to scream, but somehow, I did. My throat, paralyzed by fear, suddenly loosened and the sound burbled from my mouth. It was high-pitched and shrill. It was the sound of terror and revulsion. The sound made my throat raw. Strong hands grabbed me. Shook me.

"*No!*" I screamed. "*No!* Help me! No!"

My teeth rattled in my head.

"Birdie!" my mother yelled. "Birdie! Sweetie. Wake up. Wake up. You're having a bad dream. Birdie! Birdie!"

I stared at her, disoriented. I was in my room. In my bed. In my sweaty nightgown. I felt relief and confusion. It seemed so real. I could still smell his sour body odor in my nose. I felt the bed and was relieved I hadn't really lost control of my bladder. For the second time that week, my mother held me to her body and rocked me. I couldn't stop shaking.

"It was so real," I sobbed into her neck. "It was so real. He had a knife. And he knew about me. He knew who I was. He had been watching me."

"Shhhh," my mother said. "Shhhhh, sweetheart. It's okay. I'll never let anyone hurt you. Shhhh . . . It's okay."

My father popped his head into the room. "Everything okay, Bird? Bad dream?"

"Uh huh," I said, my sobs subsiding to sniffs and gulps of breath.

Thirty minutes later, I lay alone in my bed. I could hear the soft murmurs of my mother and father talking in the next room. I tried to make out what they were saying, but couldn't. So, I lay on my side, curled around the pillow from the top bunk, and tried to dissect the dream. If I could understand it, I thought, perhaps I could take some of the scariness out of it. I knew the events were the combination of Don Wan's drawings and my mother's fears that something would happen to us. All of the elements made sense. But rather than making me feel better, the reality of the things that caused the dream made me feel vulnerable and fragile.

I told Natalie about the dream when she came over the next afternoon.

"It was Don Wan," I said. "He was the one who grabbed me in the dream. I mean, it was him and it wasn't him. You know how dreams are, where someone is a bunch of people at once."

We were standing on the edge of the hole I had started the day before. Grace was supposed to show up at any time and I wanted to talk to Natalie about the drawings before she arrived. "So, what should we do?"

"I don't know." She stared down into the hole. "If we tell our folks, we're going to be in so much trouble. But somebody needs to do something. Drawing naked pictures of kids is weird. I mean, I knew he was a pervert, but . . ."

We were silent.

"Why do you think he drew so many of Grace?"

Natalie shrugged. "She's pretty. And she's sort of . . . sad and mysterious. You know? She always seems to be thinking something secret."

I considered Natalie's description. She was right. There *was* something about Grace that drew people's attention. Sometimes, it made me jealous, but most of the time I just chalked it up to Grace being . . . Grace.

"Do you ever wonder if she's okay?" I asked finally. "Mom always asks me about her."

Natalie nodded. "My mom does, too. And then when I tell her stuff, she just shakes her head and says, 'That poor girl' or 'What the hell is Brenda thinking?'" She raised her eyes to meet my gaze before looking uncomfortably away.

"Do you think there's anything we can do?" I asked finally. "You know, to help?"

Natalie shrugged. "Not really. I guess, just be her friend. I mean, her dad is totally busy with his girlfriend and her mom doesn't seem to care what she does or what happens to her. What do you think?"

"I don't know," I said finally. "I just feel bad for her." I looked down the street. In the distance, I could hear the sound of a lawnmower.

Grace was nowhere in sight. "Want some Kool-Aid while we wait?" Natalie's normally pale cheeks were already flushed from the heat. She grinned. "Grape?"

"Probably." I gestured toward the house. "But just to warn you, Granny's here."

"Even better," Natalie said and started toward the house.

My mother's mother was at best, eccentric and at worst, slightly crazy. Her exploits and those of her brother were known throughout Edenbridge. To be fair, my grandmother came by her craziness naturally. According to my mother, it ran in the family. The younger of two children, Granny adored her older brother Hugh, who was tall, handsome, and extremely good with numbers. Of course, by the time I met him, Hugh was just a paunchy old man who wore polyester pants and silver-tipped cowboy boots. But in his day, he was apparently the star of our small town. And wherever Hugh went, so did my grandmother. The two were inseparable—even to the point that my grandmother dated Hugh's best friend, Dale.

The trouble began when my grandmother and Dale walked into her parents' kitchen one morning and announced that they were going to get married. Apparently, Hugh, who was sitting at the kitchen table drinking coffee and reading the newspaper, stood up, looked at the ring, and announced that the marriage would happen over his dead body. He then strode out of the kitchen, out to his truck, and drove away.

"That was the last time we spoke for twenty years," my grandmother would say, shaking her head.

"But why would he do that?" I would ask. "What made him so angry?"

"Who the hell knows," my grandmother would say, lighting a fresh clove cigarette. "All I knew was that if he could act like that, I could, too. So I married your grandfather the next day. We eloped, went across the state line. My folks were so angry . . . Ach!" She waved her hand in dismissal.

This was the way of my grandmother. Everything was dramatic. She did nothing halfway. If she was told she couldn't do something, she would do it anyway. She did what she wanted, when she wanted, and how she wanted. It was challenging to the rest of us, most especially my grandfather who more often than not was responsible for tying up the loose ends left to flutter in the wake of my grandmother's vague conception. This was especially true of her collection of animals.

My mother's parents lived on five acres of land about ten miles west of Edenbridge. And it was on this property that my grandmother built her own private menagerie to which she added animals, on whims. She had chickens, ducks, a goat, two horses, a pony that collectively belonged to "the grandkids," although we never rode it, and a handful of cats that roamed the property feasting on mice, rats, moles, and whatever small birds they could bring down. And then there were the dogs.

My grandmother fancied herself a dog breeder and show person of unparalleled skill. Her dog of choice was the black and tan dachshund. And it was here that she spent most of her time and energy. To her credit, she had some skill when it came to breeding, training, and showing her dogs. She traveled around the Midwest to dog shows and frequently came home with purple ribbons and trophies that sat in limp, dusty piles on the shelf that ran along the wall of her office.

At no time would she be seen with fewer than three yipping weenie dogs jumping like dark pieces of popcorn around the inside of her car or, if they were on leashes, around her feet. And such was the case on the day she sat in my mother's kitchen wearing a Zuni-inspired shirt-dress she'd collected on her last trip to New Mexico, smoking her clove cigarettes and offering unsolicited advice about motherhood. As Natalie and I entered the kitchen, Blitz, Britta, and Edelweiss leapt from their slumber at my grandmother's feet and rushed toward us in an excited frenzy. Because of their German heritage, all of my grandmother's dogs were christened with German names.

"Come give your grandmother a hug," she said through the exhaled cloud of spiced smoke. "So, what were the two of you doing out there in the yard?" she asked as she reclaimed her smoldering cigarette and took a drag.

"I'm digging a hole to China," I said grabbing a handful of potato chips and offering the bag to Natalie. "Mom won't let me ride around town, so I'm going to see if I can dig to China."

Granny turned to my mother and raised her jet-black eyebrows. Her natural hair color was actually a light brown, but she insisted on dying her hair and eyebrows black. It was, she would tell people, a throwback to her "Indian blood." My mother shrugged.

"Maybe you should get the girls a dog," Granny said. "It would be a good watchdog, too."

My mother sighed. "Mother, for the last time, I don't want a dog. I grew up with dogs and I don't want one now. I like having a clean house. I like not having to clean up dog sh—" She glanced at me and stopped. "Excrement."

My grandmother stared at my mother incredulously. It was as if they didn't have this same conversation every time they were together. She turned to me.

"Birdie, wouldn't you like to have a little puppy?" she asked. "I just had a litter and there is one little sweetie I think you would just love. She's ornery, spunky, and just a little rotten. Her name is Hexe. It means 'witch' in German."

I looked at my mother.

"We are not getting a dog. And if we do, it's going to be an outside dog that is bigger than a cat."

Granny looked down at her dogs, made kissy noises, and began to speak in her puppy voice. "Don't underestimate the ferociousness of the dachshund." She shook her head violently from side to side, talking to them rather than us. "No, no, no. Don't do it. No, don't do it. They're ferocious. Yes, they are. Yes, they are."

I glanced at Natalie, who was watching the exchange with amusement. And, suddenly it occurred to me that maybe a puppy was what Grace needed. Something warm to curl up on her bed at night. Something sweet and loving that she could pay attention to and that would pay attention to her. Something that might protect her.

"Actually," I said. "What about Grace? I'll bet she would love a puppy. I mean, she couldn't afford to buy one from you, but if you wanted Hexe to go to a good home . . ."

Granny looked at my mother.

"Who's Grace?" she asked.

"Brenda's daughter," my mother replied and then turned to face me. "Birdie, I'm not sure that Brenda would want Grace to have a dog and I don't think your grandmother is suggesting that she wanted to give away any of the litter. She was just offering it to us."

"Yeah, but—" I began.

"No buts." My mother held up her hand. "I—" Her words were interrupted by the sound of the doorbell.

"That's Grace," I said and gestured to Natalie. "Let's go."

We hurried to the door and I pulled it open with a yank. Grace stood on the front step. In her hand, she held the transistor radio that she sometimes listened to while riding her bike. Next to her stood my sister, her hands and knees covered with pastel chalk.

"Hey," I said to Grace and then glared at Tara.

"Hey." Grace tipped her head toward Tara. "Sorry I'm late. I had to help Tara color in one of her flowers."

"Wanna see?" Tara asked.

"No," I said. "We have stuff we have to do in the garage."

Natalie and I stepped onto the porch and the three of us headed toward the garage. Tara followed.

"Sorry about this," I said as we walked. "Mom's just . . ." I shrugged. "You know . . . after yesterday . . ."

"It's cool," Grace said. "Natalie told me what's going on. So, do you think it's permanent?"

I shrugged. "Who knows? Probably." We had reached the garage and stood in the doorway. "But I was thinking . . . what if we build a tree house here? I mean, it wouldn't be the same, but . . ." I shrugged again and tried not to look hopeful. Grace laughed and I turned to see Tara mimicking my shrug.

"Go inside," I told her sharply. "Just because I have to stay at home doesn't mean I have to hang out with you."

"But I want to help."

"No," I said shortly.

"I'll tell Mom," she warned.

"Tell her what, smarty pants?" I asked.

"That you lied to her," she said smugly.

"About what?" I asked, curious what she knew—or, at least, what she thought she knew.

"You know," she said simply and then added, "About yesterday."

I narrowed my eyes, wondering what she could have overheard in my earlier telephone conversation with Natalie. I looked at Grace and Natalie and raised my eyebrows.

"I don't care," Grace said. Natalie rolled her eyes.

I sighed and looked back at Tara. "Fine. But you have to do exactly what I tell you and if you get in the way, I'm going to make you go inside."

Tara nodded happily and I turned back to Natalie and Grace.

"So, we have a bunch of wood from when Dad was trying to make some bookcases or something," I said. "I thought we could use that."

As a group, we walked to the back of the darkened garage and crowded around the pile of boards and planks.

Natalie studied them critically. "We could cut those in half for rungs to climb up." She pointed to a stack of haphazardly cut two-by-fours.

"Yeah," I pointed to several long planks of wood. "And we could use those for the floor. I don't think we have enough for walls and a roof, though."

Tara had wandered over to our father's workbench and now gestured at the folded tarp my mother had used to cover the floor when she painted the living room.

"What about that?"

Natalie grinned and nudged me with her shoulder. "Not a bad idea, rug rat."

I scowled, but said nothing.

"See?" Tara looked significantly at me. "I can help."

"Yeah, well . . ." I turned to Grace. "You want to grab those small pieces? And Nat, how about you start hauling those long boards out? I'll find some hammers and nails and a saw."

"What can I do?" Tara asked.

"You can help me," Grace said.

She looked up at me for confirmation. I rolled my eyes and shrugged.

"Fine."

We worked the rest of the morning without stopping until around noon, when Mom brought out sandwiches, Cheetos, and lemonade for lunch. We sat at the redwood-stained picnic table and ate, Grace and Tara on one bench and Natalie and I on the other.

"I think it's going to be cool," Natalie said, looking up at our partially constructed floor. "It'll be like having two houses. And we can sleep over in this one."

"Yeah," Grace said, her tone almost thoughtful. "Especially since we're not the only ones at the Nest."

Natalie and I both looked quickly at her.

"What do you mean?" Natalie asked.

Grace blinked. She looked as if she hadn't meant to speak the words aloud. She looked guiltily down at her paper plate and picked at the crust of her sandwich. "Nothing."

"That's not 'nothing.'" Natalie sounded angry. "Who else is coming to the Nest?"

"He's not coming to the Nest," Grace said quickly. "He just comes to the clearing."

Natalie looked at me to see if I knew what Grace was talking about. I shook my head. "Who is 'he'?"

"Just this boy who comes into the woods," Grace said, still not meeting Natalie's eyes. "Not all the time, just sometimes."

I leaned forward. "Who is it?"

"I don't know." Grace looked back and forth, first at Natalie, then me, and then back at Natalie. "Maybe he's new or just here for the summer."

I glanced at Natalie. Her face was growing red, though from the heat or the emotion, I couldn't tell. She assumed her interrogator tone. "What's he look like?"

Grace shrugged and pinched small pieces of crust from the corner of her sandwich. "Tall. Skinny. Brown hair."

"How old?"

"I don't know," Grace said. "High school."

"How long has he been coming around the Nest?" Natalie pressed. "And why haven't you told us about him?"

"I don't know," Grace said. Her expression seemed almost pained. "I just . . ."

"So, tell us about him now," I interrupted before Natalie had a chance to launch into more questions.

"I don't really know anything," she said. "He just hikes around the woods."

"Just hikes around?" Natalie looked significantly at me. "Sounds a little suspicious to me."

"Everything sounds suspicious to you," I said and shot her a look that told her to back off.

"Yeah, well . . ." Natalie shrugged defensively. "I'm just curious."

"Well, we need to get back to work," I reached out to collect the paper plates and napkins and then started to walk toward the house. Grace moved quickly to pick up the cups and the bag of Cheetos. Before Natalie could corner her, she followed me inside.

"Sorry about that," I said when we were in the kitchen. "You know how Nat is."

"It's okay," she said. "I just don't want her getting all weird and telling her dad. She . . . well, you know."

I laughed. "You'd think *she* was sheriff."

Grace nodded but didn't laugh with me. If anything, she looked worried.

"What's wrong?"

She shrugged and picked at her thumbnail. Grace rarely shared her personal thoughts or concerns. That she was considering doing so now was significant. My heart began to pound heavily.

"Do you think I could stay over?" she asked finally.

"I don't know." I considered asking my mother but knew the answer would probably be "no." Even though Grace and Natalie were allowed to come over during the day, a sleepover was a treat.

"Probably not," I said with a sigh. "I'm still sort of in trouble for riding out of town the other day. But I could ask."

I could hear Natalie outside talking to Tara.

"No, that's okay." Grace said "It's not a big deal. I gotta go to the bathroom. I'll meet you outside?"

Before I could reply, she turned and headed down the hallway, her shoulders hunched forward, her head down. I had the overwhelming desire to say something, to stop her, to tell her that I would ask my mother if she could stay—demand it even. But in the end, I didn't. In the end, I watched her walk away and didn't say a word.

We worked on the tree house for the rest of the afternoon until it was time for Grace and Natalie to go home. Grace left first, riding slowly off in the direction of her house. Natalie, however, hung back. I knew she wanted to talk about something, though I wasn't sure if it was the pictures or the boy in the woods. Grace had barely gotten out of sight before Natalie turned to face me.

"So, what did she say when you guys were inside the house?" she demanded.

"What do you mean?" I asked, trying unsuccessfully to play dumb.

"You and Grace," Natalie said. "When you guys went inside after lunch, what did she say?"

"Nothing," I said quickly.

"Bird, look at me." She studied my face for several seconds and then said, "You're lying."

"It's true. She just wanted to know if she could stay over."

"That's all?"

I nodded.

"So, what do you think about this guy hanging around the Nest?" she asked.

"It's kind of weird," I admitted. Natalie waited for me to say more. When I didn't, she began to pick at a scabbed-over chigger bite on her arm. I took a deep breath and forced myself to ask the question that had been on my mind all day. "So, what are we going to do about those pictures? The ones in Don Wan's stuff?"

She shook her head without looking up from the bite, which was now bleeding. "I don't know. I've been thinking about it. It's like I said before. It's creepy. What do you think?"

"I thought about telling my mom, but if I do, I'll have to tell how we found them and then I'll be grounded for the rest of the summer. And so will you guys."

"I know," Natalie said with a sigh. "I thought about that, too." She paused, thoughtful. "Maybe we should send an anonymous note."

"To who?" I asked.

She shrugged. "I don't know—my dad or the Sheriff's Department."

"Maybe," I said doubtfully. "But who's going to write it?"

"I will."

I frowned. "What are you going to say?"

"That Don Wan is holed up in the Montgomery house and that he has naked drawings of people in his stuff." She paused and then said, "No . . . that he has naked drawings of *kids* from Edenbridge."

"It might work," I admitted. "And it would be better than telling our folks."

"I know," Natalie said.

We were both silent for several seconds.

"So, we're all stuck at home, huh?"

I nodded glumly. "Grace isn't."

"Yeah." She looked down the street in the direction Grace had ridden. "I'm going to miss swimming in the creek." She raised her hand and used the fleshy heel of it to push her bangs back from her sweaty forehead. "Maybe we can figure out a way to sneak off." She walked over to her bike, pulled it upright, and climbed on. "Meantime, I'll work on that letter. I need to practice disguising my handwriting." She put her foot on the pedal and pushed off. "See you later, alligator."

I raised my hand. "After while, crocodile."

"Not if I see you first," she called over her shoulder.

And then I was alone.

71

# Chapter 8

Even as my mother insisted that I stay close to home, Grace's mother imposed no such limitations. Most of the time, as she and Reggie slept off whatever they had ingested the night before, Grace came and went as she pleased. Usually, she would end up at the Nest where she read, napped, daydreamed, or watched the lonely, dark-haired boy play with his knife. Although he didn't come every day, most mornings he would show up around 10:30 and go directly to the base of the old oak.

The routine, Grace told me later, was always the same. He would take the carefully wrapped bundle to the large rock where he had sat that first day and reverently unwrap it until it lay, blade in its leather scabbard, in his lap. Next, he would slide the blade out and examine it, running his thumb along the razor-sharp edge. He had stolen a whetstone from his grandfather's shed and now used that instead of the file to sharpen the blade.

As she had on that first day, she watched him handle the knife, shifting it from hand to hand, feeling its weight, imagining its power. She knew the heft of the knife because she had finally succumbed to curiosity and snuck down to his hiding place and unwrapped it. It was large and heavy. She held it in both hands before sliding the sharp blade out of its sheath, the earthy scent of leather filling her nostrils. Holding the knife felt wrong, she realized, though she wasn't sure why. Curiosity satisfied, she carefully rewrapped the blade and returned the bundle to its hiding place.

Often, she later told me, the boy used the knife for target practice, picking out a knot or distinguishing mark on one of the trees and then attempting to throw the knife and make it stick into the spot. He tried a variety of grips, first on the handle and then the blade. Grace watched as he marched an indeterminate number of strides from the tree, turned, and threw the knife at his target. She found herself mesmerized by the flash of the blade as it pinwheeled toward its intended target. At first, he missed most of the time. But with practice, his aim improved to the point where he was standing farther and farther from the trees at which he was aiming. As he practiced, he muttered to himself. Grace could never hear the words, just the sound of his voice. But that, in addition to his glassy-eyed look, reminded her of her mother and Reggie when they took drugs.

Grace hated what her mother had become. She knew that her friends were aware that something was going on, although they didn't ask about the details. It wasn't that they didn't care, she knew. It was simply a case of not knowing what to say if she had answered honestly. She herself didn't know what to say. How could she explain how her life had changed over the past year? Her mother's depression. Her drinking. Her boyfriend.

Grace hated everything about Reggie—the drugs and alcohol he gave her mother, his too-sweet cologne, his Village People mustache. Most of all, she hated how he looked at her when her mother was too wasted to notice. He leered, his eyes glassy and hungry at the same time. His gaze lingered on her body and her face in a way that was predatory. It was as if his ownership of her mother somehow extended to include her. More than once he had offered her a sip of his drink or snuck into her bedroom at night after her mother had passed out.

As an adult looking at childhood pictures of Grace, I can now appreciate what men like Reggie and Don Wan saw in Grace. Had she lived, she would have grown into a beautiful woman. At the age of eleven, she was gangly; tall and slender with legs like a newborn colt. But you could see that she would grow into her height and flesh out her bones in a lean, willowy kind of way. You could also see in her face that she would have become beautiful. Her blond hair was long and glossy. Her chin was delicately pointed and her teeth were slightly crooked, but these imperfections disappeared once you noticed her eyes. In my memory of her that last year before her death, her eyes were tired and ringed with dark circles. But in the school pictures taken in the years before her death, her eyes were alive and vibrant, a dark green-brown rimmed with thick, dark brown lashes.

I often consider what those eyes must have seen during the course of her short life. They were the eyes that watched her life fall apart; the eyes that saw her killer; the eyes that looked to me for the help that I was unable to give her. The realization of how I must have let her down haunts me to this day.

I remember the two weeks before Grace's death as being unmercifully hot, with air so thick and humid that it hurt to breathe too deeply. This was exacerbated by the southern winds that blew the stench from Mr. Holmes' hog farm directly into town. Everyone was on edge. Farmers feared the loss of their farms. Parents worried for the safety of their children. And we kids were chafing under the constant supervision and loss of freedom.

The only people who seemed unfazed by what was going on in Edenbridge were Puddin' Puddin' and Grace—the former who continued to ride his squeaky bike around town and the latter who spent most of her time, when she wasn't at my house or Natalie's, at the Nest. While the rest of us were kept close to home for our own safety, Grace was sneaking away from hers for the same reason.

The day before her death, Grace and Natalie came over to my house to christen the new tree house. We had finished it the day before and this was the first chance we would have to do nothing but hang out in it. I was sitting in a patch of shade along the front of the house when they rode up. Grace looked drawn and the shadows under her eyes were darker than I had ever seen them.

"Hey," she said as she coasted to a stop.

"What's shakin', bacon?" Natalie asked as she swung her leg over the seat of her bike and coasted to a graceful dismount.

"Hey," I said, though my attention hadn't wavered from Grace. "You okay?"

Grace nodded and toed down the kickstand of her bike. Natalie's face was florid from the heat and the ride. She looked first at Grace and then at me. "I saw the Schwan's man on my way over. Do you think your mom would let us have ice cream?"

"One step ahead of you." I gestured for them to follow me into the storage room where we kept the deep freezer. "Mom just bought drumsticks."

"Excellent," Natalie said. "And then we'll go up to the new tree house because I have a great idea."

I lifted the scratched, white lid of the freezer chest. Icy air billowed up and we all crowded around to take advantage of the cold. Natalie reached down to finger the white, butcher-papered parcels of the side of beef we bought twice each year. "That feels so good."

"Yeah, well . . ." I looked over my shoulder. "We better pick something or Mom will get mad about letting all the cold air out."

Still, we labored over our choices between drumstick, Fudgsicle, or ice cream sandwich, finally each choosing a drumstick and gripping it tightly in one hand as we climbed the boards nailed to the trunk of the tree, up to the tree house.

"So," began Natalie once we had settled onto the sit-upons each of us had made the year before in Girl Scouts. "I hereby call this meeting to order. First order of business . . ." She paused dramatically and Grace and I both looked up from unwrapping our ice cream cones. Natalie grinned, clearly enjoying the attention.

"What?" I raised my eyebrows. "You're clearly dying to tell us."

Natalie lowered her voice. "Did you guys hear about Don Wan?"

Natalie glanced at me and we both shook our heads.

"The Montgomery house was raided and he was kicked out." Natalie was almost unable to contain her glee. "He was asked to leave town."

I stared. "For real?"

"Yep." Natalie gave an authoritative nod. "I heard my dad talking to my mom. The Sheriff's Department got an anonymous letter. Typed." She grinned and licked her sticky fingers. I tried to catch her eye, but she continued to act nonchalant, although, at one point, I could have sworn she gave me the briefest nod—so brief, I wasn't sure I had seen it.

"Dad says he was drunk and mad as hell," she said. "He said Don tried to fight him, but Dad told him to knock it off and if he showed up in town again, he was going to arrest him."

"Wow," Grace said again. Her eyes were round and her pretty mouth was pursed. "Can they do that? Arrest him?"

Natalie nodded.

"Yeah, for breaking into the house and stuff. But not for the pictures. You can't arrest someone for being creepy."

"But he's dangerous," I said.

Natalie shrugged. "At least we won't have him creeping around town anymore."

We nodded and then for several long minutes, none of us spoke.

"So, that's my first news flash. My second one is that I have a plan so we can sneak off and go swimming in the creek."

"Yeah, right," I said. "Mom won't let me even go near the woods."

Grace licked at the dribbles of ice cream melting down the side of her cone and said nothing.

"See, that's why I have a plan," Natalie said. "We all tell our moms that we're going over to someone else's house. Grace and I will tell our moms that we're coming over here. You—" she pointed her cone at me "—you will tell your mom you're coming over to my house. Then, we meet at the Nest and go swimming. Am I brilliant or what?"

She looked back and forth between us. From the corner of my eye, I saw Grace lift her narrow shoulders in a shrug. "I don't have to tell my mom anything." Her words trailed off and she shrugged again. "I can meet you guys anywhere," she said finally.

I noticed again the dark shadows under her eyes and the way she seemed to shrink into herself. I considered asking if she wanted to stay the night at my house, but then didn't. If we were going to put this plan into action, I might be able to work it to my advantage. If I told my mother I was going to Natalie's earlier than we were supposed to meet, I could get to the Nest early and have some time alone.

"So?" Natalie's voice broke into my thoughts and I looked up, quickly.

76

"I don't think that's a good idea," I said. "Mom would know if I snuck my swimsuit out."

"I've already thought about that," Natalie said. "We tell our moms we're going over to play in the garden sprinkler—that way, when you show up with wet hair, it will be okay." She grinned proudly. "So?" Natalie said, looking first at Grace and then me. "What do you think?"

I shook my head slowly back and forth.

"Come on," Natalie said. "You know you *want* to. And we *deserve* to. We've been locked away all summer. School starts in just a couple of weeks. We deserve a little fun. And think how good the water is going to feel."

"I just . . ." I began.

"Come on, Bird," Natalie wheedled. "Don't be a scaredy-cat. Your mom will never know. There's nothing wrong with breaking the rules every once in a while. And we're not going to get caught. I promise." She turned to look at Grace. "You're in, right?"

"Sure," Grace said with a shrug.

"All right," I said with a sigh. "I'm in."

Natalie grinned and slapped me on the leg. "Excellent. We just wait until morning to tell them. That way if they talk tonight, they won't ask each other."

I pressed my lips together. If we got caught, I would be grounded. But, I told myself, it felt like I was grounded already, so . . .

"It's going to be wicked," Natalie promised. "You'll see."


I was the one who found Grace's body. As we had planned, I lied to my mother not just about where I was going to be, but what time I was supposed to be there. I told her that I had forgotten to mention it the night before but that we were all going to hang out at Natalie's house. After two weeks of us hammering together the tree house, I think she was relieved to have a day of peace. Still, she asked the requisite questions.

"It's okay with her mother, right?" she asked. "She asked permission?"

"Yeah," I answered. "Mrs. Stewart said it was okay."

"Well," she said. "If she asked her mom and it's okay with her, it's okay with me. What time are you supposed to go over?"

"Anytime after ten," I lied.

I left exactly at ten o'clock, heading in the direction of Natalie's house. My plan was to cut across to the woods as soon as I was out of my mother's sight and head to the Nest. It would be nice, I thought, if I had the place to myself. But it would be okay, too, if Grace was there. We often spent quiet time together. She would read and I would draw. There were often squirrels that raced from tree to tree, chasing each other in a frantic game of tag. Perhaps, I thought as I pedaled down the street, I could draw one of them.

It's funny what you remember in retrospect. Looking back on that day, I remember thinking how free I felt, not to be under anyone's supervision except my own for a little while. I felt light-hearted and empowered as I rode, grinning like a maniac, without holding onto the handlebars. I even whistled. I rolled to a stop as I reached the path that led to the Nest, dismounted, and walked my bike along the path.

I think I knew something was wrong before I actually saw her. It was too quiet. The buzzing of the insects that usually faded into the background was deafening in its absence. The rustling of birds and animals was missing. The woods were still. Something seemed wrong. I considered turning around but didn't.

I saw her body as I pushed my bike up the slight incline that led into the clearing. At first, I didn't realize what I was looking at. Her back was to me, and from behind, she looked like a large whitish rock. Or a large frosted slab of ice. That's what I remember thinking: It's summer and yet there's a frosted, oddly melted piece of ice out there in the woods. And for a second or two, as I walked closer, I wondered how it got there. But as I got within a couple of feet, I realized it wasn't ice. It was a person lying on their—no *her*—side. Asleep? No. Nude? Yes. Dead? I didn't know.

My heart pounded. My hands tingled and grew numb. My

heartbeat thundered in my ears. I felt sick. I felt weak, as if my legs were going to give out. And then I realized it wasn't just a body. It was a person—a person who was young and slight and . . . and familiar. The hair. That's what I noticed first—her hair. It was long and blond. I let my bike fall to the ground and stepped closer. The stillness of the woods rang in my ears.

She had died on her side with one leg pulled up under her—as if she had, in her last few moments, tried to curl into the fetal position, but lacked the energy to complete the move. Her thin arms were hugged to her chest. Smears of blood were visible on her upper arms and her hip. On the foot of the leg that was extended was a white, lacy sock. It was the only piece of clothing on her body. The rest of her clothes, her shoes—everything was strewn around the clearing.

I circled the body and realized there was blood everywhere. I looked at her face, most of which was covered by her hair. One eye, however, was visible and it stared glassily at nothing. It was deep green with thick lashes. Its gaze was unwavering.

It was Grace.

I stared back at her, too shocked to move. It was only when an ant crawled across her eyeball that I jumped back, disgusted, and threw up. My body shook uncontrollably and I sank to the ground. I wrapped my arms around my knees and stared at the scene. I knew I needed to go for help, but for some reason couldn't make myself move. I was paralyzed.

I'm not sure how long I sat there. I'm not sure how I made it from the clearing back to Edenbridge. All I remember is a blur of green on either side as I ran—and then pushing open the heavy wooden front door of the Mercantile—and then Mr. Gray trying to make sense of the sweaty, crying girl that stood in front of him trying desperately to speak.

"Grace's dead." The words came in a hysterical rush. "She's dead. She's in the woods. She's dead. There are ants on her eyes. Someone needs to get help. Grace's dead."

I remember he looked at me with a confused expression.

"Slow down, Birdie," he said and put a gnarled hand on my

shoulder. "Slow down. Now, say it again slowly."

A handful of farmers and housewives who were in the store to pick up forgotten odds and ends came over to listen.

"Grace is dead," I said in a frantic voice. "In the woods. Someone killed her. There's blood all over the place."

I began to sob and Mrs. Lempkin, who stood off to the side listening, came over and put her arms around me, holding me tightly to her slender body.

"Call Nate," I heard her tell Mr. Gray. "And Nancy. She needs to be here."

My mother arrived first. I rushed, sobbing, into her arms.

"Oh my god, Birdie," she said. "What were you doing out there? I thought you were going over to Natalie's. Oh, sweetie, what were you doing out there? Are you okay?"

I nodded as I continued to cry and tried to speak, my words coming between hiccups. "I—I lied," I said. "I wanted to—to go to the tree house. I just—we were going to go swimming. Oh—she's dead. Mom, she's dead. There was so much blood. I saw her eyes . . ."

My mother began to sob even as she rocked me back and forth in her arms.

"Shhhh," she said soothingly. "Shhhhh . . . It's okay, baby. It's okay."

"I'm so sorry—I lied," I cried. "I'm so sorry. I'll never do it again. I'll never go off by myself. I—"

My words were interrupted by the sound of a car screeching to a halt in front of the Mercantile followed by the slamming of a car door and heavy footsteps on the wooden porch of the building. The doors swung inward and Natalie's father stepped inside. He scanned the room before walking directly over to me, the sounds of his cowboy boots on the old wooden floorboards loud and hollow.

"Hey, Bird," he said softly as he knelt down on one knee. "You okay?"

I pulled my head away from my mother and looked at him through teary eyes. I wiped my runny nose on the back of my hand and nodded.

"Sweetheart," he began, "You need to take a deep breath and tell me what happened."

Mrs. Gray, who had come out from the back of the store when she heard the commotion, handed my mother a box of tissues and a Dixie cup of water. My mother held out the box, from which I took a tissue and blew my nose. Natalie's dad watched patiently.

"Why don't you take a sip of water and then tell me what happened," he said. "Just take a deep breath and start from the beginning."

"We were going to sneak off and go swimming today," I said. He nodded.

"You and Grace?" he asked.

"Me and Grace and Natalie," I said. He looked surprised, but said nothing. "We were going to all say we were at each other's houses and then meet up at the Nest at one o'clock to go swimming. But I wanted to go early and sit and draw. So, I told Mom I was going to Nat's house." I began to cry again.

"Birdie, listen to me." Natalie's father cleared his throat. "I know you're scared and you've seen something horrible, but you need to stop crying so you can tell me what happened."

"I—I know." I took another deep breath and exhaled slowly. "I went to the Nest and when I got to the clearing, I—I saw her." I tried to force down the tears that were again threatening to come. "It was Grace. She was naked. And there was . . . blood. Lots of blood and her eyes were open."

My mother gasped and Natalie's father closed his eyes and sighed. "Goddammit," he said softly. When he looked back up, his eyes were hard. "It's okay, Birdie. But I need you to listen to me for a second and I need you to tell me the truth. Okay? Did you touch anything? Anything at all?"

I shook my head.

"Is that a 'no?'" he asked.

"No," I said. "I didn't touch anything. I just looked at her and then . . ." I hesitated and then added miserably, "I threw up."

He smiled sadly and put a gentle hand on my shoulder. "That's okay," he said. "I throw up sometimes, too." He got to his feet and looked around the room at the curious faces. Word of the drama must have spread because there were now almost twenty-five people crowded into the store. Natalie's father smiled ruefully, held up his hands, palms facing outward, silencing the whispered conversations. "Folks, I need everyone here to help me out and just hang back for a while until we can get this sorted out. Please, don't go anywhere near the woods for the time being."

He looked slowly around the room, his eyebrows raised as if to elicit confirmation from everyone there. The room remained silent as he turned and walked out to the patrol car. Through the windshield, we could see him talking on his radio. A couple of minutes later, he came back into the Mercantile.

"Birdie," he said. "I know this is the last thing you want to do, but I need you to take me to where you found Grace. Can you do that, Sweetheart?"

I buried my face in my mother's shoulder and began to cry again.

"Birdie," he said gently. "I know this is scary, but I need you to show me where she is. And then you can go home. Okay?"

Still crying, I nodded.

"Nancy, why don't you two ride with me," Nate said as he gestured toward the patrol car. My mother wiped at her eyes, nodded, and kissed me on the head. Gently, she guided me toward the door.

We drove in silence the short distance to the path that ran alongside the field and disappeared into the woods. Nate put the car in park and turned off the engine. Before walking toward the path, he went to the back of the patrol car and opened the trunk. From inside, he pulled out a roll of bright yellow police tape, and a large, black duffle bag which he hooked over his shoulder. He closed the trunk and turned to me.

"Birdie," he said. "You're a brave girl and I won't make you look at her again. I just need you to show me where you found her, okay?"

We walked along the edge of the field and down the path. The woods were no longer quiet. Birds twittered and the insects had resumed their eternal hum. As we neared the incline that led to the clearing, Nate tipped his head forward and asked, "There?"

I nodded and without a word, he walked around me and my

mother, up the small hill and into the clearing. He was gone for several minutes before coming back to where we stood. He looked at my mother and nodded.

"There should be a couple of other officers here any minute," he said to her. "I think it would be best if you two went back to the patrol car and waited there. I'll have one of the officers take you home, but I need to stay here and secure the crime scene."

"Is it—" my mother began.

"Yeah," Nate said shortly as he took off his hat, rubbed his forehead furiously, and then ran a hand through his sweaty hair. His face was flushed.

My mother's eyes filled again with tears.

"Could you do me a favor and call Mary Jane?" He raised his wrist and looked at his watch. The sun caught in the face and flashed. "Christ. It's not even noon." He sighed, turned to head back down the path into the clearing, but then stopped.

"Nancy, I'm going to have to get a formal statement from Birdie," he said. "Not right now, but later. Maybe this afternoon or evening? Would it be all right if I stopped by the house?"

"Come by whenever you need to. We're not going anywhere."

Nate nodded and then looked down at me. "I'm sorry you found her, Birdie," he said. "I know she was a good friend of yours. And Natalie's. I'm sorry. This isn't something anyone should have to go through—especially a kid."

My mother and I were silent as we walked back to the car and during the short ride back to our house. Seeming to sense our mood, the lanky, young deputy spoke only to get the address and to ask if the air conditioning was cool enough. Both times, my mother's answers were brief, yet polite. As we rolled to a stop in front of our house, my mother reached out for the door handle and then pulled back in puzzlement. The handle had been removed. Having never been inside a patrol car, especially the back seat, we had no idea that the handles were removed to prevent prisoners from escaping.

Oblivious to our situation, the deputy sat in the front seat and waited. Then, realizing that we were unable to get out, he apologized, jumped out of the car, and hurried to open the rear door.

"Sorry," he said as he stood like a chauffeur escorting us from a limousine. "I don't usually transport non-criminals."

My mother smiled politely. "It's okay. We appreciate the ride."

Together, we walked silently up the front walk. My mother turned to offer a halfhearted wave as the young deputy drove away. She opened the front door and we went inside. The house was quiet and still.

"Where's Tara?"

"She's next door with your grandma."

We walked into the kitchen and my mother went directly to the kitchen phone, dialed a number, and then walked with the receiver down the hall to the bathroom so she could close the door and talk in private. The extra-long cord was stretched to its full length. After a couple of minutes, she came back into the kitchen, dialed a second number, and returned to the privacy of the bathroom.

Unsure as to what to do, I sat in one of the vinyl-covered bucket bar stools that ringed the counter that divided the kitchen from the dining room. I stared blankly at the counter, looking up only when my mother came back into the kitchen, hung up the phone, and looked at me. Her eyes were red-rimmed and worried. She stood with her hand on the receiver for a moment or two before going to the refrigerator and pulling out a can of Coke. I watched as she filled two glasses with ice and handed one to me. Deftly, she pulled off the ring tab and dropped it onto the counter. She poured most of the soda into my glass. I took a sip as she stretched to reach into the cabinet above the refrigerator for the dusty bottle of Jack Daniels. She poured some into her glass, topped it off with the rest of the Coke, stirred it with her finger, and then took a large swallow.

"Want some?" she asked.

I raised my eyebrows to test her seriousness. She shrugged, picked up the bottle and poured a tiny bit into my glass. She again used her finger to stir it. When she had finished, I took a sip. It tasted like Coke. We sat and drank in silence.

"You okay?" she asked finally. "What you saw today was . . . I can't even imagine. Are you okay? Do you want to talk? Or cry?"

I felt my eyes prickle with tears.

"I—I'm sorry I lied," I said. "I just—wanted to be alone—and then I found her and—I can't believe she's dead."

I began to cry as the shock, fear and sadness overwhelmed me—big, gulping sobs that caused my ribs to ache. My mother came around the counter, wrapped me in her arms, and rocked me until I had no tears left to cry. When I was done, we sat in silence, waiting for the next round of tears.

What I didn't realize at the time was that they wouldn't come for another twenty-plus years.

# Chapter 9

I remember very little about the weeks following Grace's murder. What I recall are just bits and pieces. Sometimes at night, I have dreams where I think I remember certain things, but when I wake, I'm still unsure if they were real events or just fabrications.

I remember that Natalie's father came to talk to me. We sat in the living room and I stared numbly at the orange globe light that hung in the corner from a decorative bronze chain designed to mask the cord. I sat on the couch between my parents. Natalie's father sat in my father's recliner. He looked tired and he smelled like sweat. He asked me to repeat my story from earlier that morning. At first, he did nothing but listen, taking notes in a battered spiral notebook. His handwriting was tight and efficient. The blue ink stood out boldly against the white, lined paper. He listened and then he began to ask questions—specific questions such as: when did I first notice the blood? Did I see any kind of weapon? Did I touch anything? How long did I stand there before I ran for help?

Although I answered as best I could, toward the end of the conversation, I couldn't think. My answers were cotton balls in my mouth. Finally, Nate closed his notebook.

"You did a real good job answering my questions, Birdie," he said. "I know you're upset, but you did a really good job. Do you have any questions you want to ask me?"

"How's Natalie?" I asked. "Does she know?"

It must not have been the question he expected because he blinked a couple of times before answering. "She knows. And she's upset and very, very sad." He looked down at his hands which still held his notebook and pen. The muscles in his jaw twitched beneath his stubbled skin. He swallowed and I could see his Adam's apple bob.

My father cleared his throat. "Nate, I know you can't talk about the investigation, but can you tell us *anything*? Do we need to be worried? What should we do?"

Natalie's father shook his still-bowed head and breathed in deeply. He exhaled and looked up. "I can't talk about the investigation as it stands right now. To be honest, this early into the investigation, there's not much to tell. We're analyzing the crime scene and everything we found there. It looks like the cause of death was blood loss due to stabbing. We found a hunting knife in the woods nearby. We're pretty sure that was the murder weapon."

My father shifted slightly in his seat. "Was she . . . ?" He glanced down at me. "Was there evidence of—"

Nate nodded.

"Yes."

"Oh no." My mother spoke the words softly. She sniffed and then asked in a louder voice, "How is Brenda?"

Natalie's father sighed. "She doesn't know, yet. She wasn't at the house. Neighbors said she and her boyfriend went into Winston. I've got a deputy at the house to alert her when they return, but as it stands now, we haven't been able to track her down. We were able to contact Stephen, though. He identified—" He glanced at me and then said, "her."

I learned later that it wasn't until almost twenty-four hours after Grace's body had been found that Brenda and Reggie returned to the house. They had "spent the night with friends in Winston." According to Natalie, when her father told Mrs. Bellamy what had happened to Grace, she became hysterical and tried to tear out her own hair. For once, I didn't think my friend was exaggerating.

It was a couple of days after Grace's murder that Natalie's father brought my bike to me. They had needed to keep it until they finished processing the crime scene, he explained, but now I could have it back. He talked to my mother and father for several minutes before opening the trunk and lifting it out. The tassels on the handlebars fluttered in the breeze and we all stood looking at it, saying nothing. Finally, my father cleared his throat and because I had made no move to touch it, my mother stepped forward and pushed it silently into the garage.

The three of us watched her without speaking until Natalie's father made a noise that sounded like "Oh." He stepped back to the trunk, reached inside, and pulled out a heavy paper grocery bag that was folded over at the top. He closed the trunk and then stepped toward me, the bag extended. I stood next to my father, but didn't reach out. I didn't want to take it. My heart pounded in fear, and I shook my head.

"It's your sketch pad and pencils," Nate said gently. "They were in the basket on your bike. I put them in the bag as soon as I could so they wouldn't get damaged. We wouldn't want your pretty pictures to get ruined." He smiled down at me and again held out the bag.

I glanced up to see my father looking down at me, a strange expression on his face. I swallowed and reached out my hand. The thick brown paper was smooth and dry to my sweaty fingers. I stared at the bag.

"What do you say, Birdie?" my mother asked as she walked back from the garage and saw the exchange.

"Thank you," I whispered. My hands trembled and I looked up at him. "Thank you," I said again, louder this time.

"Sure, sweetie," he said kindly and then stretched his arms above his head. "Well, I best be gettin'. I need to get some paper-work done and Mary Jane will have my hide if I miss dinner again."

He shook hands with my father and then climbed into the car. I watched as he drove away. There was a part of me that wanted to follow him, though I wasn't sure why. When he was out of sight, I looked down at the grocery sack. It felt heavy—too heavy to be just a sketch pad and pencils. I thought about Grace's heart inside the bag. I imagined it a purple, red mass that throbbed gently within the confines of the sack.

"Birdie," my mother called from the screen door. "Come inside."

"Okay," I said and walked slowly to the corner of the house where we kept the garbage cans for the household trash. I glanced surreptitiously around the corner of the house to make sure my mother couldn't see and then at the fence between our house and the Spencers'. When I was sure I wasn't being observed, I grabbed the silver handle and removed the lid as quietly as possible, set the bag inside, and then carefully replaced the lid. From the kitchen window, I could smell taco meat. Silently, I went inside.

I also remember the funeral. There were too many people to hold it at the church, so the decision was made to conduct the service in the junior high school gymnasium. My father had taken the day off from work, and I walked between him and my mother up the aisle between the neat rows of tan folding chairs and approached the casket. On either side, people stopped talking as we passed, watching silently to see how I would react to seeing Grace after finding her body only days before. I felt my face flush under their scrutiny and I hunched my upper body forward.

"Mom, they're staring," I whispered as we neared the casket. In front of us, several people were clustered together, staring down at Grace.

"Just ignore them," my mother said and squeezed my hand reassuringly.

I drew in a deep breath and looked straight ahead. As we approached, the people standing in front of Grace moved quickly to the side. I could feel everyone's eyes on my back as I stepped toward the coffin and looked inside. At first, I didn't recognize Grace. She looked plastic, fake. I glanced up at my mother to see if there had been some mistake—that they'd used a mannequin instead of a real body. She was staring intently down at Grace's face, but squeezed my hand again.

"She doesn't look real," I whispered.

My mother tore her gaze from Grace's profile and looked down at me. "Well, people look different when they're . . ." she hesitated and looked over my head at my father for help. I turned to look up at him and he cleared his throat.

"This isn't her, Bird," he said awkwardly. "This is just her . . . just what's left."

"Try to remember Grace as she was," my mother said. "Pick a memory of her when she was alive and happy. *That* was Grace—not this."

I nodded and tried to think of a time when Grace had been happy. An image of her at the Christmas pageant popped into my mind. Grace had never been one to sing along during practice, but that night, for whatever reason, she sang aloud. Standing next to her, I had stared, shocked by her voice which was suddenly light and pure, each note rounded and full. It was, although I didn't know the word at the time, ethereal. I had stopped singing to listen, watching as she sang the notes, her eyes closed, unaware of my gaze.

I tried now, as I stared at her serene yet artificial face in the casket, to remember the clarity and perfection of her voice that night. I thought about the hours we spent together in the Nest reading. About her Pop-Tarts. About how she looked the last time I saw her, a twisted, lifeless body in the clearing. I wanted to touch her, to pull back the high collar of her dress to see the stitched repair of her sliced throat, but knew it would be inappropriate. I wanted to say good-bye, but I didn't know how. I wanted to tell her how deeply sorry I was that I hadn't been there for her that day. I wanted to cry. Instead, I stared.

"Come on, sweetie," my mother said in a low voice as she nudged me to follow my father, who had turned and was walking in the direction of the old-fashioned wooden bleachers that lined the walls. My father spoke softly to several people as we climbed to the middle row and sat down next to Mary Jane and Natalie. There was a quiet hum as people resumed their conversations. Around me, people shifted in their seats, cleared their throats, and waited for the service to begin. After about ten minutes, the church organist began to play a hymn on the battered upright piano at the front of the gym. Everyone stood as Grace's father and his girlfriend Sally walked stiffly down the aisle to the front of the rows of folding chairs, followed by Grace's mother, who leaned heavily on Reggie's arm.

Once they were seated, the townspeople glanced at each other, wondering if, because this was a gymnasium rather than a church, the same rules applied.

Reverend Ackerman, who sat next to his wife slightly behind the podium, stepped forward, cleared his throat, and waited for the organist to finish. Because he stood, we all stood.

"A prayer," he said when the room was silent.

The townspeople obediently bowed their heads and waited.

"Dear Lord," he began. "We come to you today with heavy hearts as we mourn the loss of your daughter, Grace Annette Bellamy."

Because we didn't pray in our house, I glanced at my parents on either side of me to see what I should do. My mother stood ramrod straight, her chin high and her eyes forward. On my other side, my father had his head bent, though I could see he wasn't praying, but instead picking at a cuticle on his thumb. Still not sure what to do, I compromised, tipping my head slightly, but not closing my eyes. Rather, I glanced curiously around the gymnasium, forgetting for the moment why we were there, and instead enjoying the opportunity to stare with impunity at the top of the farmers' sunburned heads and the womens' Aqua-Netted coifs. I was so engrossed in Mrs. Haas' beehive that I was unprepared for the communal "amen." Guiltily, I jerked my eyes quickly to my lap as the congregation raised their heads.

During the service, I found myself staring not at the minister whose voice seemed to drone on and on, but at Grace's family—particularly her mother. Over the past six months, she had lost a great deal of weight. Her face was ashen and gaunt; her eyes puffy and vacant. She seemed devoid of emotion. Beside her sat Reggie, unkempt with his lank hair and wrinkled sports jacket. He sat with one arm draped over the back of Grace's mother's chair and the other in his lap. Occasionally, he would squeeze her shoulder. Grace's father, who sat on the other side of his ex-wife, was the exact opposite of Reggie. His black suit was beautifully tailored and his white shirt was starched to crisp perfection.

My parents had chosen to sit with Natalie and her mother. It was the first time I had seen Natalie since Grace had been murdered, and I could tell she wanted to ask questions about finding Grace. I knew, too, she would have information gleaned from her father, who stood toward the back of the gymnasium with other detectives and deputies studying the crowd. As the service seemed to draw to an end and the organist began to play *Amazing*

*Grace* on the school piano, Natalie gripped my hand. I realized she was crying.

"I'm going to miss her so much," she whispered.

I looked at her. Natalie rarely allowed herself to appear vulnerable and I was unprepared for the grief in her eyes. A part of me knew I should try to comfort her. But my body felt heavy. I was watching the scene as if it were on television and happening to someone else. As the hymn came to an end, the minister offered a prayer. My mother, who usually scoffed at such things, listened intently, her eyes on the minister, and even nodded at one point. My father had his head bowed. For some reason, I noticed he was tanned from yard work, although the skin along the hairline at the back of his neck was white from where the barber had clipped the hair short. I was again startled when everyone said "Amen" and stood. Grace's father and Sally walked down the aisle followed by Grace's mother, who appeared to be heavily supported by Reggie. She stared blankly ahead and at one point seemed to stumble. Reggie caught her and helped her out of the school and into the car parked directly behind the black hearse.

"That poor woman," my mother said later to Mary Jane. "She could barely walk."

We were standing together in the cemetery. It was a small, country graveyard on the edge of town and so close that many people, ourselves included, simply walked there. We were drenched in sweat by the time we made it to the graveside. Like many, we sought shade during this last part of the service; a dark green canopy had been set up for the family and there were also nearby trees. Some of the town's older residents had driven rather than walked and as they waited for the service to start, they sat parked in the gravel horseshoe drive that ran the length of the cemetery. Those without air conditioning sat with their doors open or windows down. Most smoked and talked quietly to each other.

"You're kidding, right?" Mary Jane said to my mother. "You know that wasn't all grief. I mean, I'm sure a lot of it was, but you know she was sedated—and not from a doctor's prescription."

My mother stared at her. "She wouldn't do that on the day of her daughter's funeral, would she?"

"When you're in that deep—" Mary Jane said and shrugged.

"Nate said that it was a full twenty-four hours before they were able to tell her about Grace. She and that boyfriend of hers were in Winston doing god knows what."

My mother shook her head and made a clicking noise with her tongue. She looked around at the people clustered in small groups. I followed her gaze to where my father and uncle stood talking to a knot of men.

"Where are they in the investigation?" my mother asked. "Do they have any idea who did this?"

Mary Jane seemed to consider, as she often did, how much she should share. She glanced down at Natalie, who was pretending not to listen, and then leaned in and spoke in a low voice to my mother.

"They have some leads," she said. "But nothing substantial. There was no semen from the rape. There are some hairs. Probably the best evidence they've got right now is the knife. Nate said they have a couple of partial fingerprints."

"Any suspects?" my mother asked quietly.

Natalie's mom looked carefully from side to side before answering. Her voice was low. "Don Wan. And Reggie. But you didn't hear that from me."

"Seriously?" My mother frowned.

"I told you about the drawings, right?" My mother nodded. "Well, there were apparently several of Grace. Suggestive, if you know what I mean."

My mother opened her mouth to speak when, as if by some unspoken signal, everyone began to move toward the grave. It was time for the burial. We silently joined the rest of the town.

A man in black directed the pallbearers to remove the child-sized casket from the back of the hearse and carry it to the grave. Once the casket was in place, a second man got out of the car directly behind the hearse, briskly opened one of the back doors, and then hurried around the back of the car to open the other one. Reggie and Grace's mother emerged. From an identical car directly behind theirs, Grace's father and Sally got out. The foursome walked together, but clearly apart, to the folding chairs arranged around one side of the grave. Once they were seated, the rest of us clustered around.

Natalie's father stood under a shade tree, apart from the crowd, his eyes hidden by dark aviator sunglasses. Even though his stance was casual, it was clear that he was studying the people present. Two other detectives were on either side, a respectful distance away, with video cameras. They had been present at the funeral as well. I'd asked Natalie about it when we first sat down, and she said that they videotape funerals in situations like this because often, the killer likes to attend the funeral.

"Why?" I had asked.

"Because they get a thrill from seeing everybody sad," she said. "They like seeing what they've done. So Daddy is having them film it so they can look at it later and see who was here and how they were acting."

I felt the same detachment during the graveside service as I had during the funeral itself. And, because I couldn't seem to feel anything, I watched the emotions of the townspeople as they clustered around the grave. Next to me, Natalie cried in large gulping sobs. I reached out to touch her arm, wanting to share in her grief— wanting to cry, too. But for some reason, I couldn't. I didn't feel anything.

As my eyes drifted aimlessly from face to face, I saw movement near the edge of the cemetery, along the line of trees that separated the cemetery from the school property. I turned my head and was able to make out the shape of someone standing next to one of the large oak trees, his hand resting on the trunk as he watched the graveside service. Hoping to get a better view, I shifted my weight to my other foot and leaned slightly to the side. It wasn't a man, I realized suddenly, but a boy. His eyes were partially hidden behind dark hair that needed to be cut. I studied him, wondering if this was the boy Grace had seen hiking around in the woods. He wasn't someone I recognized and he seemed to fit her description. Quickly, I glanced over to Natalie's dad to see if he had noticed the boy as well. He appeared to be in deep conversation with one of the deputies. I wondered what they were talking about. Was it the murder? Did they have new information about Grace's killer? I tried to read their expressions but could tell nothing. When I looked back at the line of oak trees, the boy was no longer there.

When Reverend Ackerman delivered the final prayer and then moved to offer his condolences to Grace's parents, everyone seemed to take a collective step backward, unsure what to do now that the scripted part of the funeral was over. Usually in Edenbridge, something like this would be followed by a luncheon provided by the church ladies at the home of the deceased's family or in the church basement. In this case, however, Grace's father grabbed Sally's arm and escorted her away as quickly as possible. Reggie and Grace's mother, too, left immediately. Unsure how to handle this break in protocol, the townspeople stood around in small groups, looking uneasily at each other. I had followed my father and two of his friends from high school to stand in the shade of one of the cemetery's towering oak trees. I looked across the gravestones to where my mother, Natalie, and her mother stood.

"Is it okay if I go over and talk to Natalie?"

My father looked down at me and then glanced around to where my mother stood, now deep in conversation with Mary Jane. "Sure." He cocked his head to the side. "You doing okay?" I nodded and he squeezed my shoulder. "Okay, well, just stay with your mom."

As I walked toward my mother, I looked over to where my grandfather and my uncle stood talking to several of the local farmers. They were all dressed in their threadbare best. My grandfather sat sideways in the driver's seat of his faded Ford pickup, his booted feet resting on the running board. He was talking animatedly about something and gestured with his finger toward Mr. Holmes, who stood with his wife and one of his sons in the shade of an elm near the gravesite. The odor of pigs that wafted in on the southern breeze and my grandfather's gesticulations created little doubt as to the subject of his conversation.

"Stinkin'... shit... ask where *he* was ..." my grandfather said loud enough for snatches of his conversation to be overheard.

I glanced at my father, who looked nervously around to where Mr. Holmes stood. Their eyes met and my father quickly looked away in embarrassment. His discomfort made my heart hurt and I wondered briefly how often he was embarrassed by his father. I glanced again at Mr. Holmes. He smiled at me and I gave him a small wave. Quickly, I walked over to where Natalie stood with our mothers, their heads bent together in quiet discussion.

"It's hot," Natalie said when I reached her side. "I'm ready to go home."

"Me, too." I gestured to our mothers. "What are they talking about?"

"Grace," she said. "And you."

"Me?" My heart began to thump heavily in my chest. "What about me?"

"Your nightmares," she said without looking at me. She paused. "Is it true?"

I shrugged.

"It would give me nightmares, too, you know," Natalie said. "If I had found her."

The numbness I had felt over the past week disappeared, only to be replaced by anger. "But you didn't, did you?" I spoke the words through gritted teeth. "*I did!* Thanks to your stupid plan, *I* found her. If we had just done what we were supposed to, none of us would have been there!"

Natalie stared, shocked at my outburst. "Birdie," she said helplessly and reached out to touch me. "I'm sorry. I know—"

"No, you don't know," I yelled, the rage welling up inside me. I stabbed a finger in her direction. "You don't know what it's like! This is your fault! It's all your fault!"

Before I could say anything else, my mother stepped between us and grabbed my arm. "Birdie," she said and then turned back to face Mary Jane and Natalie.

"I'm sorry," she said. "She didn't mean it. She's just upset. She just—"

"Don't touch me," I screamed and wrenched my arm out of her grasp. "Don't!"

I turned blindly and began to run—away from Grace's grave, away from the people, away from everyone and everything. I had gotten only a few yards away when I tripped and fell, my ankle twisting under me. Mr. Holmes, who was closest, reached me first.

"You okay, Birdie?" he asked. I tried to stand and he crouched down to help me. The moment his hand touched my arm, I heard my grandfather's infuriated yell.

"Get your hands off her!"

The words hung in the air, and Mr. Holmes froze. My grandfather hurried over and momentarily towered over us.

"I was just—" Mr. Holmes began as I scrambled to my feet.

"I don't care what you were doing," my grandfather interrupted. "Don't you ever touch her again!"

Mr. Holmes rose to his feet and stood, towering over my grandfather. His eyes were hard and the veins on his neck and forehead pulsed. I watched as his left hand closed into a fist. Mrs. Holmes, who had hurried over as well, put a warning hand on his arm.

"Leave it, Anthony," she said.

As she spoke, Natalie's father stepped between the two men.

"Edwin . . . Anthony," he said in a low voice. "I think you should both take a step back. In fact, I think everybody needs to take a step back." He said this last part loud enough for everyone in the small crowd of people who had gathered to watch the drama to hear. "I know we're all pretty tightly strung right now and this has hit us all pretty hard. But we're gonna find the man who did this."

He looked around the crowd and pursed his lips.

"It's been a tough day," he said. "The funeral's over. I think we should all go home."

Almost relieved to have some sort of direction, several of the people began to walk to their cars or back to the school. Natalie's father led my grandfather away from the rest of the group. Their conversation was short and ended with my grandfather stomping back to his truck.

My father stood next to my mother, clearly torn between walking back to the school with us and going over to talk to his father and brother.

"Unbelievable," my mother said, her voice tight with anger. "Where the hell does he get off acting like that?"

My father shrugged. "You know how he is when it comes to—" He glanced down at me and seemed to struggle for words. "—people like Holmeses." He pulled in a deep breath and let it out slowly. He had taken off his suit jacket and sweat rings stained the armpits of his dress shirt. "I'd better go talk to him."

My mother stared at my father incredulously. "You're joking."

"Nance," he said and shook his head. "Come on. Cut me some slack. I . . . I have an obligation to make sure he's all right."

"Unbelievable," she said sharply. "And what about your obligation to your family? Or, let's see, what about your obligation to set a good example for your daughter?" She pointed at my grandfather, who was retelling the story to a small group of people clustered around him as if they hadn't been there. "Is that the sort of behavior you want your daughters to see—to grow up thinking is okay?"

She glared at him for a long minute and then threw up her arms in disgust. "You know what?" She extended her hand for the keys to the car. "You're right."

"Nance—" he began.

"Keys," she interrupted, punctuating her demand with a single jerk of her upturned hand.

His mouth tightened, and they stared at each other for several long seconds before my father sighed, reached into the pocket of his pants, and pulled out the keys.

"Birdie," my mother said without looking away from my father, "Are you okay to walk?"

I nodded.

"Yes," I said in a small voice.

"This isn't over," she said pointedly to my father and then turned. "Mark my words, John. This is just the beginning."

# Chapter 10

After Grace's funeral, everything about our small community seemed to change. Everyone had a theory as to who had murdered her and why. Gossip ran rampant and truth blurred into fiction as people recounted what they suspected, what they knew, or what they thought they knew. The only person who seemed to be un-affected by Grace's murder was Puddin' Puddin'. Unfazed by what was going on around him, he continued to ride around town on his rusted bike making his engine noises. Gossips around town wondered out loud if he was the murderer, pulling plot devices from *The Grapes of Wrath*. Did he find Grace by herself and try to touch her? When she screamed, did he try to make her be quiet? Yes, they said, he had the intellect of a child, but he also had the body of a man—a body with urges and desires he might not be able to control. It wasn't, some people whispered, out of the question that Puddin' Puddin' was the killer.

"Lord knows that Otis and Susan don't keep a good eye on 'im," Randy Jenkins said to my father two days later. He had needed gasoline for the lawn mower and I had ridden to the station with him to fill the gas can. Randy was manning the pumps and sharing his observations with anyone who would listen.

My father, who had climbed out of the pickup and stood next to it while Randy filled the canister, nodded but didn't say anything. Instead, he squinted up at the late afternoon sky.

"So, who do you think done it?" Randy asked.

"Dunno," my father said.

"Your girl found 'er, right?" Randy asked, peering at me through the rear window of the cab. I shrunk down, embarrassed and not wanting to be the subject of any more curiosity. "She see anybody?" He looked straight at me, his expression almost menacing. "Did you see anybody out there?"

"Randy, leave her alone," my father said and stepped in front of him. "She's been through enough and she doesn't need to be talking about it."

Randy scowled and then turned, flipped the lever on the gas pump, and returned the nozzle to its cradle.

"Want me to put it on your tab?" he asked sullenly, sneaking a quick glance at me.

"If you don't mind," Dad said as he pulled open the driver's side door and slid inside. "I'll settle up this weekend."

Randy nodded, hawked up a gob of spittle, and spat as he walked back into the station. As we pulled out onto the street, Puddin' Puddin' rode past. He was dressed in his usual pants and long-sleeved shirt, his head down and his fingers tightly clasped around the cracked plastic grips of the handlebar.

I looked at my father, who glanced quickly at me but didn't speak.

I shared what Randy had said with my mother when we got home.

"Idiot," she murmured to herself and then said more loudly to me, "I'm sorry, sweetie." She pulled me into a hug and then pulled back and looked into my face. "I know I don't have to tell you this, but you don't need to be repeating what Mr. Jenkins said. There's enough gossip going around right now as it is."

"I don't want to talk to anybody about this," I said miserably. "You should have seen how Randy—"

"Mr. Jenkins," my mother corrected.

"Mr. Jenkins," I amended with a scowl. "You should have seen how he looked at me. It's like I'm a circus freak or something. I hate everyone looking at me, asking what I saw when I found . . . her."

"I know, baby," she said and reached out to cup my face. "I'm so sorry you had to—that you're *having* to go through this." She paused and then said, "Hey, I have an idea. What if we invited Natalie over? Would you like that? You two could have a sleepover and—"

Before she could finish, I shook my head.

"No," I said. "I don't want to see her."

"Sweetie, I know you two had an argument, but it wasn't her fault this happened," she said. "It wasn't anybody's fault. If you just talked to her, I'm sure—"

"I don't want to," I said. "I don't want to talk to her or answer her questions about what happened or . . . anything. I just want to be left alone."

My mother studied me for several seconds without speaking. Finally, she sighed and said, "All right."

"All right," I echoed. "I'm going to go to my room," I said and started down the hallway. I had only gotten a couple of steps when she spoke.

"Birdie?" Something about her tone caused me to stop. I turned to face her. Her dark eyes were sad. "I love you," she said. "I'm sorry."

I stared at her, unsure how to answer. I didn't feel anything— not love, not hate, just . . . numbness. Finally, I nodded.

"I love you, too," I said, even though it felt like a lie.

She nodded, reassured. "This will get better," she said. "Just give it some time."

After several days of listening to, and trying to defuse, the gossip, Reverend Ackerman took it upon himself to drive out to the Glenderson farmstead and talk to them about their son. According to my grandfather's eager retelling, Otis Glenderson told Reverend Ackerman he could go to hell because their son was a legally recognized adult and could do whatever the hell he wanted. Undaunted, Reverend Ackerman thanked him for his time and then drove into Winston and purchased a silver Huffy bicycle with reflectors on the pedals and wheels. Puddin' Puddin' rode it for a day before the bike was found parked on the church porch with a handwritten note that said, "We do not need your charity." Later that day Puddin' Puddin' was again seen riding the antiquated, rusted bike he had pulled out of the brush down near Settler's Creek.

"I swear, I don't know what's wrong with that family," my

mother said one afternoon as Puddin' Puddin' rode past our house making his engine sound. Surprised that my mother would say such a thing, I looked up in shock.

She saw my stare.

"Don't get me wrong," she said quickly. "I'm sure he's a nice boy, he's just . . ." She trailed off and then looked at me. Her expression was serious. "Does he ever try to talk to you?"

I shook my head.

"Has he ever tried to get you to go with him?" she pressed.

"What do you mean?"

"Like, into the woods or down to the creek?"

"No, Mom," I said. "Geez. He just rides around on his bike and pretends it's a motorcycle."

She nodded thoughtfully and then sighed as if she had made a decision.

"So, I've been thinking and . . ." she said and then stopped. "Could you go get your sister? I want to talk to both of you about some things."

I nodded, slid off the bar stool and went to the kitchen doorway.

"Tara," I yelled in the direction of my sister's room. "Come here."

"Birdie," my mother snapped, "Go *get* her."

I sighed and trudged down the hall to my sister's room She looked up from her Barbie dolls when I pushed open the door.

"Mom wants you," I said and then added wickedly, "I think you're in trouble."

Tara's blue eyes widened and she dropped the red plastic shoe she was attempting to shove onto Skipper's foot. She looked worried. "Why?" She pushed a curl of blond hair back behind her ear. "I didn't do anything."

I shrugged as she scrambled to her feet.

"I don't know," I said. "But she wants to talk to you. She looks pretty mad."

With a final worried look, she hurried down the hallway toward the kitchen. I followed at slower pace.

"I'm in here," my mother called from the living room.

Tara hurried into the living room, where our mother sat, hunched forward over a stack of index cards. She motioned for us to sit on the couch.

"I didn't do it," Tara said quickly.

Our mother blinked in confusion and then looked knowingly at me. Tara caught our mom's expression and realizing what I had done, frowned.

"No one is in trouble," Mom said, her attention once again on Tara. "I wanted to talk to both of you."

She smiled and gestured toward the couch. Dutifully, we both went over and sat. Tara, who got there first, managed to pinch my arm without our mother seeing.

"Ouch," I said loudly and rubbed my arm.

"What's wrong?" Mom said.

"Tara pinched me," I said and glared at Tara who, in turn, looked innocently at our mother.

"You probably had it coming," she said finally and winked at Tara. I frowned, angry at being the odd man out.

"Now," our mother began, "what I want to talk to both of you about is what to do if someone you don't know—or even someone you *do* know tries to . . ." She sighed and seemed to search for the right words. "We've talked about strangers," she began again. "And what to do if a stranger tries to get you to get in his car, right?"

We both nodded.

"What do you do?" she asked.

I glanced up at Mom, who was waiting expectantly for my answer.

"I say 'no,'" I said.

"That's right," she said and nodded in approval. "But what do you do if he tells you that . . . I don't know, he's looking for his puppy and needs your help. What do you do?"

"I tell him that's too bad about his dog and that I hope he finds it, but I can't help him look for it," I said.

My mother smiled encouragingly.

"Right," she said. "And what if he offers you money to help—or shows you a picture?"

"I still say 'no,'" I said.

"Good," she said and then turned to Tara. "So, what do *you* do if you're at school and a grown-up you know comes to the school and says I told him to pick you up? What do you say?"

Tara glanced at me and I shook my head slightly and mouthed the word "no."

"*No!*" she yelled, surprising both my mother and me. "I'll say 'no' and run back inside."

"Good," my mother said. "Good. You probably don't have to scream or run, but better safe than sorry." She grinned and then became serious. "What if it's your grandma or grandpa?" she asked.

Tara looked at me and I shrugged.

"Yes?" she said.

My mother seemed unsure of the answer herself. "Probably, it would be all right," she said. "But to make sure, the school should call me or, if I'm sending anyone else to pick you up, I'll call the school."

"Why would Grandpa or Grandma not be all right?" Tara asked. I wondered the same thing myself.

"They probably would be," my mother said. "I'm just thinking about why they would be coming to get you, you know? Just thinking about what would be going on that that would happen."

She waved her hand dismissively.

"Anyway," she said. "What do you do if someone tries to grab you and force you into their car?"

"We scream 'no,'" I said.

"That's right," my mother said. "But you have to be ready to fight, too. Do whatever you have to. Scream 'no' if you can. Kick or hit them between the legs as hard as you can. Go for their eyes, too." She paused. "Do everything you can to make noise, scream, scratch, hit," she said. "Because the minute they have you in their car or have you away from other people . . . well . . . just fight them. And scream. Don't yell 'help' either. Yell 'fire' or 'no' or something like that."

Her eyes were wide and serious. Her fear was suddenly palpable and its intensity made Tara begin to cry. Mom looked at both of us and realized just how much she had scared us.

"I'm sorry," she said quickly. "I know I'm scaring you." She pulled both of us into her arms and held us tightly to her. "I just love both of you so much," she whispered. "I could never stand losing you. I just want you to know what to do. I don't want either of you to get hurt. That's all."

She rocked us against her until my sister stopped crying. Although I usually didn't like being cuddled, that night I leaned against my mother, my ear to her chest, and listened to her heart as it pounded away, rapid at first and then, finally, slower. We were all scared, I realized.

It was that fear which caused me to make amends with Natalie. Deep down, I knew the blame for what happened was no more hers than mine. We had let Grace down and we had to share that burden together. Her tone was cautious when I called her a week later.

"Hey," I said when she came to the phone. "Look . . ." My voice trailed off as I searched for words. "I . . ."

"I know," she said.

"Know what?" I asked, wondering for a moment if it would really be that easy.

"You're sorry," she said. "I am, too."

I exhaled deeply, not realizing I had been holding my breath. "I am. I shouldn't have said that—at the cemetery."

Neither of us spoke for several seconds and then she said, "So, you wanna come over?"

The idea of leaving the safety of my house caused my stomach to tighten. "I don't think I can," I lied. "I'm . . ."

"Or I could come over there," Natalie said when I didn't finish the sentence. "We could cut a window into the tree house and boss Tara around." She laughed and I found myself smiling. "Come on," she wheedled. "It'll be fun."

Okay," I said.

"Right on," Natalie said. "Let me ask Mom." I heard her ask Mrs. Stewart in the background and then she came back on the line. "I'll come over after lunch."

Unlike in the past when Natalie would race madly into the driveway and then skid to a stop, on this day, the first day we spent together since the funeral, she rode sedately into the drive and stopped without any kind of show.

I was sitting in the shade of the open garage. I stood as she coasted to a stop.

"Hey," I said and smiled. It was the first time I had really smiled since Grace's death.

"Hey," she said. She was sweating and her face was ruddy from the heat and the ride over. She didn't climb off her bike, but instead stood with her feet planted on either side and looked at me, waiting perhaps to see if I was going to start yelling at her. Instead, I studied her face. Her brown eyes looked tired.

"Whatcha been up to?" I asked, unsure how to begin.

She shrugged. "This and that. Just watching TV and reading. Mom's been taking me into Winston to the library for books and . . . you know." She hesitated. "How are you?"

Rather than meet her eyes, I looked down at her fingers where they rested lightly on the curved handlebars. The nails had been chewed down, their edges ragged like tiny saw's teeth. I glanced at my own fingers, which were bloody and raw from the constant picking and chewing on my cuticles. I held them out for her to see. She nodded knowingly. It was one of the things we shared in common.

"It's kinda weird," she said and looked around.

"What is?" I asked, unsure which of the many things that had changed, was weird.

"No Grace," she said.

I nodded. "It seems wrong," I said finally. "I mean, you and I did things alone before, but she was still sort of there. Now, she's . . ."

"Not," Natalie finished for me. We were both silent.

"I miss her, too," she said.

"I had a dream that Don Wan did it," I said without thinking.

"He was going to come after us, too."

"He won't hurt us," she said. "He couldn't. It would be too fishy if all three of us were . . ." She stopped speaking and shrugged. "You know . . . if something happened to all of us."

I nodded and dropped my eyes, looking again at my mangled cuticles.

"Wanna go up in the tree house?" I asked finally, more for something to say than because I wanted to climb into it.

Natalie peered around the side of the garage and into the backyard. The tree house was invisible under the canopy of leaves. She nodded and then carefully climbed off her bicycle, used the toe of her sneaker to pull down the kickstand, and turned to follow me into the backyard.

"We did a better job with the Nest," she said once we had climbed the tree and were sitting on the platform.

"Yeah, but I don't want to go back there," I said.

She nodded, understanding my reluctance. I waited, anticipating her questions about that day, about finding Grace, about the murder scene. Instead, she picked at a jagged piece of fingernail. "I can't stop thinking about her," she murmured after several seconds.

I raised my eyes to look at her. She was hunched forward, her curls obscuring her face. I watched as she raised her hand to her mouth and then, resisting the temptation to chew on the nail, returned it to her lap.

"I dream about her at night," she said.

"What do you dream?" I shifted uncomfortably, unsure if I really wanted to hear.

"I dream about all of us together at the Nest." She laughed. "Do you remember how hard it was getting all those boards up into the tree? You had the hammer and Grace and I would tie the boards onto that rope and pull them up to you so you could nail them into place?"

I smiled at the memory. "You guys had blisters on your hands from the rope. And you complained for weeks."

Natalie nodded. "But not Grace."

"She never complained," I said and then exhaled slowly. "If she had, we might have been able to help her."

Natalie looked quickly up at me. Her brown eyes were wide. Rather than speak, she reached out for my hand and I grasped it, clutched it even. Her palms were hot and moist, though I wasn't sure if it was from the heat of the day or our conversation. The freckles stood out in stark contrast to her pale skin and I found myself mesmerized by their randomness. It was only when I heard her sniff that I realized she was crying. I looked at her and longed to hug her. For some reason, though, I couldn't make my body move to comfort her.

We were both silent for several minutes, Natalie crying and me staring off into space. The birds twittered on the branches above us, and from my mother's flower garden came the quiet hum of the bees.

I was the one to break the silence. "Where do you think she is?"

"Heaven," Natalie said automatically. "The Bible says she's in heaven, looking down on us, watching over us."

"But how do you know that?" I asked quickly.

Natalie frowned and shook her head slowly. "I don't know. It's just what happens when you die. You go to heaven with God and his angels."

I tried to imagine Grace in heaven, on a cloud with angels and a smiling, grandfatherly man with a long, white beard. "I don't know," I said doubtfully.

"The Bible says so," Natalie insisted. "You just don't believe it because your Mom doesn't believe in God. It's true, though. There is a heaven. And she's there."

"I want to believe it," I said. "I just . . . I don't know. I can't believe she's gone."

"I don't like it either," Natalie said with a final sniff. "But there's nothing we can do about it." She raised the bottom of her shirt up and loudly blew her nose. Her rounded belly showed whitely above her shorts.

"That's gross," I said as she rubbed the snot into the fabric.

Natalie grinned. "Don't tell me you haven't done it before." She looked around the tree house. "So, are we going to make that window or what? I'm thinking over there." She pointed to the wall that overlooked the Spencers' yard.

"Okay," I said with more enthusiasm than I felt. It wasn't a resolution, but it was a start. "Let's do it."

## Chapter 11

I can tell you the exact day that I began to hear Grace's voice. It was a Tuesday afternoon, almost two months after her murder. School had started just a couple of weeks after her funeral and for those of us in Grace's class, those first few weeks were surreal. There were whispers about what had happened, about the investigation. That I had discovered her body made me somewhat of a celebrity. But the fact that I didn't want to talk about it or share the details of what I had seen made some of my classmates almost angry.

Natalie, to her credit, ran interference, providing bits of information she gleaned from her father. And because of this, teachers and students turned to her for information. But as time passed and late summer turned into fall, conversations around town became less and less about Grace's murder and more about the minutiae of life. People moved on. But I didn't. I couldn't. I found myself obsessing about it. I missed her in death like I never did when she was alive. And, I was perhaps a better friend.

Even though I knew my mother would ground me forever if she ever found out, I started sneaking to the clearing in the woods to sit in the Nest and look down at the murder scene. It wasn't that I wanted to. For some reason, I felt like I had to. I was compelled. And apparently I wasn't the only one. Wads of Kleenex, drained whiskey bottles, and cigarette butts littered the ground. Some of it, I knew, was left by older kids who went "to see where they found that dead girl." But most of it was left by Grace's mother.

The thought of Mrs. Bellamy sitting alone in the woods made me sad. Finally she was paying attention to her daughter, but it was too late. I imagined Grace's mother sitting on one of the rocks, smoking, crying, and drinking. According to Natalie, she had ended her relationship with Reggie and was mourning her daughter by going to the clearing and drinking until she passed out. Natalie said her father had taken Mrs. Bellamy home more than once. I never actually saw her during these vigils. I never really saw anyone, until early September when the young man I had seen at the edge of the cemetery began to come to the clearing. He was, I was soon to find out, Tommy Anderson. And he'd known Grace much better than any of us had realized.

I was in the Nest and had fallen asleep. My nightmares had become nightly occurrences and I was perpetually tired—constantly struggling against the fog in which I seemed to move. The voice was what woke me, a whispered hiss, commanding me to wake up—that "he" was coming. I jerked awake. The voice had been Grace's and for several disoriented seconds, I looked around, expecting her to be there. Suddenly, a dark head popped into view.

"Gotcha," the stranger said with a sly grin and jerked his head in the direction of the clearing. "I saw your bike." He pulled himself through the entrance and sat with his legs dangling through the hole. There was no chance of escape. My heart pounded. My legs tingled with fear. I was trapped.

"I'm Tommy," he said as he dusted his hands off on his jeans. He glanced up. His eyes were a brilliant, arresting shade of blue that was mesmerizing. "Tommy Anderson." When I didn't answer, he cocked his head slightly and raised an eyebrow. "You're Grace's friend, right?"

I nodded, confused as to how he knew who I was.

"Which one?" he asked.

"Birdie," I whispered and then cleared my throat and spoke again, louder, "Birdie."

"Right." He nodded as if he knew all about me. "Grace talked about you. She talked about both of you, but especially you."

I was surprised. I swallowed nervously. "You were at the cemetery."

He laughed, a brittle sound that held little humor.

"Yeah. Shitty day, huh?"

"You . . . knew Grace?"

He nodded.

"She didn't tell us she talked to you," I said. "Just that she saw you walking through the woods."

He grinned almost wolfishly and suddenly I felt like he wanted to eat me up. I thought about my mother's scenarios. None of them applied here. Tommy must have seen the panic in my eyes.

"Don't worry," he said and held up his hands in surrender. "I'm not going to hurt you." He grinned. "Seriously."

"I'm not scared," I said with more assurance than I felt. "I was just . . ." I swallowed nervously and shrugged in a way I hoped appeared casual.

"I used to come here to get away from my grandparents," he said. "Grace came here to get away from her mom and that asshole." He studied me for several seconds, as if gauging how much I knew about life in the Bellamy house. "I didn't know she was here at first," he continued. "But one day I was down there practicing." He pointed down, through the trapdoor of the Nest, at the ground. "I had this hunting knife that I was trying to teach myself how to throw. And she was up here watching. She sneezed. Scared the hell out of me." He grinned. "Made me mad, too, you know? I felt like a fool. I told her to come down. And then when I saw it was just a little girl, we started talking."

"What did you talk about?"

"Lots of things," he said. "We talked about her mom and the new boyfriend. Her friends. You. My grandparents."

"Who are your grandparents?" I asked

"Bea and Elmer Sullivan," he said. "My mom is, or I guess, *was* Cindy Sullivan until she married my dad. I'm here for the summer." He smirked. "My folks sent me here to keep me out of trouble."

My scalp tingled. "What do you mean?"

He looked down through the trapdoor at the ground between his legs, shook his head, and twisted one side of his mouth into a grimace. "Long story. You don't want to know about that. It's not all that interesting."

"Did you talk to Grace about it?" I asked.

"Yeah," he admitted. "She was easy to talk to."

He stared down at his hands, his expression sad. "I miss her." Tommy flexed his fingers. "She was just a kid, but she was smart in a weird way. She understood things—know what I mean? I told her things I'd never told anybody. I don't know if it was because she was just a kid or what, but, she was easy to talk to."

His use of the past tense reminded me of the fact that she would never come back. He returned his gaze to his hands and I looked down at the flaking scabs on my knees and shins.

"I found her," I said, finally, surprised and unsure why I volunteered this information to a stranger. From the corner of my eye, I saw Tommy's head jerk upward.

"You did?" he said. "What did she—I mean, how was she— what did you do?"

"I don't remember, really. I—stared at her and then ran to the Mercantile and—I don't remember all of it. We called the police and Natalie's dad came out and . . ."

Tommy exhaled loudly. "That's . . . wow. So . . . you saw the murder scene."

I fingered the white piping on my shorts. Unwelcome images of Grace's body leapt into my mind and I pushed them away.

"Did you see the knife and her . . ." his voice trailed off, but something about his tone caused me to look up.

"I saw everything," I said, again surprised I was telling Tommy more than I had shared with my classmates or my family.

His face flushed slightly and he looked away. "What did the police say when they saw it?"

"I don't remember," I said honestly. "Natalie's dad was, I don't know, upset and I was standing on the path with my mom."

Tommy stared at me, his interest making me uncomfortable.

*"Birdie, you need to get out of here."*

The voice was unmistakably that of Grace. The back of my neck prickled as if she were standing right behind me and I turned to look over my shoulder. There was no one there. I returned my attention to Tommy, who still was waiting for details.

"I don't want to talk about it," I said and then added quickly.

113

"Look, I'm really tired. I think I'm going to go home. My mom will be waiting for me."

He nodded. "Yeah. Listen, I'm sorry. I didn't mean to push." He looked at me significantly and then said, "I'm going to be around for a couple more weeks if you want to talk or hang out. We could meet here."

"Thanks," I said quickly, eager to get away. "I don't know if I'll really be able to. My mom doesn't want me wandering around by myself after what happened. And I shouldn't come here, you know, alone."

He grinned again. "Sure. I get it. But you wouldn't be alone. You'd have me here."

I nodded but didn't reply. He shrugged and then lowered his body down through the entrance. I watched the top of his head as he climbed down and then, when on the ground, looked up. Carefully, I lowered myself to the first rung and slowly climbed down. Tommy watched my progress.

"I know I'm a little too old for tree houses," he said as I stepped off the last rung onto the ground and turned to face him. "But that one's not bad. Grace loved it. You know, she slept here when things got crazy at home."

Though I had suspected as much, I had never known for sure—hadn't asked. The fact that this stranger knew more about Grace than I did made me angry. And slightly jealous.

"I know," I lied, my tone almost defiant. "So, I guess I'll see you around."

He stepped back to let me pass.

"Yep—at least for a couple of weeks," he said again, as if I hadn't heard him the first time. "Then I'm heading back to Chicago. My dad has a job lined up for me at the company he works for."

I walked over to my bike, picked it up, and was walking it across the clearing to the path when I heard him say my name. I turned. He stood at the base of the tree, his hands stuffed into the front pockets of his jeans. His head was cocked slightly to the side. His smile was sad.

"Listen, I'm really sorry about Grace. I know she was your

friend. She cared about you a lot. I hope you know that."

"Thanks," I said.

He nodded but didn't say anything else. I turned back to the path and hurried out of the clearing. There was something unsettling about Tommy, but also something that I recognized in him— the same sort of sadness I saw in Grace. The same sort of sadness I saw in myself.

I paused at the foot of the small hill and turned to look backward. He stood in the same spot as when I had left him. He raised his hand in a half-wave and I nodded at him before turning and walking away.

Even though he scared me and even though Grace's voice in my head warned me not to, I couldn't stop myself from sneaking away to meet Tommy. His connection to Grace, his understanding about a part of her life I had purposely avoided, and his grief were like a magnet to me. I couldn't not see him. Sometimes it was for just fifteen minutes. Other times I concocted an after-school activity that afforded me a couple of hours of free time. Tommy was often already there, or, if not there, would arrive shortly after I did. Our conversations were at first stilted and uncomfortable—but after the first few times, we began to open up to each other.

It was a strange relationship. He was seventeen and I was eleven. In other circumstances, we wouldn't have had much to talk about. But in this instance, because of Grace, we seemed to be on the same level.

He did most of the talking, sharing stories about his friends in Chicago, his family, and his grandparents. He talked about wanting to learn to drive. He admitted that he had gotten into trouble more than once—that he had hurt people. But, he said, Grace's murder made him want to change.

"It's like I said that first day," he said on our last afternoon together.

He was pacing around the clearing, talking and gesticulating. In the short time I had known him, I had seen his moods swing from calm and gentle to hyperactive and talkative. We were, of course, talking about Grace.

"We connected," he said. "I can't explain it, but her death changed me. It made me want to be a better person. I don't want to make the same mistakes I did before." His eyes were intense and his face flushed as he turned to look at me. It was when he was like this that I became most uncomfortable—and it was when I most acutely felt Grace's anxiety on my behalf.

"I gotta go," I said when he finally stopped for a breath. "It's getting late and I have to go home before Mom freaks out." He paused in his pacing and looked at me as if he had forgotten that I was there. I tried to smile, unsure how to terminate our friendship. "It was . . . nice getting to know you."

"Hey, yeah," he said and his voice softened. "I'm going to miss you, Birdie. You know, you remind me a lot of her. I liked hanging out with you."

"Me, too," I said, although I wasn't sure I meant it.

"So, can I write you? Or call sometimes?" He spoke the words quickly, nervously. "I mean, just to say 'hi.'"

I thought about how I would explain to my mother letters or phone calls from a boy she had never met. My response sounded noncommittal even to my own ears. "Yeah, I'll get your address from your grandparents."

Tommy smiled, recognizing that the words were empty, and then shrugged.

"Well, Birdie," he said. "It's been nice knowing you." He moved quickly toward me, his arms spread. The sudden movement startled me.

"*Run!*" Grace's voice boomed in my head.

I wanted to scream, but all I could manage was a garbled squeak. I started to run toward the path. Tommy was quicker and cut off my escape.

"Whoa, whoa, whoa," he said as he grabbed my arm. "What are you doing? What's wrong?" He grabbed my other arm and turned me unwillingly to face him. He smelled of sweat and something spicy. "Hey, it's okay," he said softly. "I wasn't going to hurt you. I

116

just wanted to give you a hug good-bye. That's all."

My breath came in gasps and I felt the pulse throb in my temple. Tommy craned his neck and tipped his head to the side to try to look into my face. I had the strange sensation that he was going to kiss me. I kept my eyes trained on the big, white letters of his AC/DC T-shirt. After a second, he released my arms and stepped back. "I just ... well ... bye."

"Bye," I mumbled and then turned and ran out of the clearing. My heart felt like it was trying to jump out of my chest. My head pounded and I felt the contents of my stomach rising up. Too scared to stop, though, I ran until I was within a hundred yards of the Mercantile. I turned to look behind me, but no one was there. I stopped, and tried to control my breathing. He had just wanted to hug me good-bye, I told myself. That was all. Still, I shivered.

I never talked to anyone about hearing Grace's voice—not even with Natalie, who had taken me on as her personal project. While all I wanted was to be alone, she was determined to make things the way they were before Grace's death. Each day at school, we would walk the halls before and between classes, talking with other kids. Natalie carried the conversations, keeping me involved, but not requiring me to really participate. By sheer force of her personality, she kept me a part of the social structure of our small school even though I struggled to feign interest. Inside I felt flat and disconnected.

I was Natalie's project outside of school as well. She tried everything she could think of to shake me out of my haze—including devising the types of adventures that in the past, I would have embraced. "Let's climb down the concrete pillars on the Settler's Creek Bridge." "Let's sneak into the Masonic Lodge Hall and see what they have hidden in there." "Let's get Mom to take us out to Mr. Jenkins' field to look for arrow-heads." But each time, I met her suggestions with a shake of the head or a shrug or a halfhearted "Maybe later." I knew that she was trying to make things the way they used to be, but our former fearlessness had become terrifying to me.

In many ways, I resented Natalie because she had rebounded in a way that I just couldn't seem to. We handled our grief differently. Whereas I wanted to pretend like none of it had ever happened, she took it upon herself to figure out who did it despite the fact that professionals that included her father, were unable to. It became her obsession and as with anything Natalie became fixated on, those of us around her were pulled into her orbit.

"Tell me about what you saw," she would say at least once a week. "Please."

At first, I resisted, telling her that I didn't want to talk about it. But over time, her relentless questioning wore me down. It was a Wednesday afternoon shortly before Easter when I finally told her what she wanted to know. Grace had been dead for nine months.

"I wish I could see my Dad's case files," Natalie groused. It was a common refrain. "If I knew what the crime scene looked like, I might be able to see something they missed. I mean, I was her friend, after all. We knew her better than anybody. And besides, you were there. What did you see?"

We were sitting in the tree house in my backyard. Though we had originally agreed to call it Grace's Nest, neither of us called it that. For both of us, Grace's Nest was in the clearing in the woods next to Brush Creek. The tree house in my backyard was simply called "the tree house."

"Natalie, I don't want to talk about it," I said for what seemed like the hundredth time. "I've told you. I just want to forget it happened."

"But Birdie, we can't," Natalie said. "Don't you see that? We owe it to Grace. We need to figure out who killed her."

I sighed.

"Listen to me," Natalie pressed. "There's a clue there that they're just not seeing. You might have seen something that they didn't know was important." Her eyes glittered with intensity. Meanly, I wondered if Natalie really wanted to avenge Grace or if what drove her was actually having the fame that would come from solving the case. "We owe her this," Natalie insisted. "Please."

I sighed and dropped my head so that I didn't have to look at her. My hair had grown since Grace's death and I was thankful for the ability to hide my face behind a veil of mousy curls.

"Please," Natalie said again.

I was about to refuse when I felt the familiar stirring in the back of my skull.

*"Tell her,"* Grace said, her voice soft and resigned. *"You might as well."*

"But I don't want to," I murmured.

*"It's okay,"* Grace said. *"Tell her."*

"Please," Natalie said at the same time, "Tell me."

*"I'll protect you,"* Grace said. *"I won't let the memory hurt you."*

After several seconds, I nodded.

"Excellent," Natalie said. I could hear the excitement in her voice. I didn't look up—not even when I heard the zipper of her book bag being pulled open and the crackle of paper as she dug around for a notebook and pencil.

"So," she said when she had her notebook open and was ready. "What was the first thing you noticed when you went into the clearing—the very first thing?"

I closed my eyes and, for the first time since Grace's death, willingly tried to summon up the image of what I had seen. I had become so used to pushing down—pushing away—the memories that at first, it was hard to let myself remember.

"It was quiet," I said finally. "I was pushing my bike up the path and it was quiet. There were no bird sounds or bugs or anything."

"Interesting," Natalie murmured. "And then what?"

I took a deep breath and exhaled slowly. "I saw her . . . body."

"Where was it?" Natalie asked.

"Near the big rock," I said. "She was . . ." I took a deep breath before continuing. "She was on her side . . . facing the big rock."

Natalie scribbled in her notebook. "What was she wearing?"

"A sock."

The scribbling stopped. "Oh," Natalie said, her voice shaky.

"Her clothes were all over the clearing," I continued, oddly pleased that I was making her uncomfortable. "All she was wearing was a sock."

Natalie swallowed, but said nothing.

"Part of her face was covered by her hair, but I could tell it was Grace. There was blood all over the place."

In my mind, I could see Grace's pale body, the smeared blood standing out in garish contrast to the chalky skin. I shook my head to dispel the image, wondering if Grace, from her perch inside my head, could see my memories—if they were as upsetting for her to see as they were for me to recall.

"Did you touch anything?" Natalie asked.

"No," I said numbly as I remembered the glassy blankness of Grace's eye as it stared back at me—recalled the big, black ant that had crawled across her eyeball as if it were nothing special. "I just stared at her. I knew I should go for help, but I couldn't move. I couldn't do anything. I just stared. And then finally, I went for help."

Natalie cleared her throat—for once, too uncomfortable to speak. I had intentionally left out the details of Grace's eye and the ant. I didn't want anyone, even Natalie, to know about this final injustice.

"Did you see the knife?" Natalie asked. "Was there anything that seemed out of place?" They were, I knew, questions she had heard her father ask or perhaps heard on television.

"It was all out of place," I said tightly. "Nothing was the way it was supposed to be."

Natalie cleared her throat and I finally raised my gaze to meet hers. Her face and her eyes were red.

"I don't want to talk about this anymore," I said.

Surprisingly, Natalie nodded.

It was the one and only time I talked to her about what I had seen.

# Chapter 12

Slowly, inevitably, life in Edenbridge settled back into its familiar pattern. The first few weeks after the murder, there had been outrage that anyone could do something like that. And there had been fear. Hopes were high that the murderer would be caught. When no one was, outrage gave way to frustration. People's expressions were pained as they talked about what had happened. I knew, from talking to Natalie, who eavesdropped on her parents when she was supposed to be in bed, that there were suspects, but not enough evidence to charge anyone. Frustration eventually gave way to resignation. People still talked about the murder of Grace Bellamy, but as time wore on and no one was ever charged with the crime, it was more with the sense of something that had happened "in the past."

I first noticed it at the annual Firemen's Chili Supper, which was held on the third Saturday of October. It was more than a year after the murder and as I walked around the school gymnasium and looked at the tables of donated prizes and desserts, I realized conversations were no longer exclusively about Grace's murder—or even partially. Instead, people talked about the high school's football team and plans for the annual Halloween hayride. Parents had begun to relax their rules and once again, children rode their bikes around town with relative freedom. It wasn't that people forgot; it was just that the killer hadn't been caught, and their vigilance weakened. Eventually, even Natalie moved on.

I, apparently, was the lone exception.

Grace was never far from my mind. I thought about her during the day; and at night, if I didn't dream about finding her body, I dreamed of being abducted myself. Sometimes it was Don Wan and sometimes, it was a faceless dark-haired man. Sometimes he grabbed me from behind, though more often than not, he approached me from the front, his face in shadows, his voice velvety and smooth.

The dreams almost always were set in the clearing below the Nest and they were always the same. It's nighttime. A man approaches me, the orangish-red tip of his cigarette glowing brightly as he inhales.

Even though I can't see his face, I can feel his eyes watching me.

"You should be home in bed," he says. "It's way too late for a little girl like you to be outside."

In the dream, I have a good reason for being there, though I never know exactly what that is—I just know it's important.

"This is where Grace died," he continues almost conversationally as he drops the cigarette to the ground and grinds it out with his boot. "But you know that, don't you? You found her body."

He blows the smoke out in a ghostly plume. I nod but don't answer. He moves closer.

"Are you scared?"

The question is unexpected and suddenly, he's standing right in front of me.

I nod again.

"Good."

The voice is soft and although I can't see his eyes, I can see his white teeth, his cruel smile. And even though I know it's coming, the first slap always takes me by surprise. I'm shocked and confused. I begin to cry.

"Don't you dare cry," the man snarls, his lips twisted in anger.

From up in the tree house, I hear a rustling and then the sound of wood on wood. Someone is up there and is moving the milk crate we use as a bookshelf.

He slaps me again—this time with the back of his hand. I feel the bumps of his knuckles as they strike my skin. I can't stop crying.

"Stop it," he growls through clenched teeth. "You need to learn how to do what I tell you."

I struggle to stifle the sobs.

"Take off your clothes," he says. "Except your sock."

I begin to tremble so hard that I think I'm going to collapse.

"*No.*"

The word doesn't come from me. It comes from above me. It's Grace. She is climbing down from the Nest.

"*Leave her alone,*" she says. "*Take me instead.*"

"Grace, no!" I gasp. "No."

"*Birdie, it's okay,*" she says. "*I'm already dead.*"

"No!" I scream. "No!"

*"Birdie, it's okay,"* she says as she steps off the last rung onto the hard-packed dirt at the base of the tree. She walks toward me.

"No!" I repeat "No! Stop!"

*"Birdie, wake up,"* Grace says, her voice strange-sounding. *"You're having a bad dream. Wake up."*

The man, who has been watching this exchange, now reaches out and grasps my shoulders. He begins to shake me.

"Birdie, wake up."

It was usually at this time that the voice trying to wake me became my mother's. It was not uncommon to wake with her sitting on the edge of my bed, her face scrunched into a worried expression. I remember one night in particular—the night when my parents began to argue in earnest about what to do with me. It had been more than six months since Grace's murder and I had awakened everyone with my screams. My mother had come into the room and was trying to wake me.

"Birdie, baby, you're having a nightmare," she said, shaking me. "Wake up."

"No," I say again, this time, not a scream, but a murmur, uttered in one world and heard in another. The clearing, the Nest, and the man faded. I opened my eyes to see my mother's worried expression.

"Birdie, sweetheart, wake up," my mother said again, this time calmly. "Are you with me?"

I nodded as she pulled me into her arms and rocked me slowly back and forth. Over her shoulder, I could see Tara in the doorway, her blue eyes wide.

"Shhhhh," my mother said softly. "It's okay. You're safe."

Tara stared at us and then slowly approached the bed. "It's okay," she said softly, echoing our mother. "You're safe." She reached out and petted my arm. I tried to smile. "I can sleep in here if you want," she offered.

I blinked and shook my head. "That's all right," I said as I pulled away from my mother and lay back down. "I'm okay."

"Do you want some water?" my mother asked as she bent over the bed and pushed my curls back from my forehead. When I said no, she nodded and kissed my forehead.

123

"I'm okay," I said again.

Later, when Tara had been put back to bed, and the house was quiet, I listened to the murmur of my parents talking. Occasionally, I caught snatches of the conversation.

"—not healthy."

"—it'll pass."

"—don't think so."

"—needs help—professional help."

"—just . . . time."

"—too long already . . . what's it going to take?"

"—not crazy . . . psychologist . . . weakness."

I rolled over onto my side and hugged my knees to my chest.

My mother, I knew, wanted me to see a professional— a psychologist. My father, however, was more of the "pull-yourself-up-by-your-bootstraps" school of thought. He believed, as did most of Edenbridge, that only crazy people or people who were too weak to handle their own problems saw a psychologist.

"—give it some more time," I heard my father say.

"I think we've given it enough time," my mother said loudly enough for me to hear her entire sentence. She was angry.

"—calm down," my father said.

"Birdie?"

The whisper was so soft, I almost wasn't sure my name had been spoken. I rolled over onto my back and then looked at the doorway. Tara's pretty face was cast in the shadows of the nightlights that were plugged into all the outlets in my room.

"Can I sleep in here?"

"Yeah," I said and scooted to the far side of the small bed. Gratefully, Tara hurried across the room and slipped under the covers. I curled up behind her and wrapped her in my arms.

"I don't like it when Mom and Dad fight," she whispered.

"Me neither."

Tara was silent for several minutes—so long that I wondered if she had fallen asleep.

"Birdie, are you crazy?" she asked suddenly.

"I don't know," I said miserably. "I think maybe sometimes I am."

"I don't think you are," she said. "I think Grandpa is wrong."

"What do you mean?" I asked, surprised that my grandfather was weighing in on my mental health. "When did he say that?"

"Last week," she said. "When I went with Dad to Grandpa and Grandma's. Grandma asked how you were doing and Dad said you were still having bad dreams. And then Grandma said it was no wonder given what you saw and Dad said he and Mom were thinking of taking you to the doctor. And Grandpa said those kinds of doctors are for crazy people and that was more of Mom's hippy thinking."

"Hmmm," I said.

"I don't think you're crazy," Tara said. "I told Grandpa that."

"Thanks, Tara." I squeezed her against me in a hug.

"Besides," she said with a yawn, "Even if you were crazy, you're still my sister, so I would love you anyway."

I smiled a little and impulsively kissed the back of her head. In the next room, my parents were no longer speaking, though I could hear them moving around in a way that suggested their conversation had ended badly and they were still awake. Next to me, Tara began to breathe deeply. She had fallen asleep.

"I'm sorry I'm so mean to you sometimes," I whispered to Tara, even though I knew she couldn't hear me. "And even though I don't say it, I love you, too."


The nightmares never completely stopped and my father must have won the argument because I never went to therapy. Still, their frequency lessened and as Natalie and I passed from junior high into high school, life assumed a certain normalcy. I did my best to forget about what had happened, though that was easier said than done. Finding Grace's body and the burden of her continued presence within me, even though she rarely "spoke," marked me in a way that people sensed even if they couldn't identify specifically what about me was "off." As a result, I turned inward. I pushed people away. I developed a reputation for being standoffish and came to be regarded by the other kids at school as "weird." Most of my friends drifted away toward more normal companions—all except Natalie. She was the constant—an anchor, but also a reminder.

Each year, on the anniversary of Grace's death, the two of us would find a way to sneak off to the Nest. Usually, we would climb up into the tree house, clean away the remnants of leaves, and squirrel and bird droppings, and then sit quietly on the old cushions that each year grew more sour with mildew and rot. Natalie would talk about Grace or remember aloud something the three of us had done, but most of the time, we sat quietly and simply marked the passing—that was, until the summer before our senior year in high school.

It had been seven years since Grace's murder and we were at the clearing for our yearly vigil. As was often the case when my emotions were heightened, I felt Grace's energy stirring at the base of my skull—a tingling that made me feel jumpy and fragile.

"It never changes, does it?" Natalie asked as we stood at the base of the tree and looked around the clearing.

"Not really," I said matter-of-factly. "We have, though."

Natalie grinned and shot me a mischievous look. Her hair had deepened into an enviable shade of auburn and though she was still pale, she covered her freckles with makeup. She had lost the little girl pudginess and had become decidedly pretty. I, too, had changed. I had grown tall—almost as tall as my father. And my hair, which had been an uncontrollable mop when I was younger, was now held in place with barrettes or hair bands. Three years on the track and cross-country teams had given me the lean body of a distance runner.

"So, I've got a surprise," Natalie said once we had climbed up into the Nest and settled ourselves in our respective corners.

"Yeah?" I spread out the old wool blanket Natalie's father insisted she carry in the trunk of her beat-up white Chevrolet Chevette.

"Yeah." She waited until she had my full attention before unzipping her gym bag, reaching inside, and producing a bottle of vodka. "Check this out."

126

"Where did you get that?" I asked and looked nervously around.

"Borrowed it," she said with a laugh. "From my dad's liquor cabinet."

"Nat, you're going to get in trouble," I said anxiously. "*We're* going to get in trouble. We're not old enough."

"Jesus, Birdie, lighten up," she said. "Why do you think I brought it? You need to relax a little. You're so concerned about breaking rules."

"There's a reason why rules are rules," I said. "And when you break them, there are consequences."

"Uh huh," she said and twisted off the screw top. She sniffed the liquid inside, shrugged, and then raised the bottle to her lips. "Cheers."

I watched as she took a large gulp and then began to cough.

"Smooth," she said with a grin, her eyes watering.

I frowned and shook my head when she offered the bottle to me.

"Come on," she said and pressed it into my hand. "Just take a swig."

Grudgingly, I raised the bottle to my lips and drank. The first swallow made me choke and sputter. "Oh my god," I gasped as the alcohol burned a hot path down my throat and into my stomach.

"I know," Natalie said. "It's rad."

"I hate it when you talk like a valley girl," I said and handed the bottle back to her. She laughed, flipped me the bird, and took another drink. This time she didn't cough at all.

"Try again," she said. "The second one's a lot better."

Rather than argue, I took the bottle and took a swig. She was right; the second mouthful was better.

"Not so bad, eh?" She raised her eyebrows.

"Not so bad," I admitted and leaned back on my elbows. The vodka settled comfortably in my stomach and for the first time since I could remember, I felt my body relax a little. I closed my eyes and exhaled. A comforting warmth enveloped me and I smiled. When I opened my eyes, Natalie was watching me. I held the bottle out to her, but she shook her head.

"In a bit," she said and flopped back to stare at the canopy of leaves. The afternoon was bright and, surprisingly mild. I lay back next to her, our bodies at angles, our heads touching. I looked up to see bits of blue through the green.

"Sometimes I go outside and lay on the grass and look up at the sky," she said. "I stare up at the clouds or, if it's night, the stars. When I'm out at Grandpa and Grandma's, it's so dark . . . you can see every star in the sky. It's like someone tossed a bunch of glitter into the air and it's just suspended there, catching the light."

We lay for several minutes, not speaking, until Natalie finally broke the silence.

"Sometimes, I wonder if the stars are really just the souls of the dead, up there looking down on us."

I rolled my head sideways to look at her. Her expression was wistful.

"I wish she were here." She turned her head so she could look at me. I blinked, but said nothing. "Do you think about her?" Natalie asked, her gaze unwavering. "You never really talk about her. You don't really talk about much of anything."

"There's nothing to say," I said finally. "And talking about her doesn't change anything." I lifted my head, chin to my chest and raised the bottle to my lips. Vodka spilled out of my mouth and ran down my chin onto my shirt. I immediately wondered how I was going to explain the smell of alcohol to my mother.

"I sometimes think about the last thing she saw before she died," Natalie said.

"Jesus, Natalie!" I exclaimed, even though I had wondered the same thing myself. "Why would you think about that?"

She shrugged and reached for the bottle. I handed it to her and she lifted it to her lips and drank deeply. I watched the muscles of her throat work as she swallowed.

"Natalie, you weren't there," I said as she swiped the back of her hand across her lips. "You didn't see her. You didn't—"

"You can't continue to blame me, you know," Natalie interrupted, emboldened by the vodka.

"What makes you think I blame you?" I snapped.

"I can tell," Natalie said. "Ever since the funeral. I see it in your eyes. You blame me because it was my idea to lie to our parents. It was my big idea to meet up there. It was my fault that you found her."

"That's not it," I said and then stopped, unsure what "it" really was.

"But you know what?" Natalie said and stabbed her finger in my direction. "It was her mom's fault. It was Reggie's fault. It was her dad's fault. *They* were the ones who let her down. *They* were the ones who broke the rules. You and me . . . we were the *good* part of her life."

I stared at her, the warmth in my belly replaced with something else—something dark. I had accepted that Grace's voice in my head, her energy living inside me, was punishment for letting her down and for finding her body when it was most vulnerable. I cared more than Natalie and, as such, was being punished while Natalie was spared. It wasn't fair.

"Bullshit," I said, suddenly, unaccountably angry. "*We* were the ones who let her down. *We were*, Natalie. We should have been there for her. We should have helped her. We knew what was going on."

"We were kids, Birdie." Natalie threw up her hands in frustration. "Jesus, we're *still* kids."

I shrugged and we sat for quite a while in uncomfortable silence.

"I miss her," Natalie said suddenly. "Not just today. I miss her every day. I miss the three of us—the way we used to be." She reached out to touch my arm. "I miss you, too—the way you used to be."

I turned, then, to look at her.

"You've changed," she said. "You're distant and . . . I don't know. It's like you're untouchable."

I felt my anger fade at the sincerity and vulnerability of her words. "You're touching me now." I gave a conciliatory half-smile.

"That's not what I mean," she said and pulled her hand away. I could tell that her feelings were hurt.

"Nat," I began and then stopped. There was nothing I could

say—no words that would explain any of it. "I'm sorry."

She raised the bottle again to her lips.

"It's okay," she said sullenly and took another drink before handing me the bottle. She flopped back down and closed her eyes. I looked at her. She wore makeup now and the mascara made her eyelashes seem impossibly long. I wanted to touch her face—to tell her again how sorry I was. Instead, I took another gulp of vodka and lay back down next to her.

"You're going to get me in so much trouble," I said. "Mom is going to kill me."

"You?" she laughed. "Fat chance. You have to break the rules to get into trouble."

"And what do you call this?" I asked, gesturing broadly to include the Nest, the clearing and the vodka.

"I call this . . . necessary," she said with a grin.

I looked up at the leaves, stationary in contrast to the Nest, which now seemed to spin.

"Whoa," I said. "It feels like the Nest is moving."

Natalie laughed. "You should probably stop." She sat up, her upper body swaying slightly. "Whoa. We probably both should."

"I don't want to," I said, frowning as I tried to make my thick tongue work. "It feels good. I'm so . . . relaxed. I don't think I've felt like this since . . . since . . ." I threw up my hands. "A long time." I could hear my words; they were slurred despite my best efforts.

"I think you're drunk," Natalie said.

"Me, too," I said and laughed loudly. "But I don't wanna stop. I wanna stay like this."

Natalie made a face and then nodded seriously. "Okay, but we should go down to the clearing now."

Her words sounded . . . blurry.

"If we have more and try to climb down, we'll probably fall and kill ourselves."

She stood and extended her hand. I grasped it and allowed her to pull me up. The floor of the Nest seemed to tilt under my feet and I stumbled.

"Feels weird," I muttered.

*"Birdie!"*

It was Grace's voice.

"Huh?" I moved on rubbery legs to the opening in the floor.

*"Sit down,"* she said softly.

"But I just stood up," I said.

*"Birdie, listen to me."* Unlike the fuzziness of everything else, Grace's voice was crisp and clear. *"You need to sit down and scoot over to the hole. Don't walk. Scoot."*

"Okay," I said.

*"Just take it slow,"* Grace said.

"Hurry up," Natalie said from behind me. "I need to pee."

"I'm going to sit down and scoot on my butt," I said. "I need to take it slow. You can go first."

"Whatever," Natalie said as she stumbled to the entrance to the Nest, sat down, and swung her legs through the hole in the floor.

*"Tell her to be careful,"* Grace said. *"Tell her to go slow and take one rung at a time. And tell her to hold on tight before she goes to the next one."*

"Grace says to be careful," I began and then stopped.

Natalie tipped her face upward to frown at me.

"Huh?"

"I meant, if she were here, Grace would tell us to be careful," I said quickly. "You know how careful she was."

Natalie frowned and then nodded exaggeratedly.

"Just go one rung at a time," I said.

*"And tell her to hold on tight before stepping down for the next one,"* Grace said.

"And hold on tight . . . when you're stepping," I said lamely.

"On it," Natalie said and shoved the bottle into the waistband of her shorts. "Just . . . watch and learn."

Before I could reply, Natalie pushed herself away from the edge of the opening and was clumsily lowering herself down the rungs toward the ground. I crawled to the edge and watched her progress.

"Made it," she called from below. "Your turn."

I scooted to the opening and swung my legs so they dangled down through the hole.

*"Stick your foot out and put it on the first rung,"* Grace instructed. *"Now, put your hands on either side of the doorway to support your weight,"* she said. *"Go slow and push yourself forward."*

The ground below suddenly seemed very far away.

*"Don't look down,"* Grace said quickly. *"Just focus on the next step."*

I nodded numbly and pushed forward so that I was standing on the first rung.

*"Good . . . now slide your foot down to the next rung,"* Grace said.

"To your left—I mean, your right—no, I mean your left," Natalie called helpfully from below. "Sorry."

*"One rung at a time,"* Grace said softly. *"Just focus on my voice."*

"One rung at a time," I murmured.

*"That's right. And hold on tight with your hands until your foot is on the next rung."*

From below I could hear Natalie's voice, too. "You've got one . . . two . . . three . . . five more to go."

The minute I put my feet on the ground, my legs began to tremble uncontrollably and I felt as if I wanted to throw up. Unable to stand, I collapsed at the base of the tree.

"Damn," Natalie said as she unscrewed the cap on the bottle and took a swig. "We forgot the blanket."

I looked up at her and she held out the bottle. I shook my head. "I think I'm done."

She frowned down at the bottle and then sighed. "Yeah, me, too." She turned and flung the bottle into the woods. I heard it crash through the brush and land on the ground with a dull thump.

"I don't feel so good," I said, surprised at how quickly the nausea hit.

Natalie squatted down next to me and studied my face. This close up, I could see what was left of her freckles. "You don't look so good," she said finally.

"I'm . . ." I began and then stopped, turned my body, and vomited violently.

Natalie sprang back in disgust.

"Gross."

I panted, trying to catch my breath, and then felt the familiar roll of nausea as the second wave hit. And then the third.

"We need to get you home," Natalie said once there was no longer anything left for me to throw up.

I nodded miserably.

"I'm going to be in so much trouble," I moaned. "I'm drunk and I have puke all over me. Mom is going to kill me."

"I could sneak you into my house," Natalie said thoughtfully.

"I just want to go home," I said.

She nodded and leaned drunkenly forward to help me up. I grasped her hand and allowed her to pull me upright. I glanced down again at my stained shirt. Natalie looked at it, too. "Don't worry." She slid her arm around my waist and led me out of the clearing. "I think I have a T-shirt in the car."

I didn't end up getting in trouble. In the end, no one knew what had happened. After Natalie dropped me off, I staggered up the sidewalk and around back to the kitchen door. When I turned the handle, it was locked.

"Great," I muttered as I fished around in my book bag for my house key.

Inside, the house was quiet aside from the soft ticking of the kitchen wall clock. A note was pinned to the cork board by the phone. It had been written quickly but neatly in my mother's careful handwriting.

> *Birdie:*
> *Your Dad, Tara and I are in Winston.*
> *Your grandfather had a heart attack this afternoon and the ambulance took him to the hospital. I'm sorry, sweetie, but it doesn't look good. I'll call when we know something.*
> *Love, Mom*
> *P.S. There are frozen pizzas in the freezer.*

The seventh anniversary of Grace's death and the first time I got drunk was also the day my grandfather died. Despite my mother's observation that he would have had to have a heart for it to stop working, it *was*, according to the doctors, what killed him. He was sitting at the kitchen table, smoking a cigarette and waiting for my grandmother to fix his lunch when the first heart attack hit. The second occurred as the ambulance took him to the hospital in Winston, and the third as they wheeled him into the emergency room.

Although his death affected me differently than Grace's, I had the same questions about what happened to him once he was gone. I wondered, too, about his last moments. As he was dying, did his life flash before his eyes? Did he feel remorse or regret for his actions? And when he was dead, did he go someplace else or was he just . . . gone? The fact that Grace's presence lingered within me made me question the idea of death. Was there a heaven and hell? I imagined my grandfather trying to explain to St. Peter the reasons why he did the things he did—the hateful things he said to people he considered lesser than himself, his racism, his horrible treatment of Mr. Holmes and his family. I considered this as we sat in the second pew of the church, waiting for the organist to finish playing "The Old Rugged Cross."

My grandfather's funeral was completely different than Grace's. While her death had been tragic, my grandfather's was simply the end of a life. To my left sat Tara and my mother, and to my right, my Aunt Rita and two cousins, Alfred and Frank. In front of us, in the first pew, was my grandmother, flanked on either side by my father and my uncle. I studied their backs as the song droned on. My father stared blankly forward at the casket and my uncle watched the organist. My grandmother, however, stared down into her lap. From behind, I could see her bony shoulder blades poking out the polyester fabric of her black dress and I longed to reach out and run my finger along the ridge.

Next to me, Tara sniffed. This was her first funeral and she was overwhelmed—though more by the sadness of everyone around her than by the fact that she would never see Grandpa again. I looked down at her and tried to smile.

"It's okay," I whispered. "It's going to be okay."

She nodded and slipped her hand into mine. I squeezed it gently and she squeezed back.

Years later, I would remember flashes of that day, but what stands out most for me was seeing Grace. We were at the cemetery and my father, uncle, and several of the men in town were lowering my grandfather's coffin into the ground. I stood under the dark green awning with my cousins, Tara, and the adults.

It was a windy day and the edges of the awning snapped in the dry, baked breeze. I was watching the overgrown grasses along the edge of the cemetery bend and wave under the wind when I saw her. She was wearing the dress she had been buried in. I gasped and looked quickly to either side to see if anyone else noticed her, but everyone had their heads bowed in prayer. I looked back at where Grace stood. She smiled and raised her hand in greeting.

I frowned but didn't return the gesture. We studied each other. I wondered how I must appear to her with my seventeen-year-old body and my modern clothes. She looked exactly the same as I remembered. A gust of wind snapped the edge of the awning above me, though Grace's hair remained undisturbed. I frowned as I realized that this wasn't a vision I had conjured up. Grace was real—or as real as she could be. I thought suddenly about the times over the past few years when I had heard her voice. I immediately thought about the books we used to sneak from the library on ghosts—were they the cause of this, I wondered briefly? I looked at the people gathered to the right of the grave, searching for Natalie's face. As if she felt my eyes on her, she looked over at me and smiled sympathetically. I tipped my head and jerked my eyes in Grace's direction. Natalie frowned and then, understanding what I was trying to convey, looked toward where I had indicated.

Her expression registered confusion. She looked again at me, gave a short shake of her head, and raised her shoulders. I glanced back at Grace, who mimicked Natalie's gestures. Natalie couldn't see Grace. Just as she hadn't heard her when we were at the Nest the week before, she couldn't see Grace today. Grace's presence was directed toward me, I realized suddenly. Grace had chosen *me* to haunt. It was because I found her, I thought—because I recognized my responsibility in what happened. Because I accepted that I had let her down, my penance was to know that she didn't rest peacefully. The realization made my body tingle unpleasantly.

I felt my knees wobble and realized too late that I was about to pass out. My mother caught me before I hit the ground, though I don't remember it. Everyone said it was the heat and the stress of my grandfather's death. I, however, knew better. It was my body's reaction to seeing Grace and the realization of what seeing her meant.

"You're okay, sweetie," my mother said as I came to. "You just fainted."

I looked frantically from side to side, unsure where I was or what had happened. Awkwardly, I tried to sit up.

"No, no," my mother said. "Just stay down for a little bit."

Around me, the people of Edenbridge spoke in low tones, bending and craning to get a better view.

"You fainted, Bird," my mother said. "Your Aunt Rita's getting you some water."

Natalie's face popped into my line of vision. "You okay?"

I nodded.

"What were you trying to tell me before you passed out?" she asked in a low voice.

I thought about Grace standing at the edge of the cemetery and the stillness of her hair despite the wind. No one would believe me if I told them—not even Natalie.

"Nothing," I muttered.

She frowned, but before she could press the issue, Aunt Rita returned with a napkin wrapped around ice cubes that smelled like Dr. Pepper. She slipped it into my hand.

"Put this on your forehead," she said and pushed my hand to my face.

The ice felt sharp against my flushed skin. A trickle of cold water ran down my temple and into my ear. "Grandpa," I said suddenly, realizing that I had fainted in the middle of the funeral and probably ruined the service.

"It's okay, sweetie," my mother said. "They had just finished the prayer when you passed out." She looked around at the people who were beginning to disperse. "Let's get you to the car and into the air conditioning."

She stood awkwardly and several people moved to help me to my feet. Once on my feet, I looked to where I had seen Grace. She was no longer there. I craned my head to see where she might have gone, but before I had a chance to look around for her, my mother turned me toward the cars and began to lead me away. Exhaustion washed over me and I leaned into my mother. We were almost the same height. She squeezed my shoulder gently.

"It's okay, sweetie," she said again. I nodded in agreement even as I acknowledged in my own mind that it wasn't going to be okay. It was never going to be okay as long as I was in Edenbridge. The realization came as clearly as if Grace herself had whispered it in my ear. If I were to stand any kind of chance at a normal life, I needed to break the hold that Grace and this town had on me. And the only way to do that was to run away. As long as I remained in Edenbridge, I would never be free of the memories. I would never be free of her. If I were to survive, I had to run as far away as possible and never look back. And that's exactly what I did.

Part II:
1989–1993

# Chapter 13

Despite my desire to run as far away from Edenbridge as possible, being a seventeen-year-old with no job and decidedly average grades meant that I only made it as far as the University of Nebraska at Lincoln. It wasn't as far away as I would have liked, but it was someplace where I was, for the first time ever, anonymous. There was only one other person from my class who chose the same school and we didn't really run in the same circles. Only occasionally did we see each other on campus, and when we did, all that was exchanged was a polite nod or wave.

At first, I worried that Grace would follow me out of Edenbridge and because of that, I spent the first few weeks of college tiptoeing around the edges of my new life—probing the limits of who I was allowed to become. Even as I made decisions or expressed opinions, I questioned if my thoughts were really my own. But after the first month or so, I began to relax and reinvent myself. In that way, college was liberating. No one knew my parents or my parents' parents. No one knew me as the girl who found her dead friend in the woods. No one knew anything about me except what I wanted to share—and that was very little. I kept the few friends I had at a distance and cultivated a sort of detachment that gave the impression of having too much on my mind to be bothered with conversation. I worked hard to maintain that same sort of detachment, with varying degrees of success, with my family and my hometown.

Distance from my father was not hard to achieve. For whatever reason, the closeness we shared prior to Grace's murder all but vanished after her death. It was as if he were scared to be too familiar with me. And as the investigation progressed, he became more and more distant. No longer did he take me with him to the station. And as junior high flowed into high school, we became like acquaintances. We spoke, but only about generalities. And never again was it just the two of us.

My mother, however, was a different story. We spoke at least once a week although I'm not sure why, given that the script of our conversations never changed.

"How are you?" she would ask.

"Fine," I would say.

"Really?" she would ask.

"Really," I would say.

"I don't believe you. How are you *really*?"

"I'm fine."

Long silence.

"How are classes?"

"Pretty good."

"So, you're doing okay?"

"Yes, *Mother*."

She was trying to stay connected. I knew that. And deep down, in the part of me that was actually quite lonely, I appreciated it. To be honest, I'm sure I secretly *wanted* it. But I had also come to realize that ties to the past were dangerous—as were connections on an emotional level. To become emotionally involved meant being vulnerable. And that was something I simply could no longer do. Survival meant changing everything—including my name. No longer did I introduce myself as Birdie. Now, I was Rebecca—Rebecca who wore plain, too-large sweatshirts, camped out in coffeehouses, and always carried a book as defense against conversation. Unlike Birdie who felt too much, Rebecca was cool and untouchable. She observed but didn't participate. She was everything Birdie was not.

And so, it was with this carefully constructed persona that I walked through campus to biology class on that late September afternoon of my sophomore year. The air was crisp and I walked briskly, enjoying the sound of the leaves as they crunched under my feet. I breathed in the fall and suddenly, inexplicably, felt homesick. I longed, suddenly, for caramel apples and hayrides. I wanted to sit at a bonfire with Natalie and drink apple cider. It was rare that I had a longing for anything having to with Edenbridge and that realization, in itself, was enough to snap my focus back to the present.

I slowed my pace and took the sidewalk that ran along the south side of the Woods Art Building and past one of the campus's most celebrated sculptures, a bronze piece titled *Sandy: in Defined Space*. It had originally been a temporary exhibit in 1970, on loan from the artist, Richard Miller. But everyone had fallen in love with it; and when it came time for it to be taken down, the people of Lincoln raised enough money to purchase it. Each time I passed by it, I understood why. It was an evocative piece and one that always spoke to me. Something about the woman, who I could only assume was Sandy, suggested she understood me. She, too, was haunted, though by what, I didn't know.

In the sculpture, she sits nude, almost curled to fit within the confines of one side of a square box. She is positioned with her back against one side of the box, her left hand braced behind her, her right hand dangling to the side. Her face is relaxed, her eyes closed. She appears calm even as her legs are bent and propped so she can fit into the impossibly small space. She is confined, trapped. And so she makes herself as comfortable as possible.

As much as I always saw myself reflected in Sandy, I realize now I also saw Grace. When she was alive, she, too, was boxed— forced into a small space in which she had no other choice but to make herself as comfortable and as small as possible. She, like Sandy, was lonely and isolated, which is likely why, at least twice a week, I found excuses to walk past the sculpture. Sometimes, I stopped and spent time with her. But other times, like that day in October, I forced myself to hurry past with no more than a lingering glance.

My biology class was only two buildings away from Sandy and I arrived much earlier than necessary. Though I always tried to be the first to arrive, rarely was I this early. I looked down at the scratched face of my Timex and contemplated sitting outside. The bitter cold of a Nebraska winter would make me long for days like this. I closed my eyes, raised my face to the pale afternoon sun, and inhaled deeply. Something about the taste of the air again made me think of Edenbridge. I opened my eyes and shook my head. Inside was a better choice.

I hefted my backpack more firmly over my right shoulder, turned, climbed the four concrete stairs of the back entrance, and pulled open the heavy glass door. Inside, I walked quickly to the auditorium where our class was held. The doors were propped open and I stepped inside. In the seat where I usually sat was a thin, neatly dressed man about my age. I narrowed my eyes, irritated that he was sitting in my seat. His lunch was spread out on the desktop in front of him.

He looked up as I came into the room and smiled. "You're early, too," he said.

"Yes," I said coolly as I chose a seat far enough away that there was no obligation to talk to him. He nodded and returned his attention to the partially eaten sandwich—what appeared to be tuna salad with avocado slices. He glanced up, noticed my interest, and gestured toward the other half, which sat on a square of creased wax paper. He raised his eyebrows.

"No thanks," I said, appalled at the thought of taking food from a stranger.

He nodded, finished chewing, and swallowed. "I'm actually thinking about going vegetarian," he said conversationally, as if I had asked a question. He wiped at his mouth. "I don't know why, but I'm really struggling with the whole concept of eating animals. It's barbaric, don't you think?"

He reached into the plastic sandwich bag of pretzels and delicately removed one. He lifted it carefully to his lips, placed it in his mouth, and then chewed slowly. As he had with the bite of sandwich, he swallowed and then wiped at the corners of his lips. I watched, mesmerized by the meticulous way he ate. Every three bites he would pick up the sweating can of Coke with just the pads of his fingers and thumbs and take a sip. A folded paper towel served as a coaster.

"Are you sure you wouldn't like half of this?" he asked as he noticed my continued scrutiny.

"No, really, thanks," I said, quickly. "I've already eaten. I didn't mean to stare, I just . . . You're just such a precise eater." The words sounded rude and perhaps a little accusing.

He blinked several times in surprise and then looked down at the desktop and the careful arrangement of his lunch. "I guess you're right," he said finally and picked up the second triangle of sandwich with an exaggerated flourish. I watched as he took a bite and then blushed when he winked at me.

More for something to do than anything else, I opened my backpack and fished around for my spiral notebook and a Bic pen. Science was not my strong suit and the speed at which the professor moved through the material had left me more than a little overwhelmed. Already I felt like we had covered the extent of my high school biology class and we were only six weeks into the course.

"What do you think so far?"

I looked up, surprised to find him watching me.

He reached for his soda, took a measured sip, and then placed the can back onto the folded paper towel. "I hate it. In fact, I think this—" he gestured at the open textbook that lay on the desk next to him "—is the most boring, and frankly disgusting, class I can imagine." He picked up his sandwich and took another bite. Breadcrumbs fell into his lap and as he chewed, he carefully brushed them away. He tucked his chin against his chest and looked down at his shirt. His tie lay crookedly across his stomach and he carefully straightened it. His fastidiousness was fascinating to observe.

"You know I'm gay, don't you," he said when he looked up and caught my gaze. I blushed and looked quickly away.

"I didn't—"

"I'm just telling you because I don't want you to think I'm available."

I shook my head quickly from side to side. "No . . . I wasn't . . . I just . . ."

"I know." He rolled his eyes dramatically. "It's the clothes. They're so Republican. Trust me, if I didn't have to go to work from here, I'd wear something with a little more style. But no one in the Bible Belt wants to buy their fancy furniture from a fag—even though we *are* the ones who have the best eye for decoration."

I swallowed and nodded quickly as if I agreed. I had heard about gay people, of course. But I had never really met one. At least, I didn't think so. Everyone in Edenbridge talked about Phil Grant and how he liked to hire teenage boys to work around his property, but I had never personally spoken to him. He was scary, with a perpetually stubbly face and small, darting eyes. Every time I had seen him in town, he was dressed in faded overalls that stretched over his massive belly—a big man who constantly licked his chapped lips and ran his hands over his own chest. He was nothing like the man who sat near me—a man who, I realized, had asked me a question.

"What?"

"I said, Don't tell me I'm your first gay." He looked even more closely and then drew back in amazement. "Oh my god, I am, aren't I? Honey, just how small *is* your hometown?"

"Pretty small," I admitted. "Actually, very small."

He looked me up and down as he chewed the last bite of sandwich. "I guess I should have known, given how you are trying to make yourself invisible with that hair and those clothes." He leaned back and seemed to critically study me. "But don't you worry your pretty little head. Roger is going to take care of you." He pressed his lips together. "I can recognize a cry for help when I see one and you, my dear, are crying out."

"You can't see a cry, first of all," I said indignantly. "And secondly, I'm not crying out."

He snorted softly, slipped the wax paper and napkin into the empty zipper bag and stood. "Honey, from one social misfit to another . . . you're crying out. But, I can help you with this transition. Believe me. I have an eye for talent."

He walked the length of the room and threw away the remnants of his lunch. He turned dramatically, crossed his arms over his chest and studied me.

"I don't want your help," I said. "I think I'm fine on my own."

"Ummmm." He pressed his lips out and raised his eyebrows. "Okay. You keep thinking that. But—"

The rest of his sentence was interrupted by the entrance of four boys in sloppy T-shirts emblazoned with different versions of the same Greek letters, talking loudly about a party they had attended the night before. As they slid into one of the rows of desks, one of the boys gestured toward Roger and said something in a low voice that made the other three laugh loudly.

Roger ignored them and looked at me. "So, what are you doing this time day after tomorrow?"

I looked around the room as if the answer was obvious. "We have class."

"Right. So, we'll meet here."

"What do you mean?"

He arched one eyebrow and grinned. "You'll see."


I can say with complete certainty that the day Grace was murdered was the day I learned fear. When I say this, I don't mean the fear of a scary movie or a roller coaster ride, but the deep, dark, gut-wrenching fear of vulnerability. Her death brought a heightened awareness of the dangers of everything around me. Strangers. Crowds. The dark. It happened slowly, but over time I felt myself constantly preparing for the worst-case scenario in every situation. I became consumed with fear of what would or could happen if I didn't take the necessary precautions—if I didn't immediately lock the doors after I got inside my car, didn't stare down the guy in the jeans jacket or memorize the license plate of the car that drove slowly past. Walking home from night classes were the worst.

I lived with another girl just off campus in a low-rent area comprised of squatty brick buildings and once-beautiful homes that had been cut up into tiny, cheap, oddly shaped apartments. My roommate Adelle and I rented the first floor of what at one time had been a single-family home. Once, it had been beautiful. Now, however, the outside was tired, seedy, and desperately in need of paint. The inside was much better, almost cozy, with its plaster walls, high ceilings, and hardwood floors.

I had tried living on campus. My thought was that it would be safer and, by being in an all-girl environment, I wouldn't have to worry constantly about strange men. But what I quickly discovered was that living in close proximity to so many people, even girls, was too much. It was as incestuous as living in Edenbridge. I lasted the entirety of my freshman year before deciding to find an apartment with Adelle.

Adelle and I met in a cultural anthropology class. It was my first semester at UNL and the instructor—a tall, lanky man with an enormous Adam's apple and a long, black braid that hung down his back—assigned research projects that were to be conducted in groups of three. He intentionally tried to make the groups diverse and my partners were Adelle, an outspoken African-American from inner-city St. Louis, and Jin, an international student from China who was studying biochemistry.

Though I had little in common with either of them, I enjoyed the time we spent working on the project and grew to be good friends with Adelle. She was unlike anyone I had ever known—and nothing like the Holmes family back home. She'd experienced discrimination (because now I could recognize what that was), but it had been different than what had been doled out in my hometown. I can't tell you exactly why, but Adelle frightened and fascinated me in equal parts. She was easily five foot ten with closely shorn hair and enormous brown eyes. She looked and carried herself like a model, but with more than a touch of attitude. She was thoughtful and deliberate in how she approached everyone and everything, The oldest of four children, she was the first of her family to go to college. She was interested in public administration because she wanted to return to St. Louis and clean up her city, particularly the urban core. Her plan was to get a master's in public administration and work as a city administrator with a focus on urban renewal.

I had to laugh. If only my grandfather could see this, I thought. If only he could know that I was not only going to school with someone who was black, but that this someone was also my roommate, friend, and equal. I thought again about his treatment of Mr. Holmes and his family—of the things he said and his role in the harassment that occurred after Grace's funeral. There had been the confrontation at the cemetery. But what happened after was one

148

hundred times worse.

It happened in the middle of the night, two days after Grace's funeral. According to Natalie, Mr. Holmes and his family were awakened at about 1 a.m. by noises in their front yard. Mr. Holmes told Natalie's father that he looked out the bedroom window and saw four men in white sheets and hoods standing around a cross that they had just set on fire. Heavily doused with gasoline, it was quickly engulfed in flames, causing the men to yell and cheer.

"That's what you get for dirtyin' up our town," one of the men yelled up at the bedroom window. "This is your first and last warning you goddamned child killin' nigger!"

The other three whooped.

"We know you dun it," screamed one of the others, the flames making his white robe appear rose-colored. "You just couldn't resist little white girl pussy, could you, you son of a bitch?"

As if on command, the four backed away from the burning cross in the direction of the three-deep row of trees planted to form a wind break.

"You'd better pack up your nigger brood and get the hell out of here," the shortest one yelled as they retreated. "Or we'll be back! . . . and next time, no warning . . . we just bring the rope!"

Adelle was appalled when I told her about life in Edenbridge.

"Seriously?" She shook her head in disgust. "I can't believe that people can still get away with that crap. It's just . . ." She struggled for words. "It amazes me that someone, anyone, could get away with that more than twenty-seven years after the March on Washington. I have a dream, my ass." She studied me with a serious look. "So, how did you emerge so . . . enlightened?"

I shrugged and shook my head in an "I don't know" gesture.

"My mother hated that kind of behavior and she did everything she could to make sure we didn't turn out like that. After the whole cross-burning incident, she took my sister and me with her to visit Mr. and Mrs. Holmes and take them lasagna."

Adelle laughed and said, "Well, at least it wasn't BBQ or fried chicken."

I wasn't sure whether or not to laugh, so I just nodded.

"So, what happened? With the cross and the Holmes family?"

"Not a lot," I admitted. "The sheriff's department investigated, but in the end they couldn't pin it on anyone. Everyone they questioned had alibis."

"Ask me if I'm surprised?" Adelle said. "It's just another example of small town mentality at work. What happened to the family? They get lynched or what?"

I must have looked shocked because Adelle pulled back and laughed.

"What?" she said indignantly. "I'm kidding. But don't tell me it doesn't sound like something that couldn't or wouldn't happen."

"True," I admitted. "But no, there was no lynching, thank god. Just threats tossed back and forth. Mr. and Mrs. Holmes are still in Edenbridge, as far as I know."

She shook her head slowly back and forth. "God bless them because that's some crazy shit."

It was, I agreed. I didn't share it with Adelle, but knew why they stayed. Mr. Holmes told me. I had been sitting in the Nest waiting for Tommy. It was a couple of weeks after the cross had been burned in the Holmeses' yard. I had heard the footsteps on the path and assumed it was Tommy. I jumped in surprise when Mr. Holmes' head popped through the hole in the floor.

"I thought I might find you here. Mind if I come in?"

I wondered why Grace's voice hadn't warned me. I shook my head silently, scared, but also realizing I had no choice in the matter. I scooted back to give him room.

"I didn't mean to scare you," he said. "But I've seen you sneak down here several times, and . . . I just . . . wanted to see if you were doing all right."

I stared. Most of my interaction with Anthony Holmes had been limited to polite greetings and witnessing the caustic public exchanges with my grandfather. He tipped his head and looked at me kindly.

"You know, my family and I really appreciated the lasagna you girls and your momma brought over. Lots of oregano in the sauce. It was good. We ate on it for two nights." He smiled, reached into his pocket and pulled out a Snickers bar. "Want half?"

I shook my head and forced my voice not to quiver. "I'm not allowed to accept candy from strangers."

"Ummm." He slid the candy back into his pocket. "Good rule to follow."

Neither of us spoke. My heart fluttered in my chest as I watched him look around the tree house.

"You miss Grace, don't you?" He sighed and leaned forward. "It's hard to lose a friend. When I was in the army, I lost a lot of friends. One of them was Mr. Hanson. You old enough to remember him?"

I shook my head.

"He was a good man," Mr. Holmes said. "We spent a lot of time talking. He's the reason I'm here. He gave me the land. He gave me the life he couldn't stick around for."

"Is that why you stay even though everyone is so mean to you?"

His smile was gentle. "Not everyone is mean. There are lots of people here who are really, really nice. Like your family and your friend Natalie's family." He pointed a large-knuckled finger at me. "Like you. There are lots of good people here." Then he sighed. "There are also some not-so-good people."

"Don't you get mad?" I asked. "When they say things or . . . do things?"

Mr. Holmes nodded. "I do. I get awfully mad sometimes."

"What do you do? When you get mad?"

"I talk to my wife," he said after a moment's thought. "Or I go work on something . . . or I pray."

"I don't pray," I said softly. "What's it like?"

Mr. Holmes grinned. "It's like—" He stopped and seemed to search his mind for the words to describe it. "It's like a conversation with yourself, that's not with yourself. It's like talking to a good friend."

I nodded.

"You can never have too many good friends," he said. "Like Natalie or Grace."

We were silent for several minutes, each lost in our own thoughts.

"I miss Grace," I said finally.

Mr. Holmes reached out and put a large hand on my shoulder. "I know. But, there was nothing you could have done. You need to know that. Do you want to talk about it?"

He raised his eyebrows and waited for me to answer. His face was kind and for a moment, I considered telling him everything. About Tommy. About Grace's voice in my head. About the fear that I had inside me. About the nightmares. But at the last minute, I refrained. The silence became awkward. Finally, Mr. Holmes made a noise deep in his throat.

"Well, I should go. I just wanted to make sure you were all right." He slid his body toward the opening in the floor. "If you ever need anything, you just let us know. My wife, Lila, is a really good listener and you can come to either one of us if you want to talk." His smile, before his head and shoulders disappeared from view, was kind.

I think, sometimes, about what I must have looked like—a skinny, sad, confused girl struggling to make sense of a horrific experience. I never took Mr. Holmes up on his offer, but from that point on, he and his family always made a point at community events to come over and say hello. We weren't friends, but we were friendly. And I always spoke well of them when Adelle asked me questions.

Adelle and I made good roommates. In our own ways, we were both misfits, but respected each other's right to be different. She accepted that I spent most of my time in my room reading, just as I respected her right to burn patchouli incense and leave National Public Radio on all day.

The only downside to the location of our apartment was that it was several blocks south of campus with no convenient bus route. I didn't have a car, so my only option was to walk or ride my bike. It wasn't the best solution, but it was manageable as long as I didn't get held up on campus after dark—which is what happened the day I met Roger, the day I was consumed with memories of home and the day that Grace reappeared.

It was the smell of patchouli that caught my attention that night as I walked home from the language lab. I was in front of

Love Library, an imposing three-story stone building with two wings and stacks of windows that glowed with an otherworldly light. Groups of students stood outside on the steps and in the darkened alcoves, smoking and quietly talking. A girl laughed and I smiled at the sound. It was a beautiful scene. The patchouli made me wonder if Adelle was there and I considered going over to see if she was indeed outside smoking and if she wanted to walk home together. And then I heard Grace's voice. The words were whispered and indistinct, but I could tell they were a warning. The hairs on the back of my neck prickled.

"Oh, what is *this?*" asked a falsetto voice behind me.

I spun around to see a thin man, his face obscured by the dark wool blanket that was draped over his head like a shawl. He shuffled forward until he stood in the light. I could see his thin fingers twitching as they clutched the corners of the cloth bunched at his chest. It was Count Bob, one of the local cast of odd characters. Count Bob was actually named Robert, although I was unsure of his last name. Rumor had it that at one time he had been a graduate student who came from a respectable family in Chicago with money enough to pay for his academic training all the way through his doctorate. He was, by all accounts, brilliant. He was also, by all accounts, crazy. Later, they would invent medications for the types of mental issues he faced, but at the time he was in graduate school, the solution for conditions such as his was a lobotomy.

Again, this was all rumor, but the breakdown occurred while he was working on his Master's degree, the topic of which was classical versus contemporary perceptions of the vampire. His studies became an obsession—to the point that he started to believe that he was, himself, a vampire. He stopped going to classes and instead, began to prowl the streets at night, refusing to leave his apartment until after dark. Complaints drew the attention of the police department and his family. He was institutionalized and, after electroshock therapy was unsuccessful, lobotomized.

Though he never returned to graduate school, he did move back into his apartment. Some people speculated that his family preferred to pay for him to stay in Lincoln as opposed to returning to Chicago. Others said he was simply unable to function anywhere but here. Either way, Lincoln was where he stayed and eventually earned the nickname of Count Bob. I had heard about him, of course. And I had seen him from a distance, shuffling along in his house slippers, black sweatshirt, and red sweatpants with the blanket over his head. Often, he carried a large, battered paper grocery bag full of something heavy. Many people speculated that they were the books on vampires that were missing from the library. Others guessed it was his dinner. On this night, though, his hands were free of everything but the blanket.

"Ohhhh," he said in the same falsetto. "Is this a church? It looks like a church with these elegant windows and the light just poooouring out. Oh, it's beautiful. I wonder if they sacrifice virgins there? I'm sure they do." He looked at me then, his eyes glassy in the reflected light. "Are you a virgin?"

The air left my body in a soft huff, as if I had been sucker punched. I tried to move, to run, but my legs were heavy, rooted to the ground.

"I'll bet there are virgins in there right now," he said, the blanket slipping off and exposing his shaved head. He giggled. His fingers twitched. "There are books in there that virgins shouldn't read. Shouldn't read at all. They get the pretty girls into trouble."

Grace's voice, no longer a whisper, echoed in my head. *"Move, Birdie! Pick up your feet and run!"*

I lurched forward, fear balled in my throat. One shaky step in front of the other, I walked jerkily away into a darkness that was both comforting and unsettling. I could feel Grace's anxiety. I tried to increase my pace, but was unable to do more than stumble quickly along—not that there was any reason to. I glanced over my shoulder to see Count Bob, still standing in front of the library, transfixed by the light and contemplation of sacrificed virgins.

Adelle was in the living room when I arrived home, breathless and agitated. She looked up as I rushed inside and slammed the door behind me. She was sitting on a giant, purple pillow on the floor. Her algebra homework was spread around her. The *BBC World News* was blaring from the stereo speakers. Something about my expression must have alerted her that something had happened, though, because she leaned over and turned down the volume.

"Rebecca, are you okay? You look freaked out."

"I'm fine," I said quickly. "I just—" I struggled to stop my legs from shaking.

"Jesus." She rose and walked to me. "What happened?"

"Nothing. There was—I saw—" I hesitated. "It's nothing. I just don't like walking back from night classes."

"Did someone . . .?"

I shook my head at the unasked question. "No. Nothing like that. I just saw Count Bob and he freaked me out talking about sacrificing virgins and—" I shook my head. "He just looked so . . ." I faltered, searching for the right word. "Crazy," I finished lamely.

Adelle nodded and reached out to squeeze my shoulder. I pulled away, not wanting to be touched. She looked surprised, but said nothing.

"Sorry," I said quickly. "I didn't mean to snap. I'm just tired and want to go to bed."

"Okay." Adelle nodded, but I could tell her feelings were hurt. She gave me a weak smile and then gestured to the stereo. "I'll keep the radio down."

"Thanks."

I opened my mouth to apologize again, but she was already back on her pillow, her head bowed to her textbook. I turned and walked down the hallway to the safety of my room. Once inside, I leaned back against the closed door. My heart continued to thump heavily and I tried to breathe slowly. It was ridiculous, I told myself. Count Bob was harmless. It had been a trying day. I had overreacted. I told myself these things, but I knew that the truth of the matter—the thing that I didn't want to acknowledge or think about—was that Grace wasn't gone. She probably never had been. All this time she had been there, watching and patiently waiting. I'd been a fool to think I had escaped my burden. My responsibility was now, as it always had been, to Grace.

To think anything different was foolishness.

If I were honest, I would have to admit that there's a part of me that has always questioned if the voice really was Grace's. On nights when I couldn't sleep or had been awakened by nightmares of her murder, I stared at the shadows on the ceiling and wondered about the voice. I tried to imagine how it was that Grace spoke to me from the in-between world in which she was present, but also not? Was it heaven? Purgatory? An alternate plane of existence? I also considered the very real possibility that the voice was simply my own—a manifestation of my own guilt, shame, and ineffectuality.

I discussed it once with Roger who, despite our rocky beginning, became one of my few friends. He had, indeed, taken me on as a project. A human redecorating challenge, if you will. True to his word that first day, he appeared the following class period with an agenda in mind. I had reclaimed my seat in the empty classroom and was rereading my tattered copy of *A Separate Peace* when the doors closest to me were thrown open. Unlike before when he had been dressed for work, the second time I saw Roger McManus, he was dressed in black Cavaricci pants, a black T-shirt, and a black jacket with a shocking red velvet lapel and a heart sewn onto the left chest pocket. His hair, which had been neatly combed two days before, was now wild and curly.

"Ready?" He spread his arms wide.

I blinked, unsure how to answer. He looked down at his outfit and then back at me.

"You like? It's my homage to Fred Schneider of the B-52's. I modeled it after his ensemble in the 'Love Shack' video." He pronounced *ensemble* as if he were speaking French. "So, are you ready?"

I swallowed, unsure if I wanted to go anywhere with him.

"Ready for what?"

He put his hands on his hips and said dramatically, "For today. Let's go."

"But, I don't even know your full name," I said.

"Ah." He placed his hand over the velvet heart. "I'm Roger McManus. And you are . . . ?"

"Birdie." I used my childhood nickname out of habit and then corrected myself. "Sorry. No. I'm Rebecca. Rebecca Holloway."

"Great." Roger grinned. "So, now that the formalities are out of the way, let's go."

I shook my head. "I really need to stay for the lecture."

"Come on," he cajoled. "What else is college for if not to blow off class?"

"We can't. We'll miss information we need for the test."

His smile was condescending. "Really?" He tipped his head to the side and frowned exaggeratedly. "Will we *really* miss anything?" He began to walk down the aisle to where I sat. "Are you following his lectures? Are you learning anything from them? It's early in the semester, they don't take attendance, and honestly, we can get this information from the book. And it would probably make more sense." Roger now stood in front of me. He leaned down and grabbed my backpack from where it sat next to me. "Lunch," he said as he turned and headed back up the steps toward the doors. "Now. It will be fun."

I had no choice but to follow.

It was the beginning of our friendship and the first of many classes that we skipped together. Though his flamboyance scared me at first, over time I came to understand that Roger was, like me, making the best of an unhappy life. And, like me, he was hiding his true self. He gave the impression that he was worldly and experienced, but in fact, he, too, was from a small town—Shelby, North Carolina. Growing up gay, in the South, had proven to be a challenge—a "nightmare from which I am still recovering," he said frequently. As he talked about his childhood, I began to understand why.

Though he was from the South, Roger's parents were originally from Des Moines, Iowa. His descriptions of them suggested a strange combination of Midwestern values and Southern sensibilities. His father was an insurance agent, a conservative Republican, and a card-carrying member of the NRA. His mother was a stay-at-home mom who used her spare time to craft the handwoven gift baskets that constituted the

157

base of their part-time business—custom order *Baskets o' Bullets*.

"It's nouveau-niche," Roger laughed. "I don't know how they come up with these ideas, but during the week, my mother weaves these baskets that they fill with cedar shavings and whatever bullets or gun supplies the person who's receiving the basket needs."

When he told me about his parents' part-time business, I laughed.

"Oh, you'd be surprised at how popular they are. I mean, really, what do you get for the hunter or handgun owner who has everything? Bullets and cleaning supplies and accessories, of course."

The concept stemmed from his parents' own love for firearms.

"Oh, yeah," Roger said. "They have, last I knew, twenty-three guns that range from rifles and handguns to antiques. My mother's favorite is her Smith & Wesson double action Model 29 .44 caliber Magnum revolver. It was an anniversary gift from my father."

Coming from his mouth, the words *Smith & Wesson double action Model 29 .44 caliber Magnum revolver* sounded ridiculous.

"I can't believe you know so much about it."

"Honey," he laid his hand on my arm. "How could I not? She only talked about it nonstop when Dad gave it to her. It's just like the one Clint Eastwood used in the *Dirty Harry* movies. My brother is in love with it and already has asked to inherit it when she's gone—which is fine because, even if I hadn't been disowned when I came out to them, he still would have inherited all the guns. I don't want anything to do with them."

Even though he said it with his usual aplomb, his smile was sad.

"You were really disowned?"

"I was." He lifted his chin defiantly. "Lock, stock, and barrel, if you'll pardon the expression. I think my folks always suspected I was gay, but when they walked in on me and my boyfriend one day, well . . . let's just say they knew. And they didn't like it—which is why I moved out after high school and haven't been home since."

It was another similarity, because I hadn't been home to Edenbridge since moving to Lincoln.

"I moved to Des Moines to live with my mom's mom." He

grinned. "You would have liked her. She was a pagan, worshiped Mother Earth and all that. Anyway, I started school there, met a guy, followed him here, blah blah blah. And now, four years later, I'm still here, single and finally getting back to school."

"What do you do for holidays?" I asked. His grandmother had, I knew, died the year before.

"The same thing I do most of the time—get together with all my fag friends who have nowhere else to go, cook elaborate dinners, and get so drunk we don't care that our families don't want us."

Over time, I would learn firsthand just how much of this Roger did with his friends. And, it was on the heels of one of these nights after his friends had left that I confided to him that Grace spoke to me sometimes. We were lying on his living room floor, our heads on the throw pillows from the couch. Between us sat an open bottle of wine—our third. Miles Davis played on the stereo and I was well into the warm buzz of wine. I had been hearing Grace more and more frequently and drinking seemed the only way to drown her out.

"Do you ever wonder if you're crazy?"

He was lying on his back, staring at the ceiling. "Only all the time. I think it's part of the human experience—at least, for those of us who *feel*. It's part of the package."

"I think I'm crazy sometimes," I said impulsively and then added recklessly. "I hear a voice in my head—the voice of my friend who was murdered when we were kids. Once I even saw her."

I had his full attention now. Roger sat up and stared at me. He had changed into a silk dressing gown and pajama pants after the party. As he moved, the robe gaped open, exposing the smooth skin of his chest. I looked away, embarrassed.

"You've never told me you had a friend who was murdered. In fact, you've never talked about your past. I was beginning to think you just dropped out of the sky."

"You don't think it's . . . weird?"

"Which? That you never talk about your past, that you have a friend who was murdered, or that you hear voices?" He shrugged. "I don't know. I'd have to hear more first."

"It's not voices," I clarified. "It's just one voice. Grace's."

159

I took a gulp of wine and began to tell the story, the words tumbling out of my mouth. As I spoke, I felt a huge weight being lifted along with the simultaneous desire to take them back.

"I found her." I could hear the slurred sloppiness of my words. "I lied to my mom about going to play at a friend's house. And I snuck into the woods and I found her there. In front of the tree house. Naked. Dead."

Roger exhaled, and I realized he had been holding his breath. He leaned forward.

"I ran to the town store and told them. They called the sheriff's department and my mother. I don't actually remember a lot of what happened next."

I took another swallow of wine. Although I was staring at the glass, my mind was a million miles away, seeing all over again Grace's body and hearing the deafening silence of the clearing. I could tell I had had too much to drink. I worked hard to pronounce the words.

"And since then, Grace has talked to me. It's why I left Edenbridge—why I never go back. I'm vulnerable there. Grace knows it and she . . . you know." I waved my hand around my head. "She haunts me. She warns me. It's like she's watching over me or something. I hear her in my head."

I swiveled my head to gaze blearily at Roger. He looked shocked.

"Wow," he said. "That beats having gun-collecting, ultra-conservative parents any day."

"Roger," I said, irritated, "You missed the point. Do you think I'm crazy? For hearing her talk in my head? Do you think it's her or is it just me wanting to think it's her?"

He was silent, considering how to answer. "Well, I guess I see it like this. There's no reason why it couldn't be her. I mean, there's lots of things you can't see or explain. Ghosts. UFOs. Psychics. I don't see how this is any different."

I felt relief wash over me. Maybe I wasn't crazy after all.

"But, why you?" he asked. "I don't mean that in a bad way, just . . . why you?"

I shrugged. It was a question I had asked myself as well. "I don't know. Maybe because I found her. Or . . . maybe it's her job? I don't know." I hesitated and then plunged forward. "I think it's because she thought I was her best friend. I mean, that's what the boy in the woods told me."

Roger frowned. "What 'boy' in the woods?"

"After she died," I explained. "There was this boy. He was her friend, sort of. He said that they talked a lot—that she told him I was her favorite. So, maybe that's why she chose me."

Roger took a measured sip of wine. Even intoxicated, his movements were deliberate and precise. "Did they catch the guy?" he asked. "The one who did it?"

I shook my head. "No. And, I think that made it even scarier . . . 'cause . . . there was part of me that thought he might come after me next, you know . . . 'cause I found her . . . or had clues or something." I was silent, dreading the words I knew I was going to blurt out. "I feel like it was sort of my fault—what happened. I mean, maybe I could have done something. Maybe helped her. I knew things were bad for her at home, but I didn't do anything. You know?" I looked up to see Roger nodding his head. "I didn't help because . . . I guess I was scared I *couldn't* help. And now, she's punishing me or something. She protects me . . . sorta. Even though I didn't protect her. And I feel her getting stronger." I hung my head miserably. "I know that's twisted and makes absolutely no sense, but maybe she would still be alive if I had, I don't know, done something. Invited her to stay at my house that night. Told someone about Don Wan's drawings."

Roger held up his hand for me to stop. "Who's Don Juan?"

"Sorry." I held out my glass for more wine. Roger raised his eyebrows and poured about an inch into the glass. It wasn't enough and I continued to hold the glass out for more. Finally, he sighed and poured another inch into the glass. Satisfied, I continued with the story. "Don Wan was this homeless guy. He had all these tattoos and he used to draw these pictures. One day we broke into this old abandoned house. We didn't know he was staying there and we found these creepy drawings with his stuff. Of naked girls

161

masturbating. A couple of them looked like Grace. Natalie was the only one who saw them, but she told me about it later. I was scared to tell my mom because we weren't supposed to be in the house. I was selfish, I didn't want to get in trouble."

"Natalie sent an anonymous note to the police, but they didn't arrest him or anything." I used my free hand to make air quotes. "'Drawings don't count.'"

Roger held up his hand. I paused. "Who is Natalie?"

"Natalie is—was—my best friend. Her dad was a sheriff."

"Ah," Roger nodded. "I've never heard you talk about her."

"She's still in Edenbridge," I said. "Her mother has cancer. She quit school to take care of her. Anyway," I rushed on, pretending I hadn't noticed his hurt expression, "Natalie said he was one of the main suspects in Grace's murder. I guess they questioned him, but he had an alibi, his wife or girlfriend—I forget which she was. But then he just disappeared."

"What do you mean?"

"He just got on his motorcycle one night and left town." I frowned. "I still think he did it, though." I swung my head drunkenly back and forth. "If only we had done . . . something."

Roger was silent for several seconds and when I finally looked up, his expression was a mixture of surprise and incredulity, as if I were a stranger. "Rebecca, you know this wasn't your fault, don't you?" He raised his eyebrows and waited for my response. When I didn't reply, he sighed. "Have you considered talking to someone about this? A professional counselor? I think you have this out of perspective."

"Therapy is for people who are too weak to just pull themselves up and get on with life," I spat, suddenly, unaccountably angry.

"Please tell me you don't really believe that," Roger said. "Therapy doesn't mean you're weak. It's not weak to talk about your feelings—to get help working through what happened. Jesus, Rebecca."

"You don't understand, Roger," I said angrily.

His response was equally angry. "Maybe that's because you never open up. The entire time we've known each other and this is the first time you've shared anything! What the fuck?"

162

I laughed bitterly, gulped down my wine, and extended my glass for more.

"Seriously," Roger said as he filled both of our glasses. "You're so closed off. And I guess I always knew it, but not to this extent. You had this crazy life-altering event and you don't mention it until we're drunk, two years after we met."

"Roger, please drop it. It's just one of those things I don't like to talk about."

"Yeah. Clearly."

"Hey, hey, hey," I slurred. "Don't get mad. I haven't told anyone. No one."

He stared. "How can you keep all that inside? I don't understand."

"Not a lot to understand, Roger," I said, waving the hand that held my glass. Red wine sloshed onto the carpet. "There's too much to just let some of it out. So I let none of it out."

Roger grimaced at the mess I'd made and reached out to grab my hand.

"I think that's enough wine for you. And I think you're going to be staying here tonight. I'll even give you the bed."

I smiled sloppily, no longer angry.

"You're my best friend in the whole world, Roger," I said. "But listen—listen to me. Listen."

"I'm listening."

"You can't tell anyone about what I told you. You can't. I don't want people to think I'm crazy. I'm tired of being the one who found the dead girl. I'm tired of that, you know?"

"I won't tell." He tried to pull me to my feet. "Now, come on, let's get you to bed."

"I let her down, Roger," I continued as he led me down the hall to his bedroom. "I let her down when she needed me. She died because I didn't tell what I knew. I was too selfish. My fault . . . it's my fault."

The last thing I remember of that night was lying on Roger's bed, the room spinning, and thinking that I deserved to feel this bad. It was part of my punishment for doing nothing.

We never again really talked about Grace or the voice in my

head. Occasionally, Roger would try to bring the subject up, but after several failed attempts he stopped asking. I knew he had questions, and there was a part of me that wanted to answer. But something inside me recognized that it was dangerous to let those thoughts and emotions out. In retrospect, maybe I should have.

## Chapter 14

The night we got the call about Adelle, Roger was at our apartment for our Friday night get-together. As an added bonus, we had all agreed that this night, Roger was going to cut my hair. True to his promise, he was slowly but surely updating my style. My hair, he believed, was the final issue to be addressed and he had decided that after dinner, he and Adelle were going to work together to give me a new style.

We were sitting in the living room waiting for Adelle to arrive. I was seated on the hand-me-down couch Adelle's parents had given her and Roger was lounging in the oversized beanbag that came directly to the apartment from my dorm room. We were drinking margaritas.

"So, tell me what you're thinking," I said and touched my ponytail.

He grinned and shook his head. "Nope, it's a surprise." He heaved himself awkwardly up from the beanbag.

"Come on, tell me," I begged.

"No." He picked up his glass and raised it in my direction. "Want another?" He headed toward the kitchen.

"Not yet," I said as I licked the rock salt off the rim of the glass. "But don't have too much because you're not touching my hair if you're anything less than sober."

His response was made unintelligible by the clink of ice cubes being dropped into his glass. I glanced at the clock on the mantle. Adelle was habitually late, but rarely more than fifteen minutes. She was now more than thirty-five minutes late. And there had been no telephone call, which was uncharacteristic.

"Hey, Roger," I yelled, "what time does the clock in there say?"

165

"It's . . . 7:35."

"Maybe we should call Adelle," I said as he came back into the room. "She usually calls if she's running late."

Grace's voice murmured in my head, the words unintelligible.

"Let's give her another fifteen minutes," Roger said. "Maybe she got hung up at work or she is over at Thomas's." He raised his eyebrows suggestively.

Thomas was Adelle's new boyfriend. We hadn't met him, but from her accounts, he was "fine" even though he was a "corn-fed white boy." They had met as College Democrats. He was the exact opposite of the kind of guy we'd have expected Adelle to date.

"He's the type of guy that would freak my family *out*," she said. "But he's also very forward-thinking. He understands what I want to do. You know he wants to go teach in inner-city schools? He volunteers for Social Justice Now! He's living the change he wants to see."

Just as we were about to start calling around in search of Adelle, the phone rang. I hurried to answer it. The voice was deep and masculine. "May I speak to Rebecca Holloway?"

"This is she," I said.

"Hello, ma'am. This is Sergeant William Cosgrove from the university police department and I'm calling on behalf of Adelle Jackson. She was involved in an assault tonight and she asked that we call you."

I stared at the answering machine. The red Power and Ready lights glowed like two menacing eyes.

"Adelle?" I said stupidly. "She assaulted someone?"

"No, ma'am," Sgt. Cosgrove said. "She was assaulted. While walking on campus. She was taken to the county hospital. She asked that we call you."

"Is she all right?"

There was a pause before Cosgrove answered. "I'm sorry, I can't answer that question directly. But what I can tell you is that she would probably like to see a friendly face. She asked that you come to the hospital."

"Of course," I said. "What do we do when we get there? Do we ask for her or for you or . . .?"

"Go to the front desk and tell them who you are and who you're there to see. She'll probably be in one of the triage rooms."

I thanked him and stood for a moment after he had hung up, receiver still pressed to my ear. The all too familiar knot in the pit of my stomach clenched. It was happening all over again, I thought. A friend attacked. Would it have happened if she hadn't been on her way to see me? I felt the familiar sting of guilt—and something else. A prickling on the back of my neck. A soft murmur that I knew, without a doubt, was Grace. I closed my eyes and tried to will her away, but her whispers, still indistinct, became louder. So intent was I on Grace, I didn't hear Roger come up behind me.

"Rebecca?" The voice was real. And outside my head. I spun around and brandished the phone receiver like a weapon.

"Whoa, sorry." He held his hands out in front of him. "Didn't mean to scare you. I just wanted to check and see—" He caught sight of my face. "Geez, you're white as a ghost. What happened? Are you okay? What's going on?"

"It's Adelle," I said tonelessly and hung up the receiver. "She was walking through campus on her way here and was attacked. I don't know any more except that they took her to the emergency room and she asked them to call. We need to go down there."

Roger looked shocked. He reached into his pocket for his keys. "Of course. I'll drive."

As we drove to the hospital, we talked about what could have happened to Adelle. Eventually, though, we fell silent, neither of us knowing what to say. Once at the hospital, we identified ourselves at the check-in desk, and were then directed to a small, cramped waiting room. We were told that we would be allowed to see her as soon as the doctors had finished their initial examination. More than an hour passed before we were summoned.

"Rebecca Holloway?"

I looked up to see a roundish woman in her mid-forties standing in the doorway. She wore faded pink scrubs and held a blue file folder in one hand and a pen in the other.

"Rebecca Holloway," she said again, this time louder.

I raised my hand and stood. "I'm Rebecca." Roger stood as well and then, as if on cue, we both began to walk toward the woman. Her eyes skipped from me to Roger and then back to me.

"I'm Sara, the admitting nurse, and I have been asked to take you back to Adelle Jackson." She looked from me to Roger and smiled kindly. "Given the circumstances, I think maybe you'll need to wait here."

Roger raised his eyebrows.

"She has asked only for Rebecca." Sara said. "I think it's best to let them talk and then determine if she wants you to come back." She turned back to me. "If you'll follow me."

I looked at Roger, who smiled and gently squeezed my arm. "Come back and let me know what's going on as soon as you can. And give her a hug for me."

I nodded and followed Sara down the hallway toward the treatment rooms. I was unprepared for the sight that greeted me. Adelle sat on the bed farthest from the door. Her usual bravado had been replaced with a silent, withdrawn stoicism. Her face was swollen and misshapen; one eye was swollen shut, her lower lip was split.

"Oh my god, Adelle," I said as I rushed into the room. "Are you okay? What happened?"

She shook her head without answering. I tried to hug her, but she pushed me away.

"Not now," she said shortly. "I don't want to be touched."

I stepped back, unused to being the one offering physical contact and being rejected. We sat in silence for several seconds before she began to speak, her words thick and bruised. "He came out of nowhere. He came up from behind and dragged me into the bushes. He had a knife."

I felt my throat drop into my stomach. My heart fluttered in my chest and I felt my body flush. A man. A knife. A rape?

"Adelle, what did he do to you?" My voice was tight and pitched much lower than usual.

"He hit me. Twice. And he told me that if I made a sound, he would kill me."

I stood, dumbfounded, not sure what to do or say. I felt sick.

"Did he . . .?" I hesitated to ask the question, both because I didn't want to hurt her more by making her answer and also because I wasn't sure I wanted to know. She nodded, her eyes closed.

I again reached out to touch her. She recoiled and I drew my hand back to my side.

"Were you able to describe him to the police?" I asked. "I mean, did you see his face?"

"He was white, muscular, dark hair," she said. "That's all I saw. It was dark and after he hit me the first couple of times, I just . . . kept my eyes closed."

I didn't know what to say.

"I'm so sorry, Adelle," I whispered. "We'll catch him. I promise you we'll find the guy who did this."

Adelle winced as she shifted on the hospital gurney.

"They want to do a rape kit," she said numbly. "I don't know if I can stand having them down there right now. I just want to take a hot shower and make this all go away."

I stood helplessly as she began to sob.

"Adelle," I said softly, "Tell me what you need. Tell me what to do."

"Don't leave me." Her voice became panicked. "I can't be alone."

I felt her fear, her vulnerability.

"It's okay," I said. "I'm not going anywhere. I promise. And when we're done here, we'll go home. I'll make sure no one bothers you."

She sniffed and used the wadded mass of tissues clutched in her hand to daub the tears. She winced as she touched the tender flesh of her swollen eye. Bruises were already beginning to appear.

"Adelle, Roger's here, too. He's out in the waiting room. Do you want to see him or should I tell him to go home?"

She stared into space, not answering.

"Adelle," I said gently. "I need to tell him if he should stay or go."

"I can't be around him now," she said dully. "I don't want anyone to see me like this."

"Okay." I turned toward the door. Let me just go tell him not to wait, all right? I'll be right back."

She nodded and then reached out to grab my arm. "Don't tell him what happened. Just tell him I got beat up. Don't tell him about the other part."

I gently touched the hand that still gripped my arm. She flinched at the contact and pulled it away.

"I promise," I said softly. "I won't tell anyone. I'll be right back, okay?"

She didn't respond, so I turned and walked back down to the waiting room. Roger stood up as I stepped into the room. "How is she?" he asked. "What happened?"

"She was walking through campus and some guy grabbed her from behind, dragged her into the bushes behind the arts building, and beat her up."

His eyes grew wide. "Oh my god. Is she okay?"

"Bruised," I said. "And scared. She's going to be here for a while, I think. They have to fix her up and then the police are going to have to take a report, so maybe you should go home."

Roger frowned and shook his head. "I couldn't do that. Besides, how will you get home?"

I considered telling him the truth. Perhaps if he understood what had really happened, he would understand why Adelle didn't want a man—even a gay man—around her. "We can either call a cab or have the police take us back to the house. She's really emotional right now."

He searched my face and seemed, finally, to understand the situation.

"Oh," he said softly. "I'll be home the rest of the night if you guys need a ride or . . . anything. Okay?"

"Yes," I said, and then after a pause, "Thank you."

The wait for the doctors, the nurses, and the police to do what they needed seemed to take forever. The same questions were asked, the same information was written down, and after a while the faces began to blur. Adelle endured it all. She answered the questions in a dull monotone, all evidence of her usual spirit, gone. Finally, the doctors had bandaged her external wounds, the police had taken information for the initial report, and the evidence for the rape kit had been collected. Now, we sat with the female detective who would be handling the case.

"I'm Judy Sanchez," she said. "I'm a detective and I'll be handling the investigation. How are you doing? Hanging in there?"

Adelle nodded numbly. Detective Sanchez's expression was compassionate and she waited several seconds before flipping open her notepad and uncapping her pen. In bold, blue ink, she jotted down the date and time.

"I know you've been asked all sorts of questions and you've given a statement," she said. "But I need you to go through it one more time. I know you're tired and it probably feels like you're having to relive it over and over, but the sooner we can get moving on this, the better chance we have of finding the guy who did this." Detective Sanchez looked over at me and smiled kindly. "Would you mind giving us a few minutes?"

"Sure," I said and stood to leave.

"Can she stay?" Adelle asked quickly. "I don't want her to go."

I looked at the detective, who nodded. "Of course. So, if you could just tell me what happened. No detail is too small."

"It was about seven o'clock," Adelle said after a long pause. She gestured at me sitting in the corner. "I was going home for dinner and I was running late. I had been at my boyfriend's dorm and one thing had led to another. So, I was rushing. I took a shortcut through the sculpture garden and was coming up the back side of the library when someone grabbed me from behind. There are all those bushes and trees back there and he ..." She shook her head.

Detective Sanchez leaned forward, nodding encouragingly, and waited for her to continue.

"I shouldn't have taken the shortcut," Adelle said finally. "I just figured it was so close to the library and there were people around the front of the building. I just thought that it would be okay. I figured it was no big deal."

Her words again trailed off.

"He came out of nowhere," she said softly, almost to herself. "He came up from behind and he grabbed me in a sort of chokehold. He had a knife. His arms were like steel. They were so strong and I couldn't get away. I wanted to scream, but he put his other hand over my mouth. And he whispered in my ear. He told me if I fought him, if I screamed, he would kill me. He said he would slash my throat and then rape me while I bled out. He used those words, 'bled out.'" She looked at Detective Sanchez plaintively. "I didn't have a choice. It wasn't my fault."

Detective Sanchez met her gaze and smiled kindly. "No, Adelle, it wasn't your fault. This was not, I repeat, not, your fault." She paused. "I know this is hard. Can you tell me what happened next?"

Adelle closed her eyes and nodded her head slowly. The muscles in her jaw jumped. "He threw me down on the ground."

"Face up or face down?"

"Down at first, and then he flipped me over."

"And then he got on top of me and he pushed the knife against my throat and told me to be quiet. And then he hit me. He punched me in the mouth. And then he brought his fist back and hit me in the side of the head." She swallowed. "He kept telling me not to make a sound, or he'd kill me. Then he cut my tights with his knife and unzipped his pants."

Detective Sanchez pointed to the evidence bags on the counter. "Are those your clothes? Were those what you were wearing?" She consulted a sheet of paper with writing on it. "It says here you were wearing a long, denim skirt, tights, a T-shirt, and a heavy, multicolored sweater. Is that right?"

Adelle looked at the clear plastic bags that contained the clothes she had been wearing. She looked like she wanted to throw up. "Yes."

Images of Grace's body—either of what I imagined happened to her or that she had shared with me—popped into my head. I groaned softly and shifted uncomfortably in my seat.

"I know this is hard, Adelle," Detective Sanchez said. "Did you see his face?" She looked again at the paper in her hand. "It says here that he was a white male, early twenties, tall, muscular with dark hair and a scratchy voice. Is that right?"

Adelle closed her good eye and jerked her head in a quick nod. "He was wearing dark clothes. I couldn't see much of his face. It was so dark. I could hear people talking nearby, you know? They were so close. I wanted to yell out, but he would have killed me. I know he would have."

"You did what you had to do to survive." The detective's voice hardened. "You're *alive*. That's what's important."

Adelle nodded tightly, but didn't look up from her lap.

Detective Sanchez reviewed her notes and then returned her attention to Adelle, who was now staring at the wall opposite her. "What happened after the rape?" Detective Sanchez waited for several seconds before clearing her throat. "Adelle?"

"He lay on top of me for a little while," she said numbly. "I kept thinking any minute someone would walk by. . . or hear him panting. But they didn't. Then he wiped himself off with the bottom of my skirt, zipped up his pants, and told me that because I was such a good girl, he would let me live. After he left, I managed to crawl over to the front of the library and some girls who were smoking took me inside and they called the police."

Detective Sanchez scribbled in her notebook.

"What do I do?" Adelle asked suddenly, her voice cracking with fear. It was the first emotion she had expressed since the interview had begun. "What if he knows who I am? What if he figures out where I live?"

Sanchez put down her pen, stood, and moved to where Adelle sat. "We're going to do everything we can to catch him. And until then, there are things you can do to protect yourself." She looked over at me. "First, you two can talk to your landlord about changing the locks and putting additional locks on your windows." She returned her attention to Adelle.

"You might want to start carrying mace with you. Do you have a dog?"

Adelle shook her head.

"That might be something to think about. Rapists are often opportunists. Dogs are deterrents. We also offer self-defense courses. Maybe you and your friend could take one of those. You were attacked, Adelle, but you don't have to be a victim. You can be a survivor." She paused and reached out as if to touch Adelle, but then didn't. "There is no right or wrong reaction to something like this, but it's important to get help. I have a rape counselor outside who is going to talk to you, give you some information, and a list of numbers to call if you need to. You're not in this alone. There are people here to help you through this." She glanced at me. "You have friends who will help you and I promise you, we will do everything we can to catch this guy."

*"He needs to be punished."*

The voice was low with barely contained anger. I jerked my head toward Adelle. She was again staring blankly at the wall as the detective continued to talk. She hadn't spoken a word.

*"He needs to be punished,"* the voice repeated.

I swallowed convulsively, my heart racing. I knew the voice. I knew it better than my own. It was Grace.

"We'll catch this guy." Detective Sanchez promised again. She looked from Adelle to me and it was as if she, too, had heard Grace. *"We'll find him and he will be punished."*

174

# Chapter 15

It was late by the time Adelle and I arrived home. The next day, we called the landlord about installing additional locks on the doors and windows. A middle-aged man with two girls of his own, he was sympathetic to what Adelle had experienced, and did it immediately. Still, neither of us felt safe and we struggled with what had happened in different ways.

I hadn't shared the details of my childhood experience with Adelle. Roger was still the only person outside of Edenbridge that I'd told and I continued to regret my drunken confession. I considered telling her, but something held me back. And, to be honest, I was dealing with issues of my own. What had happened to Adelle that night on campus brought back all the anxiety, fear, and paranoia I had experienced after Grace's murder. It also brought back Grace. I felt her more often now in the back of my head, watching and listening. Whenever the conversation turned to progress on Adelle's case, I could sense a sharpening of her interest.

Her presence made me feel fragile and vulnerable. The insomnia returned. And on those nights in which I *was* actually able to sleep, my dreams were troubled and violent. The days were no better. When I forced myself to leave the apartment to go to classes, every shadow, every bush harbored murderers and rapists. Locked inside the safety of my home was the only place where I was able to relax, and even that was a broad interpretation of the word because I had also begun to fear the dangers inside my home.

Ever since Grace's murder, all I could think about was germs. I washed my hands several times each day and was careful about touching anything that could be contaminated. But the night of Adelle's rape, what had been a concern with germs erupted into a full-time job. We had come straight home from the hospital and Adelle had showered while I fixed drinks. As I stood in the kitchen listening to the shower running, I began to imagine what was being washed from her body. I imagined the cloudy white residue of her rapist's semen running down her legs, onto her feet, and swirling down the drain. The thought made me feel physically ill and a part of me wanted to run into the bathroom and ask her to stop—or, at least, to disinfect the tub when she was finished. But, even as I thought that, my face flushed with shame for thinking such a thing when my friend had just had her life turned upside down. I forced myself to push the images aside. But as the night progressed, I found myself obsessing about what was in my shower—to the point that I had trouble concentrating on our stilted conversation. I was barely able to wait until Adelle was in bed before I pulled on kitchen gloves and began to scrub the tub with Comet.

I hoped that over time, these fears would go away. But if anything, they became more extreme. I began to worry about what diseases or germs were being brought into the apartment by Adelle, by visitors, and by me. The thought of eating food that had been prepared by someone else made me feel so ill that I only ate food I fixed myself. No more lunches from the cafeteria or sandwiches at The Coffee House. I was sure that hair or germs were in everything I ate.

Roger was the first to notice—or, at least, the first to say anything. He came over after I had missed several classes. I responded to his knock by securing the chain on the door and then opening it just enough to see who was outside.

"It's me," he said irritably. "Let me in."

I closed the door, removed the chain, and then opened the door fully. His gaze took in my ratty track sweats, T-shirt, and bunny slippers.

"Where have you been? You realize you've missed class three times this week and—"

"Could you take off your shoes?" I interrupted. "They've been outside."

He glanced down at his feet, sighed, and then slipped off his loafers.

"Birdie, I'm starting to get a little worried about you." He never used my childhood nickname. "You're missing classes. You never leave the apartment and now you're . . ." He gestured at my outfit. "I don't know what you're doing."

He walked past me into the living room where I had been lying on the couch watching hour six of a twelve-hour *L.A. Law* marathon on Lifetime. The coffee table was littered with Diet Coke cans, the remnants of my scrambled egg breakfast, half of a turkey sandwich, and an empty potato chip bag. I stood in the doorway, my arms crossed.

"Rebecca, talk to me. You haven't been the same since Adelle's—" he paused and then amended his statement "—since what happened to Adelle."

I sniffed and wiped at my nose. "I have the flu."

"No, you don't," he said sharply. "That's a lie. You're becoming a, I don't know, a recluse and I think you need help." He gestured at the television. "I mean, you're watching Lifetime, for god's sake. How much worse can it be?"

"That doesn't mean anything," I snapped.

"Doesn't it?" He tipped his head to the side. "Seriously, and be honest, how many made for television movies with Melissa Gilbert have you watched this week?"

I blushed.

"Exactly," he said. "I think this thing with Adelle brought up a lot of suppressed issues for you. Things from when you were a kid. And rather than dealing with them, you're, well—" he spread his arms wide "—you're doing this."

"I'm fine," I said, angry that he had brought up my drunken confession.

"I don't believe you." He picked up the remote and turned off the television. "I've talked to Adelle. She said you're up all night, that you're skipping classes, that you're spraying everything down with Clorox. What's that about?"

I shrugged.

"Sweetie, you need help," he said. "You can't keep up like this. You look like hell warmed over and I think you need to talk to someone."

"I don't."

"You do and you will. Today. I've made an appointment for you at the mental health center. It's free."

"I'm not going," I said firmly. "Thank you, but I don't believe in psychiatry and I don't want to talk to anyone about this. I can handle it on my own."

Roger crossed his arms over his chest and shook his head. "No. I don't think you can. And if you don't agree to do this, I'm going to call your mother and tell her exactly what has happened and what I think is going on. I probably should do that anyway."

Following my parents divorce, my mother had fully come into her own. She cut and dyed her hair, began to take art lessons, and started seeing a psychologist. At first, my sister Tara and I were shocked.

"There's nothing wrong with it." Her tone had been defiant. "In fact, Birdie, I think you would benefit from it, too."

"I don't need therapy."

"There aren't . . . things you want to talk about?"

"I don't want to talk about anything," I said. "All I want to do is get on with my life."

It had become a point of contention—so much so that I had taken to letting my mother's calls go to the machine. Given how anxious she was to have me see someone, the last thing I needed was Roger to contact her with his concerns.

"Roger," I said quickly. "Please don't do that."

"If that's what has to happen, then I will," he said simply. "Your choice."


Laura, the therapist, was much younger than I had anticipated— and much more pleasant.

"I appreciate you seeing me," I said as I settled into the seat across from her. "But I need to be honest with you. I didn't want to come here and I don't think I really need your help."

"Okay." She pushed an errant lock of dark hair behind her ear and studied my face. "So, then, why are you here?"

I sighed. "I'm here because I didn't really have much of a choice in the matter. I know that sounds defensive, but my friend kind of . . . bullied me into coming."

"Ummm," Laura said. "And how did your friend do that? Or maybe I should ask *why* did your friend do that?"

"He threatened to tell my mother about some of the things I've been doing that seem a little . . . weird."

Laura nodded and pushed her glasses up on the top of her head.

"Weird, how?" she asked and then quickly added, "Not that you have to tell me, though it wouldn't hurt anything."

I looked at her and smiled knowingly. "I know what you're doing." I waved my index finger. "You're trying to get me to talk by pretending not to care if I talk."

Laura laughed and held up her hands. "You caught me, red-handed. Reverse psychology."

I smiled, sincerely this time. "I didn't expect you to give up so easily."

Laura shrugged. "You've already made up your mind. I can only offer you help if you want it. If you don't, well, then I can't force you to talk about what's going on. I *will* tell you, though, that if your friend went to these lengths to get you to come, he's concerned. And maybe you should look at what's going on that causes that concern. But that's your business."

This was not what I had expected.

"So, you can leave right now or you can stay and talk for the rest of your—" she glanced down at the gold and silver watch on her wrist "—forty-eight minutes. It's your decision. I do have to ask you a question before you go though—and I need you to answer honestly."

"Okay."

"Do I or your friends have any reason to worry that you are a danger to yourself or others?"

I felt my eyes widen and I recoiled in horror. "Oh my god, no," I said quickly. "I would never hurt anyone else. And I'm not going to kill myself or anything. I'm just . . . sad. I'm not dangerous."

"Okay." Laura scribbled something on the piece of paper in front of her. "Not knowing anything about you, I have to take you at your word."

She slid the paper into the file on her lap and then placed the folder on the small table to her right. With a smile, she leaned back in her chair expectantly. "So, what would you like to do with your remaining—" she glanced again at her watch "—forty-six minutes?"

*"Get out of here,"* Grace's voice whispered. The command was like a tickle at the back of my brain and it took everything I had to resist the urge to get up and run out of the room. Laura knew what to look for. She could—and would—sense that something was wrong with me if I spent too much time here.

"I probably should go home," I said. "I don't want to waste your time."

Laura laughed. "It's not a waste of my time. I have someone coming in after you, so I have to be here regardless. I have to tell you, though, I admire you for coming in today. I have a friend who is agoraphobic and she has to force herself to leave the house. She's a certified recluse. If I want to see her, I have to go there."

I wrinkled my face.

"I'm not agoraphobic. I just don't like leaving my house. I had some things happen when I was a kid . . . a friend of mine was murdered. And then my friend Adelle was just raped on campus and it just . . . brought up some issues, you know? That's all. But that's normal. That's not agoraphobia."

Laura smiled kindly. "The world can be a scary place. There are a lot of people out there who aren't so nice. How old were you when your friend was murdered?" She must have seen something on my face because she held up her hands in a defenseless gesture. "Not for the file. You've made it clear you don't want therapy."

"I was eleven," I said. I felt Grace's anxiety but continued. "She was one of my two best friends."

Laura shook her head. "Poor girl. Did they ever catch the man who did it?"

"No," I said. "They had a couple of suspects, but no one they could ever pin it on."

"That has got to be kind of scary for you," Laura said. "To know that this man is still out there and then after what happened to your friend on campus—I can understand being apprehensive about going out. As women, we have to be extra cautious."

I nodded. "Adelle is taking a self-defense class."

"That's your friend who was attacked."

"My roommate, yeah. They still haven't caught the guy who did that either. I mean, he could be anyone. He could be the guy sitting next to me in class. He could be the guy who checked me in today. He could be . . . anyone."

Laura nodded.

"Is that what scares you—that the men who did these things to your friends are out there running around free? Looking for other victims?"

"Partially." I looked past her at the bookshelves, then said, "But it's more than that. I'm scared, yes. But, I'm also, I don't know what it is. And I'm not sure I could survive something like that. Grace didn't."

Laura leaned forward. "And Grace was your childhood friend?"

I felt the tingle of Grace shifting her energy. As much as she wanted me to leave before I said too much, I could tell she was also interested in the conversation.

"Of course, you know Grace was just a girl," Laura continued. "Her attacker was a lot stronger than she was. You're a grown woman. There are things you can do to defend yourself."

"I know. I just . . ." I fell silent and Laura sat, watching me, waiting for whatever I was going to say next. Grace too, was waiting. *"Don't do it,"* she warned. *"She will think you're crazy."*

Despite her concerns, or perhaps because of them, I swallowed, took several calming breaths, and forced myself to speak. "I found her. I found Grace. At our tree house. In the woods. I found her body."

"Oh, Rebecca." Laura's voice was kind. "It makes perfect sense, then, why what happened to Adelle has affected you to this extent. Did you, after you found Grace, did you go see anyone? A professional?"

I shook my head. "My mother wanted to take me to see someone, but my father thought it was a waste of money. He thought psychiatry was a load of crap that only fools buy into." I glanced up. "Sorry."

Laura grinned. "A lot of people from his generation think that—especially Midwesterners with their 'pull yourself up by your bootstraps' frame of mind. My family still thinks I'm crazy for going into the profession." She studied me for a few moments, as if debating whether or not to say something. "So, who *have* you talked to about it? Friends? Family members?"

"No one," I said, rather more abruptly than I had intended.

Laura blinked. "No one? At all?"

"No."

"Okay. What about some other kind of outlet? For example, do you write, maybe in a journal, or do some kind of art? A lot of people who have suffered traumatic childhood events work through it by painting or sculpting."

I thought back to the day of Grace's murder and how I had lied so I could sneak away to the Nest and draw. Since then, even the thought of drawing anything made my throat tighten. I shook my head. "I'm not artistic. I'm a business major. I don't really like to write."

"Okay, what about exercise? Do you work out? The university has a nice fitness center that's free to students. You could take an aerobics class. Or maybe weight lifting. It might help with the anxiety."

I felt myself recoil at the thought of touching the dirty, sweaty gym equipment and shook my head dismissively.

We sat in silence. The clock on her desk loudly ticked off the passing seconds.

"Well, I guess I should go," I said finally and stood up. "Thank you and I'm sorry this was a waste of your time."

"I can help you," Laura blurted out. "I mean, I think I could help you if you wanted. Through therapy. And there are some medications that you could take for your anxiety and depression."

"I'm not depressed." The words came out more forcefully than I had intended. "I'm not depressed and I'm not agoraphobic and I'm not—I don't need your help."

Laura stood up and positioned herself between me and the door.

"I understand this is frightening," she said. "But you're not Grace. And you're not Adelle. You're Rebecca and you're strong in your own way. We can work together to help you realize that."

My scalp tingled with Grace's energy. I cleared my throat and tried to nod as if I appreciated her offer.

"Thank you," I said. "But I tend to agree with my father. I only came because I had no choice." I paused and Laura waited for me to continue. "Look, I think you're a nice woman, but I don't need your help. I'm fine. I just need a little time to work through what happened to Adelle."

Laura nodded and stepped aside. "Okay, but if you change your mind, I'm here. You don't have to do this by yourself. And seriously, think about finding some sort of creative outlet for your anxiety. Even if it's just, I don't know, finger painting."

She laughed and I forced my lips into a thin, polite smile. All I wanted to do was leave. "It was nice to meet you."

"You, too," Laura said. "Take care of yourself and—"

"I know," I said as I walked toward the door. "I appreciate it. But I really think this is something I can handle on my own."


Later that night as I lay in bed, I thought about my conversation with Laura. She seemed like a nice person and it was clear she wanted to help. But help with what? Or, perhaps better to ask, help with which issue? My fear of germs? How increasingly uncomfortable I was leaving the house? The fact that a dead girl seemed to be living within me? What would she have done if I had shared that little fact?

Grace laughed softly. I closed my eyes and tried to shut her out. Whereas in the past, her presence had been gentle and benevolent, as she became stronger, she also had become angrier and more cynical. I could tell she didn't trust Roger. I had felt it before, but it was especially obvious when I came out of my appointment with Laura.

To ensure that I actually went, Roger had driven me to the

appointment. As I stepped outside, I scanned the parking lot. His white Ford Escort was still in the ten-minute parking even though I had been inside much longer. I walked over and pulled open the passenger-side door. Roger had reclined the seat back and was listening to NPR. He jerked in surprise.

"So?" He released the seatback to its upright position.

"So?" I mimicked as I climbed in and buckled my seatbelt.

"What did you talk about? How was it?"

I shrugged. "We talked about what's going on and she agreed that I am simply dealing with what happened to Adelle in the best way I can. She didn't seem to think I needed therapy or anything. Just rest."

Roger studied me suspiciously. "Really. So, you're handling this like anyone would, huh?"

"That's pretty much what she said. She said that if I ever wanted to talk about anything or had a real problem, that I could come back."

"Hmm." Roger started the car. "What would you say if I told you that I don't believe you?"

"I would say that I appreciate your concern, but it's none of your business. And, I would tell you that you're wrong. I'm fine and Laura even said so."

But as I lay awake that night, my chest tight and my heart racing with the familiar anxiety, I considered the possibility that I was going crazy. I knew Grace would reassure me that I wasn't, but if she was a manifestation of the insanity, of course that's what she would say. I thought about my freshman psychology class. Did crazy people even know they were crazy? I ticked off my list of fears. Rape. Murder. Romantic intimacy. Germs. Leaving the apartment.

The thoughts swirled in my head even as I dozed—words superimposed with images. Faceless men stepped from the shadows. I was powerless. And then, as so often happened in my nightmares, I was back on the path that led to the Nest. The woods were eerily silent. The humidity was cloying. I felt as if I were drowning. I walked down the path and stood at the base of the small hill that led to the clearing. I knew what I was going to find. It was always the same.

Her back was to me, a white-blue ice sculpture. She did not yet have the swells of adulthood, although the angle at which she lay gave her a violin-like shape. It was Grace. I already knew that. The shock of the victim's identity had worn off after years of having the same dream. Still, my heartbeat thundered in my ears. My hands tingled and grew numb. I felt sick. I felt weak, as if my legs were going to give out.

As had happened when I was eleven, I stepped closer. She was on her side, one leg pulled up, one leg extended. Her arms were hugged to her chest. On the foot of the leg that was extended was the only piece of clothing left on her body—that damned sock only partially on her foot.

I circled the body. There was blood everywhere—much more than I remembered. I looked at her face, which was mostly covered by her hair. One eye was visible and it stared glassily at nothing. It was deep green with thick lashes. Its gaze was unwavering. I stared back, reacting only when the ant crawled across her eyeball. I stepped back. And then, unlike in any of my previous nightmares, Grace blinked.

"Oh my god, you're alive," I said breathlessly, amazed at this new development. "I thought you were dead, but you're . . . you're alive. Oh, Grace!"

In one smooth move, she sat up and brushed the hair from her face. *"I'm not alive, Birdie."* She picked a leaf from her hair. *"I'm dead. I was murdered when we were eleven. You know that."*

"But—"

*"No buts about it, although . . ."* She looked down at her naked body. *"I guess there is at least one butt involved, huh?"* She laughed. *"You wouldn't believe the things he did to my butt, either. You know that, don't you—what he did to me? How he raped me and sodomized me and then made me beg for my life? I am assuming you saw the police report."*

I stared and shook my head numbly.

"No," I said. "I didn't see—I mean, they wouldn't let me. But I didn't want to see it anyway. I . . . I . . ."

*"'I, I, I.' You always did have a weak stomach. That's why you need me now. You can't deal with what scares you. Like when we were kids,*

*you left me to fend for myself. Why didn't you ask about my mom and Reggie? Why didn't you tell me about Don Wan's drawings?"*

I gasped. "Was that who did this? Was he the one?"

She shook her head slowly back and forth and made a *"tsk, tsk, tsk"* sound. *"Birdie, you know as well as I do who did this."*

"No," I exclaimed. "I don't. They never solved the murder. They tried. Natalie's dad worked so hard on it. Please, Grace, tell me who did this. Let me fix this!"

*"You know,"* she said. *"If you think about it, you'll realize. But I have to go. The ants are making it too hard to think. Too hard to talk."*

"The what?" I leaned forward. "I don't—"

*"The ants."* Her voice was scarcely a graveled whisper. *"Quick, come closer. I need to tell you."* A large black ant crawled out of her nose. *"They're . . ."*

She grabbed my shoulder and pulled me close. She opened her mouth to speak. An ant the size of a peanut skittered out and landed on her chin. And then suddenly, there were ants everywhere, crawling out of her mouth, her nose, her ears. Her lips moved as she tried to speak but nothing came out. Her body shook.

"Grace!" I tried to pull away, but her grip on me was too strong. "Let me go!"

"Rebecca!" The voice was sharp and clear. "Rebecca! Wake up."

I sat up with a gasp. The clearing faded and Adelle's worried face came into focus.

"It's okay," she said. "You're safe. It's just a dream."

My body was covered in sweat and my breath came in short, strangled gasps. I felt sick and guilty.

"You scared the shit out of me," Adelle said as she pushed wet tendrils of hair off my forehead. "What can I do?"

I closed my eyes and pressed my fingertips to my temples. "Nothing," I said softly. I inhaled deeply, and shakily exhaled. "I didn't mean to wake you. It was just one of those scary, weird dreams about all sorts of stuff that doesn't make sense. Know what I mean?"

Adelle grasped one of my clammy hands in her own and squeezed gently. "Rebecca, what's going on?"

"It's nothing. Really. I—"

"Stop. You've had nightmares for as long as I've known you. But they've gotten worse." She looked down at the quilt I had brought from home. "Roger told me about your appointment today."

I studied our clasped hands and considered telling her about Grace. About the dreams. About everything. But even as I had the thought, I could feel Grace shaking her head. I forced myself to meet Adelle's gaze. I gave her hands a final, quick squeeze and then let go.

"I'm just tired. But I'm fine. Really."

Adelle looked disappointed, but also resigned to the fact that, once again, there would be no discussion of this subject. She braced her hands on her thighs and pushed herself to a standing position.

"Well, if you change your mind . . ." She pressed her lips together and then turned and walked out of the room.

I waited until the door was closed to lay back down. The sheets were damp and twisted and I considered changing them. However, I knew that the chances of me being able to go back to sleep were slim. I glanced at the clock. It was 3:15. I had once read that 3:15 was the least likely time for anyone to wake because of REM sleep patterns. It was also, I suddenly recalled, the time of night that the marching band music blared and all hell broke loose in *The Amityville Horror*. Perhaps it was an evil time of the morning.

"Now I'm just being stupid," I muttered as I rolled onto my side and reached for the book I always kept on the scuffed red milk crate I used for a nightstand. It was the same paperback I had been reading when I first met Roger—*A Separate Peace*.

The story was not a happy one, but it was one that resonated with me because I understood Gene's guilt at what happened to Finny. His split-second decision to jiggle the branch upon which Finny was balanced to jump into the water below and the guilt that he carried was not unlike the feelings of remorse that I myself harbored. Everything you needed to know about his torment was captured in the cover. Gene stands next to a towering, heavily branched tree. He is turned toward the reader, his face serious, his hands thrust into his pockets. Behind him, Finny, a pale, indistinct figure, balances on one of the lower branches, bent over as if to jump into the water below. A second figure climbs the trunk of the tree. Gene's eyes are haunted.

My copy was battered and worn from reading. It had been given to me in high school by one of my English teachers. She had recognized my love of reading and sought to encourage it by providing me books from her personal library. I had loved it so much that when I graduated, she gave it to me. In the time since, I had read it so many times that I almost knew it by heart. I found it a comfort on nights when I couldn't sleep. Tonight, however, I found it hard to concentrate. My mind kept returning to the dream and to my conversation with Laura.

Perhaps she was right. Maybe I did need an outlet—a way to take what I had in my head and exorcise it. And, maybe in doing so, I could exorcise Grace's presence as well. I got up and went to my closet, where I kept extra spiral notebooks and pens. I hadn't tried journaling before, but of all the suggestions Laura had offered, it sounded like the one that would be most safe.

I settled back into the bed and opened the cover. The blank page seemed almost too clean. It glowed with promise. I stared at it, unsure where to begin. Did I start with my childhood? With my day? With the dream I had just had? The size of the task was overwhelming and my hand trembled. What did I need to get down on paper? What should I write?

"The date," I muttered. "I should start there."

I took a deep breath and, in the top right-hand corner, scribbled the date. I sat back and studied my work, particularly my handwriting. It was too sloppy. Almost illegible. Also, the ink was blue. I had mistakenly purchased blue instead of black pens at the student union bookstore at the beginning of the semester. I preferred black ink, so I had given the pens to Adelle. Or at least I thought I had. Clearly I had missed one.

Frustrated, I ripped out the page, wadded it into a tight ball, and threw it into the wastepaper basket. Blue ink would *not* work. I climbed back out of bed and went back into my closet, where my backpack hung on a heavy metal hook. I unzipped it and rooted around for a pen with black ink. I found an almost empty Bic pen, zipped the backpack closed, and returned to the bed. Maybe, I thought, if I lay on my stomach as opposed to sitting up, I would be better able to write clearly.

"Okay," I said once I was situated, the pillow bunched up under my chin. "Let's try this again."

Angling the notebook slightly, I again wrote the date at the top of the page. This time I printed, rather than using cursive, and liked the look of it much better. I scooted the notebook up and poised my pen in anticipation of the first line. I considered again, where to begin. Immediately, my mind drifted to Charles Dickens' introduction to *David Copperfield*. I scribbled: *Whether I shall turn out to be the hero of my own life, or whether that station will be held by anybody else, these pages must show. To begin my life with the beginning of my life, I record that I was born . . .*

"Plagiarism," I said as I ripped out the page.

*My name is Birdie Holloway and this is my story,* I wrote.

"Boring and I don't go by Birdie anymore," I said, ripping out the page.

*I don't know where to begin this journal,* I wrote. The letters were sloppy and oddly shaped. Again, it wasn't how I wanted my handwriting to look. I ripped the sheet of paper from the notebook and put it with the rest of the mistakes. The fresh sheet glared brightly up at me. I tried again.

*My name is Rebecca and I don't know how to begin.*

"Better," I muttered, "but I don't think I want my name attached to this. What if someone finds it?"

Suddenly, I was gripped by fear. What *if* someone found this and read it? The thought made my stomach clench into a tight knot. They would know what happened to me. They would know about Grace. They would know about the fear I carried inside me. Suddenly, journaling didn't seem like such a good idea. I ripped out this page as well. I looked at the stack of papers. They didn't just need to be thrown away. Because of the power of their intent, they needed to be destroyed. I folded them carefully and hid them under a stack of T-shirts in my closet. I would burn them tomorrow. Journaling was out. It was too . . . honest. Too real.

I considered Laura's other suggestions. The gym was out because of the germs. Running, which I had done in high school, was also not feasible because it would mean I was outside. She had also suggested art. I hadn't drawn anything since Grace's murder. It was too closely tied to everything that had happened—Don Wan's drawings, my selfishness in sneaking away to draw, and finding Grace's body. But what, I thought, if I didn't draw? What if I simply scribbled? Let the pen go wherever it wanted. There was no agency in that. It was just . . . lines.

Before I could talk myself out of it, I placed the point of the pen onto the blank sheet of paper. My hand shook and the urge to throw the pen and paper against the wall was overwhelming. I closed my eyes, inhaled deeply, and let my hand and mind wander. Unlike in the past, I didn't try to control my thoughts. And as my mind worked, my hand moved, seemingly of its own accord. The lines were smooth and graceful. There was no control or even desire to control. It was hypnotic and cathartic and after what seemed like ten minutes, I stopped. I felt calm.

I glanced at the digital alarm clock, which read 5:05. I blinked, unable to believe it was the correct time—that more than an hour and a half had passed. I got up and padded to the kitchen. The time on the microwave read 5:08.

I turned and walked back to my bedroom. I picked up the notebook, which was covered with spirals and long curving, interconnected lines. It was a mess, but I could make out some images—a violin, an iceberg, an eye like the one on the back of a one-dollar bill, but ornamented with long, spindly eyelashes. I didn't remember drawing any of the images, although clearly I had. I felt tired. Weighted. Sleepy. I turned off the light and lay down on my bed, letting my body relax into the mattress. I sighed and turned my head to stare at the nightlight plugged into the socket next to the closet. My eyes became heavy, and before I knew it, I had fallen into a deep, dreamless sleep.

# Chapter 16

It was after ten o'clock when I awoke the next morning. I didn't feel refreshed, but I did feel better. I had already missed my first class, so rather than get up immediately, I continued to lie in bed and think about the night before. Nightmares were nothing new to me—especially ones involving Grace. But this one had been particularly disturbing. The fact that she spoke to me, that she moved—it was a new and upsetting twist. And the ants. The ants were like something out of a Stephen King novel.

I rolled onto my side and felt around for the notebook. The entire experience of drawing and losing time felt as if it hadn't happened. It was surreal. But as I flipped through the pages, I realized that it had, in fact, happened. The images were there as proof. I studied them with a fresh eye. The drawings were rudimentary and almost childlike. But something about them was mesmerizing—especially the intricate spiral. I followed its path with my index finger.

"Rebecca," called Adelle from the kitchen. "You still here?"

"Yeah," I hollered back. "In my room."

Adelle opened the door and looked in. She was dressed all in black and apparently had already been to class. "Whatcha doin'?" Her eyes zeroed in on the notebook and she pointed. "What's that?"

I looked down and tried to laugh off my discomfort at being caught, though caught at what, I wasn't sure.

"Oh, it's just some doodling I did," I said. "Last night when I couldn't sleep."

She came fully into the room and picked up the notebook. "Interesting," she said as she turned the pages. She paused, seemingly thinking about something before handing it back. "I wonder what it would look like in color? Or paint?" She continued to study the drawings. "It's almost like a labyrinth," she mused. "Or like some of those rock carvings you see in the aboriginal tribes or with the Anasazi. Some people think they're maps and others think they were used for meditation or spiritual activities." She looked up, saw my expression and grinned.

"Art History," she said by way of explanation. She laid the notebook back on the bed. "So, I just wanted to see if you were all right. You know, after last night."

"I'm okay. Tired, but okay. I eventually went back to sleep around five."

"That's good." She hesitated, as if considering whether or not to continue. "Listen, I know I said it last night, but if you ever need to talk . . ." She shrugged.

"I know." I smiled at her. "And I will if I need to." I glanced at the alarm clock. "But right now, I need to get up and go to class."

Adelle smiled. "I'm glad."

I frowned, not understanding what she meant.

"That you're going to class," she explained. "Even though they don't take attendance, it's good that you're going. Some professors figure out when you just show up for the tests. So, maybe yesterday's visit helped?" She looked hopeful.

"I think so," I said and pushed back the covers. "We'll see."



I was surprised to find Natalie sitting on the front steps of the house when I came home that afternoon. More of Roger's work? I wondered as I returned her wave.

"Hiya," she said as I reached the foot of the porch stairs. Even though she was trying to be lighthearted, I could tell she was anything but.

"Hi yourself. What are you doing here?"

She shrugged. "I needed a break from Mom, from Edenbridge." She squinted into the pale afternoon sunlight. "So, how are you?"

I swung my backpack off my shoulder, climbed the steps to where she sat, and settled down next to her. "This semester's been kicking my butt." I shrugged. "How's your mom?"

She sighed. "Depends on the day. Lately, she's been pretty bad, but they've finished the chemo, so now it's just, you know, recovery." She shrugged. "That's part of how I was able to get away, though I'm not so sure that's a good thing."

"Nat, I'm sorry," I said and reached over to touch her arm. She smiled wearily and suddenly, I realized how worn and beaten down she looked.

"So," she said in an attempt to change the subject. "Tell me about you. How are things?"

"Not much to tell," I said. "Classes, homework, you know."

She studied my face, no doubt taking inventory of the dark shadows under my eyes, my gaunt cheeks, the ever-deepening furrows of my forehead.

"You look tired."

"All-nighters," I lied. "School is . . ."

She looked pointedly at me and I knew she could tell I was lying.

"I heard about your friend," she said finally.

I snorted softly and internally cursed Roger. "Make the papers in Edenbridge, did it?"

She ignored my sarcasm. "No. Your friend Roger called me."

"Great!" I said, suddenly angry. "Fucking fantastic."

"Birdie," she said quickly, surprised by the vehemence of my reaction. She reached to put her hand on my shoulder. "Don't be mad at him. He's just worried."

I wrenched away from her grasp, stood, and stomped up the steps. Natalie jumped up and hurried to my side as I fumbled to find the right key to the front door.

"It still gets to me, too," she said softly. "I can only imagine how Adelle's attack brought back memories of what happened to Grace."

At Natalie's mention of her name, I could feel Grace's interest pique. More and more frequently I felt her there, at the base of my skull, her presence almost like an itch that was too deep to be scratched. Having Natalie present only intensified the sensation.

"I don't want to talk about it," I said shortly. I felt Grace's disappointment.

"Fine," Natalie said quickly. "You don't have to talk, but there are some things I want to say—things I *need* to say." She hesitated and then said more softly, "Things I need you to hear." She looked around the porch and then gestured toward the front steps. "Can we sit?"

"Don't you want to go inside?" I knew I sounded angry and defensive.

"In a little bit." She walked back to the steps, sat down, and patted the space beside her. "Come sit with me? Please?"

The tickle that was Grace intensified. I sighed and moved to sit next to Natalie.

"I know you don't want to talk about Grace and I understand that, but we've never really talked about it—not really. I mean, there was that one time when we were kids and then that day at the Nest, when we got drunk, but other than that, not really." She turned her head and studied me with an intensity that made me squirm. "Do you remember?"

"Yes," I admitted softly. "I do."

"And do you remember that I said some day we would need to talk about it? Well, that's today. I need to talk about it. And, whether you like it or not, I think you do, too."

I closed my eyes and bowed my head. I didn't want to have this conversation. Not today. Not ever.

"I know you blame me," she continued. "You think that if I hadn't convinced you guys to lie so we could go swimming, this might not have happened or that you wouldn't have been the one to find her. But that's not fair. I have spent more time than I can possibly tell you asking 'what if . . .' I have tortured myself with what I could have done differently. How I could have stopped it. And you know what? There wasn't anything."

I started to protest—to stand up, to leave. But Natalie put a firm hand on my arm and held me in place. I looked down at where we were joined. Her fingernails were chewed to the quick, her cuticles ragged and scabbed.

"I know what happened changed you," she said. "I saw it at school when you withdrew from everyone and everything. And I see it now. You never come home to visit. You avoid my calls and I know from talking to your mom that I'm not the only one who has noticed." Her grasp on my arm tightened. She lowered her voice. "Birdie, her death affected all of us. It damaged *all* of us. And we've all had to deal with it. You're not alone. Let the people who love you, help you."

I shook my head. "I don't need help."

"Birdie, we all need help sometimes." Natalie took a deep breath. "I take Prozac. My mom's doctor prescribed it. And it's helped. Maybe you should—"

"Jesus!" I exploded. "Why the fuck does everyone seem to think that medication or therapy or fucking talking about this is going to change anything?" Natalie jerked backward, startled at my display. "Taking *Prozac* isn't going to fix this. It's not going to *change* anything."

"But it *will,*" Natalie said quickly. "It does." She shook her head as if she were searching for the words that would change my mind. "I was having a hard time dealing with my mom's cancer. Leaving college to take care of her has been tough." Her eyes filled suddenly with tears and I stared, caught between anger and curiosity. It surprised me to know that Natalie, who was always so strong, so in control, so powerful, was also so . . . fragile. She cleared her throat and wiped at the corner of first one eye and then the other. The edge of her finger, I saw, was smudged with mascara. She wiped it on her jeans and continued. "I'm seeing a psychologist. It's helped—to talk, I mean—about Mom. Dad. Life. Grace. I was having nightmares."

Her expression, when she raised her gaze to meet mine, was knowing. Roger again. I said nothing and waited for her to make the point this was all leading up to.

"Roger called your mom. He said he wanted to surprise you by inviting me up for a girls' weekend. For fun. After he got my number, he called and said you were . . ."

"He said I was what?"

"He said you weren't sleeping well, weren't leaving the house, that you were skipping class, and that you have been very depressed since your friend was attacked," she said. "He said he thought you needed a friendly face."

When I didn't respond, Natalie reached for my hand. "Birdie, let me help."

"Natalie," I yanked my hand away before she could touch it. "I don't need your fucking help. Or Roger's. Or . . . anyone's. I just want to be left alone!"

*"Calm down!"*

I blinked at the command because it hadn't come from Natalie. It was Grace. Her voice the same as in my dream, the same as it had been when she had been alive. *"You need to stop overreacting. They already talk about you behind your back. Do you want to give them more ammunition? Just take a deep breath and chill out."*

I felt a calm—her calm—flow through me. I closed my eyes, took a deep breath, and opened them to find Natalie staring at me—her eyes wide. I felt suddenly guilty and ashamed. I felt the blush crawl up my neck onto my face.

"I'm sorry," I said quickly, my anger gone. "I . . . I don't know what hit me. I'm sorry." This time I was the one who reached out—the one who touched her arm.

*"Tell her you'll listen to what she has to say,"* Grace said. I hesitated and Grace's energy shifted, became more forceful. *"Tell her."*

"Please, Nat, I'm sorry," I said. "Maybe I am stressed out." I removed my hand from her arm and stood. "Let's just go inside and have a drink. I'll listen to what you have to say. I won't get angry again. I promise. I'm just tired from all the late nights. I didn't mean to go off on you like that."

I stooped, picked up both backpacks, and slung them over one shoulder. She still hadn't moved. I looked down at her. She nodded slowly, thoughtfully, and then stood. She reached out for her bag, but I shook my head. We walked together to the front door and I inserted my key into the lock. As we stepped into the dark entry, I pointed up the wooden stairs.

"There are two apartments up there," I said. "We have the

whole first floor."

I inserted the key into the lock on the apartment door and then pushed it open. Natalie stepped in front of me into the narrow hallway. I followed her into the living room and set the bags on the floor next to the couch.

"Nice place," she said as she studied the room. The afternoon light streamed through the window and caught in the prism Adelle had hung from the top of the window frame. Natalie wandered idly over to the mantel to look at the collection of bric-a-brac. "Not yours, though, is it?" She gestured to the mismatched candlestick holders that were covered with layers of different-colored wax from multiple candles.

"No," I said. "My roommate's."

"I didn't think so," she said and then grinned. "You'd *never* leave candle wax on your holders. I'm surprised you haven't scraped it off when she wasn't looking."

I smiled despite myself. There was, I thought, something strangely reassuring about being with people who had known you forever.

"It's good to see you, Birdie," she said suddenly, as if reading my thoughts.

"You, too," I admitted.

We studied each other as if gauging the damage of the past few years. Her auburn hair was pulled back in a banana clip, her bangs were teased into a fringe over her forehead. She was still pretty, but her looks were weighed down by the years. It was her eyes, I realized suddenly. When we were young, they had sparkled with playfulness and the promise of adventure. But now, they were simply a dull, tired brown ringed with smudges of fatigue. There were lines, too, along the outside corners that hadn't been there last time we were together. She looked, I realized with a shock, old.

"You look tired," I said.

She smiled wearily. "I *am* tired. Taking care of Mom . . ." She shook her head and smiled sadly. "Some days it's all I can do to get out of bed." She lowered her eyes and seemed to study the threadbare area rug Adelle's mother and father had given us for the apartment.

197

I cleared my throat. "I'm sorry about before."

Natalie continued to look at the carpet. "I didn't just come here for you, Birdie," she said finally. "I came here for me, too. I needed to get away—to be with someone who understands me." She sighed and glanced up at me for a second before returning her gaze to the rug. "I needed to get away from Mom's sickness and Dad's denial and Edenbridge's, well, you know what I mean."

I nodded but said nothing.

"It can be the warmest, safest place in the world," she said absently, as if she were talking to herself. "And at the same time, it can suck you in and keep you prisoner. It never lets you go."

She again raised her gaze and met mine. This time, neither of us looked away.

"You have no idea how much I envy you," she admitted. "I wish I could run away—go someplace different. Be someone different." I swallowed, unsure how to respond. She gave an apologetic smile. "Sorry. I'm just tired. I don't sleep well. Most of my dreams are pretty crappy—that Mom has died but I wasn't there, or that I'm lost in a forest and can't find my way out." She paused. "I know you don't want to talk about your nightmares, but I *need* to talk about mine. I dream a lot about Grace."

I felt Grace shift within me, as if she were leaning forward in an effort to hear every word. I tried not to touch the back of my neck.

"Sometimes I have these dreams she's still alive." Natalie said as she turned back toward the prism. The reflected light played across the side of her face. "And when I wake up, I feel sad. Let down. Like someone gave me a present and then stole it when I wasn't looking."

I cleared my throat. "I didn't know you thought about her so much."

She nodded slowly. "I have this dream. We're adults, but we're also not. We're still kids, sort of, but in adult bodies. And you and I are sitting at the Mercantile. And we're trying to decide what kind of ice cream we're going to get. And out of the blue, Grace walks up. It doesn't look like her, but it is. And we both stare at her—like we're surprised. And you say something about how we're getting ice cream and what does she want. And she looks at you and says she can't have any; they don't let them have ice cream where she is. And I remember then that she's dead." Natalie's eyes again filled with tears. "And, as soon as I realize it, as soon as I understand it, she begins to get paler and paler. She shimmers and slowly starts to fade away. We run over to her, try to touch her, but she's not solid. She's like . . . vapor. She's just disappearing in front of our eyes and we're telling her it's going to be all right—that we're going to take care of her. But we can't."

Her words began to come faster.

"We're running around trying to find something to keep her there. We're looking under trees and abandoned tires and all sorts of junk that just seems to suddenly be there. But we can't find what we're looking for."

Without tearing my eyes from Natalie, I moved to the couch and sank down. She turned her attention from the prism to look at me and I nodded to let her know I was listening—that I understood. She walked to the couch and sat down next to me. I reached out my hand and she clasped it. Her expression was stricken, her voice tight as she continued.

"We're so desperate to find some way to help her. But we can't. And I turn to you and say something like, 'What are we going to do?' And—this part is always so clear—you point to Grace and I turn to look at her. And all that's left is a whitish outline—kind of like what you see when people try to take pictures of ghosts. But Grace's eyes are still visible. We're both looking at her and then she begins to scream—this high, little girl's scream. And in my heart, I know that was probably the last sound she made when she was alive. And then she's gone."

My heart was beating wildly as Natalie finished her story. In my head, I could feel the pressure of Grace's reaction filling every space. My temples throbbed. My tongue felt thick and dry in my mouth. Natalie looked sideways at me.

"I guess that sounds pretty crazy, doesn't it?" she asked.

I shook my head.

"No." My throat was constricted and the word sounded garbled.

I cleared my throat and tried again "No, it doesn't. I ... I dream about her, too." Natalie squeezed my hand and waited for me to continue. "The thing is, I kind of think I deserve the dreams. I knew she had been sleeping at the Nest. I just ... I didn't do anything about it."

"Neither of us did," Natalie said. "And that's something that we're going to have to live with. But we can't let it control our lives."

"Do you feel like she's ..." I was about to say, "still with us," but at the last moment amended it to "in a good place?"

Natalie sighed and squeezed my hand again. "I think she's in heaven, looking down on us, watching over us. Protecting us."

I felt my heart skip a beat. Was Natalie saying she felt Grace, too?

"How do you know that?" I asked quickly. "Do you feel her with you? Hear her sometimes in your head?"

Natalie frowned and shook her head slowly. "Nothing like that. It's just a feeling I have that she's in a better place."

"But your dreams ..." I began.

"Just me working through the fact that I miss her and that a lot of things in my life are out of my control," she said. "I think it's my brain's way of processing it. That's probably what's going on with you, too."

I nodded, disappointed that she had no idea what I was experiencing.

"Birdie, I know that it's not something you want to do, but maybe you should consider going to see someone," Natalie said and then added quickly, "You don't have to take drugs. But just going to a therapist has helped me a lot. More than I ever thought it could."

"I *did* go to see someone," I said, almost angrily, and felt her flinch. I took a deep breath and tried to keep my voice calm. "After Adelle's ... after what happened to Adelle, I went to someone on campus."

"And?"

I shrugged. "She was nice."

"Are you still seeing her?" Natalie's tone was pleased and surprised. She smiled in encouragement.

"No, I'm not." I squeezed her hand and tried to pull away. Her fingers gripped mine. "It's not what I need," I said finally. "It didn't do for me what it does for you." As gently as possible, I pulled my fingers from hers and smacked my palms against my thighs. "I don't know about you, but I could use a drink. How about you take your stuff into my room and I'll get us a couple of beers?"

I stood and pointed to my bedroom door. Natalie looked surprised and slightly hurt at my withdrawal, but stood, picked up her bag, and headed toward my room. As she reached for the door handle, she stopped and turned to look back at me. We stared at each other for several seconds and I could tell she wanted to say something—to continue the conversation.

"Natalie, don't." It was a request, but also said firmly enough that it was a command. She started to protest, but, seeing my expression, pressed her lips together, nodded tightly, and opened the bedroom door. It was as if we had silently agreed to call a truce. And it was a truce we both honored until the last day of her visit. We were standing on the sidewalk next to the same dented Chevette she had driven all through high school. Seeing it now made me smile.

"It was good to see you, Birdie," she said.

"You, too," I said and was surprised to realize I actually meant it. We had spent most of our time sprawled out on the living room couch watching old movies, drinking margaritas, and eating popcorn. Grace had been present, but not as powerfully as that first day when we had talked about her. It had been nice to spend time with Natalie, but I was ready for her to leave.

"You know, if you ever need anything," Natalie began.

"I know," I said quickly. "Thanks for coming up. Sorry it was a false alarm. Roger overreacts."

She nodded, accepting my lie. "Let's do a better job of staying in touch. I know you don't want to come back to Edenbridge, but I could come here."

"Sure," I said. We stood that way for several seconds. The afternoon sunlight was warm on my shoulders. Suddenly, all I wanted to do was take a nap.

"Birdie," she said and I steeled myself for this, her final assault. "I know you don't want to talk about it, but always remember there are people who love and care about you—your mom, me, Roger. We will do anything to help you."

"I know," I said as she pulled me tightly to her. "Drive safely?"

She nodded and yanked open the car door. The groan of metal made both of us laugh.

"I'll call next week," she said after she had climbed in and rolled down the window. "Or you can call me if you want to talk before then."

She put the key in the ignition and twisted it. The engine came to life with a roar. I stepped back in mock horror. "Tell your folks hi," I said as the motor settled into a softer rumble.

"We'll do it again soon, yeah?" she asked, squinting up into the bright sunlight.

I think we both knew it wasn't true, but still I nodded and waved. She grinned and then eased the car away from the curb. The engine knocked a couple of times until she gave it more gas. I watched until she turned the corner and was out of sight before turning and trudging back up the steps to my apartment.

# Chapter 17

After Natalie's visit, I returned to my routine of skipping classes and staying inside. But instead of reading when I couldn't sleep, I found myself trying to recreate the experience I had the night I made the ink drawings. Sometimes it worked and when it did, my sleep was deep and dream-free. When it didn't, however, I lay awake frustrated or floated in a strange sort of half-sleep that was almost worse than the nightmares. It was during one of these nights of sleeplessness that I recalled Adelle's observation about labyrinths and meditation. She had suggested color. And then there was Laura's suggestion of a creative outlet. I knew I would never again draw. And I had no desire to take an art class. But the idea of something like painting—something new with no ties to the past—sounded appealing. Or, at least, it did until the next day when I found myself wandering through the art supplies section of the student union bookstore. Almost immediately I realized that I had no idea what I was looking for or what I was going to do with it once I found it. Forgotten grade school memories of construction paper, minty-smelling paste, and thick poster paints came to mind as I walked down one of the aisles.

"Can I help you find something?" A thin, scruffy man in a blue Mr. Rogers cardigan appeared at my side. His dirty blond hair was pulled back into a ponytail. He smiled and tipped his head slightly as he waited. His teeth were small, even, and very white. "You look a little lost."

"I am," I admitted and spread my hands wide. "There's just so much."

The man's smile widened. "Okay, well, tell me what you need."

"Art supplies," I said. "But I'm not sure where to start. I'm not an artist."

"That's okay." He placed his hand on his chest. My name is Jeff and I'll help. So, a couple of questions. Is this for you or for someone else?"

"Me," I said.

"Right. So, what medium were you thinking?"

I stared at him, overwhelmed and embarrassed at not knowing how to ask for what I wanted. "You know," I said quickly, "maybe this is a bad idea. I don't even know what I want. I'm a business major, not an artist."

"Nonononono," he said and reached out as if to place a reassuring hand on my arm, but thankfully, stopped before touching me. "We can find what you need. Seriously." He looked around the art supplies section. "Were you thinking drawing? Or painting? Paper mache?"

"Paint," I said with more authority than I felt.

"Great." He rubbed his hands together. "You have a lot to choose from. Oils, watercolors, acrylics, tempera, enamels." He glanced over at the paint aisle and then back at me. My expression must have told him everything he needed to know because he smiled kindly. "How about this: I'll ask you some questions and we'll go from there." He raised his eyebrows and I gave a quick nod.

"What do you want to paint? Do you care how long it takes to dry?"

"I don't know yet what I'm going to paint," I said. "It's going to be kind of stream of consciousness. And the faster it dries, the better."

Jeff rubbed thoughtfully at the whiskers on his chin.. "Okay. Do you want to be able to paint over it and do you want to mix colors?"

"Painting over it is probably good." I shrugged. "I'm not sure about mixing colors."

"Okay, are you going to paint on canvas or paper?"

"I am assuming paper is less expensive, so probably that."

"Acrylics," he said happily, as if that were the answer to everything. "They dry fast, can be painted over, and the cleanup is a lot easier than with oils because they're water-based and you can just wash them out."

He gestured for me to follow him to the next aisle.

"You'll probably want to start out with student paints." He pointed to a display. "They're cheaper because they have more filler, but I think for what you're doing, they'll be fine. I'd recommend you start out with red, yellow, blue, white, black, brown, green, orange, purple, and maybe gray." He began to pull tubes of paint out of their dispensers and hand them to me.

"And brushes," he said. "You'll need some stiff-bristled and a couple of soft-bristled. And we'll get you some paper, too. How big?"

By the time he was finished, I had more than enough supplies. I surveyed them piled on the checkout counter.

"Jeff," I said as he began to ring them up. "This is a lot. I'm not sure I can afford—"

"Shh," he said, looking around as if to make sure we weren't being overheard. "I'm going to let you use my employee discount on top of your student discount."

"Oh, Jeff, thank you," I protested. "But that's not—"

"Stop," he continued in his conspiratorial voice. "This stuff is way overpriced. Just remember: acrylic paint dries quickly, so don't put too much on your palate."

"I don't know how to thank you." I felt suddenly awkward.

He grinned shyly and said, "You could buy me a beer."

I looked up in surprise.

"Or not," he said quickly when he saw my expression.

I began to gather up the bags.

"Sorry," he said and then sighed. "This is all coming out wrong. How about this: if you need help or advice or, you know, just want to go grab a beer and talk, I'd really like that." He tore off the receipt and wrote something on the bottom of it. "This is my phone number," he said. "Give me a call sometime?"

"Thanks," I said as I stuffed the receipt into one of the bags and hefted them off the counter.

Jeff nodded and raised his hand in a weak wave. I nodded quickly and hurried out of the store.

The encounter had unsettled me. I wanted to go back to the safety of my apartment—to the familiarity of my things. Everything outside of the world I had created for myself seemed almost too busy—too full. Outside of the student union, I stopped and forced myself to take several deep breaths. The afternoon sun was mild for a change and around me students stood in small clusters or pairs, backpacks slung casually over their shoulders, talking and laughing. Everyone and everything seemed so normal.

I thought again about Laura. Maybe there was value in going to see her. *Or maybe she'll show you just how crazy you really are*, the voice in my head intoned.

"It's just a rough patch," I murmured. "It's just because of what happened with Adelle. There's nothing wrong with me that time won't fix."

Though, later that afternoon, as I sat on my bed and fingered the brushes and the tubes of paint, I questioned if that was really the case. Would time really fix this? Would "expressing myself through art" really make everything better? I imagined my grandfather and how he would sneer at the idea.

"I don't care what he thinks," I said aloud. "Maybe this *will* work."

Before I could change my mind, I went to the kitchen and grabbed a couple of trash bags. Back in my room, I spread one out on the floor and split open the other. Using masking tape, I taped it to the wall and then stood back to survey my work. Against the cream-colored wall, the filleted trash bag looked like a glossy portal to another world. I picked up one of the large squares of paper Jeff had suggested for my "canvas" and tacked it to the wall, squarely in the middle of the black plastic. I hadn't wanted to buy an easel, so this seemed like a good alternative, although as the pins ground into the old-fashioned sand plaster, I suddenly wasn't so sure.

Next I changed into old jeans and a T-shirt. Jeff had said I would need rags, so I pulled a couple of old, ratty T-shirts from the back of my closet, ripped them in half, and tossed them on the bed next to the palette and the paints. I wasn't sure what to do next, so I spread the contents of the bag onto the bed and sorted it into piles. Paints. Brushes. Palatte knife. I went to the kitchen to get the spray bottle we used for our houseplants and paper towels to blot my brush—both tips from Jeff.

Jeff.

His telephone number was on my dresser. I glanced over at the folded slip of paper and then up to the mirror I had nailed to the back of my door. I tried to see myself as Jeff would have. Roger had indeed given me a makeover and I had to admit, he had done a good job. My mother had been right. I had become pretty. Was that what Jeff had seen? Was that why he had given me his number or was it more than that? Appearances could be deceptive. Still, he *had* shown an interest and he had seemed kind.

*Kind of what?* came the nagging voice in my head.

The voice wasn't Grace's—it was my own.

"Give it up," I muttered to myself. "He'd just change his mind as soon as he got to know you."

The thought made me sad, though somehow, I understood its truth. I was untouchable—both because I didn't want to touch or be touched. Or did I? The question took me by surprise. Was that what all of this was about? It seemed too much to process, so I turned my attention to the blank square of paper in front of me, waiting for whatever image I was destined to paint to take shape.

Nothing.

I frowned and cocked my head to the side, hoping to get a different perspective.

Still nothing.

Finally, after about ten minutes of staring at the paper, I decided that it wasn't going to work. At least, not yet. I went back out to the kitchen, opened the refrigerator, and pulled out a bottle of beer. This wasn't working the way I thought it would. I was considering returning the art supplies to the bookstore when my thoughts were interrupted by the peal of the cordless phone on the counter. I picked up the handset and looked at the caller ID. It was Roger. We had spent several weeks not speaking after he'd called Natalie, but lately we were talking again.

"Guess who?"

"I have caller ID, Roger."

"Yeah, well, good for you. What are you doing?"

I took a drink from the bottle and glanced in the direction of my bedroom. "Working on a project."

"Not anymore. You're going out with me."

"I can't," I said quickly, preparing to launch into my usual litany of why I couldn't, or didn't want to, go out.

"Yes, you can. You need to get out of the house and I want to go dancing."

I took another swig of beer. "I don't like to dance. You know that."

"Well, then you can watch me," he said. "Besides, it's a gay bar."

"All the more reason—"

"—that you'll have a good time," he finished. "You need to relax a little. And you don't have to worry about anyone hitting on you or anything because they're all gay men."

"Roger, it's a school night."

"Which means nothing because you never go to class anymore anyway. I'll pick you up at 8:30."

Before I could protest, the line went dead.

I held the receiver in front of my face and considered calling him back to cancel, but then decided that it would do no good. When Roger was in the mood to go out, he wouldn't take "no" for an answer. And, he was right about going to gay bars. There, as long as I didn't touch anything, I felt fairly safe. And, I enjoyed the music.

I picked up my beer, wiped the ring of condensation from the counter with the bottom of my shirt, and wandered back into my bedroom. "I should just go," I said to myself. I studied the blank page of paper and lifted the bottle to my lips. "It's not like I have anything else to do."


Roger picked me up at exactly 8:30 and we drove downtown to the bar district and his favorite haunt, Alpha-Beta. A rainbow flag hung limply in the window, backlit by the flashing strobe lights inside. The deep throb of dance music emanated from the building as we walked from the parking lot to the club.

"Isn't he gorgeous?" Roger yelled in my ear as we entered the club and he waved to a muscular man I could only assume was his new love interest. "His name is Douglas." Roger pointed at the bar and the man nodded. "Come on." He grabbed my hand and led me through the throng of men posing and grinding to the pulsating beat of the music. When we reached the bar, Roger dropped my hand and leaned down.

"Beer?"

I nodded and he turned to the bartender, held up three fingers, and then reached into his back pocket for his wallet. When our drinks arrived, he handed one to me and watched as I pulled a wet wipe from my pocket, tore it open, and carefully wiped down the mouth of the bottle. I met his eyes.

"What? You never know."

He rolled his eyes and then turned to look at the crowd. Douglas had been stopped by a group of men who were all talking animatedly.

"So?" Roger spoke to me without taking his eyes off of Douglas. "What do you think?"

"I don't know," I said. "He's nice looking."

"And he's great in bed."

Never sure how to respond when Roger shared information like this, I simply nodded. I was about to ask how they met when Douglas finally broke free of the group of men and started toward us.

"Hi," he said as he pulled Roger into a hug. "I'm glad you made it." He smiled at me over Roger's shoulder. "Hey."

I raised my beer bottle in greeting.

"So," Roger said when they separated. "Rebecca, this is Douglas. Douglas . . . Rebecca." He winked. "She's my fag hag."

His words, despite being true, stung. I scowled.

"What?" He looked from me to Douglas and back. "It's true."

I forced myself to smile and leaned forward toward Douglas, who smiled in greeting. He was at least eight inches taller than me and I had to tip my head backward to meet his eyes. I had to yell to be heard over the pulsing beat of the techno music. "Nice to meet you."

He grinned again and the black light made his teeth glow. There were several specks of lint on his black t-shirt. He dropped his arm casually over Roger's shoulders.

"So, you guys wanna party?"

I looked at Roger who slid his arm around Douglas' waist.

"Poppers?" he asked.

Douglas reached into his shirt pocket and pulled out a sandwich bag with a perforated sheet of what looked like Daffy Duck stickers. "Better than that."

"Holy shit!" Roger grabbed the bag. "Seriously?"

I leaned in to see the bag more closely.

"I don't get it. Stickers?"

Roger laughed and handed the bag back to Douglas. "Those aren't stickers," he said. "What this fine specimen of manhood brought us tonight is LSD."

"LSD like acid, LSD?" I looked up at Douglas for confirmation.

"Yes ma'am." He grinned. "Just put one of these on your tongue and enjoy the ride."

Roger pretended to fan himself. "Some men bring flowers or chocolates, but not this one." He slapped Douglas' broad chest. "Let's do it."

"Are you crazy?" I knew I sounded like an old woman, but I didn't care. "Roger, that's against the law."

"Law, smaw." Roger rolled his eyes. "You need to loosen up."

Douglas opened the bag, removed the sheet, and tore off a couple of squares. He handed one to Roger and one to me before putting the sheet back into the baggie and sticking it in his pocket.

"You realize you just wasted a good hit, right?" Roger looked at me. "She'll never do it."

Everything about the evening and the way Roger was treating me so he could impress Douglas was making me angry. I stared at the tiny square in my hand.

"What will it do?"

Douglas grinned. "It will open up your mind." He looked at

Roger for confirmation. "Everything will feel so intense and real. It's this intellectually stimulating experience that's just consciousness-altering. It makes the unreal real, and the real . . . really, really real." He placed his own square on his tongue and let it dissolve.

I wondered, suddenly, if he had washed his hands after going to the bathroom.

"*Throw it on the floor.*" Grace's voice cut through the noise of the music. "*Just say 'no.*'"

I stared at the square of paper in my palm and then looked back at Roger. His expression had gone from playful to serious.

"Actually, I don't think you should do it. I don't think you would enjoy it."

"Are you saying I can't handle it?" I asked indignantly. Douglas looked uncomfortable and began to scan the bar for an escape from this mini-drama.

"No," Roger said. "It's just that it can really mess you up if you're not in a good space." He glanced at Douglas, who gestured toward the dance floor, and smiled in a "just a second" sort of way and then returned his gaze to me. "Listen, this was a bad idea. You didn't even want to come out and now, well . . ." He glanced longingly at Douglas who was edging away from us. "How about you take my car and head home. I'll just have Douglas give me a ride."

"Roger, I can't leave you here." I looked at Douglas, who was swiveling his shoulders in time to the music. "You don't even know this guy. I can't just take your car and go."

"Believe me, I know him plenty well and I was planning on letting you take the car home anyway. Besides, I'm not sure you'd really have that much fun. I have a feeling things are going to get a little . . . ummm . . . raunchy."

"But—" I protested.

"Please." He reached into his pocket, pulled out his car keys, and pressed them into my hand. "I'll call you tomorrow afternoon," he said, already turning to Douglas and smiling widely. "Okay, handsome, let's go."

The two disappeared into the crowd.

"Asshole," I muttered to myself. I took a swallow of my beer

211

and considered the situation. I had no desire to stay—especially if Roger was going to be completely absorbed with his new boy toy. I set the bottle on a nearby table and began to make my way toward the door.

I didn't usually go out at night by myself and was unprepared for the feeling of being completely exposed as I stepped into the darkness. Roger had parked close to the bar and I could see the car from where I stood. It hadn't seemed all that far away when we went in, but now that I was alone, it looked like an impossible distance. In the doorway, men laughed and flirted and smoked.

"Well, at least there will be witnesses," I murmured. "And maybe one of them will help me if something happens."

Remembering something I had read in the self-defense information Detective Sanchez had given Adelle, I fished my house keys out of my jeans pocket and stuck them carefully between the fingers of my left hand so that when I curled it into a fist, I looked like some sort of Transformer. Between the thumb and forefinger of my other hand, I grasped the key to Roger's car so I could open the door without having to fumble to find it.

"You can do this," I told myself as I took a deep breath and forced myself to walk. It was all I could do not to run the fifty yards to the car. My heart pounded in my throat as I took measured steps, careful to stay in the middle of the street, until I reached the car. Behind me I could hear the men in the doorway laughing. It was strangely reassuring.

"You can do this," I said again, softly, and then felt the familiar tingle of Grace's presence. She didn't speak, but I could tell she was there.

When I reached the car, I slipped the key into the lock and pulled open the door. The dome light illuminated the interior and I looked in the backseat. It was empty. Quickly, I climbed into the driver's seat, pulled the door shut behind me, and used my elbow to lock the door. I breathed heavily and gripped the steering wheel. I had done it. I had walked to the car in the dark on my own—and nothing bad had happened.

I grinned as I put the key in the ignition and started the car.

I had done it. I had taken on the night and had won—or, at least, hadn't lost. It was a small triumph, but one that made me suddenly hopeful. It felt as if it were the beginning of something significant and despite the temperature, I rolled down the window. The cold night air was refreshing after the hot club, the smoke machine, and fifty different brands of cologne.

When I got home, I immediately undressed and showered, scrubbing vigorously to remove the smell of the bar from my skin and hair and then used towels to pick up the smelly clothes I had worn. As I tossed them into my dirty clothes basket, coins and dollar bills fell from the pockets.

I bent to pick them up, and saw again the small square with the image of Daffy Duck. Carefully, without touching the ink, I turned it over and examined it. It seemed harmless enough. And then I thought about what Douglas had said, about how it opened up your mind and expanded consciousness. I turned to look at the blank paper tacked onto my wall. Trying to paint hadn't worked before, but maybe I simply needed something to kick-start the process. I looked down at the paper in my hand and wondered again what germs might be on it.

*"Don't."*

The word came like the crack of a ball striking a baseball bat. But this time, it sounded as if it had come from outside my head. I looked around the room.

"Grace?"

The room was silent—so silent I could hear the steady drip, drip, drip of the faucet in the bathroom.

I looked back down at the tab of LSD. It was dangerous. But everything was dangerous. I swallowed and, before I could change my mind, closed my eyes and pressed the piece of paper to my tongue.

# Chapter 18

Eight hours later, I stood against the wall and stared blearily around my bedroom. Smears of paint stained the walls, the door handles, the dresser, and virtually everything else. All of my clothes had been pulled from the closet and were pushed up against the underside of my mattress. My head hurt and my mouth felt dry and metallic. My sheets and bedspread were a mess of paint and paper and pencils and pens. Scattered around the room were large squares of paper with dabs and smears of paint. Several "paintings" were lined up against the wall.

Through the haze of a headache, I struggled to recall the events of the previous night. I remembered that after letting the tab of LSD dissolve on my tongue, I had grabbed the Depeche Mode mix CD borrowed from Roger, put it in my boom box, and hit Play. I waited until the music started before approaching the paper tacked onto my wall. I stared at it, willing whatever muse was supposed to inspire me to appear. Nothing came to me, so I grabbed several of the tubes of paint and squeezed some onto the palette. Next, I picked up one of the brushes and smeared it into the globs of color.

"Just . . . go with it," I had murmured. "Start small." I closed my eyes, took a deep breath, and was immediately rewarded with the image of a spiral. Tentatively, I began to play with the green and yellow and white paints, mixing them into a limey shade of green. As I began to cover the whole of the paper, I felt the first tingling of something. I remembered glancing at the clock. Exactly, I noted, thirty minutes after I had held Daffy to my tongue.

Until that first tingle, I had been convinced that nothing was happening and even laughed at the thought of Roger and Douglas dancing at the club and wondering why they weren't feeling anything. But then I felt the tingle and I knew something was about to happen—something bigger than myself. I closed my eyes and held my breath for what seemed like forever. Finally, I exhaled and was almost knocked to my knees by an intense rush of something that felt like being sucked through a straw. I was euphoric . . . powerful. I looked at my green background and realized with sudden insight that it would be wasted on a spiral. I heard myself speaking aloud as I did when I had had too much to drink. But unlike with alcohol, I didn't feel impaired. Quite the opposite. I felt immeasurably in control. My words were power manifested.

"I can see it so clearly," I said. "So clearly. I'm going to draw. No, paint. I'm going to paint and I'm . . . you . . . it's all so . . . I need more."

It was as if I was talking to another part of myself—a part that was creative and less controlled than the persona I allowed most people to see. My halves rushed together in a bone-jarring whole. I was . . . complete. I began to paint black skeletons of trees in the winter. No leaves, just trunks and branches and a tree house. "Ah," I said to myself and to the paper, "I know what this is. I know where this is!"

*"Where is it?"* a voice asked.

I spun around, startled, expecting to see Adelle. Instead, I found myself looking down at Grace, still eleven years old and angular. I felt as if the top of my head had popped off and my brains were exposed. But for some reason, I didn't mind. Grace was here—not just in a dream, but in reality. She looked both the same and very different from how I remembered her. Had she changed, I wondered, or had I?

"Grace. You're here. Why?"

*"You're going to need me."* Her tone was matter-of-fact. She looked around the room. *"What are you doing?"*

"I'm expanding my consciousness. I'm exorcising my demons."

She shrugged and nodded in the slow, solemn way I had forgotten she had. My scalp tingled and I grinned.

"I'm . . . you . . . this!" I gestured at the painting on the wall.

"This is ours!" I turned back to the painting and squinted. I tried desperately to focus, but found that my train of thought was disrupted and I really couldn't concentrate on anything long enough to complete the task. I felt her disapproval.

"I know," I said quickly, apologetically. "I need to focus. Detail. I'll do detail."

Grace watched as I crouched on the floor over a fresh piece of paper. I focused on the paper and began to paint with purpose. "You probably can't see it." I gestured at the images I was creating. "You're dead. But I can and this is so very vivid. This green, it's not just green, it's the most *intense* green I've ever seen. The lines are there. I just need to follow the sweep and curve of the lines that are there. Did you know that? That pictures are already in the paper? They absolutely are. We just have to coax them out. And that's what I'm doing now. With my hand . . . and this brush. All of my consciousness is located in my hand. It's so powerful."

Grace moved to stand behind me. I felt her peering over my shoulder at the face I was painting. Rendered in red and black, the face on the paper had one eye that was obscured with hair. The other stared blankly ahead. The image rippled under my gaze. It was all wrong. In the background, my mind registered "Stripped" playing on the CD player. I pushed the paper away and attacked a fresh sheet.

"I need clarity. I need focus—to just focus on one part. Just one."

I looked up at her face, grabbed a new sheet of paper, and then began to draw her eye complete with eyelashes. It looked like a cross between a Picasso and a second grader's rendering of the sun. I compared it to her face.

"It's not very good, I know," I babbled. "But I'm not an artist. I'm studying business."

Grace laughed. *"You have no interest in business. I've often wondered why you try to shove yourself into that box. Remember how you used to draw? And read? You're too creative to study business."* She looked at the drawing. *"Although, if that's any indication of your work, maybe you should stick to business."*

"I know! I know." I jumped up and began to pace back and forth. I could do better. I *knew* it. I felt the need to convince her—to prove my worth. "I'll try again," I announced resolutely. "I'll do it again. This one will be good. I know it will."

I sat back down, pushed the paper to the side, and grabbed a fresh sheet. Suddenly, my perception changed and it was as if I had a three-dimensional view of the scene. I was me, participating. But I was also omnipresent—an energy somewhere in the vicinity of the ceiling, watching what was happening below. I could see myself and Grace—how we moved, our interaction. I picked up the green tube of paint and squeezed from the middle, squirting out more paint. I stared at it, mesmerized. It seemed to glow with energy and life. I felt an overwhelming desire to eat it.

*"Well, are you just going to sit there?"* Grace's voice broke into my contemplation.

Using bold strokes, I created an outline of an eye. It looked more like an Egyptian symbol than Grace's actual eye, but I grinned in appreciation.

"It's beautiful." I laughed in delight. And then I saw the ant skitter across the floor.

"Oh my god, Grace." I backpedaled into the corner. "It was an ant. Did you see it? An ant—like the ones that live inside you."

Grace laughed and her eyes became hollow holes that melted down her face like candles left to burn themselves out. I blinked. What in the hell was happening?

*"I can hear what you're thinking, Birdie. Nothing you think now or ever is your own."*

Suddenly, the room seemed to bend and I felt the movement of time as if it were one of my spirals. The past, the present, and the future were connected to each other even though they happened separately, just like points on a spiral that are adjacent to each other on a two dimensional plane but are separated down the length of the spiral itself. I blinked several times. My hearing was almost painfully acute.

"I can hear my hair growing," I mumbled. "It's life growing out of my body."

"*You should draw your hair,*" suggested Grace with a wicked, eyeless grin. "*Draw it growing.*"

"You're right." I crawled out of the corner and over to the paper. I looked around and saw the earlier paintings I had scattered around the room. The eye with the rudimentary eyelashes sprang to life, jumped off the paper, and skittered on its centipede legs to safety under my bed.

"Shit. I'm going to draw my hair growing," I announced to Grace. "No, no, *your* hair growing. I'm going to paint that."

I squirted paint directly onto the paper and then blended it with my brush. Colors smeared together in swirls and trails. It was a deconstructed face, as seen through a prism. It was Grace's face, but also, not. The result was a supernatural creature with hair and bursts of light behind it. It was magical, I decided, and so I began to hum as I worked. The only song I could think of, though, was far from magical.

"I rode through the desert on a horse with no name, it felt good to get out of the rain," I intoned tunelessly over and over. Finally I sat back on my heels.

"Done." I repeated it for emphasis. "Done."

Grace crept over and studied the painting. "*It's interesting, but it doesn't look like anything, really. It certainly doesn't look like me.*"

"When did you become such a critic?" I waved my hands in front of my face. They seemed to melt and then reform and then melt again. I saw movement to my right and turned my head. It was a vine growing out of the floor and creeping along the wall. I lay back and watched, mesmerized, as it expanded and crept. Leaves, first tiny and then robust, grew from the tendrils followed by yellow, bell-shaped flowers. I thought I could smell honeysuckle and then the flowers withered and died, only to be replaced by enormous Venus flytraps that reared and snapped and wobbled on their stems. They smacked their whiskered lips. They wanted to eat me.

Grace began to sing. "*Psycho Killer, Qu'est-ce que c'est.*"

"No! Stop singing. I thought you were here to help me! Make them stop!"

"*I'm here so you don't have to do this alone. But I can't stop it. Besides, none of this is real—it's all in your head. Even I am. I'm dead—have been for years. You know the truth deep down."*

"Why are you so mean?"

*"You try being dead."*

The Venus flytrap was still writhing, the blooms snapping in anticipation.

"No!" I rolled onto my side and faced the bed, my hands clasped tightly over my ears. The eye that had leapt from the page stared out at me from under the dust ruffle, blinking occasionally with its stringy, spindly lashes. My heart galloped as I lay there, eyes screwed shut from the horrors on both sides. Strong and throaty in the voice of a woman rather than a girl, the woman she would never become, I heard Grace call my name.

*"Birdie."* Her voice had the reassuring tones of a mother trying to calm and soothe a terrified child. *"Come here. Let me help you. You know you never should have done this alone. You should have had that little faggot friend of yours stay with you. As unstable as you are, this was a stupid idea."*

"I needed to." My eyes were still squeezed shut. "I needed to get rid of all the *shit* that's in my *head!*"

She laughed. *"And you thought this would do it?"*

"Yes!"

*"Shhhhh. You'll wake your roommate, although maybe you won't. She's pretty used to your nightmares, isn't she? Did you know she's getting tired of you—and more than just a little freaked out? Between nightmares, your weird hours, and the fact that you're scared to leave the house, she thinks there's something wrong with you. And there is, isn't there? You know it deep down. You can say it's normal or make excuses, but we both know that in a lot of ways you're as dead as I am. Or wait, maybe you really did die, too, and this is your purgatory for not helping me—for abandoning me."*

"Shut up," I said miserably. "I don't need some dead girl whose mother was a druggie telling me what is and isn't real. I don't need your help. I can do this on my own."

*"Fine."* And with that, the entire room was silent—too silent. I rolled over, ready to apologize. But it was too late. There she was, lying just like she had in the woods. Back exposed. Pale skin. Smears of blood. One sock. I got to my feet and walked to where

she lay. One eye stared glassily at me. Dark green with thick lashes. "Grace?" I squatted down and stared at her. Nothing moved. No tremor. No blink. "Grace, I'm sorry. I didn't mean it. I'm sorry. Please. Don't do this."

I tentatively reached out and touched her shoulder. She was cold, like meat in the refrigerator. I recoiled, but then forced myself to touch her again, to shake her gently. Nothing. And then I realized what I had to do. I would bring her back to life by capturing her image and then freeing her. I hurried back over to the pile of papers and grabbed a fresh sheet. My movements were deliberate. I squirted paint onto the palette.

"I can do this. I understand now."

I began to paint. And what emerged was a violin on its side. No strings. No bow. Just the body. That's what it was, I realized. Grace, the stringless violin. I glanced over at her cold, still form. The green of the vine, which was again just a vine, caught my eye. I stood up to inspect it. I sniffed one of the blossoms. It smelled like cat urine. I wrinkled my nose and returned to my paper. But after a couple of strokes, I stopped. The smell from the flowers was making it impossible to breathe, let alone concentrate.

I strode to the window to let the cool night air pour in. I could hear a drunken rendition of "Margaritaville" coming from an intoxicated frat boy weaving down the street. I turned from the window and the painting again caught my eye.

"It needs another line." I hurried back to the painting and carefully added a very deliberate line. I glanced at the clock. It was 5:02 a.m. I sniffed. The room still smelled like urine. I climbed to my feet and looked around the room for something to cover the odor. My gaze settled on the green perfume bottle on my dresser. It glowed with emerald intensity. I picked it up and pulled off the cap. It smelled deep and herby. The glass bottle throbbed in my hand and I stared, mesmerized. The bottle was breathing. We just didn't know it because we couldn't *see*. Suddenly, everything in my room was alive. I could feel the atoms and the energy that was holding everything together. I walked around the room touching things and watching them exist.

"This is unreal," I said softly. "It's unreal and disturbing . . . so graphic."

I turned to look at Grace, to implore her to stop playing possum. Her body, though, had become distorted and warped like objects in the distance on a hot summer day. I was simultaneously fascinated and disgusted.

"You're like Dali's clocks." I squatted on the floor at eye level and studied her shimmering form. "Melted blues and whites." I scooted backwards to my paint supplies and, still keeping my eyes locked on her body, fumbled blindly for a paintbrush. I held the brush in front of my face. The bristles were caked with greenish paint. I mashed the tip against the hardwood floor to crack the dried paint. Flakes fell onto the paper and I blew them off. The brush was still matted with paint. Irritated, I tossed the brushes aside and squirted paint directly onto the paper.

"It was hot that day," I said. "That's right." I used my fingers to create the form. Grace's back. Grace's hip.

I glanced up at Grace periodically as I worked. Her form wavered and grew fainter, the blues fading to white and the whites becoming translucent shadows. She was disappearing— leaving me. My heart felt like it was breaking.

"So, now you're punishing me by leaving, aren't you?"

I didn't expect an answer and when I looked up, I wasn't surprised to find that she was gone. I lay on my bed, exhausted. Around me, the room slowly returned to normal. As the sunshine poured into the room, the vines shrank and eventually retracted into the floor. The eye skittered from under the bed and jumped back onto the paper. The walls once again became solid. I studied my possessions with a detached eye. I recognized things as belonging to me and as being important to me and my life, but not particularly interesting. I closed my eyes and let my body sink into the bed. I wanted nothing more than to sleep. I dozed and finally slept. A knock on my door jolted me awake.

"Rebecca."

It took me several seconds to process the sound. At first, I thought it was Grace. But as the fogginess cleared, I realized that the voice calling my name was both real and male. I rolled over and looked at the alarm clock. It was late in the afternoon. "Rebecca, it's me."

The door opened and Roger walked into the room. He looked around and let out a long, low whistle. "What the hell happened here?" He cocked his head to look at the painting of the eye and then turned to face me. "I just came by to get my car and to apologize for last night. I was an ass. Believe me when I say you didn't miss much." He turned and looked again around the room.

"You know, these aren't bad," he said after several seconds. He walked over to the picture of the spiral, knelt and picked it up. "Rudimentary and surreal at the same time—but also really emotional. And this one—" he pointed to the painting I had done of Grace and her growing hair. "—is really intense. It's like Joseph and his Technicolor Dreamcoat showed up for a—" Roger turned to look at me, his mouth open, his eyes angry. "Tell me what I'm thinking happened didn't really happen.'

I sighed. "Roger, I'm tired. I've been up all night."

He nodded. "I see that. Again, tell me what I think happened, didn't." He glared. "Rebecca, what the fuck? Are you crazy?"

"Shut up. It's none of your business."

"The hell it's not. Do you realize how dangerous that was? You're just lucky it was a weak dose." I raised my eyebrows. "Douglas got them off a guy he didn't know. We had to take two hits to really get anything." I returned my head to the pillow and closed my eyes.

"So?" He sat down on the edge of the bed. "How was it?"

I opened my eyes. His expression was worried. "It was horrible and weird and . . . not all bad, but not much good. I felt very out of control."

"Do you remember what happened?"

"That's the weird thing," I said slowly. "I do. I remember every single detail of it."

Roger waited for me to continue. When I didn't, he said, "Care to elaborate?"

I shook my head. "No. It's private."

Roger stared. "Tell me."

"No," I said again. "I don't want to talk about it."

"Why not?"

When I didn't answer, he frowned and turned away from me. His anger was palpable. When he finally met my gaze, his eyes were hard. "You make it really hard to be your friend. Do you know that?"

I looked down at my hands. After several seconds, I heard him grunt softly and begin to walk around the room. I raised my gaze to see him standing in front of the painting of the spindly eye. I looked at it as well. When I had painted it, it had seemed necessary and insightful. In the light of day, however, it was disturbing.

"It must have been something," he said finally. "I'm surprised you did something artistic, though."

"It was intentional," I said. "I was looking for an . . . outlet."

Roger nodded, still studying the paintings. I could tell he was angry—angry and hurt. His stance was rigid. After several long minutes, he sighed. "Are you hungry?"

It was a peace offering.

"Yeah. You?"

He turned, finally. His face was unreadable.

"Pizza? We could go to that place down the street where they make it in front of you."

It was one of the few places I would eat for the sole reason that all the cooks wore plastic gloves and the bank of glass windows made it possible to see them preparing the food. I wasn't so sure, though, about having it delivered.

"Or I could make spaghetti."

Roger groaned. "Not spaghetti again. You know, it won't kill you to eat food other people have prepared. Let's get pizza and have it delivered."

I could tell he wasn't going to back down, so I shrugged in resignation. I didn't have to eat any of it, I reasoned.

"Okay, but you're buying."

He grinned. "Fine. Go order it."

When I returned from the kitchen several minutes later, I found Roger was again standing in front of the paintings. "You know," he said thoughtfully. "This is some really unique stuff."

"Roger—"

"Don't worry. I'm not going to invade your precious emotional sanctuary or anything. I'm just . . . intrigued."

I stood next to him, my gaze skipping from each piece in the order it had been created. Studying them this way, as a set, I could see the progression of my trip—an embarrassing reminder of each stage of the evening.

"So, what are you going to do with your collection, Picasso?"

I had forgotten Roger was there and the sound of his voice startled me. "Throw them away," I said shortly. "They're not something I want around."

He waited to see if I was going to say anything else. When I didn't, he said, "Want me to get rid of them for you? We have a dumpster at the apartment complex. I can stick them in there when I go home."

I looked at him, surprised that he would offer and absurdly grateful that despite everything, he still wanted to help. I nodded and he began to stack the papers carefully on top of each other. When he was finished, he stood, pulled a twenty out of his wallet and handed it to me.

"I had to park down the block, but if the pizza guy gets here before I get back, this should cover it." He opened the back door and stepped onto the narrow porch. I followed, suddenly filled with gratitude.

"Thanks, Roger. For everything."

He looked surprised at the emotion and winked dramatically. "Anything for you, sugar. Anything."

# Chapter 19

"I'm surprised to see you," Laura said as I slid into the chair across from her. "I didn't think you'd come back."

I nodded but said nothing, avoiding her eyes. I knew how I must look. It had been five days since I had taken the LSD and in that time, I had barely slept or eaten. Food looked repulsive and greasy and the thought of putting it into my mouth made me nauseous. And sleep, which at the best of times had been somewhat elusive, was now impossible. Each time I closed my eyes, I was bombarded with images from my acid trip—most specifically those of Grace. It was as if she were speaking to me inside my brain. Nothing seemed real and I felt, for the first time, that I really was losing my grip on reality. In desperation, I called and asked for an immediate appointment with Laura.

We sat in silence for several seconds until Laura leaned forward and said softly, "Rebecca, what's happened? Why are you here?"

I was staring into my lap and blinked several times before raising my eyes to meet her sympathetic gaze.

"What we talk about . . ." I began slowly. "It's confidential, right? I mean, it goes nowhere but here?"

Laura nodded.

"And, if I told you about something illegal that I'd done, that stays here, too?"

"Well, that depends. If it was murder or rape or something like that, I'd be obliged to report it." She paused. "But that's not what you're talking about is it?"

I shook my head.

"Drugs?"

I looked up, startled by her perception.

"It's okay. You can talk to me about it. But you have to tell me the truth. I can't help if I don't know the extent of what we're dealing with."

"I took acid," I admitted softly. "I know I shouldn't have, but I did. I was trying to paint—to get insight into . . ." I shrugged helplessly. "I wanted to make certain things stop. But they didn't stop. They got worse. I think it changed something in my head. My nightmares became real."

"What do you mean?" Laura took off her glasses and put them on the table next to her.

An image of Grace, lying on her side, dead, popped into my brain. I gritted my teeth and struggled to focus on Laura's face.

"Rebecca, what happened when you took the acid?"

I sighed and shook my head. Even though she still hadn't spoken to me, I could feel Grace watching.

"It was horrible," I said finally. I felt a surge of panic. I wanted to run from the room. My breath and pulse came in ragged bursts, as if I had sprinted across a football field.

"Deep breaths, Rebecca. Focus on my face. Tell me what happened."

I struggled to control my breathing. "Grace came alive. And there were ants and vines. I thought I was going to die."

"Grace was your friend who was murdered, right?"

I nodded miserably.

"You said you felt like it changed something in your head. Can you tell me what you mean by that?"

I shrugged and searched for words. "I haven't been able to sleep since it happened. Or if I do sleep, I have nightmares. I see it all over again in my head." My throat began to constrict.

"Rebecca, do you need some water?"

I shook my head, closed my eyes. Grace's tortured face appeared again in my consciousness.

*Go away,* I thought. *Go away.*

"Rebecca, it's okay." Laura's voice became clearer and Grace faded somewhat.

226

"I feel like it's all happening again." I opened my eyes and tried to focus on Laura. "I dream about finding her body . . . about not helping her . . . of her dying out there alone." I shook my head almost violently from side to side. "I can't stop thinking about her," I said helplessly. "And I can't stop worrying that it's going to happen to me—that I'm going to end up the same way."

Laura reached for her pad of paper and then stopped. "Do you mind if I take some notes?"

I shook my head. "No notes."

"Okay." She sat back in her chair. "So, let's talk about Grace."

In my head, I could feel Grace's agitation. It was if she were pacing back and forth in my brain.

"You found her body?"

I nodded miserably.

"And you never received therapy for what happened, right?"

I shook my head.

Laura was thoughtful for several seconds.

"Rebecca, have you ever heard of survivor's guilt? It's when a person blames themselves for surviving a traumatic event when others didn't. They see it as their fault that they survived. I think you blame yourself because Grace died and you lived."

Grace laughed in my head and I flinched.

"It's okay," Laura said, not realizing my reaction was to Grace and not to her. "Your parents didn't know how this would affect you. But you don't have to continue to live with it—at least not to this extreme. I can help you."

I laughed bitterly and Laura's brow creased into a tiny frown. "Did that strike you as funny?"

I shook my head. "No. It's just . . ." I hesitated. "It's hard to think about."

"I know," Laura said. "But I think cognitive therapy can help."

"What do you mean?" I asked, trying not to give into the glimmer of hope I suddenly felt.

"Well, talking about what happened and then trying to change how you think about it. Probably once a week at first. And then, outside assignments—maybe having you volunteer at a rape crisis center or a women's center. Many women find it empowering to take on their fears by helping others with the same or similar problems."

The thought of being around women experiencing rape and abuse made me want to vomit. "But I wasn't raped."

"No, but you fear it. And as trite as it sounds, the best way to overcome your fears is to face them. And I would also recommend medication."

I pressed my lips together but said nothing.

"Depression goes hand in hand with survivor's guilt. We have a psychologist here on staff who would write the prescription. Have you ever heard of Prozac? I think it would help."

*"No!"* Grace was back. *"No drugs."*

"No," I said aloud. "No medications."

"Okay." Laura leaned back and crossed her legs. "We can revisit that. What about therapy?"

*"You don't need therapy,"* Grace said.

I shook my head to try to clear her from my thoughts.

"Maybe," I said aloud.

Laura smiled wanly.

"You don't seem too sure," she said.

"I'm not," I admitted. "Can I think about it? And then call you back to set up an appointment?"

Laura nodded slowly. "Or, we could set up an appointment now and talk about it more next time." I opened my mouth to protest but she held up her hand. "My concern is that you won't make the appointment. And that would be a shame because I think I can help you. Depression doesn't carry the stigma it used to. And survivor's guilt, although powerful, can be overcome."

I closed my mouth and nodded slowly.

"Same time next week?" Laura asked and reached for her spiral appointment book. She looked up expectantly, challenging me to say "no."

"Sure."

"Good." Laura scribbled my name in the two o'clock time slot and then closed the book. "I'm proud of you, Rebecca. I know this is scary, but I have no doubt that you're doing the right thing."

I, of course, cancelled the appointment the next day. And though Laura called several times to try to reschedule, I didn't call her back.

*"You made the right decision,"* Grace said one afternoon two weeks later as I walked back from class. Winter had finally arrived and brought with it several inches of snow. It crunched beneath my feet as I picked my way along the sidewalk. *"You don't need other people meddling in your life. You can fix yourself."*

"This coming from the dead girl who is haunting me," I murmured.

I felt her gentle laugh.

Despite my insulated duck boots, heavy coat, and gloves, my hands and feet felt like blocks of ice by the time I made it back to the apartment. I stomped my feet on the front porch to knock off the snow, stepped into the entryway, and clumsily unlaced them. My fingers were pink with cold.

Adelle came out of the kitchen as I closed the front door behind me and set the boots on a rubber mat just inside the door. "I can't believe how cold it is." I turned to hang my coat and wool cap on the wooden coatrack. "If I hadn't skipped so much class, I wouldn't have to go every day now."

"Once finals are over, you can start next semester with a clean slate." She held up a ceramic coffee cup. "I just made some hot tea. There's still water in the kettle if you want some." She started toward her room and then stopped. "Oh, Natalie called. She wants you to call her back."

I waited until she had closed the door to her room before picking up the phone and carrying it with me into the kitchen. I knew the number by heart, but I just stared at the receiver. She probably wanted to talk about Christmas break. Though I had managed to avoid going home since moving to Lincoln, this time there was no alternative. I had exhausted every special academic session/holiday at a friend's house/volunteer activity excuse I could fabricate. Three years had passed and I couldn't avoid it any longer. I had to go home.

"I don't know why I'm so scared," I thought. "It's not like Grace didn't follow me here anyway."

But it *would* be different. Here, I was safe. Here I had my routine. Here I was Rebecca. But there, I was Birdie. Birdie who would have to answer questions and be responsible to others. I set the receiver down on the counter and turned to the kettle. The call to Natalie could wait. I would be in Edenbridge soon enough.

As it turned out, I didn't have to worry about calling Natalie back; she called me. It was almost midnight the same day. I was awake, trying to cram a semester's worth of political science class into my short-term memory, when the phone rang. The number on the caller ID was Natalie's. Though I considered not answering, I knew that if I didn't, Adelle would. I pressed the Talk button.

"Hey," I said. "Sorry I didn't call you back. I was studying and lost track of time."

She cleared her throat. "It's okay. And I usually wouldn't call so late, I just—" She cleared her throat again and this time, it was followed by the sound of a wet sniff.

"Nat? Are you crying?"

She sniffed again and then said, "Yeah."

"What's wrong? Is it your mom? Or—"

"Birdie, I'm pregnant."

"What? But how?"

"How do you think, Birdie?" She struggled to swallow back the tears. "I've just been lonely and felt so alone. And then a few months ago, I was at the IGA in Winston and ran into Pete Wade. He was back in town because he hurt his back and lost his scholarship. We got to talking and one thing led to another and we started to . . . well, you know."

"You never told me."

Natalie was silent for several seconds and I realized that she had called several times, but I hadn't picked up or returned the call. I lifted the ring finger on my free hand to my mouth and began to gnaw on the ragged cuticle, trying to remember what I knew about Pete Wade. He had been in the class ahead of us. He was good-looking and had been on the football and basketball teams.

"It wasn't supposed to be anything serious," she said finally, as if that were an answer. "He wants to have it. He wants to get married." Her voice was tired and suddenly, she seemed very young. "Oh, Birdie, I don't want a baby. Not now. I mean, I know I can't afford to go to school full time, but I was thinking about taking some writing courses at the junior college."

"Writing," I echoed and studied the finger I had just been chewing on. A deep bead of blood had risen to the surface. I stuck it quickly into my mouth. The blood was thick and metallic. I ran the tip of my tongue over the ragged flesh.

"Have you thought about . . .?" I didn't want to say the word.

"An abortion?" she supplied. "Yeah. But, I don't know if I could do that. I think about Grace and . . ."

I stiffened as she said the name. In my head, I felt Grace's agitation.

*"She can't give it up,"* Grace whispered. *"Tell her she can't give it up."*

"I've gone over and over it in my head." Natalie began to cry. "All the options suck."

"Do you love him?" I could hear the strangeness of my tone and realized that my heart was beating faster than normal. My stomach was tight, but not from anxiety. Jealousy?

"No," Natalie said miserably. "I care about him. He's a good guy. And I think he loves me. I just—" She began to cry harder, her words coming in gasps. "This wasn't supposed to happen. I was just having some fun. It was nice to have someone looking after *me* for a change."

I felt my chest tighten, wishing there was something I could do or say to help. "I'm sorry, Natalie," I said for lack of anything better.

Grace stirred. *"Tell her not to get rid of it. Tell her to marry him."*

I blinked hard twice, three times, trying to push her away. I was feeling her emotions when all I wanted was to feel my own.

"My life will be over before it's even started," Natalie said softly. "I'll go from taking care of mom to taking care of kids. What about me, Birdie? When is it my turn?" She began to cry again. "I just feel so trapped."

"It might not be so bad," I said finally "Getting married, having a family. It might not be so bad."

Natalie made a noise that could have meant anything.

"I never wanted to have kids," she said. "I never wanted that responsibility. I don't want to have to worry about something happening to them."

"You can't think of it like that," I said, knowing she was thinking about Grace.

"Can't I?" I felt her rage and her sadness, but I had nothing to offer, had no advice.

"So, what are you going to do?" I asked again.

"I don't know," she said. "Listen, I should let you go. I know I called you, but I don't want to talk about this anymore."

I felt as if I had been given some sort of test and been found lacking. I wanted to say something—anything—that would help. "Listen, finals are over in a couple of weeks. When I'm back on winter break, we can figure this out—just like old times. We'll come up with a plan."

"Birdie, I'm almost three months along," Natalie said. "I can't wait much longer. I'm starting to show."

"So?"

"So, I need to do something quickly."

"We all had so many dreams," she said softly. "You, me, and Grace. And look at us now." She laughed humorlessly. "Grace's dead, you're a recluse, and I'm knocked up."

The truth of her words stung.

"Just, don't make any decisions, okay?"

She was quiet again and I could hear her breath, soft and irregular. She sniffed and I realized she was crying again.

"Okay," she said finally. "I'm gonna go now. I'll see you when you get home."

Before I could reply, she hung up.

I left for Edenbridge around 8 a.m., the day after my last final. I had spent the previous evening with Adelle, who was also going home for the break, and Roger, who had plans to stay in Lincoln and go out with his friends. My pace was slow, both because of the snow and because the tires on the ancient Buick my father had purchased for me the year before, were bald.

When I finally pulled into Edenbridge, it was with both relief and dread. After the hustle and bustle of Lincoln, Edenbridge seemed small and dead, despite the Christmas decorations and lights. It was as if time had stood still. The Mercantile still stood on the corner of the street, its façade faded and badly in need of paint. The sidewalks down the main streets had been shoveled and sanded so well that you could see the warped and broken sections. Randy—with the same oily rag hanging limply from the back pocket of his filthy, insulated coveralls—still manned the antiquated pumps of the gas station.

I sighed as I pulled the Buick into the driveway, put it into park, and turned off the ignition. You can do this, I told myself as I hauled my suitcase out of the trunk and trudged up the back walkway to the kitchen door. Tara greeted me as I used my key to let myself in and explained that our mother was at the nursing home where Granny had just recently been relocated.

I walked down the hallway and opened the door to my room. Nothing had changed. The shelves still housed my collection of books, rocks, and high school memorabilia. On the walls were all my old posters, including my one-time favorite of a kitten dangling from a branch with the words, *Hang in there, Baby* printed in big, happy letters at the bottom. The corners were thick with yellowed tape and riddled with holes from countless thumbtacks.

"It's like you never left."

I turned to see Tara leaning against the door frame. She was dressed in faded Levi's and an old Edenbridge Blue Jays T-shirt. At almost sixteen, she was a beautiful young woman and I envied her, not just because she was so attractive, but also because she was confident, popular, and genuinely comfortable with herself.

"Yeah," I said finally and brushed a lock of hair back behind my ear.

"Mom wants you to feel comfortable coming home," she said. "You know, like you can go away, but your things will always be here—that things will always be the same."

She stepped into the room and went to sit on the edge of the bed. Despite the cold outside, she was barefoot, and I noticed that her toenails were painted a perky pink.

"It's good to have you home, Bird." She paused and then began to pick at one of the stitches on the quilt draped across the foot of the bed.

"So, what's up with Granny?"

She pursed her lips and shrugged. "She's not adjusting well to the nursing home. She's convinced we're all trying to kill her. She refuses to eat anything she doesn't cook herself in her room and she's started hiding food under her bed. She doesn't want to shower because she thinks they're like the ones at Auschwitz."

"And people think I have problems," I said under my breath.

"What?"

I shook my head and she continued. "She thinks Gramps is still alive and is talking to her. She has whole conversations with him, but there's no one there."

I felt Grace stir in the back of my head and took a deep breath. I moved to sit next to Tara on the bed and she turned her body to face me, pulling her knees up under her chin.

"I'm just telling you ahead of time so that when Mom takes you to see her, you won't be too shocked. She's really gone downhill."

I nodded and made a note to avoid seeing my grandmother if at all possible. The thought of her mental state worried me—not just for her sake, but for my own. I closed my eyes and tried to push thoughts of hereditary insanity out of my mind. Tara leaned forward and lightly touched my arm.

"You okay?"

I nodded. "Just a headache from the drive." I gestured limply at nothing and she nodded.

"Want some Tylenol?"

I shook my head. "I just need to lie down for a little bit and then call Natalie."

Tara took the cue. "I'll let you unpack." She slid gracefully off the bed and walked to the door. Just before leaving, she paused and turned to look at me. "It's nice to have you home, Bird." Her eyes filled with tears. "I love you."

I blinked and felt my throat tighten with emotion. I swallowed and opened my mouth to tell her I loved her, too, but the words seemed stuck. I inhaled deeply and tried again to speak. My voice still failed me.

"It's okay," she said as she turned to walk out of the room. "You don't have to say it, I know."

I didn't get a chance to see Natalie for several days. Christmas preparations and family obligations on both of our parts made it impossible to meet until the afternoon of Christmas Eve. Her mother was napping and we were in her bedroom. Unlike mine, the décor of her room had changed. Gone were the posters and high school memorabilia, replaced with framed posters of Rome, Egypt, and Paris.

"I've decided to marry Pete," she said without preamble as she settled on the foot of the bed and curled her legs up under her. Outside, the snow was falling in large, wet flakes. Cups of cocoa that were too hot to drink sat on the bedside table.

"Nat, no," I said quickly. "I thought we were going to talk about it."

"I've already said yes," she said numbly. "I pretty much made up my mind right after we talked. We're going to have a simple wedding next month—just family and close friends."

I stared at her.

"It's the best decision," Natalie said resolutely. "He's a good man, he'll provide for me and the baby, and when he or she goes to school, I can start taking classes at the community college."

"But—" I began.

"I'm not giving up anything," she said defensively. "I'll still pursue my dreams—just later."

We sat in silence for what seemed like forever.

"I'd like you to be my maid of honor," she said finally.

"Of course," I said quickly. "Just let me know when and I'll—"

"It's January 15," she said.

"Oh," I said simply.

"We had to move fast," she said. "You know." She gestured at her belly, which looked only slightly more rounded than it usually did. "The bachelorette party is going to be on the 13th."

"So soon," I murmured.

"I need to do it before I change my mind," Natalie said.

I nodded, understanding suddenly the real urgency. The look of resignation on her face made my heart ache in sympathy.

*"Poor Natalie."* It was Grace. "I know," I said aloud, an answer to both of their statements.


Natalie's was the first and only bachelorette party I ever attended. I hadn't been sure what to expect, although I had seen enough movies to have an idea what it would be like. The evening started when I picked up Natalie at her mother's house. The party was to start in Winston at a bar called Jacob's Ladder.

"Strange name for a bar," I said as we pulled onto the highway and headed toward the city.

"I haven't been there," she admitted. "Peggy suggested it."

"Ah."

Peggy Norton was a girl who had been in our class and who, after I had gone away to college, had taken my place as Natalie's confidante. She was one of the bridesmaids, I quickly learned, in addition to Pete's two sisters, Sissy and Barbara, who were five and six years older than we were.

"You'll like them," Natalie had reassured me over the phone when we were talking about the agenda for the weekend. "Barbara and Sissy are nice—a little white trash, but nice."

"I don't know, Nat," I'd hedged. "You know how I am in social situations."

"I know," Natalie had said. "But this is my bachelorette party.

It's my second-to-last night as a single woman. I want you there. Please, Birdie. It's important to me."

And so I agreed to go out, agreed to be social, and agreed to be nice to Peggy. But as we walked into the bar and I saw her sitting with two women who looked vaguely familiar, I began to doubt my ability to fulfill my third promise. Peggy hadn't changed much since we were in high school together. We smiled vaguely at each other rather than hugging.

"Birdie," Natalie said after she greeted the three women. "This is Sissy and this is Barbara."

"Hi," I said with forced enthusiasm and tried to smile.

"Well, hello, Birdie," Sissy said with a look in Peggy's direction. "We've heard a lot about you." Peggy smiled, but said nothing. I shrugged and gave them a weak smile.

"Well, here I am," I said and spread my arms in a theatrical gesture. "In the flesh."

"Birdie," Peggy said with a quick nod. It was a recognition, greeting, and a dismissal all at the same time. I nodded tightly in return. Natalie watched the exchange, sighed, and then clapped her hands together. "So, let's get this party started." Her words were met with whoops and exaggerated squeals from Sissy and Barbara.

"This is going to be a night you will remember forever," Sissy promised as she looked around me and signaled for the waitress.

"We'd like a round of shots," Sissy said to the server, who looked as if there was nothing she hadn't seen or heard before. "Let's start with Sex on the Beach." Sissy nudged Barbara and raised her eyebrows suggestively. Though I didn't find it funny, I forced myself to laugh with the rest of the women.

"To Natalie," Sissy said when the drinks arrived. We all dutifully held up our shot glasses in a toast.

"To Natalie," we echoed. The drink was sweet and warm as it ran down my throat and into my empty stomach.

"Thank you, ladies," Natalie said as she raised her glass of soda water with a lime.

"Too bad you can't drink," Barbara said.

"It is," Sissy agreed. "I guess we'll just have to do it for you."

She signaled to the waitress. "A round of Slippery Nipples. Or—no, make it B-52s."

The waitress nodded and disappeared in the direction of the bar.

"So, are you excited?" Barbara asked. "Just a couple of days and then you'll be Mrs. Peter Wade."

"Love it," Sissy said and belted out another raucous "whoo hoo." I realized, suddenly, that they had been drinking before we had arrived. I looked up and caught Natalie's gaze. She smiled tightly.

"So, Birdie," Peggy said suddenly. "Tell us what you've been up to?"

"Oh, nothing much," I said. "School."

"Um," she said. "And are you seeing anyone?" She asked this last question with a touch of venom.

"Not really," I said, trying to adopt the same level of spite. "I don't have much time. Getting my degree keeps me pretty busy. But what about you? How are Ned and Abigail?"

Peggy I knew, had gone to college long enough to find a husband and get married. Abigail, I knew, had arrived almost exactly nine months after the wedding.

"Wonderful," she said and launched into a long description of her perfect husband, her perfect daughter, and her perfect life. Although I stopped listening after she uttered the word *wonderful*, for a third time, I tried to nod and make the appropriate noises at the appropriate times. Finally, she was interrupted by Sissy.

"Let's have one more round and then get out of here," she said. "There's a dance bar not far from here and I don't know about you girls, but I want to boogie!" She giggled.

The round, which turned out to be something called a Jolly Rancher, was placed in front of me.

"To Natalie's last two nights of freedom," Barbara said. We raised our glasses, though I didn't drink. Barbara noticed this and said, "Birdie, you have to drink. It's bad luck if you don't."

"I just haven't really eaten much," I said apologetically. "I need to pace myself."

"All the better," Sissy said and waited expectantly.

"You don't have to, Birdie," Natalie said and turned to Sissy. "She doesn't have to."

"No," I said suddenly, "It's fine. I want to."

I raised the glass to my lips and tipped it so the liquid poured into my mouth. It really did taste like a watermelon Jolly Rancher.

"Whoo hoo," Sissy and Barbara squealed in unison. "So, let's get out of here. The limo is waiting outside."

I felt the effects of the alcohol as soon as I stood. Carefully, I made my way to the entrance and then into the back of the limo Sissy had hired for the occasion. I said little and even put on the feathered boa she handed each of us. I laughed at Natalie's tiara. I forced myself to relax and thankfully, the next several hours passed in a blur of bars, unnaturally colored drinks, and too loud chatter. I had tried to stop drinking after the first bar, but was unable to convince Sissy and Barbara that I had had enough. I was more than a little drunk when we ended up at the final destination—a biker bar on the edge of town that Sissy thought would be "a hoot" to go to.

From the minute we entered the Jet Lag Lounge, I knew that the five of us in our party clothes and feather boas didn't belong among the denim and leather-clad bikers. Classic rock pounded out of the juke box and a cluster of bearded, tattooed men stopped playing pool long enough to watch our entrance. Drunk and undaunted, Sissy tottered up to the bar and ordered a round of drinks. Several of the men ogled her backside as she passed.

In my head, I could feel Grace stir. She was uncomfortable with our surroundings.

"Natalie, I'm not so sure—" I began, my words slurred and mumbled.

"I know," she said. "Me, too. Don't worry. We'll have one drink and then leave."

"Thank you," I said. "I think I've had too much already."

She nodded and stepped toward the bar.

"Last one for the night," she said as she accepted her soda water with lime.

"Party pooper," Barbara pouted.

"That's me," Natalie said. 'You forget, I've got a lot to do tomorrow."

"All right," Sissy grumbled. "Last one." She handed a shot—straight whiskey this time—to Peggy and then one to me.

"I can't," I said, stepping unsteadily backward, the whiskey sloshing out of the glass and onto my fingers. "I've had too much."

I looked blurrily around for a bathroom.

Natalie looked concerned.

"You okay?" she asked.

"I need to go to the bathroom," I said thickly. I could hear how drunk I was.

"Do you need me to go with you?" she asked.

"No," I said and gestured toward the back of the bar. "I think it's back there."

I turned and wove unsteadily toward the back of the bar. Several of the bikers watched me with curiosity. Others leered.

"Get a load of this one," I heard one man say. His friends laughed loudly.

"Looking for the bathroom?"

The voice was kind and I turned slightly to look up at him. His face was deeply tanned, his hair and mustache almost black in the dim light. A black T-shirt with an elaborate, fierce-looking eagle was stretched over his large belly and tucked into worn blue jeans that were cinched with a thick black leather belt.

"I think I'm going to throw up," I said.

"Follow me," he said and led me through clusters of patrons to the back of the bar where he pointed to a door with the word "Bitches" scrawled on the front in spray paint.

"Thanks," I said and stumbled forward. Despite my nausea, I was appalled at the filthiness of the room and recoiled from the thought of actually vomiting into the stool. I was considering the possibility of making it outside when my stomach rebelled. I crouched in front of the stool, making sure not to touch it, and vomited up the yeasty, sour contents of my stomach. Once the first wave passed, I stared numbly into the toilet, my face slick with sweat. I breathed heavily and waited for the second round. When nothing but stomach bile came up, I used my elbow to flush and then pulled myself to my feet. I felt better.

The man who helped me to the bathroom was waiting outside.

"I was beginning to worry," he said and tipped his head downward to look into my eyes. "Had a little too much tonight?"

I nodded.

"Way too much," I admitted. "And no food."

"Been there," he said, still studying me. His gaze was disconcerting and I began to feel uncomfortable. I could hear Sissy up at the bar, shrieking in laughter. The man glanced in their direction. "So, what exactly are you girls doing in a place like this?"

"Bachelorette party."

"And so you all thought it would be fun to see how the other half lives." Although it was said lightly, there was an undercurrent of animosity in his tone. I felt Grace stir.

"Well, thanks for your help," I said quickly and started to move toward the front of the bar. My stomach felt better, but I could tell I was still impaired. "I should probably go be with my friends."

"Oh, they're fine," he said firmly. "Stay here with me for a couple of minutes."

"I can't," I said, trying to keep the fear from my voice. "I need to go."

He stepped toward me and in reflex, I stepped backward. The wall behind me was hard and unyielding. I was trapped.

*"Birdie, get away from him,"* Grace hissed.

The man reached up and put the palm of his hand against the wall, his arm and body a barrier between me and the rest of the bar.

"Don't," I said with less bravado than I would have liked.

"What's the rush, Birdie?" he asked. At his tone and the use of my name, I jerked my attention back to his face. Adrenaline flooded my body and I felt like I was about to pass out. "Don't you want to reconnect with an old friend?" he continued. "I've been thinking about you off and on over the years. I just want to spend some time catching up. That's all."

I looked at the arm that blocked my escape and for the first time noticed the details of the tattoos that decorated his forearms—

241

dragons and naked women with angels' wings. It was Don Wan.

"I ... no," I whispered. "I can't ... I."

*"Get away from him,"* Grace yelled in my head. *"Remember the drawings? He's dangerous. Move!"*

"I've got to go," I said again and tried to move out of his grasp.

"Not so fast," he said and grabbed my arm. "I just want to talk." He grinned and lazily ran his eyes up and down my body before settling on my face. "You grew up pretty," he said. "I always thought you were a pretty little thing, but now ..." He thrust his face forward and forced his lips onto mine.

"No," I tried to say around his thrusting tongue as I struggled to get out of his grasp. "Stop."

"You know you want it," he said, his voice tight as he used his free hand to grab roughly at my breast. "You've always been a little cock tease, running around with your friends, giving me the eye. I'm just taking you up on your offer." He pinched my nipple and smiled meanly.

I gasped at the pain.

"Stop it," I said and began to cry.

*"Do something,"* Grace said. *"Knee him in the groin. Scream. Do something. He's going to rape you."*

"Get your hands off of her!'

The voice came from behind Don Wan.

"Get out of here," Don snarled without looking around. "We're talking."

"Leave her alone you stupid son of a bitch," Natalie said. "Can't you see she's not interested?"

Don swung around to face her, his features twisted in anger.

"Why don't you mind your own business, bitch?" he sneered.

Natalie recognized him almost immediately and she paled.

"Oh my god," she said quickly and then recovered. "You son of a bitch. Get away from her before I get the police involved."

"Well, aren't we all high and mighty?" Don said. "Whatcha gonna do? Call Daddy?"

"Worse than that if you don't do as I say," Natalie spat. "I was just a kid when I got you thrown out of town. Think what I could

242

do now that I'm an adult. I'll bet the boys in prison would love to get a crack at you. They don't much like rapists. Now get your filthy hands off her!"

I cowered against the wall as Don glowered at Natalie. "That was you?"

*"Don't just stand there,"* Grace said. *"Go."*

"Come on, Birdie," Natalie said as she reached out for my hand. Her gaze was locked with Don's. "Don't even think about doing anything," she said to him with a stony glare.

"Natalie," I said shakily as I stepped toward her.

"Don't say anything," she murmured, and she pulled me against her. She glared at Don, who glared back.

"We're leaving," she said to him. "In the future, keep your fucking hands to yourself."

She turned and led me back toward the front of the bar.

"I didn't . . . he—" I began.

"I know," she said. At the bar, Sissy, Barbara, and Peggy were finishing their drinks. Grace still paced agitatedly in my head.

"Didja puke?" Sissy yelled, an intoxicated grin smeared across her face.

"Leave her alone, Sissy," Natalie said. Even though she still had her arm around me, I trembled almost violently. Natalie squeezed my shoulders.

"We're leaving," she said and glanced back to where Don still stood.

"But—" Sissy said in protest.

"Now," Natalie said firmly. "You're drunk and we don't belong here."

"Natalie," I mumbled numbly. "He was going to hurt me."

"Shhh," she said in a low voice. "Let's get out of here. We can talk about it later."

We didn't talk about what had happened until after the limo dropped us off at Jacob's Ladder. After Sissy, Barbara, and Peggy left, we climbed into my car.

"He would have hurt me," I mumbled as Natalie started the car and headed toward the blacktopped road. I stared forward, watching the white and yellow lines as we sped along.

"I know," she said.

"I didn't recognize him," I said. "Not until he said my name."

"I'm surprised to see that he's back," Natalie said. "Last I heard he was in California."

"He should be in jail for what he did," I spat. "Grace hates him."

Natalie jerked her head in my direction and frowned.

"What do you mean, 'Grace hates him'?" she asked.

"Hated him," I amended quickly. "She hated him." I shook my head a little too exaggeratedly. "Sorry. Too much to drink."

Natalie nodded.

"There's definitely something wrong with him," she said finally. "Remember those drawings?"

"He said he had been thinking about me since we were kids," I said softly.

"Just bullshit to freak you out," Natalie said.

*Not bullshit,* Grace's voice intoned. *I know what he's capable of.*

"Do you think he could find me?" I asked Natalie. "Everyone in town knows where I live."

"I don't think he's going to come looking for you, if that's what you're worried about," Natalie said. "I think he was just trying to scare you. He's not smart enough to do more than that."

I nodded, unconvinced.

"Besides," she said as she slowed and pulled into the driveway of my mother's house, obviously trying to change the subject. "That's the least of what we need to be thinking about right now. I'm going to get married in less than thirty-six hours."

"Are you excited?" I asked, as she put the car in park.

"Nervous," she said after a pause.

The aftereffects of the alcohol had made me feel fragile and almost unbearably aware of everything around me. Her sadness was palpable and I wanted to pull her into my arms.

"What is it, Nat?" I asked after she didn't elaborate.

"I don't know," she said with a sigh. "I guess I'm just wondering if this is really what I'm supposed to be doing." She shook her head. "It just seems like sometimes I'm living someone else's life. Does that make sense?"

I felt Grace sigh, reminding me that she was watching even when she wasn't participating.

"It does," I said. "But you don't have to do it. You could call it off. You could—" I took a deep breath. "You could come live with me. You could start taking classes and we could live together."

Natalie exhaled deeply.

"Thanks, Bird," she said. "But I can't. I've committed to this and well . . ." She put a hand on her stomach. I saw the thin line of her lips in the muted light of the dashboard. "Even if it doesn't seem like it, this is my life. We have to play the hand we're dealt, right?" Before I could speak, she leaned forward, hugged me tightly to her, and then pulled away. "You okay to get inside?"

The moment, whatever it had been, had passed.

"I'm okay," I said and opened the car door.

"I'll bring your car back to you tomorrow morning," she said.

"I can walk over and get it," I said. "It's only a few blocks.'"

"Either or," she said. "Call me when you get up."

I nodded.

"And get some sleep," she said. "I promise that none of this will look nearly so scary in the morning."

Natalie had been wrong, of course.

And even two days later, as I stood at the front of the church and watched Natalie walk down the aisle to where Pete stood, I knew something in me had changed. I was not like other women. I would never get married, never have children, never be normal.

I found myself studying Natalie's groom as the minister spoke about commitment. Pete was still good-looking but already was becoming a little soft around the edges. He was, I could tell from our brief conversations, a nice man but not very smart. I tried to imagine Natalie's life with him and couldn't. I knew, as did she, that she was settling. She was doing what was expected and ultimately, I suddenly realized, would be just as unhappy as I was.

# Chapter 20

Everything seemed different when I returned to school that next semester. Being home, Natalie's wedding, my encounter with Don Wan at the bar, had changed me—as had my single, brief visit to my grandmother in the nursing home. Tara had told me about her slide into dementia, but to see it was terrifying. The nurse told us as soon as we checked in that Granny was having one of her "bad days."

"Get ready," Mom said as we walked down the hallway which smelled of disinfectant and stale urine. We stepped into a room where a woman sat in a chair by the window. It took me a second to realize this was Granny and not her roommate. She glared at us and pointed a knotty finger in my direction.

"Who are you?" she spat.

I swallowed. My mother and sister had tried to prepare me for this.

"It's Birdie, Mom," my mother said.

Granny narrowed her eyes.

"Here to finish the job, huh?"

I looked at my mother in confusion. She shook her head and moved toward her mother.

"Mother, no one is trying to poison you," she said. "We love you." She looked over her shoulder and motioned for me to come closer.

I swallowed again, though my throat was dry, and walked

toward my grandmother. Creases around her eyes and lips accentuated just how much she had aged. As she studied me, she narrowed her eyes shrewdly.

"They're Nazis," she said. "They pretend to be nurses and doctors, but they're not. They're studying us. Putting things in our food. And once they're done, they're going to send us to the showers."

I nodded slowly, glanced nervously at my mother, but didn't speak. I wasn't sure what to say.

"Mom, you know that's not true," my mother said wearily. She knelt so she was at my grandmother's level and reached to grasp her hand.

"What do you care?" my grandmother asked as she yanked it away, her voice both angry and desperate. "You put me in here to die." She began to weep and I involuntarily stepped backward.

My mother closed her eyes and sighed.

It was a glimpse of what I felt certain I would become. The sound of rushing air filled my ears. *This is me*, I thought almost frantically. *This is me.*

*"No!"*

It was Grace.

*"Turn and leave,"* she said firmly.

I took another step backward.

"I'll wait in the car," I muttered and turned to leave before either of them could stop me. My head down, my eyes trained on the grayish tiles in front of me, I hurried down the hall, turned into the lobby, and pushed open the door. Despite the sharpness of the air, I pulled deep gulps into my lungs and closed my eyes.

"Shit," I said.

*"That's not you,"* Grace said. *"I won't let that become you."*

"Isn't it already?" I murmured. "I hear a dead girl's voice in my head. I'm terrified of *everything*. How is that not me?"

*"You're not crazy,"* Grace said vehemently. *"You're keeping me alive. That's not crazy."*

I raised my eyes to look at the snow-covered corn field that was adjacent to the nursing facility. My breath came out in gray puffs and I was struck by the fact that everything—the field, the sky, my breath—was a shade of grayish-white that looked hauntingly familiar. I shifted my attention to my mother's Mustang. It was locked and I hadn't thought to ask for the keys.

*"You can't stand out here,"* Grace said. *"It's too cold."*

"I can't go back in there," I said.

*"You have to,"* Grace said.

"You don't understand," I said. "It's too hard. She's not my grandmother anymore. She's someone else. She's lost touch with reality."

*"What's reality?"* Grace asked.

I was about to answer when the doors opened and my mother stepped outside.

"You okay?" she asked. "I know seeing her is hard."

I could tell she was upset, too.

"I know you warned me, but I didn't expect that," I said.

"Some days are worse than others," she said. "How about I take you home and you can come see her when she's having a better day?"

She pulled me into a loose, one-armed hug and we began to walk toward the car. It occurred to me how hard it must be for her to see her mother like this.

"How do you stand it?" I asked as she unlocked the passenger-side door.

"You just do," she said softly, her eyes wet with tears as she met my gaze. "When you have no choice, you just do."


I left Edenbridge the day after the wedding and drove as fast as I could to get back to Lincoln and my familiar routine. I buried myself in the comfort of getting up, going to classes, coming home and studying. I say there was comfort, but it was in fact more like numbness—as if I was watching someone else's life play out before my eyes with no real investment in the outcome. I'm not sure how long it would have continued had it not been for Adelle.

"I need a favor," she said one afternoon, a week into the spring semester.

We had met for lunch in one of the school cafeterias and she was squirting ketchup onto her fries. I tried not to think of how many people had touched the bottle before her as I unwrapped the turkey sandwich I'd brought from home.

"Okay," I said and opened the Ziploc bag of pretzels.

"I need you to drive on Sunday," she said. We had plans to go over to Roger's apartment in the late afternoon to watch *Pretty Woman* and drink cheap champagne. "My car died yesterday."

It didn't seem like much of a favor.

"Sure," I said.

"And, I also need you to take me someplace before we go over to Roger's," she said. "I was going to go by myself, but with my car out of commission and the weekend bus route being different, I don't have any way to get there unless I bum a ride."

"Go where?" I asked, suddenly aware from the way she was broaching the subject that it might be a trip I wouldn't enjoy.

"There's a meeting at the rape crisis center," she said. "It's an informational meeting for people who want to volunteer. I was going to go and just meet you guys after." She picked up a couple of fries and smeared them in the pool of ketchup. "You don't have to volunteer," she said as she popped them into her mouth. She spoke around the food. "It should only take about an hour. Please? This is really important to me."

I took a bite of my sandwich and chewed slowly. Going to a meeting about volunteering at a rape crisis shelter was the last thing I wanted to do. But when I saw how much it meant to Adelle, I couldn't refuse.

"Sure," I said finally.

I began to have second thoughts, though, as we drove to the meeting on Sunday afternoon. Adelle smiled and talked as she directed me through the east side of town to the unassuming building that housed the center.

"It's not going to be easy work," Adelle said as we turned onto a side street. "But the thought that I'm going to be helping women makes me feel like what I experienced wasn't in vain." She touched my arm. "Thanks for coming with me. It means a lot to have the support."

"Sure," I said as I tried to fight the anxiety that was rising in my chest.

The meeting room was too warm and smelled like Elmer's glue and dust. Folding chairs were arranged in a circle and a table with coffee and pastries on it was set up along one of the walls. A half-dozen women and two men sat or stood talking in low tones. A young woman in a T-shirt that said "Take Back the Night" came over to us. Her hair was pulled up in a messy bun held in place by a couple of pencils.

"Hi," she said. Her smile was warm as she reached out to shake our hands. "I'm Nancy. Thanks for coming. Help yourself to some snacks and feel free to mingle. We'll get started in about ten minutes."

"Great," Adelle said. "I'm Adelle. We spoke on the phone. And this is my friend, Rebecca."

"Fantastic," Nancy said and reached out to pat me on the shoulder. "We need all the help we can get." She returned her attention to Adelle and was about to say something when another woman entered the room. Her hesitation suggested that she, too, was a potential volunteer. Nancy smiled at the woman and then turned back to us.

"Make yourselves at home," she said. "I need to go say hello."

We walked toward the coffee table and Adelle poured herself a cup from the silver coffee urn.

"Want one?" she asked.

I shook my head and turned to look at the people sitting in the circle of folding chairs. There were only two men. One of them looked like a hippie with grungy-looking clothes, longish hair, and a beard. The other man, however, looked oddly familiar. He was thin, with dark curly hair and bright blue eyes. I stared at him, trying to figure out how I knew him. It must have been from one of my classes, I decided as, unexpectedly, he met and held my gaze. I looked away though I could still feel his eyes on me. Tentatively, I glanced back at his face. His expression was thoughtful as he studied me.

"Want to sit?"

I realized Adelle was talking to me. I nodded and we moved to chairs that were directly across from the dark-haired man. I tried to appear nonchalant, though I wanted more than anything to study him.

"Rebecca, are you okay?"

I looked sideways at her. "Yeah, why?"

She leaned toward me and said in a low voice, "You seem uncomfortable." She hesitated. "You know, if this isn't for you, you don't have to do it. Just the fact that you came today with me means a lot."

I nodded and was about to speak just as Nancy moved to the edge of the circle and cleared her throat. "If we could get started." It was more of a statement than a question and the group grew silent.

"First, I'd like to thank you all for coming today." She smiled at each of us. "I know you all are busy, which makes it mean even more."

There was a low murmur as several of the volunteers nodded and spoke soft words of agreement.

"We all have different reasons for wanting to volunteer." It was clear Nancy was beginning her spiel. "Some of us are survivors of domestic abuse or rape." She held up a hand as if to say that was the category to which she belonged. "Others of us know a woman who is a survivor—a friend, a sister, a lover."

She paused to let her words sink in.

Adelle turned to me and smiled. I gave her a weak smile and glanced over at the dark-haired man. Our eyes met briefly before he quickly looked away as if embarrassed.

"—challenging work," Nancy was saying. "You're going to hear stories that are heartbreaking. Women are going to be turning to you in their darkest hours and it's important to remain calm and remember that they need your help."

Several people nodded.

"It also goes without saying that there are rules about privacy. You will all have to undergo background checks and sign confidentiality agreements. Whatever you hear or do here at the center cannot be shared with your friends or family. These women have been violated already. Do I make myself clear?"

Everyone nodded and Nancy smiled as if relieved to have that part of her speech out of the way.

"Okay." She turned to her chair where paper-clipped packets of paper were stacked. "If you'll all just take one of these and turn to the second page."

The meeting went on for about an hour although I already knew within the first ten minutes that I would not be volunteering. It was too real—too emotional and raw. It reminded me too much of Grace. And that's when I realized she hadn't said a word—hadn't given me any kind of sign that she was there. It was surprising and quite honestly, unnerving. I was used to having her in my head.

I contemplated this as we pulled out of the parking lot and turned in the direction of Roger's apartment.

"So?" Adelle asked. "What did you think?"

"I think it's a really great program," I said absently, my thoughts still on Grace.

"But you're not going to volunteer, are you?"

I shook my head, still not meeting her gaze.

"I am," she said. "I was talking with Nancy and I think I could make a difference."

"I think you'll be great at it."

We drove in silence.

"Becca," Adelle began. "Can I ask you something?" I felt my body tense. I knew I wasn't going to like her question. "Did something happen to you when you were younger? Were you abused?"

I felt the intensity of her gaze and forced myself to focus on the road. "No," I said more harshly than I had intended. "Why would you ask that?"

Her response was slow and careful. "I don't know. Just stuff you say or do—or don't say—that makes me wonder. You never really talk about growing up or your hometown. You don't really date. I just wondered if—"

"No," I said vehemently. "I wasn't abused."

"I'm sorry. I shouldn't have asked. I just—"

"It's okay." I wondered suddenly if Roger had shared my drunken confession. I pressed down on the left turn blinker and pulled into the parking lot of Roger's apartment building.

"I believe you," she said as I navigated the Buick into a parking

252

spot. She waited until I put the car in park and turned off the engine before she continued. "I don't need to know anything more than what you want to tell me." She took a deep breath. "I just appreciate you going with me today. I know you went to support me."

Finally, I met her gaze. Her expression was earnest as she reached out and squeezed my arm.

"We all have things we keep to ourselves," she said. "That's fine. I respect it. Just know that if you decide you want to share your stories, there are people who care. I care."

I pressed my lips together and nodded tightly. Adelle waited and in that moment, I seriously considered telling her what had happened. But then, as quickly as it had presented itself, the moment had passed.

As was always the case, I was my own worst enemy.

# Chapter 21

I wasn't prepared for what would happen after college. I had the vague impression that I would get an unexciting but secure job with a large corporation, where I would work my way up the corporate ladder. While there, I would meet a decent man, and we would marry and buy a house in a safe suburb. We would have two, maybe three, children and everything would be better. Normal. And, as my life fell into place, I hoped that my phobias would fade and I would be . . . normal. I would be like everyone else.

Like most things in my life, it turned out not to be quite that easy. Despite graduating and moving to Kansas City, not much changed. I hadn't anticipated the impact that my somewhat strange lifestyle would have on life in the real world. Unlike college classes, you can't simply skip work. And although I was able to conquer my fears and put on a front long enough to get a job, keeping it proved to be much more difficult.

I had managed to get an entry-level job as an accounts manager for Associated Wholesale Grocers, a distributor in Kansas City. Given that the city was shared by both Kansas and Missouri, I opted for an apartment in Overland Park, a suburb on the Kansas side. The one-bedroom apartment was in a quiet, recently developed part of town, where everything from the houses to the apartment complexes seemed to have been designed by the same architect.

Roger liked neither my choice of apartments nor my job.

"What are you thinking? Sales? You couldn't even leave the house to go to class. You're scared to shake people's hands for fear you'll get something. Do you really think driving around the city and interacting with people is what you need to be doing?"

"No," I said. "But that's the point. This job will force me to face my fears. It will put me in a position where I have to get out and interact with people. Yes, it involves driving around, but just around Kansas City. And, it's not sales. I am servicing accounts."

"Honey," Roger said, "Trust me when I tell you it's sales."

Roger was partially right. The job did turn out to be somewhat more sales-oriented than I had envisioned, but it also entailed customer service and helping people with their accounts. I didn't like it, but I didn't hate it. It was just part of a carefully constructed life through which I moved cautiously. Each day I would force myself to get up, leave my apartment, and interact with people. Each night I would watch television or read until it was time to go to bed.

I had come to dread bedtime. Sleep continued to be elusive and when it did come, often it brought with it unwelcome dreams that were sometimes so vivid and real, that I awoke breathless. Other times they were supernatural and warped, like lingering manifestations of my experience with LSD. I never knew what to expect. So I lay in bed, waiting and worrying and imagining worst-case scenarios. It was during these dark, lonely hours that I missed my friends the most.

That's not to say they weren't attentive—they were. As was my family. But they also had their own lives. My father continued to remain distant, but Tara and my mother called once a week. Tara was dating a guy she had met in one of her community college classes and my mother was happily working as an "intake specialist" for a women's clinic in Winston. There she helped women with everything from pregnancies to counseling about domestic abuse.

"You wouldn't believe the bumper stickers she has on her car," Tara said one night as we talked on the telephone. "Equality-this, domestic abuse-that. I'm almost embarrassed to ride with her. She's as bad as Granny. I'm beginning to think that insanity runs in our family. Granny was loony as a fruitcake and now Mom's over the top with all of this. You know she's talking about becoming a pagan, don't you?"

"A pagan," I said. "What's that?"

"It's kind of like being a witch, but they're not evil. They're all about nature and flowers and energies. They dress up in black and have—I don't know what you call them—meetings, maybe? They're outside and they dance and chant and honor the passing of seasons or something."

"Wow," I said, unsure as to how to respond.

"It's like this all-woman thing," Tara said and then continued in a stage whisper. "I'm worried she's going to become a lesbian."

I scoffed.

"Mom?" I asked. "No way."

"Well, she didn't much like Dad," Tara said. "And lots of the women in her coven, or whatever it's called, are gay."

"Yeah, well," I said and then paused. "Have you talked to him lately?"

"I called the other day," she said. "I talked to Judy long enough to find out he wasn't there."

Judy was our father's new live-in girlfriend. She had a daughter named Liza and managed a Red Lobster. According to Tara, that's where they met. My father had gone in for the all-you-can-eat shrimp and came out with a girlfriend. Aside from that, we knew very little about her.

"Oh," I said. "How's Andy?"

"Great," she said, the smile evident in her voice. "We're talking about moving in together."

"Wow," I said. "That's great. But aren't you concerned about how messy he is? And the hair in the shower and stuff?"

Tara laughed. It had a pure, tinkling quality to it that made me smile.

"No," she said. "That's part of being in a relationship. Besides, he's not that messy." She hesitated. "You should come and visit. I'd like you to meet him."

"Yeah," I said vaguely. "Maybe when things calm down here. Right now—"

"I know," she said in a tired monotone. "Work is busy."

The conversation lagged.

"Well . . ." Tara finally said. "I guess I should let you go."

"Yeah," I said. "We'll talk soon?"

"Sure," she said. "Bye Bird."

I thought often about that conversation—about what had been said and what hadn't. There was as much communication in silence as there was in words.

There is a difference between being alone and being lonely. When you're alone, there's no one around. I'm comfortable with that—and in many ways, actually prefer it. But after college, I became lonely. Not surprisingly, my friends moved on with their lives. Adelle, after about a year of struggling with the aftermath of the rape, pulled her life together with renewed purpose. She finished her degree in public administration and then took the LSAT. Her score, combined with her grades and community service, allowed her to take her pick of law schools. She briefly considered the Ivy League schools, but ultimately decided that being close to family and the issues of women's poverty, urban blight, and crimes against women as a result of these circumstances, were more important than a highbrow education.

Roger, too, moved on in search of his dream.

"I want to do big, bold, edgy interior designs," he said one Sunday exactly a month after graduation. And so, immediately after graduation, he moved to Chicago. For the first month, while he looked for work, he lived out of his car, washing in convenience store restrooms and showering at the apartments of men he met at bars, who either took him home or simply took pity on him. One of these was Duane Coston, a struggling interior designer who worked out of his apartment.

"Guess what?" Roger had a habit of calling at two or three in the morning after he returned from the bars, and this night was no exception. "I have an apprenticeship! With Duane Coston! Can you believe it?"

"No. Congratulations! Who is Duane Coston?"

"Duane Coston," Roger said exaggeratedly, "is only one of the brightest young talents in design. Granted, he's just starting out and his work is still becoming known, but the minute we met, I knew there was a connection. And after we started to talk, it became clear we had to work together." He paused to take a hit off of a cigarette or a joint. "The pay isn't great." The words sounded pinched, and then he exhaled. "But the experience will more than make up for it. And, it includes a place to live."

It was only years later that I learned that the "apprenticeship" was, in fact, unpaid and the "place to live" was either on the floor of Duane's workshop or in his bed, depending on whether or not he and Roger were getting along. Still, the experience was a stepping-stone and he used it to his full advantage. Working together, they began to make names for themselves. Periodically, Roger would send write-ups from local publications featuring their work. Their look was sharp, metallic, and industrial. Cement, found industrial parts, and cables were the backbone of their designs and quickly, they became known for not only how they designed rooms, but also their eclectic incorporation of unknown artists and sculptors.

I was much less successful. While everyone else moved forward with their lives, I seemed to remain perpetually stuck in the same place. I forced myself to go to work and to interact, but every day was torture. I always locked my car doors, always carried Handi Wipes for use after I shook hands with strangers, and always made sure to be home before it was dark. There, I would watch television or read until it was time to try unsuccessfully to go to sleep.

Nighttime was the worst for me and that, more than any other reason, was why I revisited painting. Without the influence of hallu-cinogenic drugs, it was less intense and much more cathartic. Though the experience was different, the end result was the same. To say my work was abstract was being generous. Often, the images that grew out of the paper had no particular shape or discernable features. They were spirals or mazes, shapes and curves. Sometimes they were just black lines or slashes of color. Other times, they were cool, foggy grays and blues.

Often, as they dried, I would stare at the images, scrutinizing them for clues as to what demons I was exorcising. Rarely did I come to any conclusions. Rather, each new work would end up in the closet along with my previous failures.

I was standing in front of my easel the night that Roger called with the news that would change everything. I was in a pair of paint-smeared sweat bottoms and a threadbare Edenbridge T-shirt, brush in hand, scrutinizing a painting of a broken violin-like figure when the phone rang. Knowing it could only be bad news or Roger, I picked up the receiver.

"Hi, doll!" It was Roger. I glanced at the digital clock and saw it was 2:30 a.m. The bars must have just closed. Hopefully he wasn't too drunk this time to carry on a coherent conversation.

"Hey Rog. What are you doing?"

"We just got back from the bars and lemme tell ya—" he laughed and I could imagine him flipping his hand in an exaggerated gesture. I sighed; he was well over his limit.

"Had a good time, did you?" I stepped back to study the lines I had just put on the paper.

"The best!" His words were slightly slurred. "We were celebrating."

"Oh, yeah? Celebrating what?"

Roger feigned nonchalance. "Oh, just our tremendous coup."

"What coup?" I asked, suddenly paying attention.

"Just redesigning the loft of an extremely wealthy Chicago icon who could very well make our careers." He paused. "There's just one hitch. I need a teensy-weensy, itsy-bitsy favor from you."

"Okay," I said cautiously.

"Do you remember the night you got that acid from that guy at the club?"

I put down my brush and reached for the paint-smeared Solo cup from which I drank red wine while I painted. "As I recall, 'that guy's' name was Douglas and he was supposed to be the great love of your life."

Roger snorted. "Anyway, do you remember the paintings that you did? The ones while you were, um, indisposed?"

I looked at the painting I was currently working on. It wasn't that much of an improvement from my initial attempts.

"Uh huh . . ."

"Well," he continued. "You remember how you said I could have them—the ones that I didn't throw away."

I thought back to the day after I had taken the LSD. I remembered that we had ordered pizza and that he had offered to throw the paintings away in his dumpster so no one would know they were mine, but I didn't remember giving him permission to take them.

"Actually, I think I would have remembered saying that. I thought you said you would throw them away for me."

"I did say that," he said quickly. "But then I asked if I could take some of them and you said 'yes.'"

"I don't think—"

"Well," he interrupted, "I kept them. All of them. And I have been using them in some of my more funky designs. You know, when I do stagings."

"You've done what?" I backed away from the easel and sank into the wicker chair I used to sit in and study my paintings as they dried.

"I, uh, have used several of them in my designs and they're, well, they're a hit," he said and rushed on enthusiastically. "Isn't that great? Everyone says you have a natural gift for the surreal. Especially the one with the eye. I've used it several times."

Immediately, my mind returned to that night and again I saw the eye, Grace's eye, jumping off the paper and scurrying under the bed.

"Please tell me you're joking."

"Becca." His tone was placating. "It wasn't like I intended to sell you out. I just . . . I needed something creepy and different and I knew that was it. And then I used another one of them and then people started, I don't know, paying attention. And then one thing led to another and pretty soon people were asking to buy them and wanting to meet the artist."

I stared at the wall in stunned disbelief.

"Becca."

"Don't call me Becca," I snapped.

"Rebecca," he said quickly. "I'm sorry. I know it was wrong. I know it's a violation. I know that you hate me right now and I'm sorry that I called you 'Becca.' But you need to listen to me. I need your help."

My laugh was short and brittle. "You have got to be kidding

me. There is no way in hell I would help you. In fact, I'm hanging up now."

"No! Please, wait. Just hear me out. Your work, your art, is a hit. People want it. They want to pay for it. The guy—the one I told you about that hired us? He wants to buy some of your work. He's a private collector and, well, I sort of told him that I represent you."

"No."

"Rebecca, I needed to make an impression—to get in good with him. I told him you had a collection—that you had other pieces for sale. I know you've been painting."

"No."

"Rebecca, please."

"Do you have any idea what you've done—I mean, aside from violating my trust, stomping all over our friendship, and taking my most vulnerable and raw self and putting it on display for the world to see? Actually, no. You didn't just put it on display, you auctioned it off to the highest bidder. I really am hanging up now."

And I did.

Over the next several weeks, Roger was relentless in his attempts to convince me that he was sorry. Messages on my answering machine, messages left for me at work, and even a registered letter didn't make a difference. I was resolved to never speak to him again. And then I had my first acid flashback.

I was sitting on the couch salvaged from our college apartment, petting Spencer, the fat, long-haired black cat that belonged to my upstairs neighbor. When he wasn't busy patrolling the apartment complex, Spencer made it his job to visit each of the cat-friendly residents of our building. This evening, he lay purring in my lap, his tummy full of canned tuna. *ER* was on the television and George Clooney was acting alternately indignant and sheepish. At least, he was until his words became slow and distorted and his face went from handsome to maggot-infested and then skeletal. Panicked, I began to breathe heavily. My blood pulsed in my ears. My eyes darted around the room. The few pieces of furniture and my CD collection seemed to be as they should be. But then, out of the corner of my eye, I saw a dark shape about the size of my fist scuttle along the baseboard and down the hallway toward my bedroom.

*"It's your past coming back to haunt you,"* said a voice. I looked down to see Spencer staring at me.

"Spencer?" I spoke his name aloud.

*"I can read your thoughts,"* he said, though his lips weren't moving. *"I know what you're thinking."*

I stared at him for several seconds, unsure. "You're a cat," I said. "You can't know what I'm thinking."

*"Oh, but I can,"* he said. *"Right now, you're wondering what's going on and you're wondering how we're talking when my lips aren't moving."*

I stared. That had been exactly what I had been thinking.

*"I'm communicating telepathically."*

"Really?" I asked. "You can do that?"

*"I can. And I can also see into the future. You're going to get a phone call."*

At that moment, my phone began to ring.

I blinked in amazement, looked over at the small table where the cordless phone was charging and then back at Spencer. "How did you know?"

*"It's all interconnected. The past, the present, the future."* I felt him mentally shrug. *"You need to deal with your past so you can move on with your future."* He blinked slowly and looked over at the ringing phone. *"And you need to answer that."*

I hurried over to the table, snatched the handset off the charger, and pushed the Talk button. "Hello?"

"Rebecca." It was Roger. "Please don't hang up. We need to talk."

I turned away from the table and looked back at Spencer, who was curled up, his eyes closed, sound asleep. The characters on the television were once again normal. Nothing in the apartment moved. It was as if nothing out of the ordinary had happened.

I suddenly became aware of Roger's voice in my ear. "—huge mistake and I'm sorry. Your friendship means more to me than advancing my career. You were right. What I did was wrong."

"Roger," I said distractedly, "I can't talk about this now. Something is wrong with me."

"Are you okay?" His concern sounded genuine. "What's wrong?"

"It's just . . ." It was as if the previous ten minutes hadn't happened even though my heart continued to thump rapidly. "I think I'm going crazy."

"What do you mean?" he asked cautiously. "What happened?"

I took a deep, calming breath. "I just was sitting here petting the neighbor's cat and watching TV and . . . the cat started talking to me telepathically. And the people on the television, their faces began to melt off. It was like that night all over again, but I haven't taken anything."

Roger laughed.

"It's not funny, Roger. I think I've finally—"

"You're having an acid flashback."

"A what?"

"A flashback. When you have a brief flash *back* to the acid experience."

"Back to that night," I said slowly.

"Yeah, unless you did acid some other time I don't know about. You didn't, did you?"

"So I'm not going crazy?" On the couch, Spencer, his eyes still closed, rolled onto his side and stretched his legs, toes spread, and yawned.

"It's not typical, but it happens sometimes. It happened to me, if that makes you feel better."

"Is it awful of me to say it does?"

Roger laughed softly. "No."

Neither of us spoke for several seconds until Roger cleared his throat. "So, Rebecca, I'm sorry. I shouldn't have done that without asking you."

I walked over to the counter that separated the kitchen area from the living room and took the lid off of the cut glass candy dish that no one else had wanted from my grandmother's house. I picked out several blue M&M's. On the couch, Spencer lazily began to lick his paw and rub it across his face.

"It's still not okay," I said with a sigh. I hated being angry with Roger. "And I'm still not over being upset with you, but I accept your apology."

"Thank you," I could hear the relief in his voice. "And I want you to know that I'm going to tell Daddy Warbucks that there is no collection and what he's seen isn't for sale. I don't care how much he's willing to pay for it."

"What do you mean?" I put the candies in my mouth and tried not to crunch too loudly.

"He just really wanted the pieces. I think he thought I was playing hard to get, so he just kept raising his offer."

More out of curiosity than actual interest, I asked, "How much?"

"Not a lot up front," Roger said. "But when you throw in the fact that he wants to sponsor a show so he can get first crack at the new work and then encourage his friends to buy so the value of his investment goes up—it's a lot of money. But I'm going to tell him 'no.'" He was quiet for several seconds and then began a fresh assault. "It just seemed like a win-win, you know? You could make a lot of money without doing sales."

"It's not sales," I said. "I'm an accounts manager. There's a difference."

"I know, I know. Sorry. But it's a moot point anyway." I heard the clink of ice and the sound of him swallowing. "So, are we good? Because, you know I love you and would hate to lose you. I'd do anything for you."

"We're good. It's awful when we fight."

"Thanks, *Becca*. I'll take that as an 'I missed you, too.'"

"Uh huh." I reached into the candy dish and picked out three more blue M&M's. "So, will you lose the job or project or whatever it's called?"

"It's not important," he said quickly. "We're thinking about going in a new direction, anyway. Duane is trying to incorporate a Zen dimension to our industrial aesthetic. He's calling it Yin-Yang Industrial Fusion. Calm and edgy. Balance and all that crap."

I laughed. "'Balance and all that crap' doesn't sound very Zen. What brought this on?"

"Oh, he's hanging around with this Tibetan monk or something, and so now everything is feng shui this and energy that." He sighed. "I've been thinking about trying to scrounge up the money to go out on my own. Duane is too temperamental."

"Gay men."

"Gay men," he agreed. "So, listen, I've got to run. We're going out."

"Of course you are." I laughed. "I appreciate the apology."

"I had it coming, baby cakes. I was an insensitive, selfish asshole. But I really have to go. Duane is giving me 'the look.' We'll talk this weekend, okay?"

He hung up before I could answer.

"Asshole," I muttered as I hit the End button with my thumb and turned to look at Spencer. He stopped licking himself long enough to regard me with wide, open eyes. "So, tell me the truth, can you really hear my thoughts?" He blinked and returned to his bath. I set the phone on the counter, walked over to the couch and settled back into my spot.

*ER* had been replaced by the news, so I picked up the remote and turned off the television. In the apartment above me, I could hear the squeak and thump of footsteps. I patted Spencer's back and thought about the conversation with Roger. His explanation, although by no means a justification, made sense. He was hungry for success and I didn't doubt that he was planning on using his half of the money to break away from Duane. And clearly he was trying to entice me with the mention of money.

Despite myself, I wondered how much. Enough that I could find a job that didn't require as much interaction with people? Something that wasn't sales? I shook my head at what I was considering.

"This is crazy," I said to Spencer.

He blinked, and I wondered if he really could communicate telepathically. I tentatively searched my mind for Grace. Nothing. She had been strangely absent the past few weeks, but something

265

told me that if what I was considering was dangerous, she would warn me, right?

"So, what do you think?" I asked Spencer as I stroked his back. "Do you think Roger's right? I mean, it's not like I don't have a closet full of the stuff, right? And it's not like I have to ever see it again. Once I sell it, it's gone." I searched again for Grace. Nothing.

Spencer purred under my hand and the warm rumble calmed me. I hated my job. It was exhausting to go out every day and *be* with people. The idea of being able to make money doing something that didn't require the social interaction was tempting—perhaps too tempting because before I could stop myself, I stood, walked to the counter, and picked up the phone. Deep breaths, I told myself as I dialed Roger's number.

"Roger," I said when his machine picked up. "Listen, I've been thinking about what you said and I'm not saying yes, but tell me more about what you have in mind."

# Part III:
## 2001–2004

## Chapter 22

John Lennon had it right when he said "life happens while you're busy making other plans." It's true. I had never intended to become an artist. I'm still not sure I even consider myself one. But, under Roger's management, and thanks to Gus's desire to make money, that's exactly what I became.

"Never doubt the power of the gay network," Roger said, and he was right.

Augustin Dupré, known by many simply as Gus, was the owner of several gay-exclusive nightclubs and restaurants. The product of "Old Southern money," Gus was excused from family activities and holdings in Louisiana because of his sexual orientation and his penchant for barely legal boys. In exchange for his promise to "get gone and stay quiet," he was provided with a sizeable allowance, which he spent freely.

He managed "gone" with great success but struggled with the "quiet" element of the agreement. Gus moved first to New Orleans and then to Los Angeles, where he quickly became a fixture in the party scene. Young, handsome, and full of Southern charm, he also possessed the family skill of recognizing opportunities and making money. What began as investments in clubs and restaurants later became outright purchases and, with complete renovations and the knack for appealing to the exclusive, chic Hollywood set, enormously successful business ventures. He had just begun his expansion into Chicago when he met Roger and Duane at a party.

"He wants to bring West Coast fabulous to the Midwest," Roger enthused late one night. "It's going to be amazing. And, he believes that we, well, I have just the right combination of skills and connections."

"So, explain how I fit into this?" I asked. "I'm not even really an artist. My work is crap."

269

"One man's trash and all that," Roger said. "Just trust me when I tell you that he saw your work, recognized it as unique, and saw an opportunity. And here's the great part: he thought they would be the perfect addition not only to his personal collection, but also in the private suites in his new establishment."

"What is this new establishment?" I asked.

"It's a club," Roger said. "An exclusive club and that's really all you need to know. I'm going to handle all the details. All you have to do is continue to produce those amazing canvases."

And, surprisingly, Roger *did* handle all the details. He negotiated the deals, handled all the shipping, and in the process, made himself a force to be reckoned with. Granted, it didn't hurt that he also was sleeping with Gus. But still, that didn't detract from the fact that Roger's designs were interesting and certainly different than anything anyone else was doing.

After our initial reconciliation, Roger flew to Kansas City and spent a long weekend. We talked, laughed, and made up properly. And when he left, he also took most of the paintings from my closet. The agreement was simple. He would use what he wanted in his designs and in return, give me all the profits from their sales. Also, he would act as my manager without charge.

"You're doing me a favor," he said. "Gus really wants the paintings and I really want Gus. He's willing to pay and quite honestly . . . if Gus wants it, Gus gets it. And, he makes sure other people want it."

And he was right.

With Gus as a patron and Roger as a manager, my job was nothing more than what I had been doing previously without financial compensation. There were a few nonnegotiable rules. First and foremost, my identity could never be revealed. Roger agreed, and together we crafted an elaborate story in which I was portrayed as a reclusive, tortured genius who simply went by BEC. It seemed like the perfect cover and, aside from the genius part, not too far removed from the truth. If anything, my reclusiveness only added to my mystique. Secondly, under no circumstances would I attend a show or event. I worked alone, out of my home, and once I had relinquished a canvas, I never wanted to see it again.

My mother was thrilled when I told her I was planning a career change.

"Oh, Birdie, that's great. I never thought sales was the best fit for you."

"It's not sales," I responded automatically. "But it doesn't matter because with this new job, I don't have to be out working with the public. I can work from home."

"Oh."

"What?"

"Nothing." She was quiet and then said, "It's just, are you sure that's what you should be doing? I mean, you don't really get out much as it is and—"

"Mom, please, can we not go into this right now? I know what you're going to say, but can't you please just be happy for me?"

"Oh, sweetie," she said. "I *am* happy for you. I just worry, that's all. I want you to be happy." She hesitated and then said, "So, what's this new job? Phone sales or . . ." I could imagine her sitting in the kitchen on the tall, wooden stool under the wall-mounted phone, coiling the cord around her fingers.

"It's—" I stopped. How could I explain what I would be doing? I imagined just blurting out the truth: *Well, you see, Mom, when I was in college, my friend was raped and it messed me up. So my friend Roger, the gay man, forced me to see a shrink, who suggested I paint away my fears. But I was blocked creatively, so I took a hit of LSD from this guy I met in a gay bar and when I tripped, Grace manifested herself and I started doing freaky-ass paintings of all the messed up shit in my head. Roger saw them, took them and managed to convince people they were artistic and so now I'm going to be paid to take all the crap in my head and put it on a canvas to be hung in gay bars.*

I laughed.

"What?"

"Nothing. I've been painting some since college and Roger—"

"Painting," my mother interrupted. "You've been painting? Like watercolors? Or landscapes? Or—since when have you been painting?"

"I took a class in college," I lied. "The professor said I had talent.

271

It's just a hobby, really. Or, it was. But Roger's friend, or boss, liked it and bought some pieces. And he has friends who he thinks would want to buy some, too. So, I thought I'd give it a try."

"Birdie, I had no idea. I'd love to see them. Can you send pictures?"

"Oh." I thought of the subject matter. "Actually, I already sent the canvases. And I haven't started the new work, yet."

"Are you sure you want to quit your job for this?" she asked. "It seems awfully risky. I mean, do you know this man very well?"

"I think it's something I need to try. And if it doesn't work out, I can get a new job."

"Well, you know you're always welcome here. We can fix up your room and it would be like you never left."

My stomach knotted at the thought. Short visits to Edenbridge had almost been too much for me to bear. The thought of living there for any extended period of time made me want to throw up. I swallowed and spoke in a calm voice. "Thanks, Mom. But I don't think I'll need to do that."

My next call was to Natalie.

"Seriously?" she asked. "How amazing is that? You're going to be a famous artist. Just think, your work is going to be displayed—"

"In nightclubs," I interrupted. "Don't make this more than it is. It's not as glamorous as it sounds."

"But still, Birdie, you're following your dream. Remember when we were kids? All you did was draw." Her tone was wistful and I knew what she was thinking. She never said as much, but I knew that she wasn't entirely committed to the idea of marrying Pete. Still, she had gone through with the wedding and a few months later, she had given birth to their daughter, Margaret Grace, whom everyone called Meg. Although she had assumed the role of stay at home mom without complaint, I knew it wasn't the life Natalie had envisioned for herself.

"Yeah," I said. "Sounds perfect, eh?"

"But won't you get lonely?" she asked and then quickly amended, "I mean, I know you don't go out much, but at least with your job now, you interact with people."

I felt Grace smile. Although she had been relatively silent regarding this new endeavor, I had felt her there, watching, listening, always vaguely present. And she was always interested in my phone calls home—especially to Natalie.

"You know, I think it will be fine," I said. "Let's face it. I'm better when I'm on my own, doing my own thing."

"What I wouldn't give for some time alone," Natalie said. I could hear the sadness in her voice. "I don't know the last time I had any time that was just mine."

"Are you sorry you did it?" I had always wanted to ask before now, but never got up the nerve. "That you got married and . . . you know."

Rather than answer, Natalie sighed. I waited, but she didn't continue. Instead, she changed the subject. "So, now that you're going to have more time, you should come visit. You could stay with us, spend time with me and Meg. Pete's never really here with his work schedule, so it would be just us. Like it used to be—well, like it used to be plus a toddler."

"Maybe," I said, intentionally keeping my tone neutral. "Could we play it by ear? It's just that I think these first few months are going to be pretty busy and, well . . . you know. But if I can, I will."

Natalie made a noise that could mean anything, although I recognized it as disappointment.

"I will," I insisted, knowing even as I said it that it was a lie.

"I just miss you," Natalie said softly. "I miss us. I—" She stopped abruptly and I heard the muffled sound of conversation. She had apparently covered the mouthpiece of the receiver. I listened harder, trying to make out what I assumed were Pete's words. Suddenly, Natalie was back on the line. "Listen, Birdie, I need to let you go. Pete just got home and wants something to eat. We'll talk later?"

"Yeah," I said. "And, hey, Nat, before you go . . . I . . . I miss you, too."

I waited for a reply but the line was silent. And then I realized why. She had already hung up.

At first, the money from my artwork wasn't significant. But after the initial purchases by Gus, his promotion to his friends of my work, and a decent inheritance following my grandmother's death, I was not only able to quit my job but also to make the leap into home ownership. I considered Kansas City, but ultimately, I made the decision to go someplace that was completely different—someplace where anonymity wasn't considered strange. I purchased a small cabin in the mountains outside of La Veta, Colorado.

A town of about 1,000 people at the foot of one of the Spanish Peaks, La Veta was the perfect blend of small town familiarity and pioneering independence. It was originally established as a stopover for a branch of the Santa Fe Trail that led into the San Luis Valley via the Sangre de Cristo Pass. But as people settled in the area, what started out as a utilitarian adobe fort became a shelter against the Indians and, eventually, a center of commerce. As the railroad came and went, the town grew, shrank, and eventually became an enclave of ranchers, artists, and people with summer homes—which was what my cabin was prior to purchase.

Most of the cabins outside of La Veta were small and utilitarian, and mine was no exception. It wasn't big and it certainly wasn't fancy, but its location on an isolated gravel road gave me complete privacy. For extra security and companionship, I adopted a dog from the humane society in Trinidad. Part greyhound, part yellow Lab, and part mutt, Toby was the perfect roommate. He was smart, gentle, and big enough that people were wary when they approached him.

Life at the cabin was slow and unchanging. My days were spent doing chores and odd jobs around the house and my nights watching documentaries on satellite television, e-mailing friends and family, and, of course, painting. Visitors were rare. During the first three years, my mother and sister came to visit twice. The first time was when I was in the process of moving. I had gone to the rental agency for the moving van and when I returned to the apartment complex parking lot, I found Tara and my mother sitting in the car with a box of cake donuts and paper cups of convenience store coffee.

"Surprise!" cried Tara as I climbed out of the cab of the truck. She rushed over and hugged me. "Say hello to your moving crew!"

"Hi," I said and looked at Mom, who handed me a cup of coffee. "We're here to help," she said. "Tara called last night and we decided to throw a couple of bags in the car and come help you move."

I blinked, touched at their kindness, but also nervous about having them see and handle all my things. "Wow. Thanks. I don't know what to say."

Tara grinned. "It's silly that you didn't hire movers or ask anyone to help." She held up her hands. "I know, I know, you don't want people touching your stuff. But the more I thought about it, the more I thought, 'Hey, what about us?' And this way, we'll get to see your new place and spend some time together. What do you think?"

"It's great," I said with forced enthusiasm, glad that I had shipped most of the canvases off to Roger and carefully wrapped the others in plain brown paper.

"This way, we can take turns driving and riding with you," my mother said and gestured to the rental truck. "Is that going to be big enough? And what are you going to do with your car?"

I turned to look at the truck. "It'll be big enough. I don't really have all that much stuff. I left my car at the rental place and once I get everything loaded, I'm going to go back and they're going to hook up a trailer and load the car on for me."

My mother looked at Tara and then back at me. "And how were you going to get it off by yourself? It could crush you or you could slip and fall under the hitch-thing." She shook her head. "And honestly, to think about you driving alone, hauling a car through those mountains . . . well, it's just dangerous."

"Mom," I said. "La Veta is barely in the mountains. It's the southern edge of the Rockies."

"Still, you can't do it alone. And we're not going to let you."

I looked helplessly at Tara, who shrugged, grinned, and clapped her hands together. "Okay, then. Let's get cracking."

And, as it turned out, their help proved to be invaluable—both with loading the van in Kansas City and then unloading it when we got to the cabin. When I refused to let them drive the truck, they took turns riding with me while the other followed in my sister's Toyota.

"So . . . are you excited?" Tara asked as we crossed over the Kansas state line into eastern Colorado. "It's going to be a whole new life—a fresh start."

I nodded without taking my eyes off the highway. "I am. It will be nice to just settle in and do my own thing."

"Mom's worried."

"Why now?" I glanced sideways at Tara.

"She thinks you're going to become a hermit or become so isolated in the mountains that you're going to go crazy. Of course, she's got no room to talk. She's as crazy as you are." She gasped as soon as the words came out of her mouth. "Oh, Birdie, I didn't mean that like it sounded."

"No, I know what you meant."

"That came out wrong," she insisted. "I just meant that she has her quirks, too. Just like we all do."

"It's okay," I said. "I know that my behavior seems strange to other people." I shrugged. "It's just how I am."

Neither of us spoke for several minutes and the only sound in the cab of the truck was the growl of the diesel engine and the rhythmic thunk-thunk of the tires as they passed over the highway expansion joints.

"When did you change?" Tara asked suddenly. "You weren't like this when we were kids."

I jerked my head to look at her. I had been lost in my own thoughts of how I was going to decorate the cabin once I had unpacked everything. Her face was concerned and serious. Her eyes were wide and I noticed again just how effortlessly pretty she was. When I didn't answer, she raised her eyebrows as if to say, *Well?*

I shrugged and returned my gaze to the highway. "We all change as we grow up. It's part of life."

"Hmm," she said, making it clear she wasn't satisfied with the answer.

We drove again in silence.

"Mom said it was when Grace was murdered." Tara's tone was gentle but persistent. "I sort of remember it, but not really. Mostly what I remember is being scared. And your nightmares."

I glanced at her and then returned my attention to the road.

"I asked Mom about it."

"Oh?" I tried to appear casual.

"She said it was like one of her own kids had died. And, she said she wished she had done something for Grace." She leaned forward and reached into a shopping bag between her feet for the chips she'd bought at our last gas stop. "I think that's when she changed, too."

"What do you mean?"

"She used to be so, I don't know. It's like her Mustang. She got that car after Dad—"

"Traded her convertible for that damned pickup." We had both heard the story so often it was a familiar refrain. We both laughed, united for a moment in our shared history.

"But you know what I mean," Tara continued. "She loved that car and then suddenly she traded it in for something 'safer.' Everything was all about safety."

Tara pulled open the chips, took one, and held the bag out to me. I shook my head. "I think we become more cautious as we get older," I said. "When we're young, we don't really know what's out there to be scared of."

"But it was more than that," Tara said. "I mean, don't get me wrong. She was still *way* cooler than any of the other mothers. She just seemed to become a lot more extreme and overprotective."

I laughed softly. "Extreme personalities seem to run in the family. Look at Granny—she was wide open."

"Yeah." She reached into the bag, pulled out a handful of chips, and popped one into her mouth. "You know you can always talk to me if you want to." She shoved the rest of the chips in her mouth and then wiped her fingers on her jeans. I couldn't help but imagine the grease and crumbs it left on the denim and tried not to cringe. She was trying to appear casual, but I could hear the underlying concern. My mother's approach was significantly less subtle.

She and Tara had just swapped places riding with me in the truck and we had barely gotten on the highway when she turned to me and said, "So, you're sure this is the best decision?"

I glanced at her. She was unwrapping her Arby's roast beef sandwich.

"Well, it's too late to change my mind now."

She laughed, placed the sandwich on her lap, and began to root around in the bag for the packets of Horsey Sauce she liked to dip her sandwich into. "I know it seems like I haven't been supportive about all of this, I just worry about you. It's a big step and you're moving farther away instead of closer."

"I know," I said. "But you can come visit."

"I know I can." She tore open the packet of sauce and squeezed it onto the paper. "But that's not the point. You're going to be all alone up there. You're moving into a cabin in the mountains by yourself. You don't even have a pet for company."

"I've already adopted a dog," I said quickly. "Mom, this is a good thing. It's what I need."

"But it's so far away," she said. "How am I supposed to take care of you?"

"I don't need anyone to take care of me." I scowled at the road. "When is everyone going to stop treating me like I'm this fragile thing? You, Tara, Natalie. Jesus!"

"Him, too, huh?" my mother said wryly.

It was so unexpected, I had to laugh. My mother laughed, too. And suddenly, we were friends again.

"Birdie, I don't want you to say anything," she said quietly after the moment had passed. "I just want you to listen. And then, I'll drop it. Okay?" She waited for my nod and then continued. "You're my daughter and I love you. I worry about you and that's never going to stop. You don't stop being a mother just because your children grow up." She hesitated and when I glanced at her, I saw that she was looking at her sandwich. "I don't worry as much about Tara," she continued. "She, I don't know, I just don't worry as much. But you went through such a horrible thing with Grace's death. We should have gotten you help."

"Mom, I don't understand where this is going."

She shrugged. "I don't know where it's going either. I just want you to know that I love you regardless of how you are."

"How I am," I said slowly.

"You know what I mean."

"Mom—" I began.

"I just want you to know that if I was the cause of that...because I was so overprotective, I'm sorry. I was just trying to keep you safe."

I again tried to speak but she held up her hand.

"I'm not done. I'm only saying this because of where you're going and what you're going to do. You're going to be by yourself a lot and I just worry that you're going to—"

"Become a maladjusted hermit?" I asked angrily. "Tara's already beat you to having this conversation."

"It's not just that," she said. "You're going to be up there all alone. What happens if someone breaks in? Or you get snowed in?"

"Or aliens land on the roof and beam me into their space ship and implant transmitters in my head."

"Birdie, be serious."

"I am, Mom," I said. "I appreciate your concern, but I really don't want to go into it again. I am the way I am and it was nothing you or anyone else did. I'm not going to become a hermit. I don't want to 'see somebody' and I don't want to talk about this anymore. Please?"

She sighed and finally nodded.

"Thank you. So, let's talk about something else."

"Okay," she said.

Neither of us spoke. After several minutes, I looked at her. She was staring out the bug-splattered windshield.

"Radio?" I asked.

She nodded, pushed the Power button, and began to fiddle with the knobs until Elvis Presley came on the radio. We drove without talking the rest of the way to La Veta.

# Chapter 23

With the exception of one other visit from my mother and sister, and one from Natalie, who said she just needed to get away from being a mother, I had no company at the cabin. Roger, of course, came occasionally to choose which paintings he thought he could use or sell. But other than that, I spent most of my time alone. And frankly, I was relieved. Alone, I had to make no excuses for my schedule or my behavior. I didn't have to explain why I did the things I did or the paintings I created.

Guests were emotionally exhausting—especially my mother and Tara. They wanted to be close to me, to understand me, to spend time with me. I knew that, and on some level I appreciated it. But I also knew that if they saw who I really was and how I lived, they would be much more worried than they already were. And then there were the preparations. Each time I had a guest, with the exception of Roger, I would carefully hide away my canvases and replace them with Jackson Pollack knock-offs I had done as cover. They would never see my real art, I figured, so why give them more cause for concern? I tried to enjoy these visits, but in all honestly, preferred to be alone with Toby. I got all the interaction I needed during my monthly trips into town for supplies and whatever else I needed to get by.

I was, apparently, the only one who was content with the situation. Most vocal was Roger.

"How do you do it?" he asked one night as we sat in front of the fireplace sipping wine. He was visiting to collect canvases. "Don't you get lonely? I mean, seriously, this whole mysterious recluse thing is good for business, but I'm not so sure it's good for you. I'd go crazy spending this much time alone."

"I'm happy this way," I said as I put another log on the fire and pulled the screen closed. "I have my privacy, plenty of work to keep me occupied, and Toby. He keeps me company."

Upon hearing his name, Toby raised his head and thumped his tail against the couch.

"But don't you get lonely?" Roger persisted. "What do you do for . . . um . . . companionship?"

I grimaced.

"Rebecca, you know that's not healthy don't you? Even Adelle is in a stable, healthy relationship." He had a point and I knew it. But because I had no idea what to say in response, I said nothing.

"Can I ask you a personal question?"

I turned to look at him. He was watching me over the rim of his wine glass.

"Can I stop you?"

"No." He grinned and then sobered. "Have you ever even really dated? I mean . . . ever?"

"There were a couple of guys in Kansas City that I was interested in," I lied. "But ultimately I wasn't what they were looking for or vice versa."

"Which means you didn't give them a chance." Roger raised the glass to his lips and took a sip. "What *are* you looking for?"

"I'm not looking."

"I know, but if you *were* looking."

"Well, if I *was* looking," I said with a smile, "He would have to be smart and sensitive and have a sense of who I am and what I'm about. He would have to . . . understand the things that have happened to me and how that shaped who I am today."

"Uh huh." Roger nodded encouragingly.

"And he would have to be respectful of my space and need for privacy." I shrugged. "Essentially, you, but not gay."

"It's true." He snapped the fingers of his free hand. "I'm fabulous. But in all seriousness, I meet lots of guys who are smart and sensitive. And hopelessly straight. Maybe I should introduce you."

"Or," I said as I reached for the wine bottle and poured more into first his glass and then my own, "you could resist playing matchmaker and let me just be Rebecca."

Later that night as we were preparing for bed, he pulled me into a hug. In a rare moment of weakness, I hugged him back.

"I just want you to be happy," he said into my hair as he kissed the top of my head.

"I am," I replied, my tone unconvincing.

We stood that way for a minute before I broke off the embrace.

"Mind if I check my e-mail before I go to bed?" he asked.

I shook my head.

"Nope." I gestured at the desktop computer. "It's all set up. It's a little slow, though. I need to get a new modem."

As I undressed, I could hear the telltale sound of static and beeps as the computer dialed out and accessed the internet. I could also hear Roger drumming his fingers as he waited for the connection to be made.

"You've got mail," I heard him say in unison with the America Online voice. His imitation was so accurate, I had to laugh.

The next afternoon, as he stood in the extra bedroom I had converted into a studio, making a final decision which canvases he was taking, I asked if he had heard from Gus.

"I did last night," he said distractedly as he studied the canvases. "He's in New York right now, so we e-mail rather than talk. He's looking at spaces for a couple of new clubs."

"Wow," I said. "Things *are* going well."

"Girl, don't you know it," he said as his eyes skipped back and forth between two paintings that were vague renderings of ants. He pointed to the one where the ant was crawling off the page. "This one will be perfect for this new décor we're doing down in Boystown. It's going to be very edgy and very dark."

He looked around the room and noticed several paintings propped up against the wall. Each was turned so that only the back of the canvas was visible. He pointed to the stack.

"What are those?" I followed his gaze.

"Just some things I'm working on. They're not for sale."

"Which makes me want to see them all the more." Roger strode quickly toward the stack. "If they're off limits, I need to see them."

"Wait," I keened. "Please don't! Please just . . . don't."

Roger stopped, turned, and looked at me. Something in my tone or my expression must have resonated because for once, he nodded and stepped back.

"I don't want to go into it right now," I began. "It's just something I've been working through that I really don't want anyone to see. It's—I don't even know how to begin to explain it. I don't want to talk about it."

What I didn't want to tell Roger was that the images on those canvases were more disturbing than anything I had painted in the past. Whereas before I had painted images that were in shades of whites, grays, and ice blues, these images were much more vivid and much more violent. Reds and yellows and blacks were mixed with the cooler colors to create nightmarish visions that were angry and hellish.

"Sure," he said with a nonchalant shrug. "That's fine. I can respect your privacy."

I shot him a look of disbelief and he grinned, caught out in his lie.

"Okay," he admitted and spread his hands. "Maybe not all the time, but some of the time." He glanced around the room a last time before pointing to the nine canvases he had chosen. "So, I guess that will do it. This seems to get easier for you every time we do it."

"It is," I said. "At first, it was like losing a part of myself—showing everybody what a screwed-up mess I am. But I don't have to see them once they're gone. And it's not like I am doing them for any kind of artistic satisfaction. It's just a means of getting some of this stuff out of my head. And, to be able to live up here—"

Toby's frantic barking from downstairs prevented me from completing the sentence. It was his "someone's here/this is my property, dammit/pay attention to me" bark. I raised my eyebrows at Roger and then walked over to the window. In front of the house was a shiny black BMW.

Roger joined me at the window. "Oh, yeah," he said, his voice cautious. "I may have invited Adelle to come visit."

"Really?" I asked. It had been too long since I had last seen her. The three of us hadn't gotten together since college.

He grinned, obviously relieved at my reaction. "I thought it would be fun."

Outside, Adelle was pulling a suitcase out of her trunk. I tapped on the window and she looked up, saw us, and waved.

"I should go get Toby before he has a fit," I said and turned to leave. Roger opened the window and shouted down to Adelle. "Hey stranger! Rebecca's on her way down to prevent Toby from gnawing off your arm."

As I tromped down the stairs, I could hear Adelle's laugh and an indecipherable reply. It made me smile and I realized just how much I missed seeing her in person—and how excited I was at having the three of us together again. Toby bounded out the door and immediately reared up on Adelle, who greeted him with affection. She looked up as I came onto the porch and smiled broadly.

"Hi! Surprised?"

"Absolutely," I said and hurried down the stairs to hug her. Displaced as the center of attention, Toby circled us, tail wagging, barking happily. Behind me, I heard Roger's voice.

"Don't I get a hug?"

"In a minute," Adelle said over my shoulder. "*You*, I can see anytime. But this one . . ." She squeezed me tightly and rocked me from side to side before breaking the embrace. She held me at arm's length and studied me. "Girl, you need to eat. You're skin and bones. But I like the hair."

I shrugged. "Just thought it would be nice to have a change. Toby likes it."

She smiled and then shifted her attention to Roger.

"Roger," she said formally.

"Adelle," he said with equal levelness and then grinned. "Come here."

The two hugged and for some reason, I found myself remembering the day Adelle had been raped and how she had not wanted to see Roger at the hospital. I remembered how broken she had seemed—how isolated she had made herself while she healed. And now, watching her smile and move, I could see that she was whole. It made me feel . . . something. Hope? Jealousy?

I stooped, picked up her bag, and started toward the cabin. "Who wants something to drink?"

"Me," said Adelle. "After that drive, holy hell. Girl, could you live any more in the boondocks?"

Once inside and settled, Roger built a fire in the fireplace and I opened a couple of bottles of wine—a red and a white. Adelle sat on the couch with Toby, rubbing his ears and smiling into his adoring eyes.

"Traitor," I said as I set the bottles on the coffee table and started toward the kitchen for glasses.

"Never underestimate the power of a good ear rub," Adelle said and then laughed loudly at something Roger said.

"What did I miss?" I asked as I came back into the room.

"We were just talking about the value of ear and . . . uh . . . other appendage rubbing," Roger said.

"Because Roger is a cheap tramp with a trashy mind," Adelle said.

"Cheap, but not easy," Roger said flirtatiously. "Certainly not easy."

Adelle laughed and poured wine into each of the glasses. "A toast." She picked up one of the glasses. Roger and I followed suit. "To us."

"To us," we echoed.

"*Very* different than the stuff we were drinking in college," Roger observed after we had all taken a sip and settled into our seats. I lounged on cushions on the floor.

"Well, I would hope so," Adelle said. "If we were still drinking Boone's Farm, I'd be a little worried."

I laughed. "Remember the time Roger had too much and we called the Tipsy Taxi to take him home and he opened the car door onto his head and knocked himself unconscious?"

Adelle laughed and picked up the story. "And we had to have the driver help drag him back inside because he was too heavy," she said.

"And I woke up the next morning with my face all bloody," Roger said. "Do you know I still have a scar from where the door cut my face?" He leaned forward and pointed to a small scar near the corner of his eye.

Adelle waved a dismissive hand. "You can barely see it. You should see some of my scars."

We were suddenly quiet.

"Who wants snacks?" I asked quickly and jumped up. "I've got cheese and some hard salami." I hurried into the kitchen. As I prepared the snacks, I could hear Roger and Adelle talking, their voices indistinguishable soft murmurs.

"—weird," I heard Roger say as I came back into the room. He saw me and abruptly stopped talking.

"What are you two talking about?" I asked and set the plates of cheese and crackers on the table.

"Nothing," Roger said. "Just—"

"Roger was telling me about your secret canvases," Adelle said.

I whirled to face Roger. "I told you those were off limits. You had no right to look at them."

"I know," he said quickly. "But—" he looked at Adelle, who nodded encouragingly "—Rebecca, we're worried about you. We think you need . . ." He looked helplessly at Adelle.

"Sweetheart," she said, taking over the conversation. "We love you and we want to help."

"Is that why you're here?" I glared at each of them. "Is this some sort of intervention?"

Roger and Adelle looked at each other. Neither spoke for several seconds. Finally, Roger sighed. "It's not an intervention. It's just a 'We care about you.'"

"You would do the same thing if we needed you," Adelle said.

"We just . . . you live up here all alone. You never leave. We're just worried, that's all."

"I'm fine," I said and then looked pointedly at Roger. "Fine!"

"*Calm down.*" It was Grace. "*Don't act crazy, or you'll just be playing into their hands. Take a deep breath.*"

"Becca," Roger was saying, "those canvases were disturbing. I . . ." He looked at Adelle. "We," he amended, "just want to help. You have some issues."

"You didn't seem to mind my issues when they were helping your career," I spat. "Or do I need to remind you about the conversation where you begged me to let you use my paintings?"

Roger reddened. "You're right." He held up his hands in a defenseless gesture. "You're absolutely right. I took advantage of the situation. I did. But I'm also your friend and I think you need professional help."

"Rebecca, look at it from our point of view," Adelle interjected. "These past few years, we've seen your behavior become more and more . . . strange. It's not your fault. You suffered a horrific event as a child. You weren't equipped to handle it and now it's affecting you as an adult. We're just suggesting that maybe you need help dealing with it. We just want you to be happy and have a normal life, not holed up in some remote cabin in the mountains, doing tortured paintings."

I whirled on Roger. "You told her about Grace? Jesus, Roger."

"Don't blame him," Adelle said quickly. "I asked him why you never talked about your childhood, why you never dated. I thought maybe you had been sexually abused or raped. I wanted to help. We *both* want to help. We love you."

I looked angrily at both of them. During this last exchange, Roger had moved to sit next to Adelle on the couch. Compassion and worry were written on their faces and as this registered, I felt my anger fade slightly.

"We love you," Roger echoed. "We've just seen you change over the years and it's reached a point where we think it's negatively impacting your life. You don't have to deal with this on your own. You have friends and family who love you—who want to help you."

I took a deep breath and turned to look into the fire.

"*Tell them what they want to hear,*" Grace said in my ear. "*Tell them that you'll look into therapy.*" I stiffened. "*You don't have to do it,*" she said. "*Just tell them that you will.*"

I turned back to face them. They looked like two owls on a branch, their eyes large and round.

"You're right," I said finally. "I don't sleep. I drink too much and I spend too much time by myself. You're not telling me anything I don't already know. I have been thinking about going to see a therapist. Maybe this is the nudge I need to do that."

Both Adelle and Roger exhaled in relief, and Adelle stood and came over to pull me into a hug.

"Sweetheart, we love you," she said. "I *know* how hard it is to be a survivor. And that's what you are. But you don't have to keep all that in your head. They have medications you can take. Antidepressants. Antianxiety pills. You can get therapy and work through this. I mean, look at me. I know what it's like to feel vulnerable and victimized. I know what rape can do. But I worked through it and now I'm healthy. I'm *strong*. I'm with a man who appreciates who I am and what I've been through. My experience made me stronger."

Roger stood and joined us.

"This isn't a bad thing," he said, wrapping his arms around both of us. "Unless it makes you stop painting and then we'll have to talk."

I arched back to see if he was joking, and he laughed at my expression.

"Asshole," Adelle said.

"But seriously," he continued. "You *promise* you'll look into seeing a doctor and a therapist?"

I nodded and then extricated myself from the group hug.

"So, can we talk about something else?" I asked.

Roger and Adelle glanced at each other, seeming to exchange a silent message, though what it was, I couldn't tell.

"Yes," Roger said and moved back to the couch, where he picked up his wine glass, leaned back expansively and crossed his legs. "Let's talk about me."

The rest of the visit was uneventful. We laughed and ate and discussed everything but the obvious, although Adelle tried twice to talk about Grace's death. Each time I politely avoided the conversation by saying I didn't want to talk about it until after I had worked through some of it with a therapist. Both times I said this, Grace's laugh echoed hollowly in my head.

After Roger and Adelle left, things settled back into their regular routine—working around the property during the day, watching television at night, and painting when I was unable to sleep. Roger typically came twice a year to collect paintings—in the spring and the fall—and so I was used to having the house filled with his energy and then quiet when he left. But having Adelle visit, too, though wonderful, had also been more difficult because it made the usual recalibration that much harder. For the first time in a long time, I felt not just alone but lonely.

I made more of an effort to reach out to Mom, Tara, and Natalie. They always seemed happy to talk or e-mail, but the exchanges were different. They had lives that didn't really include me. I realized it most when talking to Natalie. After having two more children, she had become increasingly busy and so our conversations were constantly interrupted by questions from the kids, catastrophes in another part of the house, and Pete. Also, there was a palpable unhappiness about her that always left me feeling impotent because I knew of no way to help her. It had started from the moment she told me about her decision to marry Pete and have Meg. But over the years, her unhappiness had become almost a physical burden that she carried with a visible weariness. I didn't realize how much until the one time she came for a visit.

She had asked if she could come visit—that she needed to get away from Pete and the kids. We hadn't seen each other since I had moved to La Veta. I almost didn't recognize the woman who climbed out of her station wagon and walked up the pea gravel walkway to the house. Toby rushed out to greet her, his stiff tail swinging excitedly back and forth.

"Hey," I said as I came down the porch steps. "How was the drive?"

She grinned tiredly and bent down to cradle Toby's head in her palms. "Longer than I thought, but good. I got to listen to something other than Barney. In fact, I brought along some of our old cassette tapes. Journey. Boston. It was fun."

She straightened and opened her arms for a hug. It was only when we embraced that I realized just how thin she had become. As we pulled apart I looked into her face. The shadows under her eyes were still evident and her hair, which was pulled back into a ponytail, was peppered with gray.

"You've lost weight," I said.

"I've taken up jogging. It's a good way to blow off some steam and I can do it around the neighborhood or at the track so I can keep an eye on the kids."

I pointed to the back of her car. "Are your bags back there?"

She nodded. "Yeah, I'll get them." She turned to walk to the car. I followed and as she lifted the hatch she glanced around the front yard and then up at the second floor windows of the cabin. "This is really nice, Birdie."

"Thanks," I said as I held out a hand for one of the bags. "I like it. My mom and Tara think it's a little too remote, but it's really perfect."

She handed me a battered brown leather suitcase, and slung a red and black tote bag over her shoulder. She pulled a blue duffle bag out and set it on the ground, closed the back of the station wagon, and followed me inside.

"So, this is it," I said as we stepped into the living room. "It's small, I know, but it's cozy. Your room is upstairs. It's the one on the left." I pointed to the doorway visible on the balcony that overlooked the living room. "The bathroom is in-between the bedrooms. I put some towels on your bed."

"It's perfect, Birdie," she said as she slung the tote bag off her shoulder and handed it to me. The contents inside the bag clinked, glass upon glass. I peered inside at the bottles of wine. "Compliments of Pete. How about you open one while I take these upstairs? The room on the left, right?"

I protested as she picked up her bags and headed for the stairs.

"I've got it," she said. "If you want to help me, pour me a drink, and keep them coming. I'll be down in a second."

Natalie did drink a lot that weekend. I, however, did not. I knew from experience that when I began to drink, I often didn't stop, and it was during those times when my guard was down that Grace was at her most vocal. I already could feel her interest in Natalie and was very careful to keep her under control. Natalie, for her part, didn't seem to notice that I wasn't matching her drink for drink—that, or she didn't seem to care.

She had come to spend time with me, but most of our time together that weekend was actually spent apart or doing solitary activities in each other's presence. Natalie went on long runs and when we were in the cabin together, we often sat on opposite ends of the couch and read. When we talked, the conversation was light and pointedly absent of references to Grace's murder, my work, or Natalie's life with Pete. It was as if we had silently agreed not to discuss the things that troubled each of us the most. But that last night, after we had finished dinner and put away the dishes, we sat next to the fire and finished the last bottle of wine.

"I'm going to leave Pete," Natalie blurted out.

I had been struggling with the fire tongs to turn a large log over on the grate when she spoke. I turned, caught off guard, and the log rolled back to its original position.

"You're what?"

"I'm going to leave Pete," she repeated and swirled the wine in her glass. I watched for several seconds, mesmerized. "I can't do it anymore, Birdie. I wake up every day and I look at him and I think, 'you stole my life.'" She snorted and shook her head almost violently. "I know he didn't. I know that. But for some reason, when I look at him, all I can see is my wasted life."

I turned back to the log, gave it a final shove, and pulled closed the mesh spark screen. I wanted to say something—*anything*—that would make her feel better. But nothing came to mind—nothing except Grace's obvious interest.

"Could you really do it?" I picked up my own glass and settled back onto my end of the couch. "Leave him?"

Natalie pursed her lips and shrugged. "I don't know," she said with a sigh. "All I know is that I can't stay with him." She took a large swallow of wine and then turned to face me. When she spoke again, her voice was earnest. "Part of the reason for coming here was to get some time away from Pete and the kids to think about this. To see how it feels to be on my own—like you are."

I shook my head slowly back and forth. "Natalie, it's not as easy as you think. My life is lonely."

"Birdie, please listen," she said and reached clumsily forward to clasp my free hand. "I've been thinking a lot about this and this is what I want to do—what I *need* to do. Birdie, this is my last chance." Her grip on my hand tightened. "If I don't leave now, I never will. Do you understand?"

I blinked several times and looked at our joined hands. Her thin fingers were clamped so tightly around my hand that the knuckles were white. She was breathing heavily. "I know it's wrong, but I don't want to be a wife and mother." She took a deep breath. "I'm going to leave Pete and the kids."

"Wait. The kids? What do you mean, leave the kids, too? Nat, you're their mother."

Natalie wrenched her hand away. "You don't have to say it like that. You don't have kids. You don't understand."

"But you're their mother."

"I know," she said miserably. "Don't you think I know what it means, my saying this? Don't you think I know what people will think—how they'll see me?" She turned and leaned forward, feet on the floor, elbows resting on her knees. "What kind of monster doesn't want her children?"

"Natalie," I said softly. "You're unhappy. You're just—"

"I know what I am," she said ruefully and drained the wine in her glass. "I know." She turned her head to look miserably at me. "I just can't do it anymore. I've thought about this a lot and I'm going to go back, talk to Pete, and try to explain to the kids. Men do it all the time."

"And then what?"

Natalie shrugged. "I'll pack what I need to get by, come back here, and figure out what to do next."

I felt my stomach contract. "Here? With me?"

"Just a few months, until I get my head straight. That's okay, right?"

"I . . . Natalie," I stammered.

"She can't live here," Grace said urgently in my head. "She'll ruin everything. You won't be able to work. She'll make messes you'll have to clean up. Think about the hair you saw yesterday in the shower drain. Do you want to wake up to that every day?"

"I need your help, Birdie," Natalie said. "I can't stay there. I don't have any place else to go."

I felt my resolve begin to waver. Grace felt it, too. I felt her shift in my head, pacing back and forth. She was anxious. *"If she is around here all the time, she'll figure out you're crazy,"* Grace said. Her voice was anxious. *"I can take care of you when it's just us, but if you let her come here, I can't protect you. She will ruin everything."*

"Nat—"

"Birdie, I can't do this anymore." She reached out for my hand and began to squeeze again. She shook her head. "I won't."

I felt a pressure build in my chest and squeezed her hand tightly. "What are you saying?" I asked hollowly. When she didn't answer, I tried again. "Natalie, what do you mean?"

She blinked several times but still didn't reply. Her eyes were dull in her gaunt face and I had a flash of her laid out in a coffin, ready to go into the ground. I fought down the terror of having another person in my home for such a long time and opened my mouth to say that she could stay—that we would figure it out. But something in me just couldn't say the words.

Instead, I sighed and said, "Let's talk about this in the morning." Natalie stared at me for several more seconds before nodding. The gesture was one of resignation.

"Sure," she said and smiled sadly. "Sure."

We didn't talk about it the next morning. I didn't bring it up and neither did she. We simply drank our coffee, silently ate our toast, and then Natalie went upstairs and brought down her bags. As I helped her carry them out to the car, I struggled to figure out what to say.

"Nat," I said as she slid the bags into the back of the station wagon and closed the hatch.

"Don't." She turned to smile at me. Her eyes were shiny. "It's okay. I just wasn't ready to go home. But I'm okay now."

"What you said—" I began but she cut me off.

"Just the wine talking." She pulled me into a hug. We stood that way for a long time. After several seconds, I broke the embrace.

"I love you," she said as she stepped back and looked into my eyes. "I know things have been hard for you, too. After Grace . . . I'm sorry I wasn't able to be more help to you." She continued to look at me and for a second, she looked like the old Natalie—the fearless, strong Natalie of our youth.

"Well, I had better get on the road," she said and walked to the driver-side door. "Thanks for everything."

"Let's do it again in a couple of months," I said suddenly. "Maybe you could come and stay longer."

She opened the door and then stepped back and pulled me into a final good-bye hug. "That would be great." She squeezed my shoulders once and then climbed into the car.

"I'm sorry about—" I said after she started the engine and rolled down the window. She held up her hand.

"It's okay. Really." She paused and reached her hand out the window. I stepped forward and grasped it. "I love you, Birdie."

I squeezed her fingers tightly. "I love you, too."

She bobbed her head a couple of times in acknowledgement, squeezed my fingers again and then withdrew her hand.

"See you later alligator." It was our old good-bye.

"After while crocodile," I responded.

She grinned, rolled up the window, and put the car into gear. I stood on the porch with Toby and waved until she had turned out of the driveway and onto the dirt road that led to the highway.

It was the last time I saw her. It was about a month after Roger and Adelle's visit that my mother called to tell me that Natalie was dead. They were doing an autopsy, my mother said, but it appeared that she had taken an overdose of prescription narcotics.

I was silent for several seconds.

"Birdie?" my mother asked. "Are you okay?"

I nodded, not considering that she couldn't see my response through the phone line. All I could think about was our talk on the last night of her visit and the stilted phone conversations since. We had never talked again about that night, and each time we spoke on the telephone, Natalie had seemed less and less engaged. She had seemed to retreat into herself, and because I felt unable to help her, I had taken to not picking up when she called.

"Birdie," my mother said again.

"Yeah, Mom, I'm here," I mumbled. "Sorry. How's her mom holding up?"

"She's taking it hard," my mother said. "She asked about you when I called her. She wanted you to know that the funeral will be on Friday."

My stomach clenched in its familiar knot. Images of Grace's funeral flashed through my mind. I hadn't been to the cemetery since my grandfather's burial. My grandmother had been cremated, so her service had been held at the funeral home. The thought of going out there now left me breathless.

"I'll have to check my schedule," I mumbled. "I want to, but I've got a lot of work . . . deadlines. There's a new show . . ."

"Birdie," my mother said. "I know you have . . . issues. And most of the time, we try to be sympathetic to them. But this isn't up for discussion. Natalie was your best friend. She loved you like a sister. You owe it to her to come back."

I was silent. I hated myself for what I had become. I needed to go to the funeral—for Natalie's parents, but also to say good-bye. Even though we never recaptured the closeness we had before Grace's death, we had held onto each other, bound together in a common orbit. Natalie had never shown me anything but unconditional friendship and had only asked for one thing in return—the one thing that I couldn't, or wouldn't, give her. The thought of her being gone was unfathomable. I felt a void—a loneliness that was as palpable as if she had physically been in my presence and then had been yanked away.

"I know," I said finally. "What time's the funeral?"

## Chapter 24

Ultimately, I didn't go to Natalie's funeral. I tried—even going so far as to pack my bag and load it into my Jeep. But then, instead of forcing myself to get into the driver's seat and start the engine, I went back inside and sat down on the couch. "Any time now," I kept telling myself. But after three days of locking the house, getting in the Jeep, and sitting in the driveway, I finally acknowledged that I wasn't going anywhere and brought my bag back inside. My mother was disappointed and angry. I sent a letter to Natalie's parents explaining that I couldn't get away, but that when I came to visit my mother, I would come see them. Her mom eventually sent a vague, polite response that made me feel worse than I already did.

That's not to say that I didn't commemorate Natalie's death. I did. I mourned privately. And I drank—a lot. I also talked to Grace. She was the one person who I thought could understand—the only one who wouldn't judge me. In the end, though, there was little she could do to make me feel better, though her idea of holding a private service for Natalie was a good one. I was midway through my second bottle of wine when Grace suggested it—*"so you can say goodbye."*

I considered the idea.

"But how would we do it? We don't have a body."

*"You don't need to have the person there to have a memorial service,"* Grace said. *"Just light some candles and put on some special music. Say a few words."*

"We could drink a toast," I said starting to get into the idea. "To her memory."

*"I don't know if you really need more to drink,"* Grace said.

*"You've had quite a bit already."*

"A fact that is really none of your business."

I could feel her shrug.

*"So, go get some candles,"* Grace said. *"And I'll pick out the music."*

I got unsteadily to my feet and lurched into the kitchen. "Candles," I muttered and began jerking drawers open. After about the fifth try, I found what I was looking for. "Got 'em," I yelled as I put several on a plate and then grabbed the matches and the bottle of wine.

*"What do you think about the soundtrack to* Eddie and the Cruisers?*"* Grace asked as I came back into the living room. It had been one of Natalie's favorite movies and she had worn out the cassette tape playing it so often. She had brought it with her when she visited, and we'd listened to it one night while cooking dinner.

"Perfect," I said. "Cheers to you, Grace!" I picked up my glass and raised it in a sloppy toast. I could tell that I was moving clumsily, so I compensated by trying to be very deliberate. I was, I knew, drunk. Again.

*"'Tender Years',"* Grace said. *"It was her favorite, right?"*

"Let me light these candles first," I muttered as I tried to arrange them on the battered wooden coffee table. My fingers felt thick as I struggled to extract a match from the box. "Why do they make them so stinkin' small?"

*"Light the candles, Birdie."* I could tell Grace was getting exasperated with me.

"I am," I said, and struck the match against the side of the box. The tip of the match flared to life. "I love the smell of sulfur."

*"Birdie, light the candles before you burn yourself,"* Grace said.

I held the match to the wick of the largest candle. My fingers trembled as I waited for it to catch. The colors of the light were mesmerizing—red, yellow, orange, and, in the center, dark blue and black. I felt the heat of the flame as it inched nearer my fingers, but still I didn't move. I didn't blow it out or drop it. I just watched in fascination as the flame began to lick at my fingertips. I was amazed that it didn't hurt.

*"Birdie!"* It was Grace. *"Blow it out. You're going to hurt yourself."*

"I was just watching it," I said as I dropped the blackened matchstick onto the candleholder. "It's like it has a life of its own." I felt Grace sigh. *You need to put some ice on your fingers. Go into the kitchen and get some.*

"No," I said almost petulantly. "I'll use this." I stuck my fingers into my wine glass and wiggled them in the red liquid.

*"That's disgusting,"* she said.

"Oh yeah, music," I said and suddenly leapt up. "'Tender Years.'" I scanned the stacks of tapes and CDs. "John Cafferty & the Beaver Brown Band," I said as I popped the cassette into the player and pressed Rewind. I winced as my fingertips came in contact with the button.

*"Told you,"* Grace said.

"Shut up," I said as the player clicked off. Using my other hand, I pushed Play. When the music began to play, I dropped my hands and walked back to the coffee table.

*"What if you used a fireplace match to light the rest?"* Grace suggested. I nodded. After the candles were lit, I knelt in front of the table and poured the remainder of the wine into my glass. I was about to start my eulogy when Grace stopped me.

*"You need a picture,"* Grace said. *"Remember the ones she sent you from her last visit? Get one of those."*

She was right, of course, and so I scrambled up and went to my desk. The pictures were in a small manila envelope in the top desk drawer. I flipped through them and extracted my favorite. It was Natalie, in profile, looking out across the mountains. I had grabbed her camera when she wasn't looking and snapped some pictures so she could have some of herself. She had a wistful expression and for a moment, I was reminded how disappointed in life she must have been.

I leaned the photo against one of the taller candles and settled back into my spot.

"Natalie," I said. It was both a question and a statement—an entreaty. I paused, wondering what to say next. I looked down at her picture. I had no idea how to start. I took a sip of wine, cleared my throat, and began again. "Natalie, I'm sorry your life didn't turn out the way you planned. I'm sorry I couldn't be . . . wasn't capable of being a better friend to you. And I'm sorry I didn't go to your funeral. I tried. I really did. But that place, that . . . town and everything that happened there . . . all of it . . ."

I shook my head and suddenly was aware of the lyrics to the song.

*Whoa, whoa tender years . . . Won't you wash away my tears . . . How I wish you were here . . . Please don't go tender years.*

"I haven't cried," I announced, though I wasn't sure if I was telling Natalie, Grace, or myself. "I haven't cried since that day."

I pushed myself to my feet and walked unsteadily to the window. "I don't think I know how to cry anymore. It's like my . . . my crying mechanism is broken." My pronunciation of "mechanism" was slurred. "I'm sorry, too, Grace. I let you down. Natalie and I let you down. The whole fucking town of Edenbridge let you down."

I spun and looked anxiously around the room. "Do you hear me? Natalie? Grace? I'm sorry!"

Toby jumped up, the fur on the back of his neck bristled. He growled and looked around for the cause of my outburst. The room was silent aside from the music and the crackling of the fire. The song had changed.

*Dark side's calling now nothin' is real . . . She'll never know just how I feel . . . From out of the shadows she walks like a dream . . . Makes me feel crazy, makes me feel so mean.*

Even in my state I could appreciate the irony.

"Ha!" I said.

Toby eyed me warily and then returned to his spot on the couch. I looked around the room. I was alone. "So, anyway, here's to you, Natalie." I raised my glass. "I'm sorry I let you down. And, here's to me, too. May I have continued success at being a failure."


The next day was painful—both because I was very hungover and because the previous night had left me unsettled. I blamed the wine and promised to be more cautious of my consumption. But deep down, I think I knew that the real culprit was my sense of guilt, loneliness, and desolation. My resolve to not drink was strong until about 6 p.m. Then with the night came my own personal darkness and my desire for a drink. I'm not sure if the wine helped or hurt, but it made everything easier to bear. Or, at least it did until I got *the* e-mail.

Hearing from Tommy Anderson was the last thing I could have expected to happen. It was late afternoon and I had poured myself a glass of red wine. I knew Adelle would be sending pictures of her trip to Florida, so I logged onto my e-mail. As I sat waiting for the internet to connect, it occurred to me that I also needed to send a message to Roger. I began to mentally compose it in my head as the AOL homepage appeared on my screen.

"You've got mail," said the computerized voice as I logged into the system. I remembered Roger and his imitation and smiled. When the page finally loaded, I saw that I had four messages in my inbox—two from Roger, one from Adelle, and one from Thomas Anderson. The subject line of the last one read: "Your Paintings."

Who is Thomas Anderson, I wondered, and how in the hell did he know about my paintings? My first inclination was anger that Roger had revealed my identity. I clicked on the message and waited for the computer to load the page.

*Dear Birdie:*

*In all likelihood, you probably won't remember me. But, I believe I would be remiss if I didn't at least try to contact you. My name is Thomas Anderson. We met in 1981 in Edenbridge. I was the young man (boy) you befriended in the clearing near your tree house after Grace was murdered. I was spending the summer with my grandparents. Does this ring any bells?*

*The reason I'm writing is because I was at a restaurant in Chicago several weeks ago and was struck by a painting I saw there. It was of the back and upper body of a nude girl. The background was a green so dark it almost seemed black. The artist was identified as BEC. I was blown away*

*by the work. I couldn't stop staring at it. And so I approached
the manager to find out where it came from. After much
conversation and bribery, I learned the name of the man
who designed the restaurant and installed the art. This was,
of course, your friend Roger who, after much coercion on my
part, eventually gave me your e-mail address. He said that
your privacy and anonymity were sacred, which is why I
hesitated to contact you. In the end, though, I really felt as if I
had no choice.*

*Birdie (or Rebecca, whichever you prefer), your work is
so evocative. It's about Grace, isn't it? I knew it the minute
I saw it—or, at least, that's what it triggered in me. I have
been haunted by her death most of my adult life.*

*I know this may seem strange and I know my attention
is completely unsolicited (and, according to Roger, likely
unwanted), but I just wanted to let you know that I have
never forgotten you. I remember our conversations and I have
always wondered what happened to you.*

*I currently live in New York and can be reached at this
e-mail address—or, if you would like to speak in person,
at the number listed below. Please know that I understand
if you don't want any reminders of that time in your life.
But if you would like to communicate, I would enjoy it very
much. I feel it only right to admit to you that I have, since
seeing the painting in the restaurant, purchased two of your
pieces. I consider them some of my best investments.*

*Most sincerely yours,*
*Thomas Anderson*

I stared at the message. Thomas Anderson. Tommy. The boy
in the clearing. I remembered him vividly. His eyes. His dark hair.
His connection to Grace. His intensity which had both scared me
and drawn me in. I sat back in my seat, shaken, though something
about his honesty and vulnerability struck a chord. He recognized
my work for what it was. I felt lightheaded. I considered my response or even if I wanted to respond. My hand hovered over the

computer mouse. To reply would open up a dialogue I wasn't sure I was prepared for. I knew nothing about this man, I reminded myself. He was a stranger who had made me uncomfortable when I was young. Did I really want to begin a dialogue with him?

"Fucking Roger and his big mouth," I said to Toby. "I should have known he couldn't keep this to himself."

I immediately opened a new message box and began to type.

*Roger:*

*Let me be clear when I say that I DO NOT appreciate you giving my e-mail address to Thomas Anderson! Our agreement was that I would remain ANONYMOUS. In case you don't have a dictionary handy, that means that no one knows who I am. Sharing my identity was NOT in our agreement, no matter how much you might think you're helping me. There are certain things that are none of your business and this is one of them. If you cross this line again, not only is our deal off, but so is our friendship.*

*I am going to politely answer his e-mail and explain that I prefer not to communicate with him—or anyone for that matter. In the future, DO NOT PUT ME IN THIS SITUATION AGAIN!*

*Rebecca*

I stood up and stomped over to the window. With the end of summer had come the cool, crisp air of autumn. The leaves had begun to change and I made a mental note to lay in plenty of supplies for the winter. In the past, it hadn't been uncommon to be snowed in for weeks at a time. And although I had plenty of firewood in the event that the electricity went out, I needed to make sure that I had enough human and dog food.

"We're going to need to run into town for supplies," I announced to Toby, who looked up and grinned—or at least what I perceived to be a grin. "We'll do that tomorrow, yeah? And we'll chop up some more firewood." I sighed and crossed my arms over my chest. "That still doesn't solve the problem of what I should do about Tommy's e-mail, though. What do you think?" Toby wagged his tail and gazed up at me with amber eyes. I reached down and he came over so I could rub his ears. "What should I do?"

I looked back at my computer and sighed. Toby's eyes lolled back in his head as I rubbed and I wished that having my ears rubbed was enough to make me happy. Part of me wanted to ignore the e-mail. It was unsolicited and there was just something about Tommy—Thomas —that made me uneasy. But there was also something about him that intrigued me. I thought about our brief conversations in the Nest the summer after Grace's murder. He had seemed so volatile—so dark. But at the same time, I was attracted to him. I blinked, startled at the word choice.

"Just a quick message," I finally said. "Just to thank him and let him know that I am very private and would prefer not to correspond. What do you think?"

Toby grunted in response, though not to my question. I bent down, kissed him on the top of the head, and walked back to the computer. The cursor arrow was positioned over the reply button. I hesitated and then clicked the mouse. My fingers hovered over the keyboard, suddenly unsure where to start. Finally, I began to type.

*Dear Thomas:*

*Thank you for your note. I usually try to keep a low profile and, as you know from your dealings with Roger, prefer to remain anonymous. But in this case, I wanted to respond. Yes, of course I remember you. And, unfortunately, I, too, think often about the circumstances that brought us together. You're correct in that many of my paintings stem from that experience. I don't think it's the type of experience that anyone gets over.*

*That said, I need to get back to work. But thank you for your e-mail. It was nice to hear from you.*

*Rebecca (Birdie)*

"There," I said to Toby, who had wandered over to the fireplace and stretched out. "That should do it. I answered his e-mail and that's the end of it." Toby looked at me with a baleful expression. "I know what you're thinking," I continued. "But I was direct, polite, and un-encouraging."

Toby regarded me for a minute longer and then put his head down on his front paws and uttered a deep, clearly uninterested sigh. The fire crackled invitingly and I weighed staying at the computer and responding to Roger and Adelle's e-mails against curling up with Toby in front of the fire. I stared at the screen. I could read their e-mails and then craft my response in my head while lying in front of the fire. Not a bad idea, I decided. I clicked on the first of Roger's two messages and scrolled down the text. I was still angry.

> *Dahling:*
>
> *I've thought about our conversation at your place and I think it's time for you to implement some of the changes you said you'd make. You need to get out more—spend more time with friends. I know you don't want to go to Edenbridge, but what about Chicago? Nothing stressful, just a quick visit. You could stay here with me and Gus—we'll make sure to sanitize the room.*
>
> *So what do you say? Come visit. I have some great folks I'd like to have you meet—and one in particular. Think on it, figure out how you're going to refuse, but know that I won't take "no" for an answer.*
>
> *Kisses, kisses, kisses,*
>
> *Rog*

I stared at the message. "No need to think about my response to this one," I muttered as I clicked on the Reply button and began to type.

> *Roger:*
>
> *Thanks, but no thanks. You're an asshole (See my previous message.)*

I next clicked on his second message which, according to the time stamp, was sent two minutes after the first.

*Rebecca:*

*In anticipation of your negative response to my earlier e-mail invitation, I'm responding with my follow-up which is:*

*This is a great idea. You need to get out and be around people. And, I've recently encountered a couple of people I think you should meet. One, in particular, is handsome, successful and, as per your criteria, "not gay" and "disease-free."*

*Gus has said he'll fly you down on his private plane if you're scared of germs from the common folk. Or, I'll fly down and drive you back.*

*Roger has spoken.*

I was considering my response to this latest missive when my inbox refreshed itself and a new message appeared. It was from Tommy. I realized he must have been online when I sent my note. I hesitated and looked absurdly from side to side before clicking on it. I wasn't sure I wanted to read what he had to say. What if he asked something that required a response?

"This is silly," I said to Toby. "Regardless of whether or not I read it, I don't have to respond. I mean, seriously, I'm an adult woman. I make my own decisions."

Toby glanced up, sighed deeply again, and closed his eyes. He gave the impression of being bored by my melodrama. I took a deep breath, clicked on the message and began to read.

*Birdie (Rebecca):*

*Hi. I'm so glad you got back to me. I worried that you wouldn't. Or that my being so forward would scare you off. I know you value your privacy—Roger was clear about that—and I want to respect that. But I also feel like we're sort of kindred spirits, you and I, because we shared this horrible experience. I don't know about you, but it has haunted me. And there is no one I can talk to about it*

*because . . . I mean, what do you say? "Yeah, when I was
17, I had a friend who was murdered?" It's kind of a
conversation stopper.*

I stopped reading. I knew what he was talking about. I understood
how that was not something you could just blurt out.

> *I respect your desire for anonymity and for privacy. I
> do. And I'm not trying to bother you. I just wanted to reach
> out—to communicate. Your art . . . I don't know . . . it was
> disturbing and upsetting, but it also made sense to me. It took
> me back to that summer when so much changed. It was like
> you expressed something with paint that I have struggled to
> figure out how to express in words all my life.*
>
> *Sorry to get all intense. I'm starting to ramble, so it's
> probably a good time to sign off. Thanks for responding.
> You're welcome to write anytime.*
>
> *Yours,*
> *Tommy*

I stared at the screen. So much of his note resonated with me. I
knew what it was like to carry an experience—that experience—around
all day, every day. I understood how it felt to have been monumentally
and inherently changed in the blink of an eye. I understood. But more
to the point, so did he. I reread the e-mail. I wanted to reply. Despite my
usual fears of strangers, of danger, of the unknown, I wanted to reply—to
have a connection with this man. I thought back to our conversations in
the clearing—our time together in the weeks following Grace's murder.
I thought about the way he paced and talked, about his sadness, about his
seemingly similar sense of loss. I fought the urge to hit Reply.

"*What are you doing?*"

It was Grace. I flushed and looked away from the computer
screen. Over the years, I had learned that Grace relied on my eyes
to see what was going on. She could read my thoughts, but only if
my guard was down and I allowed her in.

"Nothing."

*"I felt your confusion and anxiety."*

"It's nothing," I said. "I was just thinking about Natalie."

I could tell she wasn't quite buying it, but she didn't press. It wasn't until later, when she was gone, that I thought again about Tommy's note. He seemed nice enough, but there was still something about him that made me uneasy. Perhaps it was his aggressiveness—although that seemed to be too strong of a word. Maybe "assertiveness" was a better choice. Or self-confidence. He said what he thought—unlike me, who monitored every word, both externally and now, internally, to thwart Grace's nosiness.

I made myself a sandwich and searched my mind for Grace's presence. She wasn't there. I took the sandwich to the computer, sat down, and quickly began to type.

*Dear Thomas:*

*You're right. Our experience is indeed a conversation stopper—which is why I just don't talk about it. My close friends know, but that's about it. It's hard when something like that changes you so deeply, but you're unable to discuss it. I guess what I'm trying to say is that I understand.*
*Birdie*

His reply was almost immediate.

*Birdie—*

*I know you do—understand, I mean. I knew it when we were kids. You had a sad, haunted sense about you when you would come to the clearing. I see that same sadness, that same haunted quality in your work. Is that why you paint?*

I considered my response. One or two e-mails were one thing. But this was turning into a correspondence. Was that something I was ready for? Was it something I wanted? The answer to both questions was that I didn't know. Of course, I could always end the conversation, couldn't I? He didn't know where I lived or how to contact me aside from e-mail. I didn't think even Roger would have let that slip. I took a bite of my sandwich, a bracing swallow of wine, and then hit Reply.

> *Tommy—*
>
> *Is it okay if I call you Tommy? Thomas sounds so stuffy and formal.*
>
> *You asked why I paint. That's a question with a very long, very complicated answer. The short answer is that it helps me clear my head and sleep at night. How's that for honesty? I didn't set out to be an artist. I just sort of fell into it. And I really don't like to talk about my work—in part because no one knows my real identity and partially because it's, as you've guessed, quite personal. I'm not saying I won't discuss it with you, but not yet. I don't know you well enough.*
>
> *Birdie*

Again, he responded quickly.

> *Birdie—*
>
> *Yes, of course you can call me Tommy. I'm comfortable with whatever you want to share about your work. How-ever, as the owner of two of your pieces, I should admit that it lends value—solely personal—to the work to know the impetus and the circumstances. But I won't press. Some things are meant to be kept private and I respect that. We all have secrets, Birdie.*
>
> *Tommy*

I stared at the last sentence. "We all have secrets." I felt my skin tingle. Was he trying to reassure me or tell me something? I felt Grace begin to stir and quickly logged off AOL.

I fought the urge to revisit Tommy's e-mail. Even as I stood in front of my easel late that night, I considered the meaning of those words. "We all have secrets." I halfheartedly dabbed paint onto the canvas. Usually the process of mixing the colors onto the palette was cathartic. As I brushed and stroked paint onto the canvas, I usually lost track of time. Minutes would disappear into hours in the blink of an eye. Exhausted, I would suddenly stop, clean up the mess, and go to bed. But not tonight.

"We all have secrets."

After more than an hour of standing in front of the easel, I sighed and put away my equipment. I wouldn't paint tonight—couldn't paint—until I found out what Tommy meant. Carefully, I washed out the brushes, tidied my studio, and went downstairs. If nothing else, I needed to respond to Adelle and her pictures. As I waited for the computer to boot up, I contemplated how to ask what he meant.

There were no new e-mails in my inbox—just the one from Adelle. I was tempted to respond to hers first and then, just before logging off, reply to Tommy's. But seemingly of their own volition, my fingers moved the mouse to Tommy's last message and clicked. My second reading of the message lent no additional clarification. So, should I address the major question first or circle around it? I chewed on my thumb. He seemed to value forthrightness.

*Tommy—*
*You're right. We do all have secrets—or, at least,*
*private thoughts.*

I paused, impressed by my own forthrightness. How to continue, though? It was a bold admission on my part. But that wasn't what I wanted to say, was it? Or, more specifically, what I wanted to know.

*It seems like a strange thing to say, though. Why did*
*you say that?*

Before I could second-guess myself, I hit Send. Within five minutes, he replied.

*Hi—*

*I wondered where you had gone. I'm glad you responded.*
*So, you want to know why I said that. I guess because*
*it's true. I think we all have secrets—things we carry*
*around with us. I know I do. In fact, I have several, but the*
*one that seems to weigh most heavily on me is something*
*that happened that summer—the summer that Grace died.*
*I think it's part of what compelled me to contact you—you,*
*the one person who would understand what I want to say.*
*This is beginning to sound creepy, isn't it? I'm sorry for that*
*but I need to tell you something—something awful. I don't*
*know how to say it without just saying it, so, here goes.*

*You weren't the first person to find Grace. I was. I snuck*
*out of my grandparents' house the night she was murdered.*
*I went to the clearing. I had a flashlight. She was the first*
*thing I saw. At first I didn't even know what it was or what*
*was going on. Then, as I got closer . . . well, you know. It was*
*horrible. I didn't know what to do, so I ran away. To this*
*day, I feel like such a coward.*

*Rebecca, I can understand if you don't want anything to*
*do with me. But if you want to talk about what happened,*
*I think I would understand in a way that no one else could.*
*And I think it might be good for both of us. That image—the*
*image of her lying there—haunts me. If your paintings are*
*any indication, I think it haunts you, too. Am I right?*

*Tommy*

I sat back in my chair and reread the message in stunned
silence. I had no idea how to respond. He had found her before
me. He had seen her lying in the clearing, but had run away and
left her for me to find. I felt sick and angry. I didn't know what to
say. I just had to know why. Why had he run? Why hadn't he told
anyone? Without hesitation, I hit Reply.

*Tommy:*

*Why did you run away? Why didn't you tell anyone?*
*Birdie*

His response popped up a couple of minutes later.

*Birdie:*
  *I don't know how to answer your questions. I was scared.*
*I was stupid. I was worried they would think I did it. I was . . .*
*young. I don't know. I have no excuse. Sometimes the guilt*
*weighs so heavily on my chest, it's almost like I can't breathe.*
*Do you know what I mean?*
  *I'm sorry for what happened to you. You wouldn't have*
*found her if I hadn't been such a coward. Please believe me.*
*I'm sorry.*
  *Tommy*

I stared at his words. I did know what he meant and I allowed myself to consider what it must have been like for him that night. I thought about my own reaction to seeing Grace's body. I had been shocked and terrified. I quickly typed out my reply.

*Dear Tommy:*
  *I'm sorry if that last message came off as accusing.*
*I DO know what you mean. But that doesn't excuse the*
*fact that you left her there alone after everything else she*
*endured. I'm not sure how I feel about your confession. I*
*would prefer not to discuss this any more.*

I hit Send, logged off AOL, and then pushed the chair away from the computer. I didn't want to see his response, nor was I any longer in the mood to look at the pictures of Adelle's trip to Florida. The notion of sunny beaches and happy-looking people was decidedly unappealing.

My mind reeled with his confession. I felt Grace begin to stir. She sensed my anxiety, no doubt. She was used to my fixation about her death. In fact, sometimes I got the feeling that she enjoyed being so prominent in my mind. It was a power she never had in life. But tonight, all I wanted was to be alone with my thoughts and to have the chance to digest this new information.

"I'm tired," I said to Toby as I sank down next to him and reached out to pet his short, glossy coat. He grunted in his sleep and stretched out his legs, exposing his belly to the heat of the fire. I curled up behind him, tucking my bent arm under my head as a pillow. With the other hand, I gently rubbed his chest and belly. As I stared at the fire, I began to relax into the warmth of my dog and, before I knew it, fell asleep.

My dreams that night were thick, textured, and horribly vivid.

They began with a roller coaster that seemed to do nothing but climb slowly, steadily, jerkily up the track to a drop that none of us on the ride would survive. It was too steep and the force of the fall would be too much. But still, we continued to climb.

I looked frantically from side to side, trying to see around the hard foam and metal restraint that had me pinned to my seat. "It's going to rain," someone said.

I looked upward and a few tiny drops struck my face.

"I hope it doesn't make the track so wet that the wheels disengage." The voice came from the girl sitting next to me.

My heart thumped and I felt the familiar knot of fear and panic rise in my chest and then into my throat.

"I knew this was a bad idea," the girl next to me said. "But you never listen, Birdie, do you?"

I recognized the querulous tone. "Grace? Is that you?"

"Of course it's me," she said and leaned forward to stick her face into my line of vision. She looked exactly the same as she had in our last school pictures.

"Why aren't you restrained?"

"Why would I be, silly? I'm dead." She gave an exaggerated frown and then pulled a piece of bubble gum out of her pants pocket.

The roller coaster continued to clank and lurch up the incline, bringing my attention very much back to the situation at hand.

"I hate roller coasters," I said. I could hear the anxiety in my voice.

"*I know you do,*" Grace said. "*But this is your dream. I'm just along for the ride.*" She grinned. "*Get it? Along for the ride?*"

"This is a dream?" I tried to look around. "It doesn't feel like a dream. It feels real."

"*It's a real dream,*" Grace said authoritatively and pushed a strand of hair behind her ear. She moved so she was sitting casually with her arm looped over the seats in front of her.

"Grace, I'm scared."

"*I know,*" she said simply and pushed her tongue through the pink wad of gum and tried to blow a bubble.

She peered over the seat of the car in front of us and then stood up. "*We're nearing the crest,*" she said over her shoulder. "*Anything you want to get off your chest?*"

My breath began to come in short pants and I felt as if I were hyperventilating. I shook my head tightly from side to side. "I want off. Don't they have a chicken exit? At the top? For people who change their minds?"

Grace turned her body and craned her neck so she could fully look at me. "*Is that what you've done—changed your mind?*"

I nodded, though I was unsure if she was talking about the ride or something else.

She seemed to consider and then held up a hand. "*Stop,*" she yelled and immediately, the roller coaster clunked to a standstill. There was silence. The wind caused the suspended track to sway side to side. It felt like being on a boat at sea. I realized suddenly how powerless I was.

"How do I get out?"

"*Easy,*" Grace said. "*Just step out onto the scaffolding on your left. There are stairs that will take you straight down.*"

I pushed at the harness across my chest that had me pinned into the molded plastic seat.

"*Release,*" she yelled. Immediately I heard a muffled click and, with a hydraulic hiss, the restraint disengaged and rose slowly over my head. I waited for several seconds before moving. To my surprise, I found that I missed the security of the harness. Without it, I felt fragile and vulnerable. "*The steps are over there.*" She pointed.

I turned my head. Without the restraint I saw the metal handrail and the stairs that led downward. We were much higher up than I had realized. I struggled to get out of the seat. With the steep angle, my body felt like lead. Finally, I rolled to the side, pulled my feet up under me, and rose into an awkward squat. To get to the stairs, I would have to crawl out of the roller coaster, step across the gap between the track and the stairs—and I would have to stand up.

Shakily, I rose to my feet. My legs trembled and I clutched tightly to the bar that ran across the top of the seat in front of me. I stood, frozen. The wind whistled past and I felt the track sway beneath me. I looked again at the space between the stairs and the roller coaster. My hands shook as I looked past the scaffolding to the sky. It was dark, ominous. I considered the possibility of lightning.

"Go on," Grace said. "Once it starts raining, the steps will be slippery."

At her words, drops of rain began to fall.

Trembling, I clung to the handrail and stepped shakily out of the car onto the scaffolding steps. Below us the trees and buildings and other amusement park rides looked tiny and far away. The wind whistled, blowing my hair into my eyes and mouth. I wanted to descend, but I couldn't force my body to move. I looked at the roller coaster. The other cars were empty. Grace and I had been the only passengers.

"You need to move!" Grace yelled to be heard over the wind.

"We were the only ones on the ride," I yelled back. "Can't they just back down?"

"It's a one-way train, baby."

Another gust of wind rocked the scaffolding. Still clutching the handrail, I crouched down.

"Grace, I can't," I yelled. "I can't do it alone. It's too scary. I might fall."

"There's no other way down."

"Help me," I begged. "I know you can. Please."

Not responding, she continued to stare down at me. The scaffolding began to sway back and forth.

"Please, Grace."

"*Okay,*" she said finally. "*But you have to do what I tell you.*" She came down until she stood on the step directly behind me. "*You're going to have to stand up.*"

I nodded, took a deep breath, and, with both hands clutching the handrail, pulled myself into a standing position. Because she was still a girl and I was an adult, we stood eye to eye, facing each other. I was reminded of the last time I had seen her and wondered if the ants still lived inside her.

"*You're going to have to turn around,*" she said. "*But whatever you do, don't look down. Just hold onto the guardrails on either side of you and turn your body. When you do that, we'll go down together.*"

"Just one step at a time," I said. "Baby steps."

"*Baby steps,*" she repeated. "*Now, remember, don't look down.*"

I nodded and then slowly, painstakingly, turned my body until I had to let go of one of the handrails. Quickly, I jerked around so that both hands were clutching the same rail. I twisted so that I could reach out with my other hand to grasp the handrail. My heart hammered in my chest and my legs threatened to give out, but I was, I realized, now facing away from Grace and in the direction I needed to go.

"*Okay,*" Grace yelled from behind me. "*Now, take a step down. Just one at a time. Just look at the step you need to take next.*"

I concentrated on the step in front of me, lifted one wobbly leg, and stepped forward. Beneath me, the scaffolding continued to rock and sway. Slowly, I transferred the weight to my other foot and stepped down. I was one step closer to the ground.

"*One down, only 9,000 to go,*" Grace said.

We were on our fifteenth step when a gust of wind made me stumble and then fall to the side.

"Grace," I screamed as I felt my legs slide over the edge of the scaffolding, pulling my upper body with them. I reached frantically for something, anything, to hold onto. "Help me!"

"*Can't,*" she said. "*You need to help yourself on this one. Besides, why would I help someone who lies to me—someone who keeps things from me?*"

My hands clutched the pole. I felt the metal of the step cut into the skin of my chest and armpits. The rain fell harder.

"I don't know what you're talking about," I said. "Help me! Please!"

*"You were hiding something from me on the computer, Birdie. I'm not stupid, you know."*

"I know!" My grasp on the pole began to slip. "Grace, pull me up. Please! I'm going to fall!"

She tipped her head to the side and studied me as if I were a bad puppy. *"Why do you always deny me what I want?"*

"Grace, I don't know what you mean," I gasped. "Please, just help me and we can talk about this." Excruciating pain shot through my shoulders and arms.

*"I just don't get it,"* she continued as if I hadn't spoken. *"I ask so little from you."*

My fingers had begun to cramp and I found myself watching with a strange, uninterested fascination as they began their slow, tortured release of the slippery pole. Slowly, slowly, they straightened until only my chewed and fractured fingernails still clung to the pole.

The sensation of falling was not what I expected—not at first. It was silent. And it was gentle. I didn't plummet, but rather, hung suspended in the warm, balmy air.

"This isn't so bad," I thought.

*"That's because you haven't turned over,"* came Grace's voice, once again in my head. *"In just a second, the air currents are going to force your body to flip over. And when that happens, it's going to all come at once. All of the sound is going to come all at once. It will feel like you're running into a wall of sound. But, I'm here to help. I'm here to absorb the impact of this."*

I was about to answer when my body slammed into something and then was jerked upward as if I were a fish that had just taken the baited hook. The sudden rush of sound was deafening. I felt the impact in my joints.

*"Let me,"* Grace screamed, her voice sounding like mine when as a child I would talk into the box fan in my window. I tried to close my eyes, but the wind forced them painfully open.

I tried to shut out everything and focus on my memory of her face as she had looked on the roller coaster and in her school picture. I imagined her outfit, her pants, her button-down shirt. I thought about her eyes and her hair. And then, suddenly, it all just stopped.

*"How about that?"*

I blinked and looked around. I was standing at the foot of the roller coaster. It wasn't nearly as tall as it had been only moments before. In fact, it was now, I realized, only a couple of stories tall. People screamed in fear and delight as one of the other coasters rushed past.

"We made it," I said aloud and patted my chest and thighs and head.

*"Yeah. Wanna do it again?"*

I realized that the speaker was talking to me. I turned and looked up into the face of a dark-haired man. He grinned down and ran a hand through his wind-blown curls. His blue eyes twinkled. He raised his eyebrows and then looked down at his watch. On his hand glinted a gold wedding band.

*"We're not supposed to meet the kids for another half-hour,"* he said. *"We can ride it again and still have time to get a funnel cake."*

I blinked and looked around in confusion.

"I . . ." Although I didn't recognize this man, somehow I knew that he was my husband. I looked at him more closely. He looked familiar. He grinned at my scrutiny.

*"What?"* he asked and reached out for my hand.

For once, I didn't worry about germs or contamination.

"Nothing," I said and shook my head in surprise. "I just . . . you're so handsome."

His grin grew wider.

*"Thank you,"* he said and I could tell he genuinely meant it. *"It's nice to hear after a decade."*

I quickly did the math in my head. If we had been married for ten years, then we had gotten married when I was twenty. Had I gone to college? Had I graduated? Before I had time to think more about it, my husband leaned down and kissed me first on the top of my nose, then on my cheek, and then on my lips. It was a tender kiss that started out sweet and quickly became passionate. I felt my body respond, and rather than being frightened, I was thrilled at the feeling. I felt alive and eager in a way that was unfamiliar but very pleasant.

*"What say we put the kids to bed early tonight?"* he whispered in my ear. *"And then we go to bed early, too?"*

I leaned into him and inhaled his soapy, starchy smell. His heart thudded slowly and rhythmically against my cheek.

"I'd like that." I was about to say more when I heard the words, *"Mommy! Mommy!"*

I pulled away from the embrace and turned to see three children—two boys and a girl walking toward us. The girl was clearly the oldest. She was tall for her age, which I guessed to be nine or ten. She had long blond hair that was pulled back in a banana clip. Her green eyes were large and round. She was going to be a beautiful woman, I thought.

The boys were, I somehow suddenly knew, eight and six. And they looked like their father with dark, curly hair and blue eyes. I studied them in amazement, astounded that these creatures came from my body. I wanted to touch them, squeeze them, feel their bones under their skin. I felt my love for them almost bursting through my chest.

The youngest one waved something over his head as he broke into a run. *"Mommy!"* he cried. *"Mommy, look!"*

I knelt and he rushed into my arms for an enthusiastic hug. He smelled like cotton candy and little-boy sweat.

*"I won,"* he yelled. *"Look what I won!"* He pulled back and thrust a small, cheap stuffed monkey in my face. *"I won this at the baseball game,"* he said proudly. *"I knocked down all the bottles."*

*"With a little bit of help,"* said the girl. I looked up at her. She was trying to pretend she was bored and too old to be at the amusement park with her family, but I could tell she was having a good time. I pulled the boy back to me for another hug and he allowed me to hold him for several seconds before pulling away.

*"Can we go to the fun house?"* It was the older boy. I stood up and looked at him. He was quiet, I knew, and thoughtful. *"It's back there."* He turned and pointed in the direction from which they had come. *"It takes two tickets."*

"Lead the way," I said and felt a strong hand slip into mine.

We walked that way, hand in hand behind the children. I smiled happily at everyone. I was normal, I realized. I had a handsome husband who loved only me, three beautiful children, and we were spending the day at the amusement park. I found myself laughing out loud.

The man in front of the fun house looked us over and held out his hand in a bored gesture that indicated he had performed this transaction millions of times.

*"Five people, ten tickets,"* he said in a raspy voice.

I looked down at his upturned hand. The palm was large and calloused. The fingers were short, blunt, and smeared with something that looked like ink or grease. Without flinching, I placed the tickets in his hand.

*"Enjoy,"* he said automatically before turning his attention to the teenaged couple behind us. *"Two people, four tickets."*

I turned as if to say something to him but felt the older of the two boys grasp my hand and tug me forward.

The fun house was like one I had gone to when I was seven. My parents, Natalie's parents, and Grace's parents had planned a multifamily vacation to Six Flags Over Texas. We had carpooled down to Dallas, where we walked the route taken by JFK the day he was assassinated. I remembered, suddenly, standing on a downtown street corner looking up at the window in the book depository from which Oswald fired the shots. Our parents had stood solemnly behind us speaking in low tones.

*"Come on,"* the boy said, jerking me both literally and figuratively out of my reverie. We walked awkwardly on the tilting floor that rocked back and forth like flat mechanical waves and stumbled clumsily into the room of mirrors. Once inside, he dropped my hand and ran forward. I followed, my eyes trained on his small form as he navigated the confusing labyrinth. Behind me, I could hear the youngest boy chattering happily to his father.

*"Mom, look,"* my daughter said, and I turned. She moved to stand next to me. She pointed at the mirror. *"We look like sisters."*

I turned my gaze to the mirror and saw for the first time what I looked like as a happily married woman. The image that greeted me made my heart stop. It was Grace. The face that stared back at me was an adult, full-grown Grace. I blanched and stepped backward, running into the mirror behind me.

*"Mom, what's wrong? Are you okay?"*

Immediately, I heard the familiar sound of deafening silence. It was the sound of the clearing the day I found Grace's body. It was the sound of the wind as I fell from the roller coaster. It was the sound of everything and nothing at once.

I stared at the image in the mirror and it stared back at me. I blinked and she blinked. This wasn't my life—it was Grace's. Grace's memories of Dallas. Grace's family. Grace's handsome husband. None of it was mine. It was all hers. I was the one who had died.

I shook my head and watched as Grace's image in the mirror opened her mouth and began to scream.

# Chapter 25

It was the scream that woke me—and, presumably, Toby, who leapt to his feet and began to bark furiously in all directions at once. I lay still, my heart pounding, listening to him. Though loud, the sound was reassuring. This was real. Toby was my dog. This was my cabin. It was my life. What had just happened was a dream.

The cabin was gloomy with the light of early dawn and the fire, which had burned so cheerily the night before, had gone out. The room was cold and I rolled onto my side and pulled my legs toward my chest. My body shook, though I wasn't sure if it was from cold or from the nightmares. I felt strange, confused, discombobulated. The dreams, both of them, had seemed so real. Grace had seemed so real. And, in the second dream, she had taken over my body. She had been that real. How often, I wondered, did she do that? How often did she take over when I was asleep? The idea scared me.

I reached out to Toby for comfort, shushing him and making kissy noises to bring him closer. He barked once more and then padded over to me. He sniffed my face and neck and then shoved his cold, wet nose against my cheek. I reached up and pulled him down, wrapping my body around his. He groaned dramatically but endured my neediness.

We stayed like that for more than an hour, me pressed against him, my pulse slowly returning to normal. By the time I trusted myself to get up, the sun had crept over the mountains and was shining brightly into the living room. I pulled myself into a standing position and debated turning up the heat versus building another fire in the fireplace. I arched slightly to stretch out my lower back and then bent down to pull a couple of twigs from the stack of tinder next to the fireplace. Using the poker, I churned up the ashes until I had a small pile of red-orange coals. I placed the tinder on top of them and then blew. Clouds of ashes billowed up, but the coals glowed brightly. I blew again and watched as one of the coals flamed to life. I moved the twigs on top of it and then slowly, as the fire caught, fed larger and larger sticks to the flame until the fire was strong enough to add a small log. There was something satisfying about building a fire.

Toby watched and then followed me into the kitchen. Although I would have liked to think he came to keep me company, I knew that he was hungry. I looked down at him for several seconds and then opened a can of dog food and chunked it up into his bowl. He sniffed it with curiosity, then turned and walked back into the living room. I stared down at the unappetizing brown mash for a moment or two before turning to the cabinet and taking out a box of Raisin Bran. I poured some into a bowl, splashed in some milk, and spooned the first couple of bites into my mouth as I wandered back out into the living room. The computer screen was alive with flying toasters.

I thought again about the dreams and what Grace had said as I hung from the roller coaster scaffolding. She knew I was hiding something from her. She knew that I was communicating with someone and was keeping it a secret. I searched my mind to see if she was paying attention, but all I felt was quiet satisfaction. She had made her point and now, she was waiting to see what I would do. I could also sense that she was tired—that her invasion of my body and my dreams had worn her out as much as it had me. I took a spoonful of cereal and chewed thoughtfully. Perhaps she needed rest. Perhaps I could exploit that weakness.

I stared again at the computer and remembered suddenly my correspondence with Tommy the night before. Although the thought of communicating with him scared me, something told me it was important. I wondered how long it would be before Grace was asleep or not paying attention. Perhaps I could distract her by typing a long e-mail to Adelle. But then, suddenly, I didn't care what she knew. This was my life, not hers. She could invade my thoughts, invade my dreams, but at the end of the day, I was the one who was in charge. It was my body and my life—no matter how strange others might think it to be.

"Just do it," I muttered to myself as I sat down and wiggled the mouse. The screen immediately came to life and I clicked on the AOL icon. Two minutes of hissing and beeping later, the computer was connected to the internet.

In addition to the unread e-mail from Adelle, there was a reply from Roger and one from Tommy. I took a spoonful of cereal and chewed thoughtfully. I didn't want to start out with Roger's e-mails, nor was I sure I wanted to see what Tommy had to say. I clicked on Adelle's message.

> *Hey. Hope all is well. Florida was great. Sun, sand, and*
> *fun. I even tried parasailing. Not quite what I anticipated,*
> *but a good experience. How are you?"*

One thing that was both endearing and frustrating about Adelle was that she never used a greeting or a closing on her e-mails. She said what she wanted to say and then was done. I asked her once why she was so brief and she said it was because she was too busy to worry about such niceties. It made sense, but it always felt like her messages were rushed and somehow unfinished. Today's was no exception. I clicked on the pictures she had attached and waited as they loaded. Suddenly, there she was, smiling at the camera, waving, splashing in the water and flying (at least I assumed it was her) through the air. The last picture appeared to have been taken from the back of the motorboat.

"Wow," I said to Toby. "You should check this out. She looks great."

Toby raised his head from where he was curled into a ball on the couch, sighed deeply and put his head back down. I began to type.

> *Adelle:*
> *Great pictures. You look fantastic. Florida agrees with*

*you. I can't believe you went parasailing. Call me this*
*weekend?*
   *Love,*
   *Rebecca*

Next, I clicked on Roger's e-mail. It was a response to both of my angry e-mails.

*Rebecca:*
   *I have no idea what you're talking about. I haven't*
*given your e-mail address to anyone, nor do I know anyone*
*named "Thomas Anderson." There are a lot of things I am,*
*but a liar is not one of them. Well, at least most of the time*
*it's not. But in this case, I'm telling the truth. I didn't reveal*
*your identity to anyone.*
   *Rog*
   *P.S. The fact that you falsely accused me means you have to*
*make it up to me by coming to visit.*

I immediately hit the reply button and hammered out a terse response.

*Roger:*
   *He already told me that he got my information from*
*you. And it had to be you because no one else, aside from*
*Adelle, knows who I am. I've accepted the fact that what's*
*done is done, but don't ever do it again, okay? I have all the*
*friends I need. Oh, and my answer regarding visiting you*
*and Gus is still "no." I don't have anyone to watch Toby, so I*
*can't come.*
   *Rebecca*

Finally, I opened the e-mail from Tommy. The time stamp showed that it had been sent shortly after he received my response the night before.

*Birdie:*

    *I know you said you don't want to talk about it and I respect that. I'm sorry to have bothered you and brought all of this stuff up. I am just tired of dealing with it on my own.*

    *Tommy*

"*I knew it!*" It was Grace. I could feel her anger. "*I could tell something was up—that something was upsetting you. I should have known.*"

"It's not like that."

"*Really?*" Grace asked sarcastically. "*What's it like, then?*"

"He understands what I went through," I said. "From a point of view that no one—not even you—can appreciate."

"*You don't know him,*" Grace said "*And you certainly don't know him like I know him.*"

"What do you mean?" I asked aloud but there was no answer. She was punishing me with her silence. "Grace . . . goddammit, what do you mean?"

I stared at the computer. Grace was right. I *didn't* know him. But, I wanted to, didn't I? I wanted to be able to talk with someone who understood how I felt and what I experienced. Natalie had tried several times—both immediately after the murder and later when we were older. But no matter how hard she tried, no matter how much I wanted to open up to her, to share what I was going through, I couldn't. I couldn't in high school, or when she came to see me in college, or when she came to me for help that last time. I had failed Natalie just as I had failed Grace. And keeping it all inside was becoming too much.

"I don't want to do this alone," I said softly. "I don't want to have to spend the rest of my life having your dreams for you. It's not my fault what happened. It's not."

I thought about all the times Natalie had tried to talk about what had happened. I thought about the loneliness of my life. I had no one. No one had experienced what I had. No one knew the anguish and trauma—no one except Tommy. I thought about what he said about finding her body. He knew what that felt like—the shock, the fear, the revulsion, the guilt. He was someone I would never see . . . someone I would never have to look in the eyes. It was words on a computer screen. It seemed like my only salvation. I took a deep breath and began to type. I felt Grace's disapproval but, didn't care.

> *Tommy:*
>
> *I have to admit, I don't know what to say, nor am I sure why I'm writing back. You shocked me with your confession about finding Grace and I'm still not sure how I feel about it or how to respond. It was upsetting, to say the least. I appreciate your honesty and I don't think less of you for running away, although I still don't know as I really understand <u>why</u> you ran away. I say that, but the more I think about it, I guess it doesn't really matter. It's in the past. Do you ever wonder what happened that night? I pray that one day they are able to catch the bastard who did it. Until then, I guess we'll just have to live with the questions.*
>
> *I don't have any answers.*
> *Birdie*

I hit Send and leaned back in my chair.

*"Don't you think it's just a little bit weird that he would contact you out of the blue and then right away admit all of this stuff?"* As she spoke, Grace's voice became louder, more insistent.

"This doesn't concern you, Grace," I said tightly. "I don't need your help. This is about me for a change. So will you please mind your own business? For once?" The room echoed with the shouted words. Toby sat up, startled. I pushed my chair back from the computer desk and stomped into the kitchen where I threw my cereal bowl into the sink.

"Aghhh!" I yelled at the empty room. "Just go away! Please? I didn't tell him too much. I didn't tell him anything . . . and even if I did, it's none of your business. I'm tired of living in fear. You're dead, Grace. And I'm sorry. But I'm tired of feeling responsible for it! And I'm tired of my life being consumed by your death."

The room was silent. Angrily, I turned and strode out of the room. I paused at the computer when I saw that Tommy had already responded.

"I don't want to deal with any of this right now," I muttered as I climbed the stairs to the bedroom. Grace was silent, but I could feel her anger as I adjusted the water in the shower. I could tell she was waiting, biding her time. I climbed into the shower and relaxed slightly under the spray of hot water. Still, my mind raced. Grace was dead. And now, suddenly, the only other person who understood what I was going through—the only other person who had experienced the same thing—was trying to reach out to me. But then there was the niggling of doubt, of fear. Grace was right. He was too open, too in tune with what was going on in my head. It had to be a trick. But, what if it wasn't? He had come to me before, when I had been at my most vulnerable and lonely. He had been there then, so why wouldn't he understand?

*"You want to know why I'm concerned?"* Grace's taunting voice broke into my thoughts. *"Ask him about the knife."*

I opened my eyes with a start.

"What do you mean?"

I felt her mental shrug.

"Grace?"

When her voice came again, it was soft and childlike. *"Just ask him about the knife. Ask him where it came from. He knows, you know. It was his."*

I could hear nothing but her voice and the sound of the shower. Suddenly, I had an image in my head. It was of Tommy, the way he looked the summer of Grace's murder. I saw him from a great height, a height that I recognized as the Nest. But it wasn't something I had seen before. These were new images. Grace's images. I was watching the scene from Grace's eyes.

It was morning and below us, seventeen-year-old Tommy stood muttering to himself. In his hand, he held what appeared to be a hunting knife in a leather scabbard. I watched as he walked over to the large rock I had once tripped over and tore open my knee. He sat down. I couldn't make out what he was saying. All I could hear was the shower ... or was it the summer buzz of insects? The sounds merged.

I watched in fascination as slowly, reverently he slid the blade out of the cover and examined it, running his thumb along the razor-sharp edge. Slowly, he shifted it from hand to hand. In Grace's memory, it felt large and heavy. At some point I knew she had held it, examined it. The blade was sharp. The smell of leather had filled her nostrils. In our shared memory, I could smell the leather.

Below us, Tommy stood up and walked several paces from where he had been sitting and then turned. Squinting, he picked out a target and then flung the knife at it. His aim was bad and the knife somersaulted into the bushes. Grace and I watched as Tommy repeatedly retrieved the knife and threw it.

"This is not real, Grace," I said loudly and looked around the shower. "This *memory* is just you trying to mess with my head. You can't *show* me things. And you know why? Because you're dead." I spat these last words meanly. "You're trying to make me crazy so no one will want to be with me. And who knows, maybe I am ... I mean, come on ... I have a dead person living in my head." I snapped the handle of the shower down. The room was silent aside from the drip of the shower head.

"But you know what? I'm done." I yanked a towel off the wooden hook and dried my arms and legs. "I've had enough. I've given you as much as I can, but I can't do it anymore. Get out of my head, Grace! And take your visions and memories with you!"

Angrily, I stomped into the bedroom, yanked open the closet door, and pulled out a pair of jeans and a sweater. As I dressed, I considered what to do next—what would take my mind off the thoughts that crept, unbidden, into my head.

"We're cutting wood and laying in supplies," I told Toby as I tromped downstairs and unplugged the computer. "No more e-mail, no more conversations with people who aren't there, no more hassle. Just you and me, buddy."

I picked up the keys to the Jeep and unhooked his leash from the row of pegs that ran along the wall next to the door. Knowing that this meant a car ride, Toby eagerly scrambled up and ran to the door. I followed and then turned to survey the room. Going into town would be a good thing. Maybe I would force myself to chat with the people in town—or go to one of the restaurants and have a beer or a glass of wine. I went to the kitchen and pulled a wine glass out of the cupboard. I never used restaurant glasses because they weren't sterilized. I carefully slid the glass in a plastic freezer bag and then walked to the front door.

"Okay," I said to Toby as I opened the door. "Let's get out of here."

As we drove into La Veta, I was once again struck by the intersection of new and old. The fort and the depot, which were preserved as historical sites, were juxtaposed against tiny art galleries tucked into the closely situated buildings. It was a progressive community that was firmly anchored by the traditional values of hard work, honesty, and community. Everyone from the crusty ranchers to the lesbian bakery owners worked in unison to make it a place of worth and value. That was one of the things that drew me to the town. The other was the fact that people in La Veta respected each other's right to be themselves—myself included. I knew I was regarded as an oddity, that crazy artist woman who lived all alone with her dog. But no one seemed to care.

Despite the September chill, I rolled down the window so Toby could stick his head out as we drove slowly down Main Street. People milled about, their breath visible in hazy billows. It was a Saturday, I realized, when I saw the tourists ambling down the boardwalk, toothpicks sticking out of their mouths, their bellies full of hearty mountain breakfasts. I pulled into a parking place in front of Charlie's Grocery and grabbed my list.

"You wait here, buddy," I told Toby as I climbed out of the Jeep and slammed the door with a metallic clang. "I'll be right back."

I hurried into the store and began to collect the supplies I thought I would need for the next couple of months. I knew from experience that once the snow began to pile up, I could be left to my own devices for several weeks, so I filled the cart with canned goods and foods that could be frozen or stored in the pantry. As I stood at the checkout counter, the woman ringing up my items smiled at me.

"What's your dog's name?" she asked, looking at the pile of dog food and treats. She reached under the counter and pulled out a Milk-Bone dog biscuit. "You should give him this. We keep a supply for all of our canine customers."

"Thanks." I glanced out the front window and saw Toby sitting upright behind the steering wheel. He looked like the getaway car driver. His expression made me laugh. The cashier's gaze followed mine.

"That him in the Jeep?" she asked.

"Yes," I said, still laughing. "His name is Toby."

"They're like children, aren't they?" She grinned and extended her hand. "I'm Marjorie. I've seen you in here every month or so for the past couple of years and I always mean to introduce myself and then don't."

"Rebecca," I said and shook her hand quickly and tried not to think about what she might have touched before shaking my hand.

"You're that artist that lives up in that cabin way off of Highway 11, right?" she asked. "In Harry Beterman's old place?"

I nodded. "That's me."

"Nice property," she said. "Kinda remote, but still, nice. You probably get snowed in some, huh? Not many plows head up that little road."

"Well," I said, "It's not uncommon." I gestured to the pile of groceries. "But I'm ready for any emergency."

She nodded in approval and rang up the rest of my purchases.

"That'll be $279.93," she said. "Need help out with this?"

I shook my head.

Back in the Jeep, I nudged Toby back into the passenger's seat and then handed him the treat.

"That's from Marjorie," I said as he gobbled it down.

Next, I drove to the hardware store, bought rock salt and bird seed, and exchanged the empty tank of propane I had put in the back of the Jeep the week before, for a fresh one. My final stop was the liquor store, where I took my time choosing a couple of cases of wine. As I climbed into the Jeep, I looked at the clock on the dashboard. It wasn't even noon and already I was tired of interacting with people.

"I think that's enough for today," I told Toby as I started the engine, put the Jeep in reverse and backed out of the parking lot onto the main street. I rolled down the window slightly for the drive back to the cabin. The air tasted of coming snow.

Back at the cabin, I immediately began unloading the groceries. During each trip to and from the kitchen, I made it a point to ignore the blank, unplugged computer. There was, I knew, a message from Tommy. I sensed it. But I was torn between wanting to see it and being frightened of what it might say and Grace's recriminations.

"This is stupid," I said aloud as I put the last can of green beans in the pantry.

I glanced out the kitchen window at the neatly stacked firewood on the back porch. I had worked for almost a week cutting and splitting the logs. One remaining tree lay in pieces, waiting to be split into firewood. I would do it today, I thought resolutely. The physical activity would do me good and take my mind off of Tommy and Grace. I grabbed a beer out of the refrigerator, opened it, and then used an alcohol swab to carefully wipe off the mouth of the bottle. Even though it was cool outside, I soon would become sweaty and a beer was usually what I craved to cut the thirst.

Four hours, three beers, and two blisters later, I had split most of the logs and stacked them neatly on the growing mountain of wood. I had a chainsaw but preferred to use an ax. My body was tired and pleasantly sore. All I wanted was a bath, something to eat, a glass of wine, and the comfort of a fire in the fireplace. First, though, I had to deal with the issue of Tommy. It had been bothering me the entire time I was working and I had decided that the only way to deal with it was to face it head on. Moving quickly before I changed my mind, I plugged in the computer and waited while it slowly came back to life. As it hummed and whirled, I decided to skip the bath and take a quick shower. Within ten minutes I was dried, dressed, and seated in front of the waiting terminal with a glass of wine. Taking a deep breath, I clicked on the AOL icon and waited. Not only was there this morning's e-mail from Tommy, but also a reply from Roger and one from my mother. I clicked on Roger's first.

> *Dearest Rebecca:*
> *Two things:*
> *A. I refuse to take blame for something I didn't do, but I'm willing to let bygones be bygones and simply say that I don't know what you're talking about and I did not violate our agreement. Think what you will, but you're wrong.*
> *2. You ARE coming to visit. You don't know it yet. We will arrange for a dog-sitter. Or, since I'm sure you can't stand the thought of anyone in your house, we can get Toby boarded. I've checked. There are several places on the way to the airport.*
> *I will not be dissuaded.*
> *XXOO*

I considered what to say. Nothing came to mind. He wasn't going to admit what he had done. Fine. I had made my point. As for Chicago, I would deal with that later. I clicked on my mother's e-mail. Both Tara and I had been surprised when our mother announced that she had purchased a computer and that she was going to be online. But, it had turned out to be one of the best things that could have happened. By communicating via e-mail, we were much better able to keep in touch—but at a distance.

> *Hello sweetie:*
> *How are you? I was thinking about you the other day. We (the girls and I) were at coven and one of the women was talking about herbs and energy work to clear blockages in mind/body unison. I know you're against medication, but*

*what about herbs? St. John's Wort is wonderful for depres-*
*sion—not that you're depressed. And Valerian is great for*
*relaxation and sleep enhancement. I've talked to her about*
*dosages and will be sending you some in the mail. You don't*
*have to take it—just think about it. Oh, and while I'm*
*thinking about it, when I'm there for Christmas, I'm going*
*to smudge your cabin (burning sage to cleanse it).*

*Let's see . . . what else? Nothing much is going on here.*
*Mrs. Spencer from next door passed. Apparently, she had been*
*keeping track of everything everyone in the neighborhood had*
*been doing. I guess they found hundreds of notebooks with*
*notations of times and dates. Lord knows what she thought of*
*some of the things that went on here!*

*Tara sends her love. She and Andy are looking at*
*getting a timeshare in California.*

*Well, that's all I know. Write when you get a chance.*

*Love you.*

That left Tommy's message. I returned to my inbox, where it sat boldfaced to indicate that it hadn't been read. I stared at it. Grace did, too. I could feel it and I didn't even try to hide it from her. I felt my heart begin to beat faster.

"*Go on,*" she said finally. "*You want to. And you've made it clear I can't stop you.*"

Her words caused me to stop for a second. She was right. She couldn't stop me—at least not physically—from doing anything. *I* had that control.

"You're right," I said and clicked on Tommy's e-mail.

*Birdie:*

*I'm not sure there <u>are</u> answers, to tell you the truth.*
*Why did I run away? I don't know. I didn't know*
*what to do. Part of me was scared the person who did it*
*was still there. But really, I think a lot of it for me was that*
*I was scared everyone would think I had done it because it*
*was my knife—well, sort of. I had stolen it from that little*

*store on the corner. I had been using it for target practice.*
*My fingerprints were all over it. I thought if they connected*
*me to the knife . . . you know. I guess, deep down, I was just*
*a coward. I was scared. I don't know if that answers your*
*questions, but that's the best I can tell you.*
    *Tommy*

I tapped my fingers on the table as I read and then reread his reply. In my head, I felt Grace's smug satisfaction—a mental "I told you so."

"So what?" I said. "He told me about the knife of his own accord. I didn't have to ask. He volunteered the information. So what does *that* say about him?"

I thought about how to respond. I wanted to know more, but at the same time, continuing the conversation felt like playing with fire. Still, I wanted—make that needed—to know more. I felt Grace's disapproval and frustration that she couldn't stop me, couldn't control me. I clicked Reply.

*Tommy—*
    *I'm not sure what to say. I appreciate your honesty, but*
*your confession—or, more accurately, series of confessions—*
*is unsettling to say the least. How did your knife end up*
*being used to murder Grace?*
    *Birdie*

*"I can tell you,"* Grace said. *"Better yet, I can show you. Want to see my rape and murder? I know I've refused to let you see it in the past, but I think it's time you saw what really happened."*

"Go away," I spat.

*"You're going to regret this,"* she said. *"He's not who you think."*

I ignored her and reached for my glass of wine. I sipped as I waited to see if he was online and if he would reply. I didn't have to wait long.

Within ten minutes, his response appeared.

*Birdie:*

    *I don't know where to begin. I don't mean to make you uncomfortable, so I'll tell you everything and then let you make the decision about where to go from here. I don't know how much you remember about me, so I'll start from the beginning.*

    *I was at my grandparents' that summer because my parents thought my friends were bad influences. What they didn't know was that I (and I'm ashamed to admit it) was the ringleader. It was serious stuff—robbing and beating up gay men in parks, running errands for drug dealers. We never got caught, but still . . . Please understand, I'm not proud of what I did back then. It was stupid and wrong— not to mention dangerous—which is why my parents sent me to Edenbridge to stay with my grandparents. I think they were trying to figure out what to do with me and figured that Edenbridge was as safe a place as any.*

    *When you met me, I was angry. I hated Edenbridge. And then one day, I wandered into that little store. I saw the knives and I thought . . . why not? So, I stole one. I thought it would make me cool—that I could go back home and impress my friends. But I couldn't let my grandparents see it, so I hid it in the clearing, at the base of a big tree that was right near your tree house.*

    *I wanted to throw it, kind of like they did it in the movies. So I went to the clearing to practice. There was never anybody there. At least, I thought I was alone. But one day, while I was practicing, I heard someone sneeze. It was Grace, up in the tree house watching. Turns out she had been watching me practically every day.*

    *I have to admit, my initial reaction was anger . . . and embarrassment. She didn't laugh, though. Or make fun. She simply said that I was getting pretty good and asked if I could teach her how to throw it. When I asked her why, she said she needed protection. As we got to be friends, I realized who she needed protecting from and why.*

*I know this is going to sound strange, but the time I spent with her made more of an impact on me than any amount of punishment my parents could have doled out. She seemed so smart and mature. A lot of the time I forgot that she was only 11. I told her about the things I had done and she was cool. She didn't judge. And she told me about her mom and Reggie. She was scared to be at home with him there.*

*Before you ask, I don't know who killed her or why. If you ask me, I think it was Reggie. But that's just my opinion. All I know is that when I found her, she was already dead. She had been stabbed and I assumed, from how she was left, raped. I didn't know what to do, Birdie. I saw the knife and knew it was mine. Maybe she had pulled it out for protection. I don't know. All I do know is that I realized that my fingerprints probably were all over it. And, because no one knew we were spending time together, I figured people would think the worst. So, I ran. I ran back to my grandparents' house and I stayed there.*

*When you saw me that first time, I was there because I missed Grace. I just wanted to be in the place we used to spend time together. I know I probably scared you when I climbed up in your tree house. I'm sorry. After we spoke (you and me) I realized we were struggling with similar issues. When I talked to you, I didn't feel so alone.*

*I know that's a long answer to your question, but I wanted you to know everything. Grace changed my life. Her death . . . when I went back to Chicago, my perspective had changed. I understood the value of life and the devastation that comes with the taking of life. Grace made me see that.*

*I know you're a private person and you have boundaries, Birdie. But for good reason. Just know that at some point, I'd like to become friends.*

*Tommy*

I stared at the screen, dumbfounded. I thought back to that

summer and I remembered our meetings and our conversations. I knew what he meant about not feeling so alone. And then it hit me—our correspondence, our discussions, weren't chance. They were part of a larger plan. Someone or something continued to throw us together. Before, we were there for each other when Grace died. Now, as I struggled with Natalie's death, he was here again.

"Bullshit," Grace said. "You're seeing what you want to see."

"You don't know anything."

"I know more than you." I could feel her pacing. "I know that you can't trust this guy. Ask him about the other rape."

"What do you mean? What other rape?"

"You'll see," she crowed. "Natalie thinks he's trouble, too."

I blinked. "What do you mean? "Natalie's there?"

"Oh, didn't I tell you?" Grace said slyly. "She's here. Not in your head, of course. But in the great nebulousness of death."

"Can I talk to her?" I asked. "There are some things I want—"

"She doesn't want to talk to you," Grace said. "She has no time for someone who didn't take her in and then couldn't be bothered with going to her funeral."

"There were circumstances beyond my control," I stammered. "I can explain."

"She doesn't want to hear it," Grace said. "You let her down just like you let me down. You weren't there for her and you weren't there for me."

"Shut up," I said. "Just . . . shut up. You have no idea what I've been through."

"Are you kidding?" Grace said sarcastically. "I'm in your head. I know everything that's going on." She was silent for several seconds. "Natalie hates you, you know."

"That's not true."

"Oh, it is. All you have left is that fag friend of yours."

"Tommy wants to be my friend."

I turned back to the computer and pulled up the e-mail. I pointed to the last line. "See? And, you know what?" I clicked on the reply button. "I want to be his, too."

"What are you doing?" asked Grace incredulously as the message box opened. "You don't know—"

"Shut up," I said aloud.

"*Birdie, listen to me.*" Grace's voice dropped to a pained whisper. "*Tommy can't be trusted.*" She paused. "*He's the one who murdered me.*"

"Funny how it just comes up now when you're feeling threatened."

"*You never needed to know before. And I wasn't ready to tell you. But you need to listen to me now. It was Tommy. He pretended to be my friend, he lured me to the Nest, and then he killed me.*"

"You're just saying that because you're jealous!" My voice echoed through the open room. "You've always been jealous, Grace. Jealous of the fact that I had parents who loved me. That *I* was Natalie's best friend. That you died and I didn't. You're jealous and you've been punishing and controlling me ever since."

"*That's ridiculous,*" Grace said quickly. "*All I've ever wanted to do is protect you from suffering the same fate as me. Think about it, Birdie. Who has kept you safe? Who was there when you did LSD? Who takes care of you every night now when you're drunk? Me! You really have no one but me.*"

"And that's the way you like it, isn't it?" I hissed. "You've alienated me from friends and family. You've made me scared of my own shadow. Of germs. Of life. I've given up everything to you out of guilt. I've so insulated myself that I have nothing."

"*You're wrong. You're alive because of me. Admit it. You've always known it should have been you.*"

"No. There's no way it was supposed to be me. You're just saying that to make me feel guilty—to make me do what you want. But it's not going to work this time. I'm not going to let you take away someone who actually has the potential for understanding me."

"*I understand you.*"

"But you're not real," I said. "Don't you see? You're not real. I can't do this anymore. I'm sorry, Grace, but . . ." I swallowed. "You are no longer welcome here. I want relationships with real people—people who can give something back to me." I looked around the room, almost as if I expected her to appear. "I don't know if you're a ghost or . . . what. But you're dead. And I'm alive and I don't deserve to be punished any longer. I'm not going to give up my life to a ghost, so please, *leave me the fuck alone!*"

*"Fine!"* she screamed and suddenly, I felt her retreat. She didn't leave but she retreated and it was different than in the past and for the first time since her death, I felt like I had broken her grasp. I took a deep breath, sat up straighter and began to type.

Tommy—

   *I would like to be your friend, too. Please know, this is a big step for me—both to admit it and to act on it. Because of that, there are some things I need to tell you about myself—things I need to write before I lose my nerve.*

   *When Grace died, a part of me died, too. Or, at least, a part of me changed. Her murder made me begin to fear . . . things. Small things at first. But over time, they've become larger. Now, almost everything scares me—which is why I have shut myself off, locked myself away. You have no way of knowing this, but this—you—e-mailing is the first time in a really long time that I've gone out on a limb and taken a chance. You're a stranger to me. You're an unknown. You're scary. But there's something about you that makes me want to try to break free of my fears.*

   *I think Grace's death changed your life as irrevocably as it changed mine. And because of that, because of your relationship with her, you're probably the only person who can understand me and the demons I face every day. You saw it in my art and I see it in your words. We are similarly tortured by guilt, by loss, by shame.*

   *I'm tired of feeling this way.*

   Birdie

My finger hovered over the mouse. One click was all it would take to send this e-mail. One click and I would be putting myself out there, opening a dialogue with this man. I waited for Grace's voice. Nothing. I was free to make my own decision. I hesitated, and then clicked the button.

# Chapter 26

I didn't hear from Tommy for several days—though it was through no fault of his. The storm I had felt coming while in La Veta, struck with full force. It was by no means a blizzard, but it was enough to knock out the electrical lines and make the gravel road to my cabin impassable.

"Looks like it's just you and me, buddy," I said to Toby as I stepped onto the back porch for an armload of firewood. The cabin was constructed for year-round residency, meaning that it was well-insulated and small enough that the fireplace could heat most of the house. The absence of electricity wasn't that big of an inconvenience. The hot water heater and stove were powered by gas and the water was pumped from a well that had a backup gas engine. All in all, the lack of electricity wasn't bothersome unless you counted not being able to watch television or read in bed a hardship—which I didn't. Over the years I had become accustomed to being without power and usually enjoyed the simplicity of lounging by the fire with a good book and looking out the window at the falling snow. This time, however, I was anxious. I had taken a huge step—had gone out on a limb and was feeling very nervous and vulnerable. I wanted to read Tommy's reply.

"Wouldn't it figure." I sank down next to Toby on the couch. In one hand I held a glass of red wine; in the other, my dog-eared copy of *To Kill a Mockingbird*. Toby raised his head at the sound of my voice, stared at me for a couple of seconds, and then groaned and curled into a tight ball. I smiled, pulled a blanket over my feet and legs, and opened the book. It was a copy I had purchased in college. I had read it countless times—almost as many as I had read *A Separate Peace*. I was fascinated by Harper Lee, both because of her story and also because of the parallels in our lives. Like me, she had been a tomboy. Like me, she had grown up in a small town full of colorful characters. And like me, she was a bit of a recluse who seemed to struggle with her identity. Her connection with Truman Capote had inspired me to check out several of his books from the library. But after the first couple of pages of *In Cold Blood*, I didn't read any more.

Even as I began to read, my mind wandered. My eyes took in the familiar words, but my brain didn't process them. I wondered about Tommy, about his reply and what he could misconstrue about my lack of response to his almost certain immediate reply. I considered his words and what he would say, all the while waiting for Grace's chiding voice to break in. Still, nothing. It was a welcome relief, this silence. But it also seemed weird. After so many years of living with her voice, of sensing her invisible hand guiding my life, I felt oddly untethered. I thought again about my argument with Grace.

"She's just jealous," I said aloud. "She's jealous that I'm still alive, and that I am becoming friends with the one person, the secret person no one knew about, that she thought was hers—Tommy. She was in love with him."

Suddenly it was all so clear. I stared at the fire as the pieces of the puzzle fell into place. Jealousy was the reason she tried to get me to avoid him just after her death. Jealousy was the reason why she didn't want me communicating with him now. The realization softened my anger.

"I'm sorry, Grace," I murmured as I looked away from the fire and down at my book. I felt triumphant at having worked it out, but also very sad. My sadness or Grace's, I wondered before realizing that it didn't really matter. After so many years, they were one and the same.

The next four days passed slowly—not because we were snowed in, but because I was eager to read Tommy's response. I had taken a huge risk, admitting what I did, and I wanted to hear from him, wanted to read his reply. But I couldn't and so instead, I paced the cabin, stared out the windows, and busied myself outside by hauling firewood from the woodpile and stacking it on the back porch. Toby watched with a bored expression.

I was dozing when the electricity came on. It was a dark Wednesday afternoon and I had curled up on the floor in front of the fireplace with my book and a cup of hot tea. The combination of the fire, tea, and Toby snoring softly beside me made me uncharacteristically drowsy and relaxed. I put the book aside and closed my eyes. I didn't realize I had fallen asleep until I was jarred awake by the artificial glare of the lights and the loud British voices of the BBC newscast on the radio. Toby leapt up and growled in all directions, startled as well.

"Looks like the electricity is back on," I said, as much to myself as to Toby. I stood up and turned off the lights and radio. I had grown accustomed to the more natural light provided by the candles and the fireplace and wasn't ready to give it up. I considered lying back down and seeing if I could go back to sleep when I realized with a jolt that I could access my e-mail. I hurried to the computer and pressed the power button. While waiting for it to boot up, I retrieved my cup of tea, which had grown cold as I napped, and put it in the microwave.

"I have to admit," I said to Toby, who had followed me into the kitchen. "Being able to use the microwave is a lot faster than boiling water."

By the time I had reheated the tea and returned to the living room, the computer was glowing warmly. I sat down, clicked the AOL icon, and waited as it connected and my inbox appeared. I had two messages from Roger, one from Adelle, and four from Tommy. I resisted the impulse to read them first and instead, clicked on the first of Roger's e-mails.

*Hello Sunshine,*

*No response to my last message, so I thought I'd just check in and see if I had worn you down, yet. As added incentive, because I know you hate to fly, I've decided to fly out, make the trip to and from Denver with you and then fly back on my own. Good plan, no? If I don't hear from you within the next week, I'm going to make the reservations without your input. Best say "yes" now, missy.*

*Rog*

Before answering, I decided to see what his second e-mail had to say.

*Me again,*

*Just wanted to let you know that we're using several of the pieces I got when I was there last in the new restaurant. Also, Gus has convinced one of his business acquaintances to purchase the red on black spiral series. I only got two of them, so could you ship the other one in the set? Or, better yet, I'll just get it when I'm there for our trip to Chicago— save on the shipping costs. You've got three more days to decide when you're coming to visit.*

*Rog*

I didn't want to go to Chicago. Roger knew that, but he also thought if he could just continue to force me out of the house, it would keep me from becoming a full-fledged recluse. I debated the options and finally decided to bite the bullet.

*Roger,*

*I know you think you know what's best for me, but I just don't want to come to Chicago—especially in the winter. Please, please, please can't we put this on hold and revisit it in the spring? I would feel better about it that way. As for the third in the red on black series, I will ship it as soon as I'm no longer snowed in. It probably will be a couple of days from*

*now. The electricity has been off and might go off again, so
if you don't hear from me, don't worry.*
   *I promise we'll revisit this in the spring, okay?*
   *Rebecca*

Next I clicked on Adelle's message, which was written in her
typical, abbreviated style.

   *The pictures were taken by my friend, Lana. Parasailing
   was fun, but SCARY. Working on a big case, so I might not
   call this weekend, but we'll catch up soon. Promise.*

I had no response, really—not that a response was necessary.
Adelle and I were close, but in a distant sort of way. We would go
for long periods without talking and then pick back up as if no time
at all had passed. It was, we agreed, the perfect friendship in that
regard. I smiled, closed out of the message, and then took a deep
breath. It was time to read Tommy's e-mails. I took a big gulp of tea
and clicked on the most recent.

   *Okay, now I'm worried. Please respond just to let me
   know what's going on.*
   *Tommy*

Second most recent:

*Birdie,*
   *Are you okay? I didn't mean to offend you.*
   *Tommy*

Third most recent:

*Birdie,*
   *Hi there. Just checking in to make sure my earlier
   e-mail didn't upset you. Your silence is making me a
   little uneasy. I know some of the things I may have said*

*were surprising, but they weren't meant to offend. Let*
*me know where your head is, okay?*

   *Tommy*

And finally:

*Dear Birdie,*

   *If I were to tell you how often Grace pops into my head,*
*you would think I was either crazy or obsessed. I know this*
*isn't going to make sense, but I hear her in my head sometimes,*
*guiding me as if she were my guardian angel. She helped me*
*turn my life around.*

   *I'm glad you want to be friends. I agree with you that*
*we have a lot in common and no one but the other can*
*understand what we experienced that summer. It feels good*
*to talk about these things. It makes me realize that there*
*always has been a part of me that has been closed off. But*
*since we've been writing back and forth, I don't feel that*
*way. I don't feel so alone.*

   *Thank you.*

   *T.*

I smiled, relieved at his response, and strangely excited to reply
to his note. Eagerly, I hit the reply button and began to type.

*Tommy—*

   *Not to worry. You didn't offend me at all. I just hadn't*
*received your e-mails. I live in the mountains in Colorado.*
*My cabin is fairly remote and when winter storms hit, I'm*
*often snowed in without power. It's not a huge deal and*
*usually I like being alone with just Toby, a fire in the fire-*
*place, and a glass of wine. But, when that happens, I'm cut*
*off from the rest of the world—no phone or internet. That's*
*why I hadn't responded, not because of anything you said.*

   *I know what you mean about Grace being in your*
*head. She's in mine as well. I feel like sometimes it's her life*
*rather than mine (talk about sounding crazy . . .)*

I hesitated. Should I write that? It sounded a little crazy. It was divulging too much. I tried to imagine how it would sound to him and, for a moment, almost missed Grace's counsel. Better to make my own decisions, I thought. I reread what I had written. Tommy had shared, hadn't he? Perhaps he was as nervous and careful with his replies as I was with mine. But still, he was a stranger and Grace had been correct in her observations that he was too open, too assertive. And it *had* been his knife, hadn't it? I sighed. There were just so many unknowns. Better to play it safe, I thought and deleted the last line.

*I have to admit, it is nice to feel like I'm not the only person who has had this experience. My friends and family are great and they want to understand. But they didn't see her. They didn't/don't feel the same responsibility that I did/ do. You said she told you about her family—about what was going on. She never told me—never told any of us what was going on. And we didn't ask—or at least I didn't. I didn't want to know. I know that sounds silly—I mean, what could an 11-year-old have done? Nothing. But I could have asked. That's probably what I regret most.*

As I hit Send I waited for Grace's presence to make itself known—to make me fearful. But nothing happened. No condemnation. No dark thoughts. No recrimination. Just silence . . . and a warm tingle of . . . what? Excitement? Anticipation? Happiness? For the first time in a long time, I felt . . . free.

It was several hours later by the time Tommy responded. While I waited, I picked up the cabin and changed the sheets on my bed. Every hour or so, I took a break from cleaning to log onto my e-mail to see if Tommy had responded. Each time my heart beat a little faster in anticipation and each time my stomach dropped in disappointment when I saw that my inbox was empty. I had about given up hope and was about to start dinner, when I checked and found a message waiting. Eagerly, I clicked on it.

Birdie,

Thank goodness you're not angry! I was worried. I read and then reread my e-mail to you looking for clues as to what I might have said that would have upset you. I thought maybe I had shared too much or scared you off. Please know that if I share too much or ask too many personal questions, you can always tell me. I hope you know that. I never want you to feel uncomfortable.

So, your remote little cabin in the mountains sounds lovely. I love the image of you and your dog sitting by the fire, sipping red wine, and watching the snow fall outside. It sounds cozy. It also sounds like you have the privacy and the serenity that you need and want and the freedom to work when you need and want. I'm not so lucky. My job forces me to interact with people all the time. Make no mistake—I love what I do, but it's exhausting. I'm in the import/export business. My company imports indigenous handicrafts from craftspeople and artists from all over the world and then sells them in the United States for fair prices. In addition to the initial payment they receive, I return a portion of the profits to the artisans and their communities. It really is a win-win situation for everyone involved. I make a nice profit from the sale of their goods, they get a fair price for their work, and the customer gets quality crafts in addition to feeling good about themselves for paying fair-trade prices.

It's a great job, but it makes for a lonely life, too. It's hard to maintain a relationship when you're traveling and working all the time. I spend a lot of time in the office. In fact, that's where I am now. And across from me is one of the two paintings of yours that I purchased. Your use of flat, gray, dull colors lends such starkness to the work. Your style is so evocative. It's simple with a dreamlike quality.

So, how remote is your cabin? Are you near any towns? I have this image of that town in Northern Exposure—you know, all sorts of quirky characters.

Anyway, I'm glad you're not upset with me and I

*hope you write back soon. Or you could call. My number is*
*attached.*
    *Tommy*

As I finished reading his e-mail, I felt the familiar knot of fear in my stomach. He wanted to know more about my life. Grace's warning crept into my head, but I pushed it aside. He had shared details with me, hadn't he? It was only natural, only polite, to ask about my life. But still, why did he want to know? Did he have an ulterior motive?

"Stop it," I said aloud. "He's just being friendly. That's what friends do. Think about when you first got to know Roger. Same thing."

But was it, I wondered? Roger was gay. He wasn't a threat. I sighed. This was new to me and I wasn't sure I wanted to answer. But, at the same time, I *did* want to answer. It felt good to be able to share. Tommy wanted to be my friend. I hit Reply.

*Tommy—*
    *Hi. You're in your office and I'm in the living room of my cabin. As I type, a fire snaps and crackles in the fireplace and I'm sipping a glass of wine—yes, as you correctly guessed, red. I tend to prefer cabernets and zinfandels. I don't much like merlots—too soft. I take it you're a wine drinker as well?*
    *I have to admit, I looked forward to your reply all day. As I cleaned up the cabin and took care of odd jobs around the house, I took breaks to see if you had replied. It's funny, but that sense of anticipation was kind of exciting. It's not something I'm used to. I like having something to look forward to.*
    *My privacy is wonderful, but like your work, it can also be lonely. There is a difference between being alone and being lonely and lately, I've been more in the second camp. It's by my own choice, I know, but that doesn't change the fact that sometimes I miss having friends and family close by.*
    *Your business sounds interesting. I like the fact that*

*you're looking out for the interests of the people who make
the art and do the work. I wondered when I saw the name
of your company, Conscientious Imports, what it meant.
Now I know. I'm not surprised. You seem to be very aware
and sensitive to others.*

I stopped typing. Was saying that too forward? I deleted the
last two lines and then reconsidered. It was what I thought, wasn't
it? So why not say it? I chewed thoughtfully on the inside of my
lower lip and then retyped the sentences. Best not to dwell on it
too much, I thought, and contemplated what to say next. I should
ask questions about him. Not only would it allow me to learn more
about him, but it would deflect the attention from me. I began to
type.

*I'm surprised you're not married—or haven't been in
the past. I'm sorry your previous relationships didn't work
out. What happened?*

*I'm flattered that you've hung my work, but at the same
time, would really prefer not to talk about it. It's complicated
and I'm sure we'll discuss it someday, but not now. As, I'm
sure you know from your conversation with Roger, he and I
don't discuss the work, who has purchased it, or what anyone
thinks of it. Apparently, my anonymity, isolation, and
tendency toward reclusiveness add to the mystique. At least,
that's what he tells me.*

*Anyway, I know this is going to sound odd, but, I
would really prefer not to give you my mailing address.
And also, no phone calls. This is all new to me and right
now, I think e-mail is the best way to communicate. It is
what feels most natural and safest to me.*

*Still, I look forward to hearing from you,*
*Birdie*

I felt good about the exchange. I had made my boundaries clear,
but at the same time, made myself available for more conversation.

It was a bold step, though I didn't expect Tommy to realize this. Surprisingly, though, he seemed to completely understand. His reply came about an hour after I sent my message.

*Birdie,*

*Believe me when I tell you that I respect your desire for privacy and solitude. I would never want you to share more than you're comfortable with. I am willing to take this at whatever pace you'd like and share only what you're comfortable with.*

*Now that that's out of the way, let's talk about other stuff—like wine. I couldn't agree with you more. Merlots ARE too soft. I like big cabernets with lots of tannins. And I like to pair them with thick, juicy steaks. Do you like steak? I don't eat it often, but when I do . . . man, oh man . . . it's so good.*

*So, I have a confession to make and you can ignore it if you want to or just stop reading here. But, the more we talk, the more I respect and enjoy you. You are a complex and delightful woman. I am enjoying getting to know you. Do you have a picture? I would love to see it if you do.*

*T.*

After reading his e-mail, I sat back, slightly breathless. I appreciated his honesty, but it also scared me, because the more he wrote, the more I wanted him to write. His words made me giddy. It was a feeling unlike anything I had ever known—exciting, but also dangerous. I considered what that meant. I reread his last paragraph, particularly the line, *The more we talk, the more I respect and enjoy you.* That was how I felt. But should I confess that as well? How would he take it? Would it be too forward? Misinterpreted?

I decided to take a chance.

*Tommy—*

*I didn't stop reading. Thank you for your "confession." I, too, enjoy our conversations. You seem to really understand*

*me and where I'm coming from. It's a nice feeling after so
many years of feeling misunderstood. I'm sorry that you
probably don't get the same catharsis out of it that I do. Just
know that I appreciate our correspondence and I appreciate
your kindness and sincerity.*

*Pictures . . . um, no, I don't have any recent pictures
of myself. I don't like to have my picture taken and that,
combined with the fact that I'm alone most of the time . . .
well let's just say there aren't that many pictures around of
me. I would love to see one of you, though.*

*As for steak, yes, I do like it, although it's hard for me to
eat meat sometimes because I think about the animal it once
was and that makes it hard for me to eat it. Still, you're
right. When paired with the right wine, it's delicious.*

I sat back and reread what I had written so far. It was good—
casual, honest, revealing. I felt empowered and bold. There was something more I wanted to say, but I wasn't sure how. I wanted to tell
him how much I appreciated him—both now and when we were
kids. But how to write it? How to express such a strange sentiment
so seemingly out of the blue? My fingers hovered over the keys and
then, moving almost of their own volition, I typed.

*I have a confession, too. As strange as this might sound,
your e-mail and offer of friendship came at a very opportune
time. I was feeling very isolated and alone—much like when
I was a kid and you found me in the tree house. In fact, you
seem to have a knack for turning up when I need a friend. In
an earlier note, you thanked me. I'd like to return the favor.
Thank you.*
*Birdie*

I hit Send before I had time to reconsider. His response was
immediate.

*Birdie,*
*It's my pleasure. And know, I get as much out of this as*

351

*you do. I'm glad that we're friends. It means a lot to me—*
*as do you.*
   *T.*

I stared at his message and felt a tingle . . . or perhaps a prickle of . . . something. Anticipation? Expectation? Attraction? I shrugged off the feeling and pushed myself away from the computer. I needed to take a break. Too much was happening too soon. Tommy's words, although comforting, also made me uncomfortable.

I took a deep breath. Time, I thought. I needed time. And he needed to know that. Quickly, I scooted the chair forward, back to the computer desk.

*Tommy—*
   *Thank you for your note. This communication—this*
*outlet—means a lot to me. And so do you. I recently lost a*
*friend and right now, I do need your friendship. But it's a*
*little overwhelming. I don't usually let people into my life*
*so quickly or easily. Would you mind if I took a step back*
*to process all of this? It may not make sense to you, but*
*I've got some issues I need to work though. I may be out*
*of communication for a little while. You've done nothing*
*wrong. It's me. I'll be in touch.*
   *Birdie*

I again pushed myself away from the desk. This time, though, I stood and walked to the kitchen. I opened a bottle of wine and poured myself a sizeable glassful.

Out in the living room, Toby groaned, shifted, and went back to whatever dream he had been having. I smiled and fought the urge to curl up with him.

I walked out of the kitchen and stopped at the computer with the intention of turning it off. Before I could, though, a message from Tommy popped up. The subject line read: "I Understand." I clicked on the message.

*Birdie,*

*I completely understand. This has got to be a lot for you to take in. Just know that I'm patient and will be here after you've taken time to get used to the idea of our friendship.*

*I'm here when you need me.*

*Tommy*

# Chapter 27

Over the next couple of weeks, I spent a lot of time thinking about Tommy and the role our correspondence was beginning to play in my life. I made lists in my head and on paper—pros and cons. Issues and concerns. I tried to be as honest as I could, but kept coming back to the conclusion that no matter how much he scared me, I liked communicating with Tommy. And I liked being free of Grace's control. I could still feel her there, in the background watching. But she didn't speak and I felt as if she knew that she had been rendered powerless. I was in control and I liked it. I did things I typically wouldn't do. I initiated contact with friends, surprising them by calling out of the blue and chatting about what was going on in their lives. I experimented with painting that wasn't focused on Grace's murder. I called my mother and sister rather than e-mailing them. After the second call in as many weeks, my mother asked suspiciously, "Birdie, are you okay?"

"Yeah," I said. "Why?"

"Well, just—you seem different," she said. I knew that *different*, in this case, worried her.

"No, I'm great," I said.

"And everything is okay?" she asked.

"Yeah," I said.

"Work is . . ."

"Going well," I said. "I talked to Roger yesterday and it seems that interest is still high in my work."

"How's Toby?" she asked.

"He's good," I said. "Asleep on the couch. We've had a lot of snow, so he's kind of in hibernation mode."

"Good," she said.

"I was just calling to see how you were doing," I said. "You know, get caught up on what's going on. Finalize plans for Christmas. I talked to Tara earlier. She said you guys would drive out on the 22nd and stay until the 26th?"

"As far as I know," my mother said. "Last I heard, we're leaving for Breckenridge the day after Christmas. Andy is itching to hit the slopes."

"Sounds good to me," I said. "I'm looking forward to seeing you guys. It's been too long."

"Sweetheart," my mother said. "Are you sure you're all right?"

"Yes," I said with a laugh. "I'm great. I'm making some changes in my life, that's all. It's a good thing."


Later that night, I contacted Tommy. I had thought about everything that a friendship with him entailed and decided that despite my fears, I was ready to try. We would take things slowly—get to know each other in small bits. And in the process, I was going to put Grace to rest once and for all.

His response was everything I could have hoped for.

*Birdie—*

*I can't tell you how glad I was to get your note. It's been a long two weeks and I've been worried I wouldn't hear from you again—that I had scared you off with my confession about the knife and finding Grace and the person I was back then. I really missed your e-mails. It made me realize how much I enjoyed our correspondence.*

*I agree that we should just write when we can and get to know each other as it happens. I'll let you be the one to set the pace on that.*

*So, how have you been?*

And that's how our friendship began. We e-mailed back and

forth, sometimes several times a day, sometimes every few days. There was still the underlying intensity of our shared experience, but there was also casualness. I asked more questions than I answered and Tommy, to his credit, never pushed. He shared a great deal and I, with my newfound resolve and freedom from Grace, shared what I could.

The time passed quickly and before I knew it, the holidays were in full swing. In town, the merchants had hung wreaths, garlands, and Christmas lights everywhere. During my trips into town, I found myself caught up in the holiday spirit. The aroma of pumpkin bread and spices hung in the air around the bakery. At home, I drank spiced tea and, for the first time since I had moved into the cabin, went into the woods and chopped down a small pine tree to decorate. Toby, who sensed that something was different, jumped around barking excitedly as I hauled the tree inside.

"It's about time we had a real Christmas tree, isn't it?" I asked as I stood back to gauge how straight or crooked the tree was in its holder. I wanted it to be perfect because this was the first year my family was coming to spend Christmas with me. In the past, I had driven to be with them or, as more often was the case, made plans to drive to be with them and then canceled at the last minute with the excuse that I was snowed in. It wasn't that I didn't want to see them. It was simply that leaving the safety of the cabin was too frightening. Whether or not they had finally caught on, this year the plan was for my mother, sister, and Andy, now her husband, to come two days before Christmas and then leave for Breckenridge the day after Christmas. My mother planned to shop at the outlet malls while Tara and Andy skied. I had been invited along, but declined—both because I couldn't ski and also because I knew by then I would be ready for some time alone.

"Deck the Halls with boughs of holly, fa la la la la . . . la la la la," I sang to Toby as I hung the multicolored lights on the tree. I already had twined garland along the banisters and the railing and was finally tackling the task of decorating the tree. The trees of my youth had included blinking lights, multicolored bubble lights, tinsel garland, and glitter-covered ornaments. I wanted to create that look in my own tree and had ordered lights and ornaments online to be shipped to me. They had been sitting in boxes near the fireplace for weeks as I waited to cut down the tree.

Two hours later, I stepped back and surveyed the results. The tree looked exactly the way I wanted. Lights of all colors twinkled and glowed, reflecting off the tinsel and the mirrored surfaces of the ornaments. The bubble lights gurgled softly as the light heated the tubes of colored water. All that remained were the hand-quilted stockings I had ordered last month from one of the shops in town. The workmanship was excellent and our names were stitched on them: Birdie, Toby, Mom, Tara, and Andy.

As I opened the box with the stockings inside and pulled them out, the phone rang.

"Hi, doll," came Roger's voice.

"Hi," I said, happy to hear his voice. "What's up?"

"I was wondering if I could come up after the New Year and get some new pieces," he said. "I have a collector in LA who is interested."

I hesitated, the old desire to avoid interaction flaring. But then I stopped. This was the new Birdie, I reminded myself—the more social Birdie.

"Sure. I've got some new stuff you might be interested in."

"Really?" he said. "What is it?"

"It's happier," I said. I had been prepared for Roger to react enthusiastically.

"Oh. Really?"

"Yeah. Brighter colors. Not nearly as dark."

"But you're not going to stop the other stuff, are you?" he asked. "I mean, that's what people like."

I was surprised and a little shocked. "I thought you'd be happy I was doing something lighter."

"Oh, no, I am. I am," he said quickly. "It's just that your darker work is so popular."

"Roger, this is a big step for me."

"I know it is and I'm excited to see it." He laughed. "Sorry. You know me. I just get single-minded."

"Asshole," I said teasingly.

"Listen to you," he said. "What's got you in such a good mood?"

"Lots of things. It's the holidays."

"You hate the holidays."

"Not this year," I said. "Mom, Tara, and Andy are coming here and I chopped down a tree."

"Well, that was awfully butch of you."

I ignored the jab. "So, what are you doing for Christmas?"

"Gus and I are going to go to Paris," he said. "So, look, I've got to run, but we're on for the first part of January?"

"Sure."

"And Becca . . ." I could hear the smile in his voice. "I'm happy for you. You sound good."

"I am," I said. "I really am."

The day before my family was set to arrive, I cleaned the cabin from top to bottom. I considered switching out the current painting I was working on, but after looking at it for several minutes, decided that it was fine for them to see. There wasn't anything upsetting about it. The thought made me smile.

I had told Tommy about the new work and when we corresponded that night, I told him I had opted to leave the work out for my family to see. *It will be the first time I have let them see my real work,* I wrote. *For the first time in a long time I don't necessarily feel like I need to shield myself from them.*

Later that evening, I sat in the living room wrapping gifts and watching a documentary on the History Channel. As I finished wrapping the last gift, I sat back and surveyed my work. The cabin looked warm, festive, and inviting. All that remained was to change the sheets on the queen-sized bed in my room, which was where Tara and Andy would stay. The extra bedroom that doubled as my studio was ready for my mother, and since I would be sleeping on the couch, I had fresh sheets in the storage cupboard to make it up as a bed. Everything was ready. I took a sip of wine and smiled. For the first time since childhood, I was actually excited, rather than dreading the holidays. I raised my glass in a toast to myself.

"Here's to you," I said and laughed delightedly. "And to me."

The next morning, as I was hanging a wreath on the front door, a silver SUV turned off of the rutted road that ran past my cabin and pulled into my gravel drive. Toby leapt from the porch and ran toward the vehicle, barking madly. Visitors were rare and he never missed an opportunity to bark and jump. The passenger-side window was lowered and I could hear my mother's voice from the back seat.

"Will he bite?" called Tara from the passenger seat.

I smiled, waved and shook my head.

"No," I called back. "He's all bark and, well, you know."

After Andy put the SUV into park, rolled up the windows, and turned off the engine, my mother and sister got out and walked over to where I stood.

"Hi," I said as we hugged and kissed in greeting. "Welcome to Shangri-La."

Both looked dubiously at the cabin and then back at me to see if I were joking. Like most of the people in my life, my family only vaguely understood my choice to live in solitude. Each time we were together, they would, at different times, approach me with names and contact information for psychologists or therapists, always insisting that it was "just something to think about" and reminding me that no longer was there a social stigma attached to mental health issues or medication. I was sure that both Tara and my Mom were carrying business cards in their coat pockets, already contemplating how they would broach the subject this time.

"I'm teasing. Come on in."

"Hey Birdie," called Andy from the back of the SUV where he was grabbing suitcases and gift bags overflowing with tissue paper and tightly curled ribbons. "Amazing weather, huh? Heard Breckenridge got some fresh powder. Should be good skiing."

"Yeah," I said agreeably. "You want some help with those?"

"Nah. I've got it. You girls go on in. I know Tara has been wanting to use the bathroom for about forty-five minutes."

Tara nodded vigorously.

"That's because someone wouldn't stop," she said loudly enough for him to hear and then in a normal tone to me, "He was racing against the time he estimated it would take to get here."

Andy grinned as he walked past, his arms laden with gifts. He was the perfect husband for my sister. He was easygoing, kind, and agreeable to just about everything. His only flaw was that the only thing he talked about was sports. Who beat who in which sport. Who was injured and how. What coach was rumored to be leaving which team for another. Andy was a veritable encyclopedia of sports information—information that he shared at length and without encouragement. For me, although I liked Andy, having conversations with him were a mind-numbing exercise in endurance that necessitated a very large, very full glass of wine. He gave me a bone-crushing hug as he headed back out to the car.

"Hey, Birdie," he said. "Remind me to tell you about the new skis I got for Tara and me. They're the same kind used by the US Olympic ski team. They're sweet."

Inside, my mother was looking around the living room with approval. "It looks good," she said and came over to hug me. "How are you, sweetie? Doing okay?"

I nodded and she kissed me on the cheek.

"Good." She studied me appraisingly. "Really, how are you?"

"I'm fine, Mom," I said, and for once, meant it.

"Um hmmm," she said disbelievingly. Her gaze wandered around the room, taking in the decorations and landing on the tree. "The tree looks good. It looks like—"

"The trees we used to have when we were kids," interrupted Tara in delight as she came down the stairs. "Even the ornaments." She grinned at me. "And these stockings, they're great. They look like the ones Granny used to have. Where did you find them?"

"I had them made," I said.

Tara studied me. "Are you feeling okay?"

"Yeah." I smiled at her. "Of course I am. Why?"

"You just seem different. Sort of . . . happy all of a sudden." She studied me harder and then grinned triumphantly. "You're in love. You're seeing someone, aren't you? You *are*! Mom, look at her. Birdie's seeing someone."

"No," I said quickly, suddenly defensive. "I'm not."

I saw my mother and sister exchange a look.

"Okay," my mother said with a hint of a smile on her lips. "That's okay. When you're ready."


The Christmas holiday passed quickly. The first night we all sat around the fireplace drinking wine, snacking on cheese, and talking about family and friends. I tried to be casual as I steered the conversation to some of Edenbridge's older residents.

"That's too bad about Mrs. Spencer," I said.

"I know," my mother said. "But she was older than dirt when *I* was a kid."

"And what about those notebooks?" Tara said. "I can't imagine sitting in your house all day doing nothing but writing down the date and time of everyone's activities. Talk about crazy."

"I wonder if she wrote down every time we were too loud," I said with a laugh

"If so, she's got a lot of entries," Tara said. "Back when we had that Slip'N Slide we were outside screaming all the time."

I smiled at the memory.

"Hey, what ever happened to Mr. and Mrs. Sullivan?" I asked.

"Oh my gosh, I haven't thought of them in years," my mother said. "They're still in Edenbridge—I know that."

"They had a grandson that was about my age, didn't they?" I asked casually.

"Oh, I think they have a couple of grandkids," my mother said. "I know they have great grandkids because they had two of the little girls with them at the store one time."

"Wasn't one of them named Tommy?" I asked.

My mother shrugged. "I don't remember. That's what happens when you get old. Memory is the first thing to go."

I forced a laugh and then said, "I just seem to remember him visiting one summer. Tall. Dark hair. Blue eyes."

My mother thought for a minute and then shook her head to indicate she didn't recall anyone by that description. "Doesn't ring a bell," she said and then grinned. "But if you pour me another glass of wine, maybe it will come to me."

After everyone was in bed, I filled the stockings and then pretended to be asleep when my mother and sister both crept downstairs to do the same thing. The next morning, we got up late, opened presents, and drank coffee. Later, we made a huge dinner of turkey and stuffing that left us full and sleepy. Andy watched ESPN while my mother and Tara napped on the couch. I snuck over to the computer to check my e-mail and found a message from Tommy.

> *Birdie:*
>
> > *Merry Christmas. Hope you're having a great time with your family. I spent the day with some friends down in the Village. We ate too much and probably drank too much as well. I probably shouldn't be e-mailing, but I wanted to say hello and tell you that I couldn't help but think about you several times during the day. I hope you're well and on this day, I hope you know that I value you and what you've brought to my life.*
> >
> > *Merry Christmas my dear, dear friend.*
> > *T.*

I smiled and sighed.

"So, what's his name?" asked Tara who had been watching me from her place on the sofa.

"I thought you were asleep."

"So, what's his name?" she repeated. "Or do I have to come over there and see for myself?"

"Thomas," I said quickly, unwilling to let her see his message to me. "And it's not what you think. He's just a friend."

She shifted on the couch, smiled patronizingly and then closed her eyes again. "Okay," she said. "If you say so."

I watched her for a moment and then began to type out a reply to Tommy. Every once in a while I looked up to see if Tara was watching me.

*Tommy—*

*Merry Christmas to you, too. It's been great having everyone here, but I'm ready to have the place to myself again. I'm not used to having so many people around. We ate too much, too. I feel as stuffed as the bird.*

*It makes me happy that you thought of me today. You crossed my mind, too. My mother and sister even accused me of having a boyfriend (HA HA).*

*Well, I'm off to eat leftovers. Have a nice night,*
*Birdie*

As I hit Send, I glanced up to see Tara again watching me. She raised her eyebrows and gave me a knowing look.

"What?" I hurriedly clicked on a message from Roger with the subject line of "Greetings on this Pseudo-Christian Holiday Based on Pagan Dates."

"Nothing," she said. "Just that you seem different. Happy. Like you're finally living life. I'm glad, that's all. I'm glad there is someone out there who can bring that out in you. It's just nice to see you happy—like you've put the past behind you. It's good."

"It is good," I agreed as I began to scroll through Roger's annual Christmas tirade. "It's very good."

Her words were echoed by my mother the next morning as we watched Andy pack up the SUV.

"You seem happier and better than I've seen you since you were little," she said as she hugged me good-bye. "I haven't always agreed with your decision to move up here by yourself or to not get professional help, but now that I see you like this, maybe I was wrong. Maybe you made the right decision."

"It was the right decision. I needed to be alone to work through things. And I think I have. I've turned a corner. The things that were haunting me seem to be gone. I can't explain it. They just are."

My mother smiled and hugged me again. "Will you work on getting out more often? Or, what about coming with us? You don't have to shop or ski. You could just spend time with us."

"I would love to," I lied. "But I've got things I have to do here. And I have Toby. You guys go have fun. I promise, though, I'm going to make it a point to get out around people more. It's the next thing on my agenda."

"Well . . . okay," she said as she began to root around in her purse. "I gave you the numbers for the hotel, right? If you need anything or change your mind, you'll call? Are you sure you don't want to come? You could bring Toby. Lots of people bring their pets."

"Next time. I'll come next time."

Andy leaned out the driver-side window. "The sooner we hit the road, the sooner we're on the slopes—not that we're in any rush, Birdie."

My mother quickly gave me one last hug and we walked together to the SUV. I opened the back passenger door for her to get in. Tara leaned out the window and gave me a clumsy hug.

"Love you," she whispered. "It's really nice to see you happy."

"I love you, too," I said and impulsively kissed her cheek. "Bye, Andy. Bye, Mom."

I stepped back and Andy carefully executed a three-point turn and began his slow, cautious crawl down the drive to the road. Toby gave a brief, halfhearted chase and then returned to the porch. I inhaled the cold mountain air and watched as Andy signaled and pulled onto the road. My mother's hand appeared briefly out the window in a final wave. And then they were gone.

# Chapter 28

The days after Christmas passed quickly. The weather was beautifully clear and the views of the mountains were breathtaking. I said as much in my e-mails to friends.

*It sounds lovely,* came Tommy's reply. *I just wish you had a camera that would allow you to send a picture of it. I'd love to see your view.*

The simplicity of my life was an ongoing joke between us. Although our e-mails were still in many ways, superficial, we were beginning to discuss more serious things. This became especially true on New Year's Eve. Like me, Tommy had opted to stay in and we had decided to ring in the New Year together online. Each of us had our televisions on to *Dick Clark's Rockin' New Year's Eve* and we were going to watch the ball drop together—first in Tommy's time zone and then in mine. We both had purchased sparkling wine for our New Year's toasts.

*Got your television on?*

We had gotten to the point where we no longer bothered with names.

*I do,* I replied. *You?*

*Yep. I'm ready for the toast. I've been working on it all day in my head.*

I laughed.

*I didn't know we were doing formal toasts,* I typed.

*We are—though I'm less worried about that than I am about how we're going to manage the kiss.*

I felt myself stiffen as I read the words. I didn't know how to respond. I didn't know if I wanted to respond. Why did he say that? Tara's words came back to me: *She's seeing someone.* That wasn't true. Tommy and I were just friends—weren't we?

*What do you mean?* I typed.

His response came several minutes later—long enough for me to finish my glass of wine and pour another.

*I'm not going to lie, Birdie. I'm offering friendship, of course. But I hope you will consider more. I've had a bit to drink, so I'm probably saying more than I would otherwise, but I feel like I need to get some things out in the open. I have thought about you constantly over the years, wondering where you were and what you had become.*

*I know we've only been communicating for four months, but I feel that we have such a connection—like we're the only two people who understand who the other is, deep at their core. When all those days went by and you were unavailable (snowed in without power) I was going crazy with thoughts of why you weren't answering. And it was then I realized how much you mean to me—how much you've always meant to me.*

*I know this is going to sound crazy, but I think this could easily become more than friendship for me. That's not to put pressure on you. I realize that it's probably the last thing you want to hear. But I feel like it's something I need to say. Just think about it? Please?*
            *T.*

"Holy shit," I muttered in disbelief. I turned to look at Toby, who lay snoring on the couch. "This changes everything."

I was stunned. Overwhelmed. Frightened. More as a reflex than anything else, I grabbed the computer power cord and yanked the plug out of the wall, my heart thudding so violently in my chest that it felt as if it might explode. I took a deep breath to calm myself and as I exhaled, I tasted the vomit in my throat. I was about to throw up. Quickly, I rushed for the front door, threw it open, and hurled my upper body over the porch railing. Wine and stomach bile gurgled out of my mouth in a violent torrent. The sky was a gray-black against the snowy ground. My ragged breath puffed in misty clouds. The cold air felt good on my sweaty skin.

What was he telling me? Was he falling in love with me? I felt the familiar fear welling up, but also, despite my violent reaction, a tingle of . . . what? Excitement? No wonder Grace had reacted the way she had. She had sensed how he felt and she was jealous. I waited for her to confirm my realization, but she remained quiet in the background, watching and waiting. She had planted the seed and now she was just going to wait and see what I was going to do.

I shivered, cold, but not wanting to go back inside. I wanted to walk. I wanted to think. I needed the fresh air. I wiped my mouth on the back of my hand, pushed myself away from the railing, and went back inside. I grabbed my coat from the hook. Suddenly awake, Toby jumped up and rushed over to me. I grabbed his fleece off the hook, pulled it over his head, and then clipped the underside below his barrel chest.

"Let's get some fresh air," I said. "Just for a little bit."

It was one of those amazingly silent and crystalline nights in which you could hear the light snow that was beginning to fall, land on the trees and the ground. The thick blanket of snow from the past few days made everything glow. I gulped in the cold air and watched as Toby raced down the area I had cleared and then bounded headfirst into the foot-high snow drifts.

I had to respond to Tommy's message. I knew that. I just wasn't sure how. I let my mind wander through the various emotions his e-mail had evoked. Fear, of course. Confusion as to where this had come from—where *he* had come from. It—he—this—scared me. I didn't even really know this man. And Grace was right. He'd just appeared out of the blue. Of course she would say that, wouldn't she?

It was odd that he had tried over the years to find me, but at the same time, I had wondered about him, too, hadn't I? So, perhaps it wasn't so strange. But, what did I know about this man? What did I know about any kind of relationship outside of platonic friendships? I had spent so much of my life hiding from the world—protecting myself from vulnerability, from crime, from anything that made me uncomfortable. I didn't know how to respond to his . . . what? Attention? But, I wanted to. That was part of what was so frightening, wasn't it? I wanted to. I wanted to see where this could go. I was tired of having my most significant relationships be with a dead girl and a gay man.

I twirled crazily. It made no sense. I wanted a drink. I wanted to shout. I wanted to laugh and cry and . . . explode. Calm, I thought. I need to calm down and think about this rationally. I took a deep breath. None of this was making any sense. It was all too sudden. I tried to slow my mind and examine my own feelings. What did I feel about Tommy? I liked him. I knew that. But he scared me. He always had. But was that my fear or was it Grace's? I liked him and yes, if I were to be honest, I did feel attracted to him. I felt like he understood me. I felt like he and I shared . . . something. But was it just a childhood experience? Was it guilt? Was it . . . what was it?

And my attraction to him—I knew it was emotional. But was it physical? Could it be physical? I was still a virgin. I hadn't even really done more than kiss a man. Could I have a sexual relationship? Did I want to? It was terrifying, and I wondered what Grace was thinking about this. I wasn't sure what to do. I had to consider that aspect of it, too. There were no easy answers. I stamped my feet and Toby raced past me and bounded back onto the porch, ready to go back inside.

"Okay, okay, okay." I turned back toward the cabin. "I need to get some clarity."

Once back in the cabin, I pulled out a notebook and a pen. I was going to make another list.

"Let's answer some questions," I said aloud.

Do I like him? *Yes.*

Am I attracted to him? *Yes.*

Is it emotional attraction? *Yes.*

Is it physical attraction*????*

Could I fall in love with him? *Not sure what that means.*

Do I want to act on it? *Not sure.*

Does he scare me? *Yes.*

Why? *I don't know him. He's an unknown. I don't trust men.*

Do I want to pursue this?

I stared at the last question and realized I had no answer. I was, I thought, quite possibly making a big deal out of nothing. He had said only that he thought he could feel more than friendship. But what did it mean? It was nothing I could deal with now. I had to think about it. I had already told him I needed time to process my feelings. He probably thought I was crazy, anyway, reacting that way just about his desire to be friends. But, if he knew I was a bit of a recluse and accepted it . . . *and* . . . if he understood that much of it stemmed from what happened when I was eleven, he might be accepting of my hesitance.

I stood up, walked to the kitchen, and grabbed the bottle of wine. Without bothering with a glass, I tipped the bottle up and took a huge swallow. It felt warm in my empty stomach. I waited to see if I would be sick again, but felt no nausea. I should eat, I thought, but decided instead that food would get in the way of getting drunk. I wandered over to the couch and sank heavily down. The fire needed more wood, I realized as I took another swig of wine. And then another. And then another.

"Here's to the fire," I said loudly and raised the bottle in a toast. I was beginning to feel the effects of the wine. "And here's to you, Grace," I said, tauntingly and also a little drunkenly. "Happy New Year! Here's to you and your ability to completely fuck up my life."

I raised the bottle to my lips only to find that it was empty.

"I need more," I muttered and heaved myself off the couch and staggered into the kitchen. "Necessito mas vino!"

As I stumbled back into the living room, I again realized that the

369

fire needed more wood. With single-minded purpose, I carefully set the bottle on the mantel and picked up several logs from the pile next to the fireplace. One by one I stacked them on the grate.

"Perfect," I said finally. I grabbed the bottle and sank down in front of the fireplace. Toby uncurled himself, stretched, and came to sit next to me as I proceeded to drink until I passed out.

The next morning was terrible—not just because of the hangover that made me swear never to take another drink—but also because during the night, the electricity had gone out and so had my fire. My body registered the frigid air in the cabin as my mind took inventory of the pain behind my eyes, the nausea in my empty, wine-soaked stomach, and the nasty taste in my mouth.

I groaned as I rolled onto my side and heaved my body into a sitting position. Once upright, my head whirled and I snapped my eyes shut to keep from vomiting. The idea of going back to sleep was appealing, but I also realized that with the electricity off, I would need a fire in the fireplace. I pried open my eyes and looked around the room. Toby had burrowed under a blanket on the couch. The empty wine bottle lay on its side next to the hearth.

I groaned again and pulled a Duralog out of the oak storage box next to the fireplace. I typically only used them in emergencies— when I needed to get a fire going immediately, but in my condition, building a fire from scratch was beyond what I was capable of. I struck the match on the side of the box and held the flame to the corner of the wrapping. It took immediately and I sat back, relieved. The rest could wait.

Several hours later, I was functional. My stomach had stopped threatening to rebel and the headache had lessened to a dull throb. I had showered, eaten a couple of pieces of toast, and was drinking my second cup of herbal tea when I remembered why I had had so much wine in the first place. Tommy! Just the thought of his name made my stomach jump. He had told me he was interested in something more than friendship. I closed my eyes and tried to remember his exact words. "I think this could easily become more than friendship for me."

The same thrill, the same fear, the same turmoil as when I had first read those words hit me. Even though I had banished her, I found myself missing Grace's insight. With her in my head, I didn't have to think. I didn't have to make decisions on my own. But now—now that she was gone—I walked to the desk and picked up my list of questions and answers.

I studied the sheet of paper and tried to reconcile the mixed emotions the questions had evoked. Eventually, I knew I would have to respond to Tommy's message. The question was, what would I say?

By the time the electricity had come back on, a week had passed. In that time, I had worked through many of my concerns. It wasn't easy. At first, I struggled, lost without Grace's familiar voice to point out every single caution and thing to fear. But as time went on, I began to think for myself. And eventually, I realized that I was tired of being scared. I wanted to at least have a friendship with Tommy. And should something else happen . . . well, I would cross that bridge when I came to it. I felt relieved to have made a decision. It was frightening. But it was also exciting.

I waited for several hours after the electricity came back on to open my e-mail. There were several from my sister, one from Adelle, and one from Roger with the subject line: Need to Reschedule My Trip. I considered reading it first, but decided that I should respond to Tommy instead. Even though I had rehearsed what I wanted to say, actually typing it was much harder. I leaned back in my chair and closed my eyes. I simply had to tell him the truth. I slid my hand to the mouse, opened a blank e-mail and began to type.

*Dear Tommy—*

*Happy Belated New Year. The power was out again or I would have responded sooner. Although, even as I write that, I'm not sure I would have because I didn't know what to say. Your e-mail took me by surprise. Over the past week, I've thought a lot about what you wrote and I'm . . . overwhelmed.*

*I've asked myself lots of questions—hard questions. And, I tried to be brutally honest with myself when I answered. There is a lot I don't know about you—and vice versa. But, what I DO know is that I like you and I am emotionally attracted to you. I don't know what that means, aside from wanting to know you better. I've never allowed myself to take a chance on letting someone in, which is why your mention of our friendship becoming something more, scares me. I haven't ever really been in a romantic relationship before. I know that sounds strange coming from someone my age, but it's true.*

*Wow. Talk about confessions . . .*

*Tommy, I appreciate you telling me how you feel. And I'm sorry that I can't say that I feel the same way. I guess what I would like is to just continue e-mailing and getting to know each other—at least for now. Is that okay with you? Let's just be friends and see where it goes. I know that if anyone can understand why I feel this way, it's you.*

*Birdie*

His response came within minutes.

*Birdie,*

*I'm glad you wrote back. I was worried I had said too much. I've been hovering around my computer since I hit the Send button.*

*OF COURSE it's fine for us to take this slowly and get to know each other. I want you to be comfortable with this and with me. I just had perhaps a little too much to drink while we were e-mailing and let my emotions get the better of me. Still, I'm relieved to have put that out there. And I thought it was only fair to let you know that my motives*

*for continued correspondence might not be all that they*
*appeared to be.*

*As I said before, I feel like we have such a connection—*
*that we could be good for each other. I meant what I said. I*
*will give you all the time you need. For now, the ball is in*
*your court. I'll let you set the pace.*

*I'm glad your electricity is back on.*

*Tommy*

And that's how our romance began.

We continued to correspond, but it was different than before. It was more intimate and even as I struggled to trust him, I found myself constantly holding back. Often, we e-mailed late into the night. No longer did I need to paint to be able to sleep. Now, I had Tommy. It seemed like we discussed everything under the sun— our likes and dislikes, our favorite foods, how we reacted to important events in our lives. I told him about my college experience and how Adelle's rape had an impact on me. He told me about building his company and how the murder of his fiancée several years earlier almost derailed his life.

*It shattered me. I lost interest in work, in life, in . . .*
*everything. To lose her that way was too much—especially*
*after what happened with Grace.*

When he explained what he meant, I could see why.

*Angie was walking home one night from her job bartend-*
*ing. She lived just a few blocks away. She was almost home*
*when someone apparently tried to rob her. She made pretty*
*good tips at the bar and all I can figure is that they had been*
*watching her. Knowing Angie, she refused to give him her*
*money and he stabbed her, took her purse, and then ran off. She*
*bled to death on the sidewalk. I got worried when she didn't*
*call me to tell me she was home all right. By the time I got to*
*her apartment, the police were down the street working the*

*crime scene. They never caught the guy.*

*I was devastated. To lose someone you love to such a senseless crime is horrible. And then to be unable to catch the bastard who did it? But then, I don't have to tell you that, do I? You know better than anyone the impact that can have on a person.*

Within a month, though I hadn't admitted it to *him*, I had begun to admit to myself that perhaps my feelings were more than friendship as well. He had sent me a picture of himself. Remarkably, he looked much the same as he had when he was seventeen, although older and broader -shouldered. The picture had been taken at sea. Tommy was seated at the back of a sailboat with his hand on the rudder. He was smiling and squinting into the sunlight. Lines crinkled along the sides of his eyes. His skin was tanned and he looked fit. His tousled dark hair was longer than I remembered . . . and curlier. He had become a handsome man, and I told him so.

*Thanks, he wrote. But you're seeing what you want to see. I'm average on my best days. I know you said you don't have any pictures that you can e-mail, but can you at least describe yourself to me?*

I hesitated—not because I didn't want to tell him what I looked like, but because I had no idea how to describe myself. I went to the mirror and stared at myself, trying to see my face and body like a stranger would. Tall, slender, angular—that was all true. My face was nondescript. I had a decent, slightly wind-chapped complexion. Long, wavy sandy-blond hair in need of a trim. Nice, straight teeth thanks to four years of orthodontics. All in all, I surmised, an average, though not unattractive, woman.

I sat back down at my computer and thought about how to describe what I had seen in the mirror.

*I'm not sure how to describe myself. I'm five-eight and about 140 pounds. I'm thin but not skinny. My hair is kind of a dirty blond and it's long. I haven't had a haircut in years. A lot of the time I keep it in a ponytail or just twisted into a bun. I used to have bangs, but I have sort of let those grow out. I'm fairly light-skinned and I usually don't wear makeup since it's just me and Toby. All in all, I would say I look like an older, paler, much more tired version of what I looked like as a kid.*

His response was kind.

> *You sound as beautiful outside as I know you to be inside.*

I found myself glowing with pleasure. "He thinks I'm beautiful," I told Toby as I twirled around the living room. "What do you know?"

I can admit that I got caught up in the feeling of falling in love—the emotions of it. The tingle of excitement at the thought of him. The anticipation of his e-mails. I was also in love with the realization that I could be like everyone else—that I was able to fall in love. It was an exciting first for me.

Eventually, I shared my revelation with Tommy. He had described a run through Central Park with such detail and passion that I felt as if I had been there with him.

> *Tommy—*
> *You write with such wonderfully vivid detail. I love reading your words. It made me feel like I was on that run with you. Your ability to so fully describe scenes and people and experiences is one of the many things I love most about you. Thank you for sharing your world with me.*

His reply was teasing.

> *So, you love me, huh? 'Bout time.*

My reply was far less playful.

*That's not what I meant.*

He responded immediately.

*Birdie, I was just teasing you. But, what would you
say if I told you that I loved you?*

I blinked in disbelief. He had said it. He said he loved me.
My stomach knotted and my breath quickened. It was just like the
movies. But instead of watching someone else have their soul mate
profess love, it was happening to me. It was my turn. Before I could
lose my nerve, I began to type.

*I guess that I would say that I . . .* I hesitated and
then typed the words . . . *love you, too. You've become my
dearest friend and my feelings for you are . . . more than
just friendship. I don't know how to describe it. It's such
a new and amazing feeling. I'm just not sure how to deal
with it.*

I waited anxiously for his reply. I didn't have to wait long.

*Seriously? Does this mean what I think it means? I
can't believe it!! I love you, too. You know, if you called me
on the phone, I could tell you in person. No pressure. Just a
thought.*

He had suggested talking on the phone before, but I had resisted.
It would have made it seem too real. But now, having just confessed
how I felt, it felt silly to avoid talking to him. If you're in love with
someone, it's only natural to talk to them on the phone. Rather than
respond to his e-mail, I stood up and walked around the room. Toby
watched from the couch.

"This is it, Toby," I said as I walked purposefully into the
kitchen, picked up the receiver, and, with shaky fingers, dialed
Tommy's number. Before it rang, though, I hung up.

"I need to think about what I want to say," I said to myself.
"I need to practice." I walked around the room and tried different
greetings. "Hi . . . Hello . . . Hi, it's Birdie . . . Bet you're surprised to
hear from me . . ."

I paced the length of the kitchen and then went into the living
room. Toby again looked up.

"Hello," I said in a lower-than-usual voice that could possibly
be construed as . . . sexy? "Is Tommy there? . . . May I speak to
Thomas, please . . . Hi."

Practicing wouldn't help, I realized. I just needed to do it. Once
more, I dialed his number. The phone rang. The pounding in my
head was deafening. My heart beat in my throat. I waited through
the rings. After the fifth ring, he picked up.

"Hello?" The voice was smooth and deep.

I froze. My words lodged in my throat. My breath came in
short pants.

"Hello?" he said again, this time, much more of a question.

"Hi, it's me," I said in a rush. My voice was anything but calm
or sultry. It was slightly shrill to my own ears. "It's Birdie. Holloway.
From Colorado. We've been e-mailing."

I rolled my eyes at my stupidity.

"Oh my god. Hi. I'm so glad you called. I . . . I didn't expect you
to so soon, but I'm so glad you did. I . . . Hi. How are you?"

"I'm well," I said. "I just decided to pick up the phone and call.
I hope that's okay. Are you busy? Can you talk right now?"

He laughed. "Birdie, I am never too busy for you. I'm so glad
you called. And, before we talk any more, I just want to tell you how
much your e-mail earlier meant to me. I love you and I'm so excited
to know that you feel the same way."

"I love you, too," I said shakily.

"Well, now that that's out of the way," he said smoothly. "How
are you? What are you doing right now?"

And so we began to talk. And talk. And talk. It was as if we had
known each other forever. We talked about everything with an intimacy
that never ceased to amaze me. We also began to talk about the future
and how and when we should meet. It became clear that we both were

anxious to see each other in person. Our conversations had evolved from e-mail almost exclusively to the telephone.

"How about Valentine's Day?" he asked one night. I was lying in front of the fire, the phone cradled against my ear. Toby lay curled up against my side. "You could come to New York and we could go out for a romantic dinner—go to the top of the Empire State Building."

"God, that would be amazing," I said wistfully. "But I don't like crowds and leaving the cabin, even for you, would be hard. I mean, I'm just not sure I can do it. And it's a little soon, don't you think?"

He was silent for several seconds. We had talked about my reclusiveness and my phobias. He understood and assured me that it wasn't a deterrent.

"Okay," he said finally. "How about I come to you? I could come to La Veta, I could stay at one of the hotels, and we could spend the weekend together."

I considered his words and the prospect of meeting him suddenly seemed very real. The thought was simultaneously exhilarating and terrifying.

"Wow," I said softly.

"What?" he asked in alarm. "Are you okay? What's wrong?"

"It just occurred to me that we're actually going to meet face to face," I admitted. "And I'm a little scared. Not of you, but just of the reality of you. What if you don't like me or don't find me attractive?"

He laughed warmly. "Not a chance. You are beautiful to me. I am in love with who you are on the inside, not your exterior. I'm in love with your complexity and your fears and your vulnerability. Seeing you in person is only going to intensify that."

I smiled at his words. "How is it that you're so perfect?"

"I understand you because we are the same person." He paused. "How's that for romantic?"

"Ummm," I said, stretching languorously. "That's nice."

"So?" he persisted. "What about it? Your place? A long weekend?"

I was silent.

"Say yes."

I stared at the fire, imagining the two of us sipping wine and toasting each other. I tentatively left myself open for Grace's voice warning me to stay away, but heard nothing. I could still feel her there, deep in my brain, watching. But she no longer commented or gave any indication of what she thought.

"Come on, Birdie," Tommy persisted, charmingly. "Say yes."

I smiled. "Yes," I said, finally. "Let's figure out when you can come for a long weekend."


"Well, it's a done deal," Tommy said the next night. "I just got a reservation at that little bed and breakfast... the Ranch House Inn. I got the room with the cowboy motif."

My heart beat faster at the thought of him being so near—of actually speaking to him in person. "But we didn't talk about dates."

"We didn't, but I didn't schedule the reservation until April," he said. "That gives us a couple more months to get to know each other better."

"April," I said numbly.

"Yes. April. Birdie, if I had waited for you, it would have been next year. You're worth it, but I don't want to wait that long. And deep down, I don't think you do either."

"But—"

"No buts," he said. "Consider this a goal. I figure if we have a set date, we have something to work toward. And if it isn't the right time—if you're not ready, we'll just cancel. But I don't think that will happen."

"You sound so sure," I said.

"I am," he said. "And remember, we're going to make this work one way or another."


We talked a lot over the next two months and as time passed, I found I was sharing more about myself. One night, after too much wine and conversation, I even came close to confessing that I believed Grace lived inside me. But something stopped me. Grace? Pride? The realization that if he knew how I really was he'd change his mind?

I needed to talk to someone. I considered calling my sister. She had figured out even before I had that Tommy was more than just a friend. And she was the only person I knew who was happily married. I also considered calling Roger. Granted, his relationship with Gus was anything but conventional, but they had been together for several years. In the end, though, I did neither. I think more than anything, I wanted to see if it would work first. There was a part of me that wanted to surprise everyone—to say, "Look at me, I really *am* okay."

I also wanted to make sure Grace didn't try to ruin it for me. She still remained in the background of my mind. She never spoke, but I could feel her watching. And more than that, I could feel her anger, her jealousy, her frustration—especially when Tommy told me he loved me.

"I'm sorry," I murmured one night after I got off the phone with Tommy. I didn't want her back in control, but after so much time together, I felt her absence in my life. I wished she could be happy for me; though, when I thought about what it must be like to be in her situation, I knew I would likely be feeling the same emotions. It was a new kind of guilt—guilt that was heightened when Tommy said things like, "I'm so excited to be able to hug you."

It was a week before his scheduled visit that he confessed he was nervous.

"Me, too," I said. "Actually . . . a lot. I know why I am, but why are you?"

I had come to know that the silence that followed my statement meant he was thinking.

"I guess for me, it's because we've waited so long and I have built this up so much in my head," he said finally. "But at the same time, I know this is it. You're the right woman at the right time and meeting you is just a formality, as far as I'm concerned."

I idly stroked Toby's muzzle. We were sitting in front of the fire.

"What?" Tommy asked when I didn't say anything.

"There's something I'm worried about," I admitted. It had been weighing heavily on my mind for several weeks and I had been trying to get up the nerve to tell him.

"Just one thing?" he teased, and I laughed.

"Well, one big thing."

"Okay," he said. "Lay it on me."

I was silent, unsure how to start the conversation—loath to say the words.

"Come on, sweetheart, you can tell me anything."

I took a deep breath and tried to speak. The words seemed trapped in my throat.

"Birdie, just say it. Whatever it is, we can work through it together."

"I'm a virgin," I blurted out.

Tommy was silent for several long seconds.

"Did you hear me? I said I'm—"

"A virgin. And?"

"I've never had sex," I said. "I don't know what to do and if you're coming here for that . . . well, I'm not sure I can give you what you want."

Tommy laughed and I found myself angry at his reaction.

"You think that's funny?"

"No," he said and then amended his answer. "Yes. I mean, is that really what you think I'm after? Sex? Do you really think all of this is because I expect you to put out?"

"I'm just saying that I—" My words trailed off, flustered.

"Birdie, what I want from you is so much more than just sex. I have no expectations, no ulterior motives. Right now, I just want to look into your eyes, hold your hand, and kiss your lips." He paused. "That's all right, isn't it? Kissing you?"

I thought about it. There would be germs, of course. But that suddenly didn't seem like such a big deal. They were Tommy's germs.

"Of course that's okay," I said and then added almost shyly, "I'd like that."

"Good. So it's settled, then." It wasn't a question, but a statement.

"Yes," I said. "It's settled."

# Chapter 29

Exactly one week later, I sat anxiously on the couch and stared at the phone, willing it to ring but also dreading what would happen when it did. He had to be close by now. Maybe he was already in town, checking into his room, getting ready to dial the phone. I picked up the receiver to make sure there was a dial tone and then quickly returned it to its cradle.

"This waiting is killing me," I said to Toby, who lay sleeping at the other end of the couch. "He should be here by now, right?"

I stood, walked to the window, and ran my fingers nervously through my hair. I had done the math of Tommy's trip in my head so many times that I was repeating it from memory.

"He got into Kansas City at 6 a.m.," I murmured. "His flight to Denver was scheduled to leave at 10 a.m. and it was a two and a half hour flight. With the time change, that would put him in Denver at around 11:30 my time. Get unloaded, get his bags, rent the car—say 12:30. It's a three-hour drive here and he would need lunch and maybe a bathroom stop—four o'clock. And then check-ing into the hotel—4:15."

I looked at the cuckoo clock ticking away on the wall going into the kitchen. It had been my grandfather's; and each day, the first thing I did as I went into the kitchen to make coffee was pull the iron pinecone-shaped weights down on their chains. The hands read 4:30.

What if he changed his mind? I wondered. Or what if he was in an accident? He wasn't used to the twisting Colorado roads. What if he was going too fast and hit a patch of ice? A storm had moved through the area two days before. Road crews would have cleared the highways and roads, but if someone wasn't careful . . . my heart began to thump and I felt sick. Calm down, I told myself. Be rational.

"Maybe I should just call the hotel and see if he's there or if he called with an arrival time," I muttered. "Just to check."

I reached under the counter and pulled out the phone book. After finding the right page, I scanned the listings, and then, with my finger marking the number, reached for the phone.

"Hello?" said a male voice in my ear. "Birdie? Is that you? Hello?"

"Hello?" I asked, confused.

"Birdie? It's Tommy."

"Tommy?" I blinked in surprise. "That was so weird. I was just going to call the hotel to see if you made it all right."

He laughed, a warm, inviting sound. "I just dialed your number. It didn't even ring and then, there you were. It must be fate."

"It must be," I said, happy to hear his voice and then suddenly nervous. "So, are you here? In town?"

"I am. And I'd like to take you out to dinner—that is, if you're still interested."

"I would love to have dinner."

"Okay, so where is a good place to eat? I couldn't tell when I drove through town."

"How about the Timbers Restaurant," I said. "It's about a half-mile from your B&B."

"Perfect." I could hear the scratch of him writing down. "Want to meet me at the hotel? It's a little cold to walk a half-mile, but we could drive over. Or we can meet at the restaurant. It's your call."

I hesitated. Where *would* it be best to meet? The hotel? That would give us more privacy for our first meeting, but it also would mean the awkwardness of the trip to the restaurant.

"Birdie?" he asked, interrupting my thoughts.

"Sorry," I said. "I was just trying to figure out a game plan."

"Umm hmm." I could hear the smile in his voice. "How about we just meet at the restaurant? You can check me out there and decide if I look like a serial killer."

I sighed. "How did you know?"

"You forget," he said. "I know you. And I know this is a big step for you. Give me forty-five minutes to shower, shave, and change out of these clothes?"

"Forty-five minutes," I said. "I'll see you at the Timbers."

"I'll get directions from the front desk. I can't wait."

As I hung up the phone, I closed my eyes and leaned my head against the cupboard door. I was excited, scared, anxious, and eager, all at the same time. I took several long, deep breaths. I showered, changed clothes several times, and put on makeup. I was ready.

"Maybe I'll just get there early and have a glass of wine," I said aloud. "I'll get our table, sit down, have a drink, and be nice and calm when he gets there."

The restaurant was almost deserted when I arrived. The servers were setting up for the evening dinner crowd as I approached the hostess stand. A dark-haired woman in black pants and a white shirt stepped quickly forward.

"Hi." I smiled. "Two for dinner. Something maybe . . . toward the back?"

The hostess smiled, her teeth an even white line. "I understand. Something romantic?"

I blushed. "Well, sort of."

She nodded and flipped her long, black hair over one shoulder. She gestured to the dining room and said, "How about you choose where you'd like to sit and I'll follow."

We walked into the dining room and I chose a booth near the back, but not too close to the kitchen.

"How about here?" I said as I slid into the seat facing the door. "And, could we get a bottle of your nicest cabernet?"

She nodded, laid the menus on the table, and disappeared into the bar area. Several minutes later she returned with a bottle of Silver Oak Cabernet, two red wine glasses, a corkscrew, and two glasses of water. I watched as she performed the wine service and nodded my approval. She poured small amounts into each of the glasses and then smiled as if to ask if there was anything more she could do. I nodded and reached for my purse.

"I know you're not our server," I said as I rummaged around for my wallet. "But would it be all right if I give you my credit card now, before the dinner—so there won't be any confusion as to who gets the bill?"

She nodded and waited as I dug the card out of my purse.

"I'll make sure Kallie gets it," she said. "She'll be your server. She's new, but she's good and I'll make sure she knows what's going on."

I sipped the wine. It was excellent. I slid the knotted napkin from around the neck of the bottle and looked at the label. 1997.

"Good year," a voice said from above me.

Startled, I looked up to find myself looking into the bluest eyes I had ever seen. They were more startling and more amazing than I remembered. My heart stopped as I stared at him.

"Hi," I whispered and then cleared my throat. I stood up. My legs trembled. I smiled, my pulse racing and my breath coming in short ragged pants.

"Hi," he said with a warm smile and stepped toward me. We stood, looking at each other. Finally, he reached down, grasped one of my hands, and leaned forward to kiss me on the cheek. He smelled of soap, starched shirt, and deep, herby forest. He was everything and nothing like the boy I'd met twenty years earlier.

"Shall we sit?" He gave my hand a firm squeeze. I looked over to see the hostess and a server watching us.

"Birdie?" I looked up into Tommy's eyes, taking in his dark, curly hair that was just beginning to gray, his long eyelashes, the laugh lines on either side of his mouth.

"Yes," I said, slightly breathless.

"Shall we sit?" He grinned.

"Oh, yes," I said quickly. "Of course."

"Good," he said, but continued to stand.

"You're so tall," I said stupidly. "You grew up and filled out. You're a man."

He laughed. "It happens." He gestured again to the booth and

I realized he was waiting for me to sit first.

"Sorry," I said and quickly slid into my seat.

He slid into his side of the booth.

"Wine?"

"God, yes," he said. "Please."

I laughed and he raised his glass.

"A toast," he said and held up his glass. "To us."

"To us," I echoed and touched my glass to his.

As we sipped, I stared at him. He was perfect—his eyes, his square jaw, his well-sculpted hands. He, too, was studying me. I was about to ask what he was thinking when a young red-headed woman came over to our table. She smiled.

"Hi," she said. "My name is Kallie. I'll be your server tonight. How is the wine?"

I looked at Tommy, who grinned and nodded his approval.

"Everything is great," I said. "Perfect, in fact."

"Good," she said. "Ummm . . ." She seemed unsure what to do next.

"Do you have any specials?" I asked helpfully.

She nodded and pulled a black notebook out of her long, bistro-style apron. "We have two specials tonight." She cleared her throat. "We have an eight-ounce gorgonzola-encrusted beef filet with garlic mashed potatoes and grilled asparagus spears. Also, we have baked salmon with a rosemary, wild mushroom, and cabernet reduction sauce. That comes with whipped parsnips and pan-fried potatoes prepared with fresh rosemary and olive oil."

She looked up. I looked at Tommy.

"Both sound really good," he said pleasantly. "But you sold me on the steak. So, I'd like the filet, medium rare, and a house salad with a balsamic vinaigrette dressing."

"Yummm," I said, suddenly ravenous. "That does sound good. I'll have the same. But make my filet medium and instead of balsamic vinaigrette dressing on my salad, I'd like, actually, you know what? I'll have the vinaigrette dressing, too."

"Okay, so you want . . ." she trailed off, pen poised over the pad of paper.

"Two of your filet specials—his medium-rare and mine medium,"

I said. "And we'll both have house salads—the ones with the field greens—with balsamic vinaigrette dressing."

She scribbled furiously and then looked up.

"That's all?"

"That's all," said Tommy with a grin.

"Okay," she said and repeated our order back to us. "Two filet specials—one medium-rare and one medium. Two house salads, both with balsamic vinaigrette.'

"Perfect," I said.

"I'll get the salads right out," she said.

"Actually," I said, blushing self-consciously as Tommy reached across the table and twined my fingers into his. "There's really no rush."

She nodded and glanced to where Tommy was sitting. "Okay. How about you just signal me when you're ready for the salads and we'll go from there."

Tommy and I both nodded.

"So," I said once we were alone.

"So," he repeated, a slow smile spreading across his face. "We're here. Am I as scary as you thought I'd be?"

I shook my head and smiled back.

"Not at all. You're . . . It's amazing to see you in person. To see you smile instead of just hearing it in your voice."

"I know what you mean," he said seriously. "I have been looking forward to this day for months. To actually see you sitting across from me is—" He shrugged. "It's unreal. It's like I was lost and now I'm not anymore." He caressed my fingers with his thumb.

"I feel that way, too," I said slowly. "You don't know this about me, but who I am when we talk, isn't the person I usually am. I mean, I'm not the type of person to talk to men I don't know—let alone let them hold my hand." I gestured at him, at our clasped hands. "I don't do things like this."

Tommy stared at me, his expression serious, his blue eyes intense. "Well, first of all, you're not with a man you don't know—you're with me. And maybe you've never done this before because you hadn't found the person you were supposed to do this with." He paused, thoughtfully. "We were missing our other halves."

I felt my eyes tear up.

"I have always felt like Grace was my other half," I mumbled to our clasped hands. Tommy was silent and I looked up suddenly to see that he was frowning.

"What do you mean?"

"Nothing," I said quickly. "Just talking gibberish."

"I don't believe that. Tell me what you mean."

"How about later? Maybe after dinner and after we've had a bit more of this." I raised my glass, took a sip and reached for the bottle. "More?"

He shook his head. "Not yet."

"So, how was the trip?"

"It was good," he said as he reached for my hand. "It's always weird going from the Eastern time zone to Mountain or Pacific time. It's like a gift of time."

"But then you lose it when you go back," I pointed out.

Tommy grinned. "True, but better to gain more time to enjoy with you and lose a couple of the hours I would spend missing you."

I blinked.

"That sounds like a line, doesn't it?" he asked.

"Maybe a little," I admitted.

He laughed and then grew quiet. We both stared at our joined hands.

"Birdie," he began, his voice serious. I cautiously raised my gaze to meet his. "I was going to wait to do this, but I can't."

I felt my heart begin to beat in my throat and my hands grew suddenly sweaty.

"Birdie, I love you. I've been waiting for months to say that to you—to say it in person." He was silent. "Please look at me."

I gulped a breath of air and raised my eyes to meet his. Everything about his expression showed he meant it. My eyes began to sting with tears. I reached for my glass and took a long swallow.

"Birdie?" His voice was kind. "What's wrong?"

I shrugged, unable to speak.

"I didn't mean to upset you," he said. "I'm sorry." He pulled his hand away and muttered angrily. "I knew I should have waited."

"No," I said thickly. "You didn't do anything wrong." I grabbed for his hand. "Really. I just wasn't prepared for how that would make me feel. I'm just happy. And it's been so long since I felt that."

"Oh, sweetheart," he said and I could hear the sadness—no, pity—in his voice.

"I'm sorry," I said. "I don't know what to say."

"You could start by telling me that you love me, too. That is, unless you've changed your mind."

I gasped. "No. Of course not. Please don't think that."

"Okay," he said and reached out to touch my face. Somewhere, in the back of my mind, I realized that I not only didn't mind it, I liked it. And, suddenly, I realized that I more than loved him—I trusted him.

"I love you, too." Saying the words surprised even me. "It terrifies me, but I do and I can't help it."

He smiled sheepishly and looked around the restaurant, which was beginning to fill up. I followed his gaze. "What say we skip dinner and get out of here?" He smiled. "Unless that makes you uncomfortable."

I shook my head. "I think that's fine."

"We could go to my hotel," he said and quickly added, "You wouldn't have to come to my room unless you wanted to. There's a sort of library-sitting room off the front—"

"How would you like to meet Toby?" I interrupted.

He raised his eyebrows in surprise. "I'd like that a lot, but only if you're comfortable with it."

"I wouldn't have asked if I wasn't," I said even though I wasn't sure.

"All right, then."

I searched the room for Kallie. She was taking an order, but when she turned, I caught her eye. She immediately came over.

"Ready?" she asked.

"We'd like the check," said Tommy, reaching into his back pocket for his wallet.

I held up my hand and smiled triumphantly. "Too late. I already gave her my card."

"I can't let you do that," he said. "This was a $100 bottle of wine."

"I insist. Put that away. It's my treat." I turned to Kallie, who was watching the exchange with a small smile. "Have you put in our orders yet?"

She shook her head. "You wanted to wait, right?"

"We did," I said with a smile. "But I think we've changed our minds about dinner. I think, if you haven't turned the order in yet, we'd like to just pay for the wine and go."

"Okay," she said and then asked carefully. "Was everything okay?"

"Everything was fine," I said. "We just decided to eat in. So, I think the hostess gave you my card. Could you just put the wine on that?"

"Sure," she said with a shrug. "I'll be right back."

As she walked away, I smiled at Tommy. "Do you like ham? I have leftovers at home."

"I love ham," he said. "Especially if it's in a sandwich."


Two hours later, the ham was gone and Tommy and I sat on the couch, pleasantly full.

"Oh my god, that was good," he said and licked his fingers. He sat back and sighed happily.

As soon as we had walked into the cabin and I had introduced him to Toby, I went into the kitchen and put the ham in the oven. Next, I opened a bottle of wine and removed two glasses from the cupboard. As I came back into the living room, I smiled. Toby was curled into a ball on the end of the couch, sleeping contentedly. Tommy stood in front of the bookshelf studying the titles. He turned as I came into the room.

"He must feel really comfortable with you," I said and gestured to the dog. "He usually barks and jumps when new people are here."

Tommy shrugged and grinned sheepishly. "Children and animals. They both seem to like me."

"Ah," I said and poured wine into the glasses. "How about a fire?"

He nodded eagerly. "I was going to start one, but I didn't want to be presumptuous or mess with your stuff without asking."

"Thank you," I said, genuinely touched.

As I laid the fire and lit the tinder, we talked about the titles on my shelf.

"You seem to like the classics," he said. "More 'thinking' sorts of books than what I usually read."

"What do you usually read?"

"I'm a Clancy man all the way," he said. "Or Grisham—you know, airplane reads." He sipped his wine. "Nice choice."

"Thanks," I said and turned back to the fire to feed kindling into the flame. I didn't offer to show him the rest of the place, and he didn't ask. He seemed to understand that for the time being, I wanted to stay in the more public part of the cabin.

Once the fire was going, I returned to the kitchen and checked the ham. It had already heated through, so I pulled out a knife and cut off chunks of meat, which I put on a plate with pickles and crackers.

"Dinner is served," I said as I came back into the living room and set the plate on the coffee table. I realized I had forgotten silverware and napkins.

"No need," Tommy said and reached out to pluck a piece of meat from the plate. "Let's eat with our fingers."

"But—"

"It's fine," he said and pulled a neatly folded white handkerchief from his back pocket. "We can use this."

"My dad used to carry a handkerchief," I said. "I didn't know men still did that."

"I do." Tommy grinned. "It reminds me of my grandfather. And speaking of grandfathers, I haven't had ham that good since I lived with my grandparents."

"It's smoked by this old guy who lives outside of town," I said.

"He smokes all his own meats in this old smokehouse. I try not to think about how unclean it probably is because it tastes so good. I get it at the local grocery store."

"It's amazing." He sighed contentedly. "Life seems so simple here. I love it. The food, the air, the people. Did I tell you the woman who checked me into the bed and breakfast managed to tell me her whole life story in the span of about three minutes? There is such an authenticity here. I can see why you love it."

"I don't really know all that many people in town," I said. "For me, the seclusion and the anonymity are the main draws. People let each other be themselves here."

"You are pretty remote. No neighbors?"

I shook my head. "Nope. We're the end of the line up here."

He smiled and reached for his wine glass. "This was kind of like a picnic."

"With a fire." I gestured to the fireplace.

"With a fire," he agreed. "And no ants."

Involuntarily, the image of the ant crawling across Grace's glassy eyeball flashed through my mind.

"No," I said quickly and shook my head to dispel the image. I could feel the effects of the alcohol. In addition to the wine at the restaurant, we had consumed a bottle with dinner and were well into a third bottle. I tipped my head back against the couch and closed my eyes. When I opened them, I saw Tommy's handsome face.

"You're so good looking," I said, fully aware of the fact that I was slurring my words.

Tommy grinned. "You're drunk."

"I am," I agreed happily. "How did that happen?" I stared into his eyes, unable to look away. And suddenly, the atmosphere changed. I wanted him to kiss me—I wanted it more than anything. I realized I had been waiting for it even as I feared it.

"I'm going to kiss you, now," he said, as if reading my thoughts. "I've been waiting all night—waiting for you to be comfortable and ready. But I can't wait any longer. I need to kiss you. Is that okay?"

Still staring deeply into his eyes, I nodded and then said thickly, "I'd like that. I'd like that more than you could possibly imagine."

He leaned closer. I could feel his warmth and smell the woody scent of him.

"Like a forest," I murmured. "You smell deep and woody like a forest."

"Ummm," he said as he rubbed his cheek against mine, scratchy against smooth. His lips lightly touched my eyelids, my temples, my cheeks, and then, finally, softly, my lips. Our first kiss was light and feathery and fleeting. I gasped and I heard him laugh softly. And then he kissed me again, this time more firmly, though his lips were still gentle.

"Oh my god," I whispered when his lips left mine. "That was amazing."

"Thank you."

"Could you do that again?"

"Of course," he said and kissed me again.

I lost track of time. It could have been minutes or hours.

"Wow," I said when we finally pulled apart. Both of us were breathing heavily.

"Where did you learn to kiss like that?" he asked.

I blushed.

"You," I said finally.

"Me?" he asked. "What do you mean?"

"I've never kissed anyone like that before," I admitted. "I mean . . . romantically."

He pulled back and studied my face. "Are you telling me I'm the first guy you've kissed? Really?"

I couldn't look at him and instead focused my eyes on one of the buttons of his shirt. I nodded in embarrassment.

"I'm . . ." He seemed to struggle for words.

"I know." My words thick from the emotion and the wine. "It's pathetic."

"No," he said quickly. "No, it's . . . you misunderstand. Birdie, I'm honored."

I raised my gaze to his earnest face. "I'm honored that you chose me for your first kiss. And, I hope to be your first in other ways, too."

"I want you to kiss me again," I said as I closed my eyes and tipped my head slightly backward. I felt his lips again brush mine before he moved to kiss my jaw, the spot below my earlobe, my neck.

"Mmmm," I said, amazed at the sensation.

"We're just getting started," he said softly. "By the time I'm finished with you, you'll be begging me to stop."

"You mean begging you *not* to stop," I murmured with a little smile. "I'll be begging you *not* to stop."

"No, begging me to stop." He moved away from me and I opened my eyes to see him looking at me with a strange expression. I blinked. "You'll be begging me to stop," he continued. "Just like Grace did that night in the clearing after we made love."

"Tommy," I said sharply and drew back. "That's not funny. Why would you say something like that?"

His face hardened—his laugh lines becoming chiseled parentheses around the thin slash of his mouth. There was nothing soft about him now. "Because it's true."

"This isn't funny," I repeated.

"It's not supposed to be funny," he said. "We were lovers. That night—the night she died—we kissed for the first time. And then we made love—just like we're about to do." He grinned, though there was no humor in the expression. "Oh, she said she didn't want to, but she did," he said. "They always do. And it was beautiful. She cried out of joy and happiness. She wept with pleasure."

"Tommy," I said sharply, "You're scaring me. This isn't funny. Please don't play this game with me."

"It's not a game, Birdie," he said, his voice soft and soothing, as if he were calming a frightened animal. "Grace and I were in love. And now, you and I are in love. I'm going to make you mine forever. I thought you wanted that."

I stood up quickly and took several clumsy steps backward.

"Tommy, you're scaring me," I said, my voice shaky. "I think we've both had too much to drink. I would like you to leave."

"You don't want the only man who's ever paid attention to you to leave." He smiled and shook his head. "Not really."

"Get out!" I yelled.

Toby, who had been asleep by the fire, jumped up at the tone of my voice and growled warily.

"Get out," I said again. "Now."

"But Birdie," Tommy said, his tone placating. "I just got here. I came all this way. I didn't mind. I did it because I love you. I'm in love with you. I just wanted you to know everything about me before we got started. And I wanted to come clean about Grace. I don't want there to be any secrets between us."

"Get out!" I yelled and pointed to the door. "Now!"

"Birdie, just let me show you how much I love you."

He walked slowly toward me. I thrust my hands out and began to back toward the kitchen.

"Birdie," he said softly in mock reproach. "Come here. I'm not going to hurt you. I just want to love you. That's what you wanted, wasn't it? Someone to love you unconditionally? Someone to love you forever? Someone who . . . what was it?" He paused as if trying to remember. "Oh, yeah, someone who had the strength to get past your demons and see your inner beauty. Isn't that what you wanted?"

"No!" I yelled and shook my head furiously from side to side. "No! I don't want that."

"Oh, but I think you do," he said with a sly smile. "That's why I'm here, isn't it? I think you have some unresolved issues and we're here to work through those together."

He shook his head sadly.

"You should have listened to your family and friends, Birdie. You should have been seeing a therapist for some time."

"I am fine," I spat angrily.

"Fine?" he said and cocked his head quizzically to the side. "Really? You're fine? Is that why you hear Grace in your head? Is that why you've locked yourself up in a cabin in the middle of nowhere? Is that why you invited a killer into your home for sex?"

"What are you talking about?" I asked, shakily. "What do you mean?"

"You still don't get it, do you?" he asked and shook his head. "Unbelievable." His voice became hard. "I killed Grace. And I'm going to kill you—after we make love, of course. Which, incidentally, I need to tell you, I think you are sorely in need of. To be in your thirties and still a virgin? What's that about?" He laughed spitefully. "But maybe you were just saving yourself for me. Was that it?" He resumed his slow pursuit.

For each step he took closer, I took a step backward until I reached the darkness of the kitchen. My breath came in small, short pants. I considered trying to run and hide. But where? He could find me in the cabin. I would freeze out in the woods—and anyway, my chances of outrunning him were slim. Was this how Grace felt—trapped and vulnerable?

*"Take a deep breath and stay calm."* It was Grace.

"Grace," I breathed in relief. She was here. She would save me.

"Yes," Tommy said as he continued his slow advance. "Grace. She is what brought us together, you know. It was her death that allowed me to find you."

*"Back into the kitchen and get the knife from the ham,"* Grace whispered. *"Let him get close. Let him think he has you where he wants you and then stab him as hard as you can in the belly."*

I nodded.

"See?" Tommy said knowingly. "You realize it now, don't you?"

I had backed fully into the kitchen and he stood in the doorway, his form a silhouette against the light of the living room.

"So," I said as I continued to creep backward. "We're going to make love and then what?"

I could hear the smile in his voice as he continued his slow pursuit. "You'll see," he said. "It will be beautiful."

I felt the counter against my back.

"Gotcha," Tommy said softly as he continued forward. "No place else to go. I guess we'll just have to pick up where we left off. Don't worry, though. I'm a very accomplished lover. And we have all night."

He stepped forward and bent his head to kiss me. His eyes slid closed and I felt his soft lips again on mine.

He didn't seem to notice or care that I didn't return the kiss.

"Now!" Grace hissed in my head. "Now!"

In the darkness of the kitchen, Tommy hadn't seen my fingers close around the handle of the butcher knife. He didn't realize my intent until it was too late. With Grace guiding my hand, I thrust the blade deeply into the side of his belly and then twisted it.

Tommy pulled back with a hiss and then looked down at the blade protruding from his side. He stumbled backward and then looked at me in disbelief. Fumbling, he grasped the handle, gave a grunt, and then heaved the knife from the wound with a sticky, sucking sound.

"So, you want to skip the foreplay, huh?" he gasped, the bloody knife clutched in his hand. "Fine by me. Post-coitus is the fun part for me anyway."

He lunged forward, one hand pressed to the bloody wound, the other wielding the knife. Still trapped against the counter, I feigned right. But I wasn't fast enough. I felt the blade slice my arm.

"Nice try," he grunted and grabbed me with his other hand. It was slippery with the blood from his wound. "Come here," he sneered and lunged with the knife again. This time I felt it cut across my palm.

"No!" I screamed and brought my knee up as hard as I could into his groin. He gasped and fell to the ground. The knife clattered to the floor and I kicked it away.

*"Call 911!"* Grace said. *"Call them and tell them you need help."*

I stumbled into the living room, picked up the cordless phone and punched in the numbers.

"9-1-1, what's the nature of your emergency?" It was a woman. Her voice was calm.

"There's a man in my house," I screamed into the phone. "He tried to rape me. I stabbed him. I need help. He murdered my friend."

"Okay, ma'am," the woman said. "Calm down. Are you in a safe place?"

"No! He's on the floor in the kitchen! He's—"

*"Run!"* Grace screamed in my head. *"He's up and he's got the knife again. Get to the Jeep!"*

I dropped the phone and raced to the door. My purse and keys were on the side table and I grabbed them as I fumbled with the doorknob. My hands were sticky with blood, shaky from fear and clumsy from the wine.

"*Hurry!*" Grace's voice was urgent. "*He's coming.*"

I turned to see Tommy staggering into the living room. I wiped my hands on my blouse and tried again. It turned and suddenly, I was outside on the porch. I ran to the Jeep.

"*It's locked,*" Grace said.

I fumbled with the keys. They all looked alike.

"*That one,*" Grace said as my fingers closed on the largest key on the ring. I couldn't make my hands stop shaking. I turned to see Tommy lurching through the open door. He leaned against the doorframe, one hand clutched to his belly. From the other hand dangled the knife.

"Shit, shit, shit," I yelled as I finally managed to get the key into the lock and turn it. I yanked the door open, climbed inside, and used my elbow to push down the lock once I slammed the door closed.

"Please start, please start, please start," I prayed as I turned the key in the ignition. For once, the engine roared to life.

"*Go!*" screamed Grace. "*Now! Drive!*"

I threw the Jeep into gear and cranked the wheel. Tommy still stood clutching the doorframe of the front door. Our eyes met as he struggled to take a step forward and then collapsed. In amazement, I watched as he crawled across the porch and attempted to pull himself into a standing position.

"*He's trying to get to his car.*"

I punched the accelerator and the vehicle bucked forward before almost immediately catching a patch of ice. The Jeep fishtailed wildly and then caught traction and leapt forward. As I struggled to maintain control of it, I saw Tommy opening the door of his rented car.

"*Lights,*" Grace yelled as we spun out of the turnaround and onto the drive. Quickly, I flicked on the lights and drove jerkily toward the road. In the rearview mirror, I could see the blink of headlights coming on.

"*He's following us. Gun it. Now!*"

I cranked the wheel and turned onto the rutted, snowy road.

Although much of the snow was now melted off, what remained had melted during the day and then turned to ice once the sun went down. Breathing in gasps, adrenaline coursing through my body, I drove down the rutted road, the Jeep bucking and slipping from side to side as I hit patches of ice.

"We're going to wreck," I said. "I've had too much to drink. There's ice all over. I need to slow down."

"*You can't.*" It was Grace's voice, although not from my head. I looked at where she sat in the passenger's seat. She still looked eleven. "*Unless you want to end up like me, you can't. You should have listened to me. I am the only person who can take care of you.*"

"I know," I said miserably, nodding. "I know. I'm sorry. I just . . ."

"*I know about the loneliness,*" she said. "*But you're not alone. You'll never be alone. You have me.*"

I glanced in the rearview mirror and saw headlights in jerky pursuit.

"He's still there," I said. Grace turned to look out the back window. Her face was illuminated by the light of the dash. She was beautiful.

"*He's losing blood,*" she said. "*He will lose consciousness soon. A wound like that bleeds out pretty quickly.*"

"How do you know?" I asked as I struggled to keep the Jeep under control.

"*I know.*"

"Where are we going?" I asked. "It's 2 a.m. There's no place open."

"*Sheriff's department.*"

I glanced back and noticed the lights had disappeared.

"I think we lost him," I said as the Jeep hit a rut and bounced sideways.

I cranked the wheel to compensate and then felt a second wave of fear. "Oh my god, Grace. We left Toby."

I pulled my eyes from the road to look at her. She was about to speak when the front wheels of the Jeep hit a patch of ice and slid drunkenly to the side. I jerked the steering wheel and the back began to fishtail. I pumped the brakes hoping to slow the skid, but that only seemed to make it worse. Almost as if it were in slow motion, I felt the Jeep buck, lurch to the other side and roll out of control.

As I bounced around in the cab, I realized I had forgotten to put on my seatbelt.

"Shit," I thought as my head smashed into the windshield and I began to lose consciousness. "Wouldn't you know it would come down to this?"

# Chapter 30

The events following the accident are still unclear. I've been told that I was brought into the emergency room unconscious. A trucker apparently had seen the lights of my Jeep as I bounced down the incline and radioed for help. Sheriff's officers responding to my 911 call were close by and called for paramedics. The scene apparently hadn't been pretty. Firefighters had to cut me out of the wreckage and I was airlifted to the hospital in Colorado Springs, where I was treated for a broken leg, a broken arm, numerous broken ribs, head injuries, and a punctured lung. According to my mother, I drifted in and out of consciousness for about a week.

My recollection is much less cohesive. What I remember is captured in flashes. I remember the Jeep spinning out of control and then hitting my head repeatedly as it rolled. I remember waking up in the Jeep. It was upside down and I was on the roof. I remember touching my head and then staring at my hands. They were covered with blood—though I wasn't sure if it was mine, Tommy's, or both. I recall a pain that shot all the way up my leg into my hip as a man and a woman loaded me onto a gurney. I remember that a helicopter circled overhead and I could see snow falling in the beam of the powerful blue-white light that shone down on us. And when I turned my head, I saw Grace standing off to the side watching silently. She nodded encouragingly.

I also remember struggling to tell the doctors about Tommy—that they needed to send the police or sheriff's department to my cabin, and someone needed to take care of Toby. I could hear their voices discussing my condition, but no matter how hard I tried, I couldn't seem to speak.

Several days later, I woke to the light of the morning sunshine streaming through the window of what appeared to be a hospital room. My mother sat in a chair by my bed, her chin to her chest as she slept. She looked pale and very tired.

"Mom?" I croaked. My throat was dry and my voice raspy. I wondered briefly if I had swallowed glass from the windshield. I tried again. "Mom?"

She awoke with a start and blinked uncomprehendingly at me for several seconds. "Oh my god, Birdie." She jumped to her feet. "Shh, don't talk, sweetie. You had a tube down your throat to help you breathe. I'll get the nurse."

She rushed out of the room and moments later, a woman in pink scrubs rushed in. Behind her were my mother and sister. The nurse smiled and studied me over the top of her glasses.

"Looks like someone's awake," she said kindly. "How are you feeling?"

"Not good," I rasped. "How long have I been here?" I looked down at the casts on my leg and arm. "What happened?"

"It's okay, honey," my mother said. "You were in a car accident. You hit some ice and your Jeep went off the road."

"Oh my god," I groaned as it all came back to me. Tommy. The knife. "I was trying to get away from Tommy. I stabbed him. He was at my house. You can't let him get away. He killed Grace. He tried to kill me. He stabbed me twice."

I tried to pull myself out of the bed but was stopped short by an excruciating pain in my side. I gasped.

"You have broken ribs and a punctured lung," said the nurse gently. "You're not going to be able to go anywhere for a while. Just calm down and don't move around."

"You don't understand." I looked wildly around the room and met my mother's eyes. "You have to call the police. They need to arrest him or something. He was chasing me in his car. You have to go get . . . oh . . . " I began to cry. "Oh, Mom. I killed him, didn't I?" I reached wildly for her hand. "I didn't mean to, but he was going to rape and kill me just like he did Grace."

My mother squeezed my hand reassuringly and exchanged a

look with my sister, who had come into the room and now stood on the other side of the bed, slightly behind the nurse.

"Sweetie, just lie back and try to relax. There's no reason to get upset. It's okay."

"No," I said forcefully. "It's not okay. He was chasing me in his car. I think he passed out. You can still catch him. He . . . he tried to kill me. You've got to believe me. You've got to send the police."

Then I remembered Toby.

"Oh my god," I moaned. "You've got to get Toby. You've got make sure he's okay. Tommy may have gone back to the cabin!"

I began to sob. My mother patted my arm.

"Sweetie, calm down," she said. "Look at me. Look in my eyes. It's okay. It's all okay. Andy is at the cabin and is taking care of Toby. He's fine."

I looked frantically around the room. If Andy was at the cabin, then the situation must be under control. I felt myself calm slightly. "So, they found Tommy? Was he still alive? Is he in jail?"

My mother glanced again at my sister and then looked back at me.

"Birdie, sweetheart, listen to me." Her voice was soft and calm. "We talked about this last time you were awake. Remember? You didn't kill anyone."

"Yes," I said emphatically. "I did! Tommy Anderson. From Edenbridge. I stabbed him! He was going to kill me like he did Grace! Grace saved me!"

My mother sighed and looked at the nurse, who was poking at the beeping machine next to the bed. The nurse pressed a final button and then looked down at me. "Rebecca, listen to me. You need to take a deep breath. This machine keeps track of your vital signs and right now, it's telling me that you need to calm down. Okay? Now, I need you to answer a couple of questions for me, okay?"

I nodded helplessly.

"What's your name?"

"Birdie," I rasped. "Rebecca Holloway."

"Good. Do you know what year it is?"

"2004."

"Excellent." She scribbled something on the chart she held in her hand. "Do you know where you are?"

"I'm assuming the hospital."

"Do you know why you're here?"

"I wrecked my Jeep," I said and began to feel the panic rising again. "Grace and I were trying to escape from Tommy and I hit a patch of ice."

"And who is Tommy?" asked the nurse, her eyes flicking up to meet my mother's. "Deep breaths, stay calm."

"Tommy Anderson is a man I was e-mailing," I whispered with exaggerated patience. "I knew him when we were young. He came to visit me and then he tried to kill me. He killed my friend Grace when we were kids. He was the Sullivans' grandson."

I directed this last bit of information toward my mother, who looked at my sister. Tara shook her head and shrugged. My mother then looked at the nurse, who nodded, as if giving my mother permission.

"Sweetie, I'm going to tell you something and you need to stay calm and listen to me, okay?" My mother squeezed my hand gently. "You've had a nasty bump to the head. You're okay, but I think it's made you a little confused. We talked about this last time." She paused. "We're still trying to understand who you're talking about."

"Tommy Anderson," I said, exasperated. "The Sullivans' grandson. He murdered Grace. And he just tried to murder me. Why won't anyone listen to me?"

"Birdie," my mother said gently. "Reggie murdered Grace. Remember? He was arrested two weeks after the murder."

"No," I wailed. "It was Tommy Anderson. We've been e-mailing. He was in town when Grace was murdered. He was with his grandparents. He got my name from Roger and we've been e-mailing. You have to listen to me. He killed Grace. He tried to kill me. I stabbed him. I stabbed him in the stomach. There is blood all over the house. He chased me in his car."

"Shhhhhhh," my mother said softly, reassuringly. "Shhhhh. Sweetie, listen to me. You're confused —from the accident. We checked with Mrs. Sullivan. Their grandson, Tommy, died when he was sixteen. He was killed in a gang fight in Chicago two years before Grace's murder. And we've talked to Roger; he didn't give your name to anyone."

I wrenched my arm away from her hand in protest. "No," I insisted. "Tommy was at the Nest after Grace's murder. It was his knife that was used to kill her. He *told* me so."

"Birdie, Grace stole the knife from the Mercantile to protect herself from Reggie. That came out during the trial."

"But, he said . . ." I began.

"Sweetheart," my mother said softly, "We've all been to the cabin. There is no blood anywhere. You're confused. There is no Tommy."

"But the e-mails," I said plaintively. "Check the e-mails. They're all on my computer! He came to visit. He was staying at the Ranch House Inn. He had a rental car. Look for the reservations. We had dinner. At the Timbers. Ask the waitress. Kallie. She saw us together. Ask her."

Tara put her hand gently on my leg.

"You were at the Timbers Restaurant, but you were there by yourself," she said gently. "They called us after the accident was reported on the local news. They said you were drunk. You came in, drank a bottle of wine, talked to yourself, and then left. They were going to try to stop you from driving, but you left too quickly. We found the receipt."

"But it wasn't just me," I insisted. "Tommy was there. We were going to have dinner. We both ordered the steak but decided to go back to the cabin and eat leftover ham." I looked wildly around me. "Mom . . . Tara . . . you've got to believe me. We fought. I stabbed him. There's blood everywhere. For god's sake, check my e-mails."

"Sweetheart," my mother said. "We *did* check your e-mails. You told us to the last time you were awake. Andy checked them. There weren't any from a man named Tommy. Just a lot of e-mails you wrote that were never sent. You have to believe me, sweetie. There is no one named Tommy."

"You're wrong," I yelled despite the pain in my throat and the weakness of my voice. "You're wrong! You're wrong!"

The beeps on the monitors next to me began to speed up again.

"You need to calm down," the nurse said. "Deep breaths."

"I don't want to take any deep breaths," I hissed. "You won't believe me and I'm not going to stay here—not while there's a killer on the loose! He cut me for chrissake. Look!"

I held up my hand to show them where I had been cut trying to defend myself. But as I did so, I stopped and stared at my hand. There was no injury, no cut, no bandage.

"But it was there," I insisted and then looked up at my mother. She looked sad. "This is bullshit!" I ripped the IV out of my hand and struggled to get out of bed. The nurse punched a button and two other women rushed into the room. My mother and sister stepped back while the nurses struggled to restrain me.

"Let me go!" I yelled. "You can't do this! I need to get out of here!"

I felt the prick of the needle and looked down as the nurse in the pink scrubs depressed the plunger on the syringe. I felt cold and then warm . . . and then very, very heavy. My head began to swim and as I faded once again into unconsciousness, I heard my mother's voice.

"Well, at least it was better than last time."

When I woke up, it was evening. My sister was in the chair next to the bed flipping through an outdated copy of *People* she must have snagged from the waiting room. I blinked and then remembered what had occurred last time I was awake. Nothing made sense. I struggled to sit up but realized I had been restrained. As I moved, Tara smiled at me.

"Hey there." She put the magazine down and came over to put a hand on my arm. "How are you feeling? Let me go get the nurse."

"No," I rasped. "No, not yet. Why am I in restraints?"

"They were worried you would hurt yourself. You ripped out your IV last time." She looked nervously at the door. "I think I should go get the nurse. Mom and Dad would want me to."

"Dad's here?"

"Yeah, can you believe it?" she said. "He flew in yesterday and was here last night. He's at the cabin with Andy right now, but he'll be here tomorrow morning." She paused and looked again at the door. "I really should go get the nurse."

"No," I said. "Not yet . . . Please, just tell me what's going on. I don't understand what's happening."

"Well—" She hesitated.

"Please."

"You were in a car accident," she said. "They had to cut you out of your Jeep and they brought you here. You're in the hospital in Colorado Springs. You've got a bunch of broken bones and a concussion and your lung was pierced. You're lucky to be alive."

I struggled to remain calm.

"What about Tommy? Is he dead? Is he in jail?"

Tara stared at me for several seconds and then quickly looked away.

"At least tell me that Toby's okay."

"Toby's fine." Tara's expression was hard to read. "He's at the cabin with Andy and Dad."

"What about Tommy?" I asked again. "Did they find the body? Are the police going to arrest me? It was self-defense, Tara."

Tara squeezed my hand and looked deeply into my eyes. "Birdie," she said and then sighed. "We don't know what you're talking about." She put her hands up as I started to protest. "No, wait, hear me out. Listen. As far as we can tell, there is no one named Tommy. You didn't kill anyone and there are no e-mails from anyone named Tommy. There are a bunch of e-mails from you to someone named Tommy, but they were never sent."

"But he came here," I protested. "He and I had dinner together. People saw us. He came back to my place. He tried to kill me."

"Birdie, you were alone at the restaurant. Everyone who saw you there says you were completely alone. And there is no sign of a struggle at the cabin—just a knife on the floor in the kitchen. From the ham."

I tried to shake my head, but the pain was too much.

"You've got to believe me," I pleaded. "He killed Grace. He told me so."

"Reggie killed Grace," she said. "Don't you remember? Natalie's father arrested him. There was a trial. He was found guilty. And then after the trial, Grace's mom committed suicide—a drug overdose. Remember?"

'No," I said emphatically. "No, that's not what happened. They never found the killer. It was Tommy. He was there that summer. He met me in the woods. We talked."

Tara shook her head. Her expression was a combination of fear and disbelief.

"Birdie, listen to me," she said patiently. "There is no Tommy. No one outside of you has ever seen him."

"Grace did," I insisted. "She did. She watched him practice throwing his knife in the woods. They were friends."

Tara balked. "How do you know that?"

"She told me so," I said triumphantly.

"When?" Tara asked, furrowing her brow.

"Lots of times," I said. "She warned me that Tommy was dangerous, but I wouldn't listen. She was the one who saved my life when he came after me with the knife. She takes care of me. She always has."

"Birdie, what are you talking about?" asked Tara. "What do you mean she was the one who saved you? That she talks to you?"

"Just what I said," I replied. "She talks to me. Ever since she died, she has been in my head. She warns me of danger. She has kept me from being raped several times. She protects me. She saved me from being murdered by Tommy."

Tara stared at me, her mouth slightly open. She glanced at the door.

"What are you saying?" she whispered.

"I'm saying that Grace saved me from the man who murdered her."

"Reggie—"

"Tommy," I corrected.

"Tommy didn't murder Grace," Tara said. "Reggie did. There is no Tommy."

"That's not true!" I exclaimed. "Jesus! Why won't anyone listen to me? I stabbed him. There's blood all over the cabin. Just go there and see! You have to believe me."

'Shhhh," Tara said. "You need to stay calm, or they'll sedate you again. Listen to me. We've all been to the cabin. There is no Tommy."

"There is!" I yelled. "There is!"

Within seconds, a nurse bustled into the room. She glared at Tara and then turned to me.

"No one believes me," I told her. "She is trying to tell me that what I know is true, isn't."

"Rebecca, please calm down," said the nurse firmly.

"I *am* calm," I insisted. "I *am* calm. I just want someone to listen to me. Why won't anyone listen to me?"

"We're listening," the nurse said. "We're listening."

"No!" I screamed. "You're *not!*"

A second nurse came into the room. In her hand was a syringe. She handed it to the first nurse. "It sounded like it was time for this," she said.

"No!" I yelled. "No! I don't want it. No!"

This time the nurse inserted the needle into the port on my IV and depressed the plunger. I struggled against the restraints.

"No," I said weakly and began to sob. "No! You don't understand! You can't do this. I need to get up. We need to catch Tommy! I . . . need . . ."

# Epilogue

My family and friends will tell you that I'm not the most reliable of storytellers. And I can tell you that's simply not true. Granted, my story might not hold a lot of weight given that I now spend my days as a guest at the Manor Woods Psychiatric Hospital. But what I'm telling you is the truth. Grace knows it. I know it. And Tommy, wherever he is, knows it too.

He thinks he's gotten away with something. But he hasn't. We've hatched a plan, Grace and I. We have figured out what we need to say to get out of here and when we do, we're going to go someplace where Tommy can never find us. I know everyone thinks I'm crazy. And, I guess that's fine. They can tell me I didn't experience what I know for a fact I did. And there's nothing I can do about that. But I know the difference between imagined and reality.

I know because Grace told me so.

# Acknowledgments

Sandra Moran passed away November 7, 2015. She had finished her final edits of *State of Grace* but had not written the Acknowledgments. I, therefore, open with a sincere apology if I omit someone who was actively involved in the development of the story.

I will let Sandra publicly speak, though, to her beta readers: Elizabeth Andersen, Kathy Belt, Deborah Bowers, Patricia Decker, Rebecca Maury, Jane Montgomery, Stephanie Smith, Stacie Valle, and Annie Yamulla. Here is an excerpt from an email she sent to them on September 14, 2015: "Let me begin by thanking you from the bottom of my heart for all of your hard work and help on *State of Grace*. I just finished implementing all of your edits and the wonderful/amazing/perfection thing about them was that even though many of you caught the same errors, individually you all focused on other things, like over-attribution, holes in the story, etc. You're all superstars and I cannot thank you enough for all of your help."

A special thank yous to Ashley Fletcher, who read even more versions of *State of Grace* than *Letters Never Sent,* and to Elizabeth Andersen for lending her eagle eye to the final manuscript.

Sandra was able to work with her friend and mentor, Ann McMan, on the cover design for the book. She *loved* the cover, as she did all of the amazing covers Ann did for her books.

There are no words that can express the gratitude Sandra's family and I have for Bywater Books' willingness to publish *State of Grace* exactly as Sandra had left it. This was incredibly important to us.

Sandra ended each new book's Acknowledgments with a bigger tale than the last of her mother's long labor and the career her mother had to give up to have Sandra. Had she the chance, Sandra would have ended these Acknowledgments with an even bigger tale than the one in *All We Lack*.

I end it with this … Thank you, Cherie, for so adeptly raising Sandra and teaching her how to love unconditionally. So many lives have been forever changed by her ability to express love. Mine most of all.

–Cheryl Pletcher

# About the Author

A native Kansan, Sandra Moran was born on December 20, 1968. Her varied employment history spoke to her sense of intellectual adventure. She worked as a political speechwriter, a newspaper journalist, and an archaeological tour manager. She authored five novels, *Letters Never Sent, Nudge, The Addendum,* and *All We Lack. State of Grace,* the first novel written by Moran, is the last to be published.

In addition to her writing career, Sandra served as an assistant adjunct professor of anthropology at Johnson County Community College in Overland Park, Kansas. She was diagnosed with Stage IV cancer in October 2015, and passed away in hospice care less than one month later on November 7, 2015.

### Recognition for *Letters Never Sent*
Edmund White Award for Debut Fiction,
Publishing Triangle Awards (Finalist)
Rainbow Award for Historical Fiction (Winner)
Rainbow Award for Lesbian Debut Novel (Winner)
Rainbow Award for Best Lesbian Novel (Finalist)
Ann Bannon Popular Choice Award (Winner)
Golden Crown Literary Society General Fiction Award (Winner)

### Recognition for *Nudge*
Thorpe Menn Literary Excellence Award (Nominee)

### Recognition for *All We Lack*
Ann Bannon Popular Choice Award (Finalist)
Golden Crown Literary Society General Fiction Award (Finalist)

NOTE: All author proceeds from the sales of *State of Grace* will be donated to the Legacies of Lesbian Literature Project.
*www.crowdrise.com/legacies-of-lesbian-literature-project*

# Tangled Roots

"Deeply engrossing and quite beautiful, Martin's talent for creating human characters that could walk off the page into real life will leave her audience craving more." —*Foreword Reviews*

"The writing is decisive and incisive, the storyline engaging and enraging." — *Curve Magazine*

*Tangled Roots* by **Marianne K. Martin**

Print 978-1-61294-053-3
Ebook 978-1-61294-054-0

**www.bywaterbooks.com**

# Backcast

"*Backcast* is a memorable story about the unbreakable strength and resilience of women. Skillfully executed, the story is easy to become emotionally invested in, with characters that are guaranteed to entertain and enthrall." —*Lambda Literary Review*

"I love Ann McMan."
                    —Dorothy Allison, author of *Bastard Out of Carolina*

*Backcast* by Ann McMan

Print 978-1-61294-063-2
Ebook 978-1-61294-064-9

**www.bywaterbooks.com**

**Bywater BOOKS**

At Bywater Books we love good books about lesbians just like you do, and we're committed to bringing the best of contemporary lesbian writing to our avid readers. Our editorial team is dedicated to finding and developing outstanding writers who create books you won't want to put down.

We sponsor the Bywater Prize for Fiction to help with this quest. Each prize winner receives $1,000 and publication of their novel. We have already discovered amazing writers like Jill Malone, Sally Bellerose, and Hilary Sloin through the Bywater Prize. Which exciting new writer will we find next?

For more information about Bywater Books and the annual Bywater Prize for Fiction, please visit our website.

www.bywaterbooks.com